ALONE WITH THE HEIRESS

Sara eyed him carefully, while taking another tiny sip of brandy. The flickering firelight accentuated the classic angles of his face, the strong line of his jaw, and the noble bridge of his nose, making him seem even more handsome. In his loose white shirt, sitting casually on the sofa with a drink in his hand, he seemed the epitome of masculinity. The thick lashes that fringed his eyes closed briefly.

Then he turned and looked directly at her. "I don't know what we're thinking doing this."

"I like it," she whispered, settling back against the sofa.

"You like it," he said, echoing her words. He shook his head in disbelief before taking a sip of the brandy.

"Yes, I like it." Sara continued in a pragmatic tone, "No one is here. No one will know. If the storm is as bad as you say, I'm sure my mother and Aunt Colette will stay the night at their sister's house instead of trying to get back home. We're not really doing anything wrong. It's all completely innocent."

"I've never met anyone quite like you, Miss Fleming."

"I think you should call me Sara now."

"If you call me Christopher."

"Agreed . . ."

Books by Kaitlin O'Riley

The Hamilton Sisters

SECRETS OF A DUCHESS

ONE SINFUL NIGHT

WHEN HIS KISS IS WICKED

DESIRE IN HIS EYES

IT HAPPENED ONE CHRISTMAS

TO TEMPT AN IRISH ROGUE

HIS BY CHRISTMAS

The Hamilton Cousins

THE HEIRESS HE'S BEEN WAITING FOR

Collections

YOURS FOR ETERNITY

(with Hannah Howell and Alexandra Ivy)

AN INVITATION TO SIN

(with Jo Beverley, Sally MacKenzie, and Vanessa Kelly)

Published by Kensington Publishing Corporation

The HEIRESS HE'S BEEN WAITING FOR

KAITLIN O'RILEY

ZEBRA BOOKS
KENSINGTON PUBLISHING CORP.
http://www.kensingtonbooks.com

ZEBRA BOOKS are published by

Kensington Publishing Corp.
119 West 40th Street
New York, NY 10018

All Kensington titles, imprints, and distributed lines are available at special quantity discounts for bulk purchases for sales promotion, premiums, fund-raising, educational, or institutional use.

Special book excerpts or customized printings can also be created to fit specific needs. For details, write or phone the office of the Kensington Sales Manager: Attn.: Sales Department. Kensington Publishing Corp., 119 West 40th Street, New York, NY 10018. Phone: 1-800-221-2647.

Zebra and the Z logo Reg. U.S. Pat. & TM Off.

First Printing: September 2018
ISBN-13: 978-1-4201-4463-5
ISBN-10: 1-4201-4463-4

eISBN-13: 978-1-4201-4464-2
eISBN-10: 1-4201-4464-2

10 9 8 7 6 5 4 3 2 1

Printed in the United States of America

To Christopher
For bringing love back into my life.
Yet.

Acknowledgments

I can only write about a large and loving family, because I am blessed to have one myself. As always, I must thank Jane Milmore, Shelley Jensen, Maureen Milmore, Janet Wheeler, Scott Wheeler, Jennifer Malins, Greg Malins, Adrienne Barbeau, Billy Van Zandt, and Yvonne Deane. A very special thank you goes to Chris Robinson and he knows why.

To my CH family (especially Cela, Gretchen, Lynn, Jenny), I thank you for always being there for me and for making work a pleasure.

I thank my agent Jane Dystel and my editor John Scognamiglio for over ten years together and for encouraging me to continue writing. I couldn't do this without the two of them!

And thank you to my readers for loving the Hamilton family as much as I do.

~
Note to Riley
I love you more.
(Don't tell me what to do!)

1

Overboard

May 1894

Sara Fleming's only recourse was to fling herself over the side of the ship and into the ocean.

She was a captive. Trapped. Held against her will. Hot tears pricked her eyes and her heart pounded wildly in her chest.

With expensively gloved fingers clinging to the railing, she stared down at the gray water sweeping below her, the salt spray splashing up and stinging her cheeks. Despair surged through her and the idea of throwing herself over the railing and into the sea seemed her only option. If only she had jumped sooner, before the ship had left New York Harbor! She would have had a much better chance of swimming to shore safely then, but she was only just realizing they were not returning to port. It was more than likely too late to jump now.

As she glanced backward, the bustling, crowded city that was her home faded farther and farther from view.

Sara would surely drown before she made it back to land, her heavy mauve brocade dress weighing her down, pulling her into the cold depths of the Atlantic Ocean. Perhaps drowning would be preferable to being held against her will and carried away to God only knew where? Outrage flooded through her veins.

How had this happened? How had she been so foolish as to get taken away like this? It wasn't fair! She hadn't done anything to deserve being treated so cruelly. So viciously.

Trapped! Good heavens, she was trapped. There was no way out. Nowhere to go. No way to return home. She might as well jump into the swirling sea below her.

Her heart ached too. She couldn't see how she could possibly go on without him. There hadn't been a chance to say good-bye to him, not even a hastily penned note. The very thought of him ringing the bell at her New York town house this evening to take her to the theater as they had planned and discovering that she had sailed away, caused tears to spill down and sting her cheeks. Great sobs of longing and grief wrenched from her chest.

Then she burned with impotent fury at her heartless parents.

They had tricked her!

She never would have suspected them of such an underhanded maneuver. They lured her out to sea under false pretenses. It would surely qualify as kidnapping if they weren't her very own parents!

"Come see your father's new ship," her mother had suggested innocently enough that morning, a bright smile on her face. "The *Captain's Daughter* was christened yesterday and he wants you to see it."

Sara had felt slightly guilty that she had missed the ship's christening, because she had been an attendant in her friend Jennie's wedding. It was doubly disappointing since the name of the new steamship was in reference to her.

So like any trusting child, Sara had acquiesced, never imagining she would be callously whisked away against her will. How many times had she visited one of her father's ships before? She'd spent most of her young life on the decks of one type of ship or another, sailing around the world with her parents. The past two years they had been staying at their town house in New York City, and so the prospect of seeing her father's newest steamship was exciting to Sara, as it always was. But it all had been a ruse. A clever ruse to lure her away from the man she loved.

Stunned that her mother and father had tricked her so easily, Sara was deeply wounded by their betrayal. Oh, she had not been unaware of their disapproval of the man she loved, but she assumed that they were merely being over-protective, believing that no man was good enough for their precious daughter. They had not been overjoyed by her courtship with Alexander Drake, but they had not forbidden it either. They were friendly with him, cordial even. So their deception this afternoon came as a devastating blow.

Her eyes looked longingly back at the grand city she loved and called home, while the tears continued to spill down her cheeks. Somewhere in that New York hustle and bustle of buildings and streets and people, Alexander alone was waiting for her, the man who held her heart. She should be with him now.

It wasn't fair! It simply wasn't fair!

A frustrated scream of helpless rage welled within her, surging much like the waves that crashed below against the hull of the elegant ship. How could they do this to her? Their only daughter! Didn't they care about her feelings? She was no longer a child, but a grown woman of twenty. Why, she would be turning twenty-one in the fall! How dared they treat her this way? Maybe she *should* throw herself over? They would be sorry then. When she was no longer alive, they would regret hurting her and breaking her heart.

The vast water swirled cold and dark gray, far below her.

She placed her stylishly and expensively booted foot upon the polished railing of the boat, gripping tightly with her kid-gloved hands. If she pushed up, she could swing her legs over the side, taking her long, heavy skirt with her, and just slip quietly into the sea and disappear forever. Her absence might not be noticed for hours, since her parents thought she had locked herself in her suite in a fit of temper.

But when they finally discovered she was gone, her mother and father would be wracked with regret and guilt over what they had done to her. And it would serve them right, because they had hurt her far worse than they could imagine.

The time was now or never. She took a deep breath and—

"Stop being so melodramatic, Sara."

Startled, she turned to see her mother standing beside her.

Although her facial expression was one of annoyance, Juliette Hamilton Fleming was an unmistakably beautiful woman. With her dark hair elegantly coiffed under a fashionable bonnet and wrapped in an expensive fur jacket to ward off the chill of the early May sea air, her heart-shaped face was relatively unlined for a woman in her forties and her blue eyes were clear and full of life. She carried herself with grace, ease, and confidence. People always said that Sara favored her mother, but Sara didn't see the resemblance at all.

Juliette stared at her daughter in sympathetic understanding. "It's not the end of the world. And he's certainly not a man worthy of throwing yourself overboard."

Ignoring her mother, Sara turned her face away. Slowly she removed her foot from the railing. She continued to stare off at the sea, feeling more than a bit embarrassed to be caught contemplating something so foolish.

"I know you're upset with us," Juliette continued, "and to be honest, I would be upset too if I were you. Believe it or not, I am sorry for hurting you like this."

Sara glanced at her mother for the briefest of moments. As she looked back to the horizon, New York was no longer visible at all and her heart sank. Her parents had betrayed her. Most dreadfully. Sara didn't know if she would ever forgive them. She wiped at the cold tears on her cheeks, the wind whipping loose strands of hair around her face.

"It had to be done. He wasn't the right man for you. There were things you were not aware of and he would have only broken your heart. Please trust your father and me in this matter." Juliette's voice held a firm note.

"Trust you?" Sara flung back, her voice incredulous. "You tricked me! You and Father deceived me! You led me to believe we were just look—"

Juliette placed a calming hand on Sara's arm. "I am terribly sorry we hurt you, but I am not sorry about what your father and I did today. It's our duty to protect you. And you definitely needed protecting."

"Protection from what? From the man I love?" Sara cried, an anguished sob wrenching her throat. When would she ever see Alexander Drake again? Would he understand that her parents had taken her away against her wishes? Would he know that she had not left of her own volition? Would he think she had simply run off? Would he forgive her? Would he still love her? Doubt and heartache filled her with sorrow.

Her mother gave her a rueful smile. "You'll thank me for this one day, I promise you."

Sara looked away again, trying to stop the tears that were

welling again. How dared her mother be so nice to her? "I shall never forgive you for this." Her words were icy.

"How you feel now is quite understandable," Juliette said softly, patting her daughter's arm in an attempt to comfort, not patronize.

Sara was too upset to speak. Her parents were wrong. So terribly, terribly wrong. They had deliberately ruined the only love of her life. How could she ever forgive them for doing this to her? How could she continue to go on? Her every moment was consumed by thoughts of Alexander Drake.

It wasn't possible to forget him, and even if she could, she wouldn't ever, couldn't ever, love anyone else. He was far too handsome. With his deep green eyes, golden blond hair, captivating boyish smile, and dashingly romantic ways. Oh, when he looked at her, she knew he loved her. She could see it in his eyes.

Now poor Alexander would be frantic with worry over her, brokenhearted too. He would wonder where she had gone to and would be desperate to find her . . .

Finally Sara gave a defeated sigh. "Can you at least tell me *where* we are sailing to?"

A delighted smile lit her mother's face and her eyes danced with happiness. Juliette answered in one word, which explained everything. "Home."

Of course, that's where they were headed! But with her parents, they could have been sailing to China or Australia for all she knew. However, Sara also understood that home meant London for her mother. Juliette had been born and raised in England and only moved to the United States when she'd married Sara's father, Captain Harrison Fleming.

Sara had been to London many times, and she loved it there too. Her heart lifted slightly at the thought of visiting Devon House and seeing all her Hamilton cousins again. It had been over two years since she was last there. Under normal circumstances she would be looking forward to a wonderful visit with her mother's family, but now . . .

Now all she could think about was that she had been callously ripped from the man she loved.

Alexander had been on the verge of proposing to her. She had known that with every fiber of her being. He'd even said that he had something important to discuss with her. What else could it have been except marriage? They had begun courting last fall. He'd proven his love and constancy to her. And just when the most exciting experience in her life was about to happen to her, just when the handsomest, most dashing man in all the world was about to ask her to marry him, her parents carried her off against her will! She didn't even have time to send a message to Alexander before the ship set sail.

Another sob caught in her throat at the thought of him.

"You'll be happy and have fun in London, Sara," her mother offered gently. "The Season is just beginning and there will be plenty for you to do. We'll even get some new ball gowns made. All your cousins will be so excited to see you and introduce you to their friends. And, of course you know, Mara will be thrilled."

Yes, thought Sara, seeing Mara again would be wonderful. Her closest cousin and dearest friend was guaranteed to be very sympathetic to her current plight. Mara would understand her heartbreak and comfort her and commiserate with her, which was just what Sara needed now. Yes, she looked forward to seeing Mara! In spite of the circumstances, she had to admit to herself that it would be fun to see her cousins Phillip and Simon again. And Aunt Colette and Uncle Lucien. Of course, Uncle Jeffrey was always great fun. And the little girls must be so grown-up by now!

Still . . . Her heart was not in this trip to London.

All things considered, she would rather be in New York as planned, attending the theater with Alexander this evening, looking into his divine green eyes and knowing he would kiss her when she agreed to be his wife. That special excitement, that romantic thrill, that she had been yearning for her whole life had been cruelly stolen away from her. Now she longed only to be with the love of her life. Her Alexander. Oh, how she missed him so much already! Pined to be in his arms . . . to have him tell her again how he loved her and couldn't live without her by his side . . .

"How are my two beautiful girls doing over here?"

Her father's voice startled Sara from her musings of Alexander's kisses.

Captain Harrison Fleming stood beside her, his eyes moving between his wife's face and his daughter's, assessing the situation with concern. He was a tall, handsome man, his tawny hair tousled by the wind and his skin golden from years at sea.

Juliette Fleming gave her husband a rueful smile. "Well, Harrison, I managed to prevent our daughter from throwing herself overboard."

Harrison looked at Sara with disappointment in his eyes. "*Drowning?*" He shook his head in disbelief. "Quite honestly, Sara, I expected better from you."

A sting of embarrassment flooded her cheeks. Disappointing her father was definitely not something Sara was used to doing. She adored him and was inordinately proud of him, and in turn he was immensely proud of his only daughter and doted on her.

He was a self-made man, her father. Born into hellish poverty in the slums of New York City, Harrison Fleming survived a brutal childhood with hard work and determination. He made his way up in the world, becoming a successful and wealthy shipping magnate. After he married Juliette Hamilton, the three of them spent a great deal of time sailing around the world on his clipper ship, the *Sea Minx*. Oh, how Sara had loved that ship! She knew every inch of it by heart, from its lofty sails to the polished railings. This new steamship was lovely to be sure. But it wasn't the same as the clipper ship.

Sara and her father enjoyed a close bond, and when she was a child, he had always indulged all of Sara's whims, even against her mother's wishes at times. He used to let her run wild about his ship, from climbing the rigging and chatting with the sailors to sitting beside him at the helm. He'd even had a little captain's hat specially made for her to match the one he wore. Sara was the captain's daughter and loved every minute of it. She and her father had had many adventures, as her family traveled the world together.

But in spite of everything, Sara wasn't ready to forgive him for what he'd done to her this day. She was still far too angry with him.

"I didn't truly intend to jump," Sara protested coldly. "Mother is exaggerating." And to be perfectly honest, when all was said and done, Sara was more than likely *not* going to throw herself into the ocean, and her mother did have a tendency to overstate the facts of any situation.

"I know you're angry and hurt, Sara," her father said, not unkindly. He placed his hand under her chin, forcing her to look up at him. "And I understand why you're upset with us, but your mother and I only did what we thought was best for you."

She had heard that before. But they *didn't* know what was best for her. It was infuriating to be told that she didn't know what she wanted. That she couldn't decide for herself what was best. In their eyes she was simply a silly little child who couldn't think for herself, not a grown woman who knew her own mind and heart. She pulled away from her father. "Well, you are both quite wrong on this account."

Her parents exchanged a secretive glance between them.

Sara was used to that behavior. Her mother and father were still ridiculously in love with each other, even after more than twenty years of marriage. Often it felt as if they spoke a different language that only the two of them could understand. It was simply a part of who they were. Sometimes Sara felt a little left out by their connection to each other, slightly jealous even. She'd always longed to find the kind of love her parents shared.

And she believed that she'd found such a relationship with Alexander Drake. The way he treated her, the words he whispered in her ear . . . Sara knew he loved her. And she loved him. Everything about him was perfect.

But now her parents had destroyed it all in one fell swoop. Or so they both thought.

"I just don't understand why . . ." She gazed at them. "What has Alexander done that is so terrible? Can you at least tell me that much?"

"We shall tell you when the time is right," Harrison said in a tone so firm that Sara knew it was fruitless to pursue the answers now.

For whatever reason, her parents had made up their minds that Alexander was somehow a threat to her and yet Sara knew without a doubt that they were wrong. "How long are we staying in London?" she managed to ask, desperate to change the subject.

"As long as it takes." Juliette looked at her with unflinching frankness and there was no mistaking her meaning. Her parents intended to keep her captive on the other side of the Atlantic Ocean, far out of reach, until Sara forgot all about Alexander Drake.

Sara took a deep breath, the sea air bracing and invigorating her, as it always did. Once again she turned her eyes to the horizon. So this was how it was going to be. Her mother and father thought this was over. That they had won.

But it wasn't even close to being over.

As soon as she got to London she would secretly send a message to him, informing him of what happened. Letting him know where she was. Alexander Drake would come for her. And he would come right away, she knew that much. It was merely a change of plans, that's all. They would be married in London instead of New York. For of course he would still want to marry her. She believed that with all of her heart.

No matter what her parents thought they had accomplished or believed they had changed by taking her to London, this was far from over.

Sara knew how to weather a storm. She wasn't a captain's daughter for nothing.

2

All Ashore

There was a flurry of activity at Devon House when they arrived in London and Sara knew immediately that they were not expected. So her parents' abduction of her was not quite the well-planned plot she assumed it was. If Aunt Colette was not aware they were coming to stay, perhaps her parents had made the decision to take her away quite suddenly?

"What a marvelous surprise! It's simply wonderful to see you!" Colette Hamilton Sinclair exclaimed in utter delight. She wrapped them both in warm embraces. Pretty and petite, her aunt looked remarkably similar to her mother. "Where is Harrison? Did he come with you? Why didn't you let us know you were coming? I would have had everything ready for you!"

Juliette's eyes met Sara's briefly. Then she hugged her sister. "Oh, we wanted to surprise you," she said airily with a wave of her hand. "Harrison is still down at the dock making sure everything is in order. You know how he is when he's with his ship, checking every last detail, but he'll be along shortly. Sara and I just couldn't wait to see you! Besides, everything is always perfectly ready at Devon House!"

Footmen dressed in the Devon House livery were busy taking the trunks and baggage up the wide staircase to their rooms. It had been two years since Sara was last at Devon House, but the beautiful white marble mansion had not changed a bit. Elegant and imposing, it was the family town house of her uncle, Lucien Sinclair, the Marquis of Stancliff. Fond memories of playing with her cousins in the many rooms and along the long corridors flooded her and she couldn't help but smile. Devon House was like a second home to her. Sara hugged her aunt Colette tightly.

"My goodness, Sara, you've grown into a beautiful woman! You remind me of your mother at that age." Colette turned to her younger sister. "Truly, Juliette, your daughter is the exact image of you at twenty."

"She does look a little like me, doesn't she?" Juliette agreed, a note of motherly pride in her voice.

"Most definitely. I'll send word to the girls that you've arrived. They will be just as surprised and thrilled as I am that you're all in town." Aunt Colette gave detailed instructions to the butler. Then Sara's pretty and stylish aunt ushered them down the wide hallway. "Well, your timing is excellent nonetheless! Phillip and I were just sitting down to tea! Come to my drawing room. Lucien and Simon are out this afternoon, but Phillip is here and has a friend with him." She turned to Sara with a sparkle in her eye. "Oh, this is wonderful! Phillip's friend is quite handsome, Sara. Do you have a beau?"

"As a matter of fact, I d—"

"No, she doesn't," Juliette said smoothly, cutting her

daughter off before Sara could properly answer and say she did indeed have a beau.

Anger and annoyance surged within her again, overwhelming the initial joy she felt at being back at Devon House. Sara gave her mother a sharp look. Her aunt was already trying to play matchmaker and she hadn't been in London a day! Sara was not interested in meeting any Englishman, no matter how handsome.

Her heart was already taken by Alexander Drake!

Sara gave a heavy sigh, reluctantly following her aunt and mother down the stately corridor. She was certainly in no mood for this, but she pasted a smile on her face.

"Well, if you're staying for the Season, which I can only assume that you are, we can certainly remedy that situation! We shall have men fighting over you, Sara!" Colette said with a knowing glance.

Juliette said softly, "We're not sure yet exactly how long we're staying in London."

"Well, you know you're welcome to stay at Devon House as long as you like, but you must promise not to leave at least until Yvette and Jeffrey's annual masked ball next month! You haven't attended one in years, Juliette! And now Sara is old enough to attend!" Aunt Colette was fairly bursting with excitement, as she ushered them into her large and elegant drawing room. Two gentlemen were seated in comfortable chairs at a table.

"Look who I found on our doorstep!" Colette announced with a flourish.

"Why, it's Aunt Juliette! And Cousin Sara!" A good-looking young man of twenty-three or so immediately stood and hurried across the room to greet them. A wide grin lit his face and his green eyes sparkled. There was a bit of the

Hamilton look about him, but he clearly favored his father, with his dark hair and broad shoulders.

"Phillip!" Sara and her mother both cried in unison. He hugged and kissed his aunt and then turned to Sara.

She squealed in delight as her eldest cousin wrapped her in a hug and then twirled her around in excitement. They had been fond playmates from an early age and adored each other. Sara more often thought of Phillip and his younger brother, Simon, as her very own brothers. As an only child she often wished for siblings and clung to her beloved Hamilton cousins to fill that void. Her terrible mood evaporated instantly upon seeing her beloved cousin.

Phillip Sinclair, who was also the Earl of Waverly, put her down and Sara cried, "I'd have recognized you anywhere, Phillip! You look just as handsome as ever."

"And you!" The exuberant young man paused to take in the changes in his younger cousin over the last two years. "And you, Sara . . . But my Lord, it's hardly possible but you have grown even prettier since I saw you last!" he commented with his usual, easygoing charm, his smile lighting up his face.

Sara simply laughed at his words. Phillip always had that way about him. He could captivate anyone and lighten the mood in any situation. Sara always felt happier just being in his presence.

Turning his attention to the other gentleman in the room, Phillip said to him, "Did I ever tell you about my pretty American cousin from New York? Sara, let me introduce you to my good friend, Christopher Townsend, the Earl of Bridgeton. This is my aunt, Mrs. Harrison Fleming, and her daughter, Miss Sara Fleming."

Sara glanced toward the gentleman who stood somewhat uncomfortably in the presence of this unexpected little family reunion. He was much taller than average, with jet-black hair and the deepest brown eyes she had ever seen. Aunt Colette was quite right when she mentioned that Phillip's friend was handsome. This Christopher Townsend, the Earl of Bridgeton, was very handsome, indeed. Sara was not so despondent over Alexander Drake that she couldn't admire a fine-looking gentleman. Of course, she preferred Alexander's golden-blond, boyish looks to this man's dark and commanding appearance. Admittedly, Lord Bridgeton's height was impressive, as was the cut of his clean-shaven jaw, and the quiet power of his presence. His handsomeness was thoroughly different from that of Alexander Drake's. Sara almost wished she could study the two men side by side to do a proper comparison.

Phillip's friend stepped toward her, and taking her hand in his, said, "It's a pleasure to meet you, Miss Fleming. And no, Waverly never mentioned he had such a beautiful American cousin."

"Why, thank you, Lord Bridgeton. It's nice to meet you also." She gave him a mischievous smile. "But I must admit I'm a bit suspicious of your character if you're friends with the likes of my cousin."

Lord Bridgeton laughed heartily. "I couldn't agree with you more, Miss Fleming. You're quite right to be suspect, but he has his good qualities too. As do I." He turned to Juliette. "Mrs. Fleming, your daughter is very charming."

Her mother laughed. "Sara can be very charming when she wishes to be."

Joining in their laughter, Phillip stated, "I'm giving you fair warning now, Bridgeton, you're out of your league with my cousin Sara."

Sara gave both men a playful grin, one she'd used countless times on her many admirers back in New York.

"Let's all sit and have our tea, shall we?" Colette suggested, indicating the sofas and chairs as they took their seats. "They are bringing more of everything, including the tea cakes."

"It's wonderful that you're here, Sara," Phillip said some time later after they'd exchanged more pleasantries and answered questions about her family's crossing of the Atlantic. "There's so much happening in town and so many parties coming up. And Aunt Yvette's masked ball is in a few weeks! You'll have a wonderful time here in London with us. You must join us tomorrow evening. We're attending Lord and Lady Abbott's ball, and we'll escort you and show you off to everyone, won't we, Bridgeton?"

"Of course, we will," Lord Bridgeton agreed.

Sara still found it difficult to reconcile the fact that she was not in New York with the man she loved. Instead she was in a drawing room in London having tea with her family and a handsome stranger who looked at her with intent, steady eyes.

While trapped on her father's ship for a week, Sara had plenty of time to consider her unusual situation. She had calmed down after her initial upset and then weighed her options. She simply had to bide her time, until Alexander came to rescue her. And he would come for her.

She had written a letter to him ready to be posted the first chance she could escape her mother. Sara wasn't foolish enough to ask one of the servants to do it, either on the *Captain's Daughter* or here at Devon House. Even her lady's maid, Leighton, couldn't be trusted not to tell her mother. If Sara acted agreeably enough and didn't show her anger and didn't mention Alexander Drake or New York, her parents would believe she had forgotten about him. They would lower their guard, never suspecting that Sara was planning to elope with Alexander.

She had it all figured out. She would simply play along with them. By being the obedient daughter, and doing all her mother and father asked of her without a fuss, they couldn't question her behavior. She had hidden her anger and her hurt feelings from them under a cool façade of calm, which left an icy cold silence between them now. So much so that Sara wondered if things would ever be the same between her and her parents again.

But Sara smiled brightly at her cousin Phillip and Lord Bridgeton, ignoring the watchful gaze of her mother. "That would be lovely, Phillip. Of course, I shall be happy to accompany you both tomorrow evening. How could I refuse an offer from two such handsome and charming gentlemen?"

At that moment the drawing room door burst open and before Parkins, the Devon House butler, could announce their newest guest, a petite blonde flew into the room. Sara jumped to her feet in delight at the sight of her cousin, Lady Mara Reeves. Seeing Mara's sweet face again almost made the trip to London worth it. Her heart filled with affection for her dearest friend, the two girls hugged each other amidst joyous squeals and laughter.

After another round of greetings and introductions, they all sat back down.

"We just got word that you arrived," Mara explained to everyone, her slight Irish accent lilting her words. "You nearly missed us. Mother and I were leaving for Ireland in the morning! She's home now, rearranging our plans, for of course we shan't be going now. She'll be over as soon as she can to see you, Aunt Juliette. She's just as excited as I am at your visit, but I simply couldn't wait another moment to see you! So I rushed right over."

Phillip exclaimed with excitement, "Well, now I can escort my two beautiful cousins to the Abbotts' ball tomorrow night. For surely you'll join us as well, Mara, won't you?"

"Oh, yes, please do!" Sara cried, urging her reticent

cousin to join them. "It will be so much more fun to have you there with me!"

Her mother and Aunt Colette encouraged her as well.

With a shy glance, Mara smiled, unable to refuse her aunts' and cousins' request. She replied a bit hesitantly, "Well, I suppose that would be all right."

"Then it's all settled," Phillip declared. "The four of us, and Simon too, will attend the Abbotts' ball together tomorrow evening. This shall be a fun Season after all, won't it, Bridgeton?"

For the briefest instant Sara caught the glance of Christopher Townsend, the Earl of Bridgeton. His brown eyes glinted and he smiled enigmatically. "Yes, it will indeed."

Later that evening, Sara Fleming and Lady Mara Reeves sat curled up on the large, cushioned window seat upstairs in Sara's lovely guest bedroom at Devon House.

"It's the most romantic story I've ever heard." Mara stared at her cousin with her wide, gray-green eyes. "Truly, Sara, it has all the markings of a great romance."

"It is rather romantic, isn't it? I hadn't thought of it that way before . . ." Sarah said quietly. "I've been too upset."

It was so nice to finally talk about what had happened to her. She had been alone aboard ship with her own thoughts for too long. How grateful she was to have a sympathetic ear! And even better that it was Mara here with her now, listening intently to her travails and completely understanding her plight.

Mara was her dearest friend in the world. Oh, to be sure, Sara had many friends in New York, but only two dear friends. There was Jennie Goodenough, who lived just across the street from her in Manhattan and was probably her closest confidante. And there was also Amanda Ellsworth. Sara spent most of last summer at Amanda's family's grand house in Newport, consoling her friend because her fiancé had callously broken off their engagement. But Jennie and Amanda would never be as close to her as Mara was. Mara was family.

"Of course it's romantic, Sara! You've been whisked away by your parents and he has to come to find you!" Mara gave a wistful little sigh.

Frowning, Sara continued, "But it's only romantic if he receives my letter and rescues me. Otherwise it's just terribly tragic."

"Oh, he will come for you. If he loves you as you say he does, he'll come." Mara nodded in support of her dearest friend.

"He simply has to come for me. He just has to. I don't know what I shall do if he doesn't." Sara bit her lip, worrying.

It was difficult to imagine just what Alexander Drake was thinking at this moment. He had declared his love for her, so of course he must miss her and long to be with her as desperately as she longed to be with him. He must realize she was taken away against her will. If only she didn't have to wait so long! Her letter couldn't even be posted until tomorrow.

She didn't know how long she could contain herself. But she must remain calm. She mustn't arouse any suspicion. There was no doubt in her mind that her parents would lock her in this very room if they suspected that Alexander Drake was coming to London to see her.

"You won't forget to post it, will you?" Sara asked, gesturing to the letter she had given her cousin.

"I promise," Mara agreed with the utmost solemnity, holding the sealed envelope in her hands. "I shall take care of it first thing in the morning." She tucked the letter safely into her reticule.

"Thank you so much!" Sara gave her cousin a grateful hug. "Now, Mara, you must tell me . . . What has been happening with you? I've done all the talking this evening. Your last letter said you were bored and wished to spend more time in Ireland, perhaps in the bookshop?"

All of Sara's aunts managed the family's business. Hamilton's Book Shoppe was the original store opened by her grandfather, Thomas Hamilton. Under the care and direction of her aunts Colette and Paulette, the shop had done so well they had opened a second store, the Hamilton Sisters' Book Shoppe. Aunt Paulette, Mara's stepmother, even opened a Hamilton shop in Ireland as well.

Sara's mother, Juliette, had never cared much for books and had gone to live in America instead. Sara often wondered what it would have been like to grow up living above a little bookshop in London with a bunch of sisters with her all the time. It seemed rather quaint and charming, compared to her own upbringing as an only child traveling the world with her parents. Sara could barely imagine living such a sedate life herself, and simply could not picture her mother living that kind of quiet life at all.

But Sara did love Hamilton's Book Shoppe and took great pride in her aunts' accomplishments. It was a rare thing indeed for women to own and operate their own businesses and do it so successfully! Sara always made a point to visit at least one of the shops when she was in London. Her favorite was the Hamilton Sisters' Book Shoppe, the store where she met Mara for the very first time when they were little girls. They had become instant friends that day.

"I'm afraid I have nothing half so interesting to tell you . . ." Mara shook her head of soft blond curls.

"Oh, there must be something interesting!" Sara responded with a note of hope in her voice. "Surely there is a handsome young man you're pining over?"

"No, there isn't."

"You've already had your coming-out, so you must have had scores of offers . . ."

"No offers," Mara said quietly.

"That's ridiculous!" Sara refused to believe it. "How is such a thing even possible? You are beautiful and sweet and smart. Any man would fall in love with you in an instant. You're every man's type, blond and petite! Not to mention that you're Lady Mara Reeves, the daughter of the Earl of Cashelmore!"

Mara sighed heavily. "There simply wasn't anyone . . . I never met anyone who seemed special enough to me. Yes, there were gentlemen who expressed some interest in me. They were all nice enough, of course, but just . . . I don't know, Sara . . . They were rather ordinary." Mara's voice had a hint of sadness.

"Ah, yes, that I can understand." Sara nodded sympathetically. "To fall in love a girl has to meet someone extraordinary. Back in New York I had dozens of men declaring their love for me, but when I first met Alexander, I simply knew. I just took one look into his gorgeous green eyes and I knew he was special. In an instant I realized that he was the man I would be with for the rest of my life and that he felt the very same way about me. There we were, in the middle of Central Park surrounded by dozens of people, and we could only stare at each other. He looked so handsome too, with his golden hair and boyish smile. I could barely breathe! Oh, but listen to me going on and on about myself again! Forgive me?"

Mara giggled as if they were little girls again. "You always talked more than enough for both of us."

"That is true!" Sara had to smile at the honesty in her cousin's words and her reference to the time years ago when Mara didn't speak at all. Having opposite personalities was more than likely what drew the two girls together. Sara knew she could tell Mara anything and trusted her implicitly. Now Sara wanted only the best for her cousin. "But please don't give up hope, Mara. That extraordinary man is out there for you. We just have to find him."

"I hope so." Mara looked slightly doubtful, her delicate brows creased with worry. "I think my parents were a little disappointed that I didn't find a husband last year, although they would never say so to me."

"Of course they wouldn't! Your parents are wonderful and understanding and they love you. They are not like other parents who only wish to secure financial gains or social connections through their daughter's marriage. I know Aunt Paulette and Uncle Declan well enough to know that they want only for you to be happy. They would never force you to wed someone you didn't wish to marry."

"Oh, I never suggested they would do that to me!" Mara interjected, not wishing to cast aspersions on her parents. "My father has ever only wanted the best for me. I just think they wished I had received an offer. They worry about me and believe I will never marry, and perhaps I shan't. But it saddens me to think that they are worried over my future."

Sara sat up and squeezed her cousin's hand tightly in support. "Well, while I'm here, let's make the best of the Season, shall we? Let's attend all the parties and balls with Phillip and Simon, and this time *I* will be on the lookout for a special gentleman who will be the perfect match for my most beautiful cousin!"

"Oh, Sara, your enthusiasm is almost contagious! How I've missed you!" Mara smiled gleefully. "But I don't see how your presence will suddenly cause scores of extraordinary men to appear at Lady Abbott's ball tomorrow evening and fall in love with me!"

"True," Sara admitted thoughtfully. "But at least you'll have more fun here in London with me than if you were to go to Ireland for the summer as you had planned."

"Point taken," Mara conceded a bit reluctantly. "We shall see what happens." Then she added, "It truly is lovely to have you here, Sara. Today was the best surprise!"

Sara grinned with happiness. "And here's to Sara and Mara, together again!"

3

Adrift

Christopher Townsend, the Earl of Bridgeton, wasn't expecting to meet anyone that afternoon. Least of all someone like her. It was just a random moment. Unplanned. Unforeseen. And yet not unwelcome. In fact, deep down he felt the focus of his existence shift. Like a landslide. Or a tidal wave. Suddenly the landscape of his world was entirely different the minute he met the beautiful American girl.

It had started off as just an ordinary day. He had been out riding earlier that afternoon with his friend Phillip Sinclair, the Earl of Waverly, when they made an unplanned stop at Devon House, and Phillip's mother had invited them to stay for tea. Lady Stancliff was a charming woman, and although the two young men had other plans for the afternoon, they'd been unable to refuse her gracious request to stay and join her. Besides, they were always hungry and the freshly made tea cakes were too delicious to pass up.

Then Miss Sara Fleming entered the drawing room and had quite literally taken his breath away. She breezed in, self-assured and sophisticated, and looking more beautiful than any woman he could ever recall meeting, and then she recognized her cousin.

A joyous smile lit her angelic face and it felt as if the sun had burst from the clouds. Her excited laughter and lilting voice washed over him and he suddenly couldn't move. Or think. Or do anything but stare helplessly at the stunning young woman in front of him. Her flawless skin, perfectly turned nose, sparkling blue eyes fringed with long dark lashes, and silky black hair that framed her exquisitely heart-shaped face, all graced a petite and curvaceous little figure. That she was saucy and a bit impertinent only added to her charm. Perhaps it was the American influence in her, but she was like no other woman he had ever met.

And just like that, Christopher Townsend, the Earl of Bridgeton, was escorting her to a ball the very next evening, along with her cousins. The Earl of Waverly, and his younger brother Lord Simon Sinclair, Lady Mara Reeves, and Sara Fleming were attending one of the largest balls of the Season together. They made a lively, young group. Although he wasn't officially their escort, Christopher felt protective over both ladies.

Lady Mara Reeves was a pretty little thing too, with her soft, blond hair, wide, luminous eyes, and lilting accent. But for Christopher, the quiet beauty of Mara Reeves was completely eclipsed by the very vibrancy of Sara Fleming's incandescent beauty.

"Isn't that Edward Wickham over there?" Phillip asked him with a jovial grin, gesturing across the ballroom at an old school chum they both knew.

"Yes, it is. We'd better head over and say hello to him," Christopher said.

As their small group meandered through Lady Abbott's massive ballroom, filled with glittering candles, elegant tables laden with gourmet delicacies, and gorgeous floral arrangements, while costly and fashionably dressed noble and wealthy guests milled about, Christopher knew he should have been having an enjoyable evening. As a handsome, entitled young man of the nobility in the company of beautiful ladies, why wouldn't he have a good time?

Yet he only had one thought weighing heavily on his mind.

The message he had received earlier from Griggs, his estate manager, left an icy cold knot in the pit of his stomach. Now he had no choice but to return to Bridgeton Hall in the morning.

"Lord Bridgeton, you're looking far too serious for such an event."

Startled, Christopher turned his attention to the beautiful young woman gazing up at him. His heart actually skipped a beat. It was ridiculous.

"Yes, you are much too serious for an evening such as this." Miss Fleming's expression was somewhat puzzled.

"I must apologize. I'm afraid you caught me woolgathering, Miss Fleming." He gave her a smile. She was such a tiny thing. In a gown of palest blue that matched the exact color of her eyes, with her silky, dark hair and fair skin, she looked angelic, but she still couldn't disguise the true passion in her nature. It was as if it just sizzled below the surface of her cool exterior. Perhaps that was what he found so intriguing about her?

"There's no need for an apology, Lord Bridgeton," she said sweetly. "You just have a slight look of worry about you. I hope all is well."

Surprised by her astuteness, Christopher added that particular attribute to her physical appearance. She was totaling up quite nicely.

The orchestra began playing a waltz and he held out his arm to her. "Would you care to dance with me, Miss Fleming?"

"Oh yes, thank you. I love dancing and adore waltzes!"

With graceful movements, Sara Fleming stepped lightly on her feet and followed him to the dance floor.

An enchanting fragrance wafted around them as she moved and Christopher couldn't place it. Something floral and light. He had no idea about such things. He only knew the scent would be forever etched in his mind as associated with Sara Fleming and this night.

"Oh, this is one of my favorite waltzes." She sighed happily as she spun in his arms.

All the songs sounded the same to him, but her sheer delight in the music amused him. "I couldn't tell one waltz from the next. What's the name of it?"

"Don't you know?" She seemed amused when he shook his head. "It's been around for ages. It's called 'Tout à vous.' It means 'yours very truly.' Isn't it lovely?"

What was rather lovely was holding her in his arms. "I couldn't agree more, Miss Fleming."

"How long have you known my cousin Phillip?" she asked, making polite conversation.

"Oh, Waverly and I have been friends since we were at school together. And I've gotten to know his brother very well too over the years. The Sinclairs are both good men. I was aware they had a large extended family, but this is my first time meeting you and Lady Mara, of course."

She flashed him a flirtatious grin. "Disappointed?"

"Quite the opposite, Miss Fleming."

Seemingly satisfied with his answer, she asked, "Do you live in London?"

"I spend a lot of my time here, but also at Bridgeton Hall, my family estate in Sussex."

"I'm sure your home must be lovely."

"I've been told it's quite nice." Enjoying the feel of her in his arms, he asked, "Did you grow up in New York?"

"Yes, mostly. And at our country house in New Jersey, where I was born," she explained. "But I spent most of my life sailing around the world with my parents, aboard my father's ship. We traveled everywhere when I was younger. China. Brazil. California. And of course, we made frequent visits to London to visit my cousins."

Impressed with her extraordinary upbringing, he asked, "And how long will we have the pleasure of your company in London this time?"

"I'm not sure as yet. It's up to my parents to decide." She gave a little sigh.

"I see," he said. "That sounds a bit mysterious."

She smiled enigmatically, her eyes sparkling. "I suppose it is."

The girl had secrets of her own. Interesting. "So what is your life like in New York, Miss Fleming?" he asked.

"I suspect it's much like it is in London," she explained as he twirled her around the floor. How elegant and graceful she was! "We do the same kinds of things in New York that you do here and have the same sort of entertainments. Parties, musicales, soirees, suppers, dancing, the theater."

"Which city do you prefer?"

"Oh, New York, of course!" Her laughter floated around him like a song.

"Why is that?" he asked. "If they're the same, I mean. Large, bustling cities."

"It's the people who are different," she explained with the utmost sincerity. "It's the people who matter. Although I do love my many aunts, uncles, and cousins dearly, all my close friends are back in New York. The people I love are there. And I miss them. All of them." A shadow crossed her pretty face. "Quite a lot."

Christopher noted her expression carefully. She clearly missed more than just her friends. "Any one person in particular?"

She gave him a sideways glance. "Of course."

His heart thudded in his chest at the look in her eyes. The

man who held this woman's heart was a lucky man indeed. And if he were that man, he certainly wouldn't have allowed a beautiful woman like Sara Fleming to cross the ocean without him by her side. Why was she in London and not in New York with this man?

"I'm sure he misses you terribly," he said quietly.

Sara suddenly lost her footing and stumbled but Christopher caught her before she fell, steadying her with his arms. For the briefest instant he held her so closely he could feel her heartbeat against his chest. It passed too quickly, and he almost wondered if it happened at all.

Sara responded to his remark by flashing a mischievous smile. "I'm sure he does."

As the dance ended, Christopher pondered her rather flirtatious answer. Neither moved from their place on the dance floor. They remained motionless and he still held her in his arms. There was something very special about this girl and he couldn't for the life of him explain what it was or why he felt this way.

He'd danced with dozens of beautiful ladies before. None of them had left him feeling so off-kilter. So unsure of himself. Was it because she was American? Was that what made her seem so different? So exceptional? Was it her unusual upbringing? Or her incredible self-confidence?

He'd certainly had his fair share of attractive women. Christopher Townsend wasn't some rube from the country. He was an earl, for crying out loud, and a very handsome one at that. Beautiful women fell over themselves to be with him. In fact they fell right into his bed. And quite often.

Suddenly the image of Sara Fleming naked in his bed, smiling playfully and giving him one of her seductive sideways glances while tangled in the sheets, flashed through his mind. He couldn't quite breathe.

"And what about you, Lord Bridgeton?"

"*Me?*" he asked, startled from his illicit thoughts by her question.

"You asked me, so it's only fair that I get to ask you," she pointed out, her eyes twinkling. "Is there any one lady in particular for you?"

He stared down into her light blue eyes. How easily he could drown in those eyes! As for her question . . . If only there was someone in particular for him. A woman he cared for. A woman who meant something to him. Another image suddenly flashed in his head. Of a beautiful blue-eyed wife holding a child in her arms. He shook himself from the startling reverie.

Managing a careless air, he presented her with his signature smile. "Possibly, Miss Fleming. Quite possibly."

Gracing him with a look that clearly stated that she wasn't the least bit satisfied with his answer, she rolled her eyes. Once again, he was surprised that she was so astute. Impressed even. Or perhaps she was simply a lucky guesser.

"Thank you for the dance, Lord Bridgeton."

"You are very welcome, Miss Fleming. It was my pleasure." Christopher truly despised dancing, but he could have danced with Sara Fleming all evening without a moment's hesitation. After guiding her back to where her cousins had gathered near the refreshments, he released her with great reluctance.

Christopher then spent a good portion of the evening chatting with his friends, playing a little cards, and dancing with ladies who made no secret of the fact they had designs on an eligible earl. All the while he couldn't help watching the lovely Sara Fleming as she danced with other gentlemen, a pretty smile on her face. However, his mind kept going back to the message he'd had from Griggs, his estate manager. It could only mean bad news. The worst possible news. As long as he had tried to ignore it, Christopher would have to face it all tomorrow.

At one point he wandered outside for a bit of fresh air, thinking to clear his head. While breathing in the cool May air, he walked along a garden path, his shoes softly crunching the gravel beneath him. Lady Abbott had wonderful gardens.

To the outside world he knew he presented a façade as a carefree and young lord, wealthy and eligible, from a long and distinguished family lineage. Part of that was true. Part of it was a lie. Christopher had no choice but to lie, and to keep up the charade of being happy and wealthy.

Sighing, he thought how ridiculous his life had become. The complications from his father's death last year were more than he'd expected. Instead of freeing him as he'd always dreamed of, the death of his father only seemed to make his own life worse. And more confining.

Christopher smiled ruefully into the night shadows. Self-pity was not becoming on any man. And definitely not on him. There were plenty of men who would give their own lives to switch places with him. Oddly enough he often wished he could trade with any one of them and go off and live a life of simplicity and freedom. Live his *own* life.

Now that was it. His own life . . .

What a tempting thought that was! What would living his own life entail?

Suddenly Christopher stopped, in disbelief at the sight in front of him. No, it couldn't be.

But there she was.

The lovely Sara Fleming sat alone on a marble bench under a tree, staring up at the stars. Her pretty face was illuminated by the moonlight on her soft, ivory skin, and her pale blue silk gown shimmered around her. He watched for a moment while she was unaware of his presence, transfixed by the expression of longing and sadness on her face. This was not the flirtatious and careless American girl he had danced with earlier this evening. There was a tangible aura of sadness around her now.

What could have this beautiful girl looking so melancholy, when earlier she was vivacious and bubbly, the very picture of happiness? If he had to guess, it would certainly have to do with her mysterious gentleman in New York. He couldn't ignore the slight pang of jealousy he felt in his chest at the sight of her so clearly longing for this man. He was quite certain that no one had ever missed him that much in his life.

"Miss Fleming?" he said as softly as he could, hoping not to startle her.

She gasped at the sound of her name, clearly disquieted. She peered up at him. "Lord Bridgeton?"

"Yes," he responded, walking nearer to her. "I'm very sorry to intrude. Are you well?"

Sara gave him a half smile and nodded her head.

She should not be alone out here in the garden. A young lady could easily lose her reputation this way. He asked, "Can I escort you back to the house?"

She shook her head and surprised him by patting the bench beside her, inviting him to join her there.

"What are you doing out here all alone?" he asked, but he did not sit down. "You should return to the ballroom with the others."

"Yes, yes, I know," she said softly, gazing up at him with her blue eyes reflected in moonlight. "I just needed a moment or two to myself."

"You were looking far too serious just now."

She arched an elegant eyebrow. "Using my own words against me, are you?"

He smiled wryly. "They fit the occasion."

She sighed, but made no move to rise from the bench. On an impulse he accepted her earlier invitation and sat down beside her. She obviously wished to talk to him. Who was he to deny her?

"Well, Miss Fleming, if you don't mind my asking, why are you out here looking so terribly sad?"

She looked at him knowingly. "I have a feeling you may have already guessed, Lord Bridgeton."

"Would I be correct in assuming it has to do with a certain gentleman in New York?" he asked with a raised brow.

"Yes . . ."

"Has he broken your heart?" For some reason the idea of any man hurting her made him irrationally angry.

"Oh, no!" She shook her head. "Quite the opposite. In fact, I fear I may have broken his heart, although through no fault of my own."

Something she had said earlier suddenly made sense to him. "Your parents? They brought you here to separate the two of you?"

"Yes, and I miss him dreadfully," she confessed, her voice tinged with longing.

So the man had not willingly let her leave. Then again, what man would? But Christopher wondered what it was about this man that had prompted her parents to take her away. He had met both Mr. and Mrs. Fleming and they seemed like very reasonable and likable people. The fault had to lie with the man in New York. He mustn't be good enough for her. But looking at Sara Fleming right now, he doubted any man was good enough for her.

Christopher said, "I can only imagine it's not half as much as he misses you."

"That's very kind of you to say."

"I'm certain it's the truth. And I'm just as certain that he must love you very much."

"Thank you," she whispered. "I simply wish to return home to him. I hope I don't sound ungrateful, since everyone has been so lovely to me since I arrived, including you,

Lord Bridgeton. However, I left my heart with him so I cannot be truly happy until I am with him again."

"That's quite understandable," he said to comfort her. Yet he suddenly wished he could pull this beautiful woman into his arms and make her forget all about the man in New York.

Very slowly she placed her gloved hand over his and looked into his eyes. "Lord Bridgeton . . . I would beg your discretion in this matter, for I've told no one else and I've no wish for this to be known. I don't know why I even spoke of it to you. I suppose you caught me at a weak moment." She paused, gazing at him. "Although we just met and I barely know you, for some reason I feel as if I can trust you."

Oddly touched by her confession, he said, "You have my word, Miss Fleming. I shall keep your secret."

"Thank you," she murmured softly.

A silence fell upon them, and her small hand still covered his. They stared into each other's eyes. As they sat in the moonlight, alone in the garden, he felt his heart thudding wildly in his chest. Such an unusual sensation this girl evoked in him.

"You have your own secrets as well, Lord Bridgeton, haven't you?"

He nodded. "It seems we share a similar predicament. To others we have every reason in the world to be happy, outwardly. Yet there are things no one knows about that prevent us from being so."

"That's remarkable, is it not? That even the people closest to us have no idea how we truly feel . . ." Her voice was sad.

"Yes."

"What is it that troubles you?" she asked in a whisper. "A woman?"

"No, it's not a woman." He sighed. "I wish it were that simple, actually."

She looked at him in understanding. It felt as if her eyes peered into his very heart. Completely unnerved by it, his walls went up.

He cleared his throat. "Miss Fleming, it is past time you went back inside. It wouldn't help your situation at all if we were discovered out here alone together. Besides, your cousins must be wondering where you are by now."

Suddenly the intimate spell they'd been under was broken. Sara promptly removed her hand from his and stood up. "You are quite right. I should go inside."

He rose from the bench, feeling strangely bereft. "You go ahead first. I'll wait here."

Nodding, she turned to leave. Suddenly she spun around, whispered, "Thank you," and placed the lightest of kisses on his cheek.

Stunned, Christopher watched her walk away, a shapely figure in pale blue silk fading away in the night.

4

Charting a Course

"So you simply packed up and left? Just like that?"

Paulette Hamilton Reeves, the Countess of Cashel-more, asked in amazement.

"We had no choice. As soon as we suspected the man's true intentions and that he planned to propose to her, Harrison made up his mind to leave the next morning. I barely had time to pack for either of us," Juliette Hamilton Fleming explained to her four sisters as they gathered in Colette's private sitting room later that same evening.

"It's a terrible reason to have you visit us, but I'm still glad you're all here," Lisette Hamilton Roxbury offered sweetly, her smile somewhat rueful. The third of the five sisters was the busy wife of Quinton Roxbury, a leader in Parliament, and the mother of three children, including twin boys.

"My question is this: Does Sara know the real reason you decided to leave New York?" Colette asked. The eldest of the five Hamilton sisters had taken on the role of matriarch of the family since their mother had passed away. Although her coffee-colored hair held the slightest touch of gray, her unlined face would never lead anyone to guess she was the mother of two fully grown and very handsome sons.

Juliette shook her head with determination. "Not yet. Harrison is waiting for some way to prove it to her, show her evidence, so that she will believe us. All we have now are our suspicions based on what Harrison's friend told us about him. Just before we left, Harrison hired an investigator to get to the bottom of things. As soon as the investigator sends us something, we will explain everything to her. It was bad enough that we took Sara away from him to keep her safe. But it will break my daughter's heart when she learns the truth about the man she thinks she's madly in love with and destined to be with. I wish I knew a better way, but for now she's terribly angry with us."

"Yes, I'm sure she is, as any young girl in love would be," Yvette Hamilton Eddington, the Duchess of Rathmore and the baby of the family, agreed, her stylishly coiffed head bobbing. "Sara doesn't want to believe anything ill of the man she loves and she's too young to understand that you are only doing what's best for her. And as the mother of three girls, I hope we are never in such a position, but if we were, I know Jeffrey and I would do whatever we had to in order to protect them from an unscrupulous suitor."

Paulette added with a touch of humor, "Oh, Juliette, I just shudder to think what you would have done had *Maman* done such a thing to you when you were Sara's age!"

"*Maman* never would have cared enough to stop me, even if she could have," Juliette said with unflinching honesty.

The sisters grew somewhat somber at the truth of Juliette's words, and at the memory of their melodramatic and manipulative mother. Of course, Genevieve La Brecque

Hamilton, with her French manners and flair, loved her daughters but she had made their life together far more difficult than it needed to be in their little rooms above Hamilton's Book Shoppe. There was no disagreement that the girls had done more for one another than either of their parents had ever been able to do for them.

The family had been on the brink of destitution before Colette's sheer determination had made their bookstore a success. Eventually her marriage to Lucien Sinclair, now the Marquis of Stancliff, had provided the Hamilton sisters with another level of financial stability and safety at Devon House.

"I still miss *Maman*," Lisette said in a wistful tone. "And Papa too."

"We all miss her and Papa," Juliette continued pragmatically, "and we loved them both very much. But it doesn't mean we can forget how trying *Maman* could be or how she had little to no interest in anything we did or thought. Paulette and Yvette, you were both a little too young to remember just how dreadful things were. Or how desperate our situation was when we were about to lose the shop and had nowhere to go and no one in the family to help us. You may not recall the many late nights that Colette and I worked our fingers to the bone redesigning the bookshop after Papa died, while Uncle Randall threatened to marry us off to the highest bidder. *Maman* cared about herself first, us second, and Papa and the bookshop not at all. It was just how she was. Can you even imagine her coming after me when I left for New York with Harrison? Or forbidding me to go? For my own good?"

Slowly the other four women shook their heads. They knew their mother all too well. She had passed away many years ago now, and as much as they loved her, they still vividly recalled her dramatic fainting spells and French-laden diatribes, and her reluctance to deal with reality.

"You did as any mother would do," Yvette stated firmly, breaking the thoughtful silence. "You protected your daughter, Juliette. She may be angry with you now, but one day Sara will see that you only had her best interests at heart. I would do the exact same thing with any of my three girls, I promise you that."

"Jeffrey wouldn't settle for anything less," Colette said with a meaningful smile. "He's the most overprotective father I have ever seen."

"It's been an endless source of amusement to me, Yvette, that our darling Jeffrey Eddington, the Rogue of All Rogues, was blessed with three beautiful daughters to torment him!" Juliette said with a wicked glint in her eyes.

Paulette agreed heartily, "Truly. It's just altogether too perfect."

Yvette laughed in acknowledgment. She was quite aware of her husband's reputation with women before their marriage, but he was also the most devoted, the most protective, and the most charming of men. One by one, Jeffrey had managed to play an instrumental part in each of her sisters' path to the altar. But Yvette had been the one to marry Lord Jeffrey Eddington, the very handsome and illegitimate son of the Duke of Rathmore, who turned out not to be illegitimate after all. Although the Hamilton sisters had practically adopted Jeffrey as their very own brother right from the start, while he was still a reputed rake and rascal, Yvette had fallen in love with him and Jeffrey had reformed his ways to have her.

Now little Yvette Hamilton, the baby of the family, was the Duchess of Rathmore and the mother of three adorable daughters. "Oh, believe me, I derive a great deal of pleasure out of watching him squirm. And the girls haven't even had their debut yet! They shall lead him on a merry chase, indeed. Especially little Vivienne."

"Poor Jeffrey," Lisette lamented, as she was always the most sympathetic of the sisters. "He's never been anything but wonderful to all of us, and here you all are, taking great delight in his misery as a worried and caring father."

"Oh, Lisette!" Juliette taunted her younger sister. "Jeffrey was always the kindest to you! You've no idea the teasing and torture he heaped upon me!"

"But you deserved it!" Paulette pointed out. Now the Countess of Cashelmore and the proprietor of several book-shops, the fourth youngest Hamilton sister divided her time between her husband's ancestral home in Ireland and her bookstore there and raising their daughter, Mara, and son, Thomas, in London.

"That's very true. I was a bit outrageous at times, wasn't I?" Juliette admitted with pride, and then her expression grew dark. "Unfortunately, I fear that my daughter has in-herited my willful streak. Perhaps Harrison and I raised her too permissively. We may have brought her to safety in London for the time being, but if she is anything like me . . . I don't trust her not to do something reckless to win him back."

"Like sneaking off in the middle of the night to stow away on a ship bound for New York?" Colette asked with a raised brow. "And scaring her family half to death with worry, wondering where she was?"

The five sisters grew thoughtful at the memory, for they all recalled Juliette's wild and headstrong nature and how she ran off in the middle of the night to stow away on Cap-tain Fleming's ship bound for America simply for a bit of adventure. It turned out to be the ship of her future husband and it all worked out wonderfully in the end. But at the time, the entire family had all been sick with worry over her. And it had been Jeffrey Eddington who had gone to search for her.

Colette's pointed reference to Juliette's reckless past hit its mark.

"Exactly!" Juliette declared, but her pretty face was lined with worry. "You've no idea the sleepless nights I've had over this. I'm terrified she will try something as foolish as I once did to get back to New York."

"Oh, the apple doesn't fall far from the tree, does it?" added Lisette, her eyes dancing with merriment.

"Yes, yes, I know. This is my punishment for my past behavior and the anguish I put you all through," Juliette said. "But honestly, girls, I have to say, aside from sailing off to America, I wasn't any more outrageous than each of you. Think about it. We Hamilton sisters did not follow the most conventional paths."

"You have a point there." Paulette actually laughed aloud. "I for one cannot deny that."

Each of the sisters nodded knowingly, thinking back on their pasts, before they were married.

Colette ventured softly, "Sara could be just like us . . ."

"That is why I worry. So what are Harrison and I to do about her?" Juliette asked, her voice filled with seriousness. "We can't keep Sara under lock and key while we're here either. Which was Harrison's original intent, by the way. I managed to persuade him not to do so. We can't lock her up, not if we want her to meet a man she likes better and who makes her forget all about Alexander Drake. I don't wish to punish Sara, for she didn't do anything wrong. She simply happened to fall in love with the most dreadful man."

"Well, we can certainly make sure Phillip and Simon keep a close eye on Sara," Colette offered. "My boys tend to be protective of her anyway. I'm sure they will watch her as if she were their own little sister."

"Yes, that would help." Juliette nodded, a glimmer of hope in her eyes.

"Of course, it will." Colette continued, "And Phillip and Simon both have lots of wonderful young friends to introduce her to, like that Lord Bridgeton that you met yesterday. The Season is just beginning. There is so much for them to do and endless rounds of events for them to attend together. The boys can certainly keep Sara occupied. I'm sure they are all having a lovely time at Lady Abbott's this evening, even as we speak. Let's have Sara come to the bookshops while she's here and really learn the business. It will be good for her. Paulette and I will look after her and Mara will be there too. Sara will forget all about this man before you know it, and New York will seem like a million miles away to her."

All the sisters agreed that Colette's suggestion was a good plan.

Juliette eyed Paulette carefully. "Then there's Mara."

"Yes," Paulette said, biting her lip. "That could be tricky. I'm sure Mara knows everything by now, or at least Sara's version of it. And I've no doubt my daughter is highly sympathetic to Sara's situation and will likely do all she can to support her."

Ever the hopeful one, Lisette asked, "Can't you explain the situation to Mara? She's reasonable enough to want to keep Sara safe. Wouldn't she tell you if Sara were up to anything dangerous?"

"Oh, no," Juliette and Paulette both said in unison, knowing the very close bond between the two young girls could not be broken.

Paulette continued, "I couldn't ask Mara to do that. Besides she would never betray Sara. She's too devoted to her. Sara was the one who brought Mara out of her silence, remember?"

Sara and Mara had been as thick as thieves since they were four years old and nothing, not even the great span of the Atlantic Ocean, had come between their friendship over the years. When they first met, the fact that their names had rhymed had been an endless source of amusement to them, a marvel that seemed to bind the two little girls together. With two such opposite personalities it was amazing that they were so close. For each of Sara's outgoing and confident ways, Mara was equally quiet and shy.

"It will be good for Mara to have Sara here," added Paulette thoughtfully, aware of her stepdaughter's introverted personality. "Perhaps she can draw Mara out of her shell. Last year's Season was not what we had hoped. Declan and I worry for Mara and we just want her to be happy. She's so withdrawn at times."

"Would it be so terrible if Mara didn't marry?" Lisette questioned.

"No, not at all . . . Not if that was what she wanted," Paulette explained. "We were only leaving for Ireland because she didn't wish to participate in another London Season, which was fine with us. I think she's simply scared. And that's why I'm so glad that Sara is here now. Mara trusts her and would do anything for her. With Sara here, Mara will join her in attending parties and balls. Sara's high-spiritedness has always been a good influence on Mara. They tend to balance each other. I was happy when I heard that Mara agreed to go out with her cousins this evening."

Colette smiled with confidence. "Well, I believe this could be a wonderful experience for both girls."

"Yes," Juliette said quietly. "But we shall have to watch over the two of them carefully."

"Yes, most assuredly," Paulette said.

"If you hear of anything—anything at all—you'll let me know?" Juliette asked her sisters, her eyes filled with worry.

"Yes, of course." They all agreed to watch over their eldest niece, who was a Hamilton girl, just like them.

5

A Sinking Ship

"So that's it? Only six more months?" Christopher Townsend, the Earl of Bridgeton, incredulously questioned his estate manager the next morning.

The balding man slid the open, leather-bound ledger across the wide oak desk to him and pointed to the figure at the bottom of the page. "Yes, but that is only if you are very careful and strictly follow the budget I've laid out for you. And that is also providing that no emergencies arise on the estate, either. It's taken me the better part of the year to sort through the tangle of double accounts, expenses, and debts your father has accrued. It pains me to say it but it has come down to this. You need to sell the estate to pay all the creditors or find a massive influx of cash immediately. But six months is all you have left, my lord."

The grim news hit Christopher like a violent punch in the gut. As he eyed the meticulously inscribed numbers in the ledger, they seemed to dance a jig across the page, taunting him. There it was. Written documentation of his father's monumental failings. Proof of the crushing debt he had inherited. Of course, he had been aware that the estate was not in the best of shape, but he thought he would at least be able to get the finances back on track. He thought it would be manageable. He ran his fingers through his dark hair, sighing heavily.

Six months.

The situation was even worse than he'd imagined.

If only his investments would come through. With what little money he'd managed to scrape together, Christopher had invested in a small shipping company last year, but so far he hadn't reaped any profit and he had no idea exactly when he would. It was a strong company and he believed it would succeed eventually, but apparently not soon enough to save Bridgeton Hall. Or his sisters.

Or himself, for that matter.

"The numbers are not good, my lord. And there is the matter of my own family to consider as well . . ." The man looked quite uncomfortable and his round cheeks reddened. He cleared his throat before speaking again. "I have sought out another position, my lord."

"You have?"

"I have accepted a new post as the estate manager at Green Briar Manor in Yorkshire, starting at the end of the month."

"Yes, I understand, Griggs." Christopher tried to hide his disappointment.

"I am sorry, my lord, but I must think of my family. I have six children."

"Of course you do. And I shall be sad to see you go. You've been a great help to me and have served the estate well, given the very difficult circumstances. I wish I could retain your services. But as you see . . ." Christopher held up his hands. He too would more than likely abandon the sinking ship if he were in the manager's position. It was self-preservation. Unfortunately for Christopher, he couldn't jump ship when he was the captain.

"I wish you the best of luck, my lord. And if I may say, it's a terrible shame how your father ruined this estate," Griggs said. "Bridgeton Hall was always the pride of the county. It is now clear to me why he went through so many managers over the last years of his life. None of them could prevent him from spending unwisely and hiding expenses and the gambling debts. He seemed bent on destroying—"

"Yes, I'm well aware of my father's destructive nature, thank you," Christopher interrupted. No one needed to explain to him the carelessly selfish and dangerously reckless ways of his father. He had learned that firsthand at a very early age.

The former Earl of Bridgeton, James Townsend, had been a cruel and vicious man who made the lives of his wife and children a living nightmare. After he died last year, Christopher believed they were finally free of his domineering and abusive ways. Yet his father had left them with a shocking surprise. He'd spent virtually all the money and left his wife and children with a nightmare of a different kind.

In spite of all that Christopher had done in the past year to salvage their financial situation, it wasn't enough. He had budgeted and cut expenses, his own and that of his mother and sisters. He had sold most of the family's valuable possessions. But it barely made a dent in the mountain of debt his father had accumulated.

There really was no option left except to sell his family's ancestral home. Or marry an extremely wealthy woman.

Humiliated and sick to his stomach at being in this position, Christopher thought of his two younger sisters and he knew he had no choice. As much as he hoped to avoid it coming to this, he would have to find a rich wife. And quickly too. Marrying her by the end of the summer.

"Thank you, Griggs. I will miss you. I wish you and your family all the best in your new venture." Christopher stood and shook the smaller man's hand. He truly was saddened to see his estate manager leave. Especially since he could not afford to hire a new one. But he now had more pressing business to take care of.

As Christopher watched Griggs leave the office that once belonged to his wastrel of a father, he turned to stare out the tall windows that framed the elegant room. The familiar rolling vista of green lawns spread out before him. Acre upon acre of rich farmland and fertile pastures. This beautiful countryside belonged to him, but for how much longer? Could he manage to save it? He simply had to. He could not be the earl who lost the family estate.

Christopher Townsend, the seventh Earl of Bridgeton, needed to marry well.

Lord, how he hated being in that position.

But he hated his father even more for placing him in this abhorrent situation. Fortunately, Christopher had managed to keep his family's dire financial straits a secret. For the time being, at least. Everyone thought him an eligible bachelor, the heir to a respected earldom. No one suspected that the massive manor house was mired in debt and on the verge of crumbling to pieces. The vast wealth that the first earl had accumulated and had sustained generations of Townsends was all but gone. Thanks to none other than his father, the sixth earl.

There really was nothing left now.

As Christopher looked out on the lush and verdant acres thick with the green of spring that surrounded the Townsend property, he marveled that no one had guessed his awful secret. At the ball last night he had taken note of the ambitious mothers hovering around him and calculating his worth, while whispering to their debutante daughters about him, "He's an earl! And a young, handsome one at that. Smile prettily for him now!"

Then there were the young ladies themselves, already smitten with him, waving their fans and batting their eyelashes, trying to get his attention. They preened and fawned to gain his favor and hopefully win a dance with him.

Christopher was used to being thought of as a catch. He'd spent his entire life as the only son of an earl, knowing full well he would inherit everything when his father died, but he'd never really had to consider what that actually meant before. It was simply a fact of his existence. Women wanted to marry him. Being a tall, good-looking man only added to his appeal. But he never thought he'd have to make the mercenary consideration of how much his future bride would be worth. How much *she* would bring to the marriage.

Now if he could only wed a suitable lady before anyone could discover his bankrupt coffers. How those ambitious mothers would turn up their noses at him if they only knew the truth! Still, he had his title. An earldom was nothing to sniff at, and his earldom was now for sale to the highest bidder, apparently. It was all he had to offer to his future bride. He could make her a countess in exchange for her money.

And she needed to bring quite a lot of that.

His mind started calculating a list of the wealthy women he knew. It was shockingly short. There was a wealthy, pretty widow he was acquainted with. Perhaps she'd be interested in gaining the title of Countess of Bridgeton. But the thought of marrying her left him feeling a little cold inside.

Yet, he desperately needed a rich wife.

The image of Sara Fleming's beautiful face flashed in his mind.

There was something about that American woman. He felt a connection to her. And she felt it as well. He knew she did. She had confided in him so sweetly last night. And she'd kissed him! On the cheek, but still. It was a stunning gesture.

It was a shame she was planning to return to New York and to the man she loved. That was a woman he wouldn't mind marrying, whether she was rich or not. Come to think of it, he had no idea if her family even had money, but seeing how her father was merely an American ship's captain, he doubted it very much.

He knew her cousin Phillip Sinclair's family had money. One only had to look at Devon House to know that. And Phillip, an eligible earl like himself, would inherit all of that and become the Marquis of Stancliff one day. There was also their other pretty cousin, Lady Mara Reeves, whose father was the Earl of Cashelmore. There was certainly money there, and an estate in Ireland as well.

Christopher's stomach churned in uneasiness. Thinking of his friends' net worth was abhorrent to him.

He sighed heavily, and his glance fell back to the accounting ledger on the polished desk. It was this stately desk at which generations of Townsend men had sat and managed the vast Bridgeton Hall estate quite well.

Until his father.

His miserable wretch of a father.

A soft knock on the door drew his attention and he looked up from the ledger as the gentle rustling of skirts accompanied his younger sister into the office.

"Good morning, Christopher," she said, trying to smile.

His heart constricted at the sight of her. Almost seventeen years old, Evelyn Townsend was pale, thin, and frail. The Townsend family height had skipped over her and her slight frame added to the delicacy about her. Thick brown hair framed her sweet face, accentuating the whiteness of her skin and her large brown eyes. There was a nervousness about her, as if she were a tiny brown bird that would startle and fly away at any moment. Physical appearances aside, Christopher knew his sister had a backbone of steel running through her.

"Evie," he said, as she stood wringing her hands. With another heavy sigh, he sat down in his chair on the other side of the desk.

"I saw Griggs leave." She frowned, her brows furrowing. "How bad are things?"

"Not so terrible," he managed to say with a half smile.

"You're lying to me, aren't you?"

He shook his head, hoping to convince her. The last thing he wanted to do was worry her any more than she already was. Her life had been hard enough. He only wanted to make things better for her and for Gwyneth. "No, no, of course not. We definitely have some time to make changes, but the good news is that I don't think we shall have to sell Bridgeton Hall after all."

"What are you going to do, Kit?" she asked, her brown eyes narrowing on him, while she called him by his childhood nickname.

"I, my dearest Evelyn, intend to acquire a very rich wife."

With a defeated air, his sister collapsed onto the wide leather chair behind her. "Oh, Kit, no."

"Oh, yes. I'm twenty-three years old. It's high time I married and started a family. Carry on the Townsend line and all that, don't you agree?" He gave her a wide grin. It was forced and she knew it.

Evie shook her head. "This isn't right at all."

"It will be fine, I promise," he said, wishing he believed his own words. "I'm returning to London tomorrow to go about the business of finding a suitable candidate. Once

I'm married and we've shored up the family coffers and my shipping investment pays off, we won't have to worry anymore. I can give you your debut, and then Gwyneth can have her turn."

"I hate him for this."

There was no reason to state whom she hated. They both knew. Christopher shrugged. "I hated him long before this."

"I did too," Evie added, somewhat defensively. "You very well know that. But I hate him even more for how he left things. And for what he's making you do now."

"I'd marry eventually anyway, you know. I might as well marry now, to someone who can help us. It has to be done."

"You don't have to do this, Kit. Let's just sell Bridgeton Hall. It's full of painful memories for all of us anyway. We can sell it, pay off everything, and with what's left over, you and Gwyneth and I can go live somewhere else." Evie gestured to the house. "Far away from here."

The intensity in his sister's words startled him. They also echoed his very own thoughts from the night before. "Is that what you really want, Evie?" he asked softly. "To leave here?"

Her warm brown eyes glinted with unshed tears. Sadly she nodded her head. "Sometimes, yes. Sometimes it's all I think about. Going far, far away from here."

Christopher could hardly blame her for wanting to flee. He had at least been able to escape to boarding school for months on end, while in his absence his two defenseless younger sisters had been left to bear the brunt of their father's abuse. He'd only been able to protect them when he came home for summers and holidays. Then Christopher could target his father's rage away from the girls and onto himself. He always felt guilty when he returned to school, leaving them to manage on their own, but also relieved to be away from his father. However, when Christopher was gone, poor Evie bore most of the horror herself in an attempt to spare little Gwyneth.

"What about Mother?" he asked, arching an inquisitive brow.

"What about her?" Evie flung at him with more strength than it looked like she possessed.

"Where will she go if we sell the estate?"

"I don't care," she said with emphatic malevolence. "I hate her as much as I hate Father. In fact, I almost hate her more because she let him do those things to us."

Silence descended upon the room, the soft morning sunlight giving way to the gray clouds that wafted across the sky. Christopher had mixed feelings about his mother. Perhaps as the oldest, and as the only son, he had memories of Maeve Townsend when he was very young. He recalled his mother hugging him, the soft scent of her perfume enveloping him, as she sang a sweet lullaby before bed. She smiled more often back then and laughed with him. He wasn't exactly sure when things changed or why. But it seemed to have been sometime after Evelyn was born that his world went dark and became filled with anger and fear and abuse.

"I suppose she could come with us, wherever we go," Evie said grudgingly, jutting out her delicate chin. "But I honestly don't care what happens to her."

Christopher nodded, as if in agreement. He didn't want to get into that kind of discussion with his sister now. In fact he avoided discussing their childhood at all costs if it could be helped.

"Well, we can't very well toss Mother out onto the street," he said pragmatically. "We shall just have to manage. In any case, we're not going away, at least I'm not. And once I marry and have the resources we need, you won't have to worry about anything. You don't have to have a come out or even get married if you don't wish to. I can send you wherever you want to go, Evie. You can travel. You know I'll always take care of you and Gwyneth. And Mother."

The tears that had rimmed her eyes now spilled down her pale cheeks. "Oh, Kit," she cried. "How can you be so good to me when I'm so hateful? I apologize. Please forgive me."

He stood and walked to where his sister was seated. He patted her shoulder and placed a light kiss on the top of her head. "You're not hateful. And I understand. More than you know. Please don't worry. I'll take care of everything."

An anguished sob escaped her and it tore his heart in two. He suddenly realized how hard Evie's life had been, trapped in this house with their neglectful mother and abusive father, day in and day out. Year after year, with nothing to break the monotony, her life and her well-being had been at the mercy of their father's malicious and mercurial whims. While he'd had the opportunity to go away to school and later university, and even a brief trip abroad, his two sisters had been imprisoned in this nightmare. No wonder Evie wanted to flee.

How had this thought never occurred to him before?

"Why don't you and Gwyneth come to London with me tomorrow?" he blurted out before he could stop himself.

"Oh, Kit, do you mean that?" Evie's sweet face glimmered with hope.

He did mean it and he wasn't sure why. Or what bringing his sisters to London would accomplish. It wasn't as if he could afford to buy them a new wardrobe or anything. He just thought it would be nice for them to be away from their mother and Bridgeton Hall for a little while. He realized how little freedom his sisters had, and how restrictive a woman's life could be. Women really were the prisoners of the men in their lives. "Yes, go get packing and come stay at the town house with me for a few days. I'll tell Gwyneth."

"I haven't been to London since I was a little girl and Gwyneth has never been. But Mother will never allow it," whispered Evie, fear creeping back into her eyes.

"I'm the head of the family now, aren't I? I control the estate and what money we have left. I'm the earl now," Christopher said with authority he finally felt for the first time in his life. "If I want to take my sisters to London, I will. And there's nothing Mother can do to stop me. We shall leave first thing in the morning."

6

A Little Leeway

"Uncle Jeffrey, thank you!" Sara exclaimed with wonder at the wriggling bundle of golden fur in her arms. "He's just darling!" The small puppy licked her face with his tiny tongue and she could not stop giggling.

"Your mother will be furious with me for giving him to you, but that's part of the fun!" Jeffrey Eddington, the Duke of Rathmore, grinned wickedly at his godchild.

"Well, I love him already and I think he loves me," Sara cried, cradling the fluffy little Yorkshire terrier in her arms.

"Papa, why didn't you get us a puppy?" Victoria Eddington asked with an injured air. The pretty ten-year-old placed her hands on her hips in indignation.

"Because, my sweet girl, it's much more fun to annoy your aunt Juliette than it is to annoy your mother." He playfully tweaked his daughter's cheek, causing her to lose her serious grimace and laugh. She clearly adored her father. "Besides, isn't it wonderful to give Cousin Sara a present that she loves so much?"

"Papa, where did you get him?" Six-year-old Vivienne

demanded, her wide green eyes staring up at the little dog Sara held.

Sara moved to sit on the divan where she could better manage the excited puppy and allow her three little cousins to sit beside her. They were adorable in their matching pink dresses with white lace smocks and pink ribbons adorning their blond ringlets. The girls immediately climbed up and began to pet the tiny dog, squealing in delight as they did.

Uncle Jeffrey smiled at them. "A friend of mine, you know Lord Deane, don't you? His wife's dog had puppies a few weeks ago and when I ran into him yesterday he asked if I wanted one. I immediately thought of Sara. And then when I saw this little chap, I knew he would be perfect for her."

"What are you going to call him, Sara?" Violet asked. She was the oldest of the Eddington daughters, and at twelve was the calmest of the three. "He needs a name, Sara."

"Yes, he certainly does need a name," Sara agreed, as she stroked the soft golden brown fur. The puppy curled up in her lap, content to be adored by the girls. "What do you think we should call him?"

"He's so small. How about Tiny?" suggested Violet.

"He's just a baby so he won't always be tiny," Victoria countered. "I think we should call him Fluffy, because he looks like he has fluffy stockings on his feet."

"No, with that dark fur on his paws he looks like he's wearing little black boots." Vivienne announced excitedly, "Let's call him Boots!"

"Oh, that's just perfect, Vivvy!" Sara declared. "That's exactly what we shall call him." She smiled at the girls and they nodded their blond heads in agreement. "Boots."

"Since I named him, I get to play with him whenever I want," Vivienne explained in a bossy tone to her older sisters. "So that makes him my puppy too."

With a quick swooping motion, Uncle Jeffrey gathered up Vivienne in his arms and swung her around. "He's Cousin Sara's dog, little missy," he reminded her gently. "And don't you forget it."

Vivienne squealed with glee, her bubbly laughter filling the room, causing the puppy to spring off Sara's lap and chase Uncle Jeffrey's feet.

"Put me down now, Papa!" Vivienne demanded, while an overexcited Boots yipped at them.

"What in heaven's name is going on in here?" Aunt Yvette called over the din as she entered the drawing room. When she saw the puppy racing around the room, she exclaimed in dismay, "Oh Jeffrey, you didn't!"

Sara loved all her mother's sisters and Aunt Yvette was no exception. With her pretty ways and fashionable style, Sara adored the youngest of the five Hamilton sisters. The last time she was in London she and Aunt Yvette had the most amazing shopping spree! Between Aunt Yvette and Uncle Jeffrey, Sara felt at home when she was with them. It was also fun to act as a big sister to the little girls. And of course, Violet, Victoria, and Vivienne simply idolized their cousin Sara.

"Juliette will be very cross with you for giving Sara a puppy! You know how much she dislikes pets." In spite of scolding him, Aunt Yvette couldn't help but smile at the gleam in her husband's eye. "Yet I suppose that's exactly why you did it." She kissed his cheek and shook her head. "Come now, girls, your music teacher has just arrived. You can see Cousin Sara again later before supper. And if you're very good, perhaps she'll read you a story before you go to bed later. Now come along," she prodded them against a chorus of protests.

Eventually she had herded the three blond girls from the room, leaving Sara alone with just Uncle Jeffrey and Boots.

"I can't thank you enough, Uncle Jeffrey. I've always

wanted a dog of my own, but Mother disapproved," Sara said, as she scooped the puppy back into her arms to settle him down.

The little dog wanted no part of it. So she set him back down on the thick Persian rug. Idly, she tossed one of her leather gloves to him. He scurried to retrieve it and raced back to her. He clasped the soft kid glove tightly between his teeth while she pulled gently. Loving the game, he continued the little tug of war over her glove. Which was no doubt ruined now. But he was so cute, what did it matter?

"Oh, I just love him!" she declared.

"You're very welcome, my dear." Uncle Jeffrey made himself comfortable in a large armchair, casually crossing his legs. He rested his gaze upon her and said softly, "But I gather that's not the only love you have on your mind, is it?"

The smile left her face and Sara felt her cheeks burn. "I suppose they told you all about why they dragged me to London?"

He shrugged. "More or less. Your parents are simply concerned for your welfare, that's all."

"And I also suppose that they asked you to talk some sense into me? Is that what this little conversation is all about?" Her words came out much harsher than she intended them to.

Uncle Jeffrey threw back his head and laughed. "You are so like your mother, Sara. You really have no idea."

"I've heard that all my life," she responded sullenly, hating that she sounded like a petulant child.

He grinned at her, his eyes dancing. "You should take that as the compliment that it is definitely intended to be. Your mother is a remarkable woman, as are all the Hamilton sisters. And like it or not, Miss Fleming, you are half Hamilton yourself. So count yourself very, very lucky."

Sara rolled her eyes. She'd heard enough about the Hamiltons to last her whole life. Uncle Jeffrey meant well, but she was in no mood to hear about them, especially when she was more than a little put out that her parents had seen fit to share the details of Sara's personal life. Even if it was only with Uncle Jeffrey.

"And that eye roll!" Jeffrey laughed again. "If you stuck out your tongue, it'd be like I'm going back in time, sitting across from Juliette Hamilton all over again. You remind me of the first time I met her. She was just about your age too."

Sara turned away from him, focusing all her attention on Boots.

Ignoring Uncle Jeffrey was a difficult thing to do. Being charming and fun, he had always been her favorite uncle. But she did not wish to discuss her parents, nor her intimate personal affairs, with him. She finally freed the glove from the puppy's mouth and tossed it toward the doorway. Boots scampered to fetch it, sliding across the polished wood floor once his tiny paws left the security of the rug. After grabbing the glove in his teeth, he ran back to her and dropped it at her feet. And the game began again.

"In spite of what you are thinking, I did not invite you here this afternoon to talk about your parents, Sara. I know you are upset about what they did, but I want you to just consider something." Uncle Jeffrey leaned forward in his chair. "I've known both of your parents for a very long time and I am positive that you mean the world to them. Do you really believe they dragged you across the Atlantic Ocean, knowing that doing so would surely break your heart, simply because they don't like the man you've fallen for?"

Stunned by his words, Sara turned to stare at Uncle Jeffrey, her plans of ignoring him completely forgotten.

"Don't you think perhaps . . . just perhaps . . . that they have a very good reason to do what they did?"

"Well, if they had a good reason, they should have told me what it was! I only know that they didn't even give him a chance," Sara said heatedly. "He loves me and I love him, and I don't care what they say. I only want to be with him. He's all that matters to me. He—"

"So tell me all about him." Uncle Jeffrey sat back in the chair, relaxing as if settling in for a good long chat. He presented her with a warm smile and an attentive gaze.

Sara had expected an argument with him, to debate the wrongness of her parents' actions. She had not expected him to seem genuinely interested in her romantic affairs. Tossing the glove to an impatient Boots once again, she sighed. "Uncle Jeffrey, I can't imagine that you wish to hear about any of this."

"Of course I do. You're the daughter of my dearest friends, my eldest niece, and my godchild as well. I've watched you grow from a strong-willed toddler into a strong-willed young woman. And I'll have you know, I'm quite skilled at assisting romances that seem doomed. Just ask your mother and your aunts." He winked at her. "Perhaps I can be of some help."

"The only way you can help me is to convince my parents to take me back to New York."

He nodded agreeably. "I could do that . . . if . . ." Then he paused. "If I believed this gentleman of yours was worth going back to."

Warily, she looked into Uncle Jeffrey's eyes. She wanted to believe he would persuade her parents but she wasn't entirely sure she could trust him. Then she figured she had nothing to lose at this point. "First, can you tell me why we left in such a hurry? I didn't even have a chance to tell him good-bye. What do my parents know about him that I don't and they apparently don't wish for me to know? They won't even discuss it with me."

"I think that's a fair question to ask." He thought for a moment. "Are you sure you are prepared for the answer? Whatever it may be?"

Sara hesitated. She hadn't considered that point. What if the problem wasn't what she thought it was? What if there was something truly dreadful about Alexander Drake, too dreadful for her parents to tell her? Was he a danger to her? Had they discovered he had a secret, sordid past? That he had committed robbery? Or even worse . . . a murder? She shook her head at her wild imagination. It was preposterous. She loved Alexander. She couldn't ever love a murderer or a criminal. She would have sensed something that terrible about him deep in her heart. Certainly, she would just *know* if something were wrong. He had held her in his arms and kissed her, for heaven's sake! He couldn't possibly be a criminal, let alone a murderer.

"Oh, I know exactly what they think," Sara spat out the words that had haunted her. "My parents believe he is only after my money. Apparently, my inheritance is worth so many millions of dollars that no man could possibly love me for myself with that amount of money dangling over my head."

Uncle Jeffrey grew quiet, which was surprising.

"So exactly what am I expected to do?" she asked, unable to suppress the slight hitch in her voice.

Looking away, Sara turned her attention back to Boots, who insisted on continuing their game of fetch. For what seemed like the hundredth time, she tossed her now tattered glove across the room. It landed behind an oversized armchair and the puppy scurried underneath the chintz trim in search of it, emerging with his little black button nose covered in dust.

"Yes, you are in a complicated situation, my dear."

Uncle Jeffrey spoke to her as an adult. He did not patronize her. Sara found the change refreshing. Boots trotted back, looking up at her with his adoring eyes. She scooped him from the floor and brushed him off. He must have been tired from his exertions because he curled up in her lap and fell fast asleep, the warmth of his little body calming her. She gently stroked his soft, golden fur.

"The danger of being a beautiful American heiress is that there are definitely men who will want to marry you solely for your money, Sara. Plain and simple. It is a considerable amount of money, so don't ever underestimate its appeal."

"I am quite aware of that fact," she whispered ruefully, although it was interesting to hear what an adult other than her parents had to say about it. She was somewhat intrigued by Uncle Jeffrey's point of view.

"What you need to do is to determine whether whatever-his-name-is . . ."

"Alexander Drake."

"Whether . . . this Alexander Drake . . . loves you for your money or not. So when you write to him to tell him that you are in London"—he winked slyly at her—"you might mention exactly why your parents felt a separation was necessary."

"What are you suggesting?" Sara was surprised that her uncle was aware of her letter writing to Alexander. Had Mara told him?

"I'm suggesting that you act responsibly. Facts are facts and the fact is you are blessed and cursed by money. Your considerable fortune is your responsibility and you must beware of scoundrels simply out to squander it. As I said, sweet Sara, there are men out there who would do just that very thing. If I were you," he continued calmly, "I would tell Mr. Drake that your parents will disinherit you if you marry him."

"They would never do that!"

"I know that," he said earnestly. "And you know that, but your young man is not aware of that fact. Presented with that situation, it would be interesting to see what he would do, don't you think?"

Sara shook her head vehemently. "But that is so cold and calculating! I could never lie to him in such a manner."

He raised an inquisitive brow. "Are you afraid to learn that he wouldn't choose you over the money?"

"Of course not!" she protested. But suddenly she was struck with uncertainty and it felt as if she were doused with icy cold water.

"Then you should have no trouble telling him so. If he'll marry you without the money, as you say he will, then there is nothing to fear for you will know without a doubt that he loves you more than your millions. You can tell that to your parents. They will bless the union and you'll get your man and your money. On the other hand, if he bows out . . . then you know the truth about his character. And it's good riddance. He doesn't deserve you. Either way it's always best to know the truth about him." Uncle Jeffrey paused, looking at her pointedly. "Don't you agree?"

Sara remained silent as her uncle's quite reasonable words sunk in. Could it be that simple? If Alexander agreed to marry her knowing she hadn't a penny to her name, her parents couldn't object to him. And of course he would still want to marry her!

"But I've already written to him, asking him to come to London."

"Then send him another letter, informing him of your parents' plans to disinherit you. Let's see if he still comes for you."

"Oh, he'll come for me. He loves me, not my money. He's a lawyer and will be successful in his own right one day. He told me so."

"Then you have nothing to worry about," he said with ease.

"And when he comes to London, you'll help me explain

to my parents? You'll be on my side, Uncle Jeffrey?" she pleaded with him.

"Of course, I will. As long as I see that he is a man of character and worthy of a wonderful woman such as yourself, you have my word."

Flooded with relief by his rational solution to this silent stalemate with her parents, Sara was about to question what he meant by "man of character" when he continued speaking.

"In the meantime, while you're waiting for him to arrive, you may as well enjoy yourself in London." He grinned mischievously.

"What do you mean?" she asked, a bit puzzled by his remark.

"My dear girl, no one in London knows that you are a wealthy heiress. So why not have some fun while you're here?"

"Uncle Jeffrey!" Sara was a little shocked at his suggestion.

"Meet some young men and see what it's like to live life unburdened by a fortune. You will certainly see who your friends are. You can be plain Miss Sara Fleming, our poor little American cousin." He paused for a second. "Can I tell you a secret?"

She nodded almost breathlessly, this conversation with her uncle becoming more fascinating by the minute.

"Before I was the Duke of Rathmore, I was believed to be his illegitimate son."

Sara gasped. Boots opened sleepy eyes and glared at her for startling him awake. She continued to pet him.

"It's true. Most people wanted nothing to do with me. They turned up their noses at me. Boys taunted and made fun of me at school, calling me all sorts of sordid names and generally making my life miserable, as young boys are wont to do. That's when I met your uncle Lucien and he became my friend, in spite of my circumstances."

Sara hated to think of her handsome uncle as a little boy, being teased and cast out by everyone. It was difficult to get her head around it, especially imagining Uncle Lucien and Uncle Jeffrey as young boys.

"When I was older, there were no women trying to snare me into matrimony, because I had no prospects. And that is exactly why I loved all your aunts so much. They didn't care that I was illegitimate. Those sweet, wonderful Hamilton sisters accepted me as I was and loved me for my charming self and made me feel as a part of their family when they had nothing to gain by associating with the likes of me. When it was discovered that I was not illegitimate after all and stood to inherit my father's dukedom . . ." He paused for dramatic effect. "Well, you can only imagine how my drastic change in circumstance altered my social standing."

"Why, Uncle Jeffrey! I hadn't the faintest idea about any of this!" Sara was stunned. How had her mother and father never told her this story about Aunt Yvette's husband?

"Of course you didn't know. But the reason why I'm telling you all of this is so you will look at your time here in London as a little gift. No one will suspect that you are an heiress and you can discover that you are liked for yourself and not your money."

Mulling over his plan, she had to admit it had its merits. Everyone in New York society knew her father had millions and that she was the sole heir to the Fleming fortune. She had always been popular and sought after, but within the wealthy circle of her friends, they were no different from her. She had taken her position in life for granted. Now she wondered if all the gentlemen she'd ever met looked at her and merely saw dollar signs. She supposed some of them had. Thinking on it now, it would be fun to learn how she would be received if people thought she had nothing to offer in the way of a dowry.

"But Uncle Jeffrey," she pointed out. "I was with Phillip and Simon two nights ago at Lady Abbott's ball and was introduced to dozens of people. Surely they already know about my fortune?"

"Oh, I can easily squelch any of those rumors and start different ones. As the Duke of Rathmore I can casually mention to the right people that at one time your father had money, but through mismanagement or bad investments, he lost it all quite recently. I can even add that you're in rather desperate straits and are seeking a rich husband!"

Sara laughed aloud. "Uncle Jeffrey, you're terrible!" But he was wonderful, really. Talking to him made her feel hopeful about everything again. It was all going to work out perfectly. She would prove to her parents that Alexander Drake loved her for herself and not her money.

"What do you say, Sara?" he asked, with a wicked grin. "Are you game?"

"Oh, yes!" she said, nodding and thinking it might be fun. She always enjoyed parties and social gatherings, and she had nothing else to do while she waited for Alexander to arrive. Suddenly the image of Christopher Townsend flashed into her mind.

Why had she confided in him the other night? It was rather reckless of her to tell him about Alexander, but there was something about Lord Bridgeton. He had sought to comfort her. For some inexplicable reason, she felt she could trust him, almost as if he was a kindred spirit. He understood what she was feeling, because he felt the same way. She wondered what it was that worried him, for something clearly troubled him as well. The allusion he made to them possessing only outward happiness struck her deeply.

The drawing room door opened and Captain Harrison

Fleming strode in, causing Boots to suddenly jump from her lap and race across the room, yipping in indignation at being disturbed.

"Hello, Papa." Rising from her seat, Sara went to give Uncle Jeffrey a hug. "Thank you for everything," she whispered to him.

"My pleasure," Jeffrey said, pinching her cheek. Then he turned to one of his oldest friends. "Harrison has appeared so it must be time for supper."

"Juliette and I just arrived and she's chatting with Yvette now. What, may I ask, is *this*?" Sara's father glared at the little dog that wagged its tiny tail excitedly at his feet.

Sara exchanged a mischievous glance with Uncle Jeffrey. "Oh, that's Boots," she said with a casual tone, then added, "Papa, Uncle Jeffrey just made you a pauper."

Harrison look confused while trying not to step on the excited puppy. "What on earth are you talking about? And when did you acquire a dog?"

"Just today," Sara answered, feeling somewhat amused that for once she had the upper hand over her father. "Papa, Uncle Jeffrey and I decided that while I'm in London, it might be best to keep the fact of your millions a secret."

Nodding in agreement, Harrison lifted Boots from the floor and held the squirming little puppy in one hand. "I think I see the wisdom in that. You'll brook no argument from me."

Sara smiled and Jeffrey gave her a quick wink. She felt as if they were coconspirators and it felt good to have someone on her side. An ally, so to speak.

"Why in blazes do you have this drowned rat of a dog, Eddington?" Harrison questioned, clearly puzzled by the tiny ball of fur. "You can't even really call this a proper dog." Boots licked his face and her father laughed.

"Boots is *my* dog, Father," Sara stated with a satisfied smile. "Uncle Jeffrey just gave him to me."

"Uncle Jeffrey just gave him to you . . . ?" Harrison echoed in disbelief. Slowly he turned to Jeffrey. "Juliette will lose her mind."

"Oh, I know!" Jeffrey laughed with glee. "I'm counting on it!"

7

Currents

The little silver bells over the door of the Hamilton Sisters' Book Shoppe jingled as Sara Fleming entered. She beamed with pride as she glanced around the beautiful bookstore her mother and her aunts owned. Clean, airy, and filled with light, the artfully arranged shelves of books were the shop's signature selling points. Most bookshops were dark and dusty places, but not Hamilton's. Attractive and comfortable seating areas invited shoppers to peruse books at their leisure. The bookstore was adorned with gorgeous paintings and even boasted a light refreshment area, where fragrant teas and freshly baked scones and tiny cakes were served.

Sara could still recall the day this particular shop opened. She and her parents had just arrived from New York for the grand opening and she was so happy to be off the ship and excited to play with Phillip and Simon. She was about four years old at the time and the brand-new store was a magical place to her. It was also the day she first met Mara. Yes, this shop held fond memories, indeed.

Striding with purpose, Sara held Boots carefully in her arms, as the tiny puppy looked about with inquisitive eyes. She had promised to meet Mara and Aunt Paulette here today and to help out in the shop for a while. Apparently, it was considered enriching for her to become familiar with the family business. So to please her parents and play the obedient daughter, she agreed to spend the afternoon with Aunt Paulette and learn how the bookshop was run.

One of the women who worked in the shop, wearing the signature dark green Hamilton apron, smiled and told her that her aunt was waiting for her upstairs. It was one of the things that made Hamilton's so special. Her aunts only hired women to work in the shop. Sara made her way toward the staircase that led to the private offices on the second story.

"Oh, you have a puppy!" Mara exclaimed with delight as she descended the steps just as Sara was about to go up.

"Isn't he darling?" Sara cried, feeling more than a bit proud of her adorable pet. She had grown inordinately fond of him in a short amount of time. "He's the sweetest thing and so good too. Uncle Jeffrey just gave him to me yesterday!"

"He is just the sweetest little thing I've ever seen!" Mara eagerly took the small puppy into her arms, while he happily licked her face. "What do you call him?"

"Vivienne named him Boots and—" Sara stopped, surprised by the sight in front of her. Then she couldn't help but smile. "Oh, good afternoon, Lord Bridgeton!"

She'd forgotten how tall the man was. He looked quite handsome in his dress coat, and his top hat made him appear even taller. He seemed genuinely pleased to see her as well. Sara was suddenly glad she was wearing her favorite periwinkle blue-and-white striped walking dress, which she knew favored her eyes and showed off her slim waist. On her head was a darling periwinkle bonnet with white ribbons.

"Good afternoon, Miss Fleming. Lady Mara." Christopher Townsend grinned happily at them. "It's wonderful to see you both. Please let me introduce you to my two sisters, Lady Evelyn Townsend and Lady Gwyneth Townsend."

It was then that Sara noticed the two young women standing with him. Lord Bridgeton had sisters. That was quite interesting.

Both girls seemed very quiet, not very fashionable, and definitely younger than Sara was. The older one looked rather pale and nervous and the younger sister, who had to be about fourteen or fifteen, appeared a little overwhelmed by the entire situation. Yet the family resemblance was clear, the dark hair and fair skin. However, there was something fragile and a bit sad about them, but Sara couldn't pinpoint what it was.

As greetings were exchanged and more exclamations were made over the cuteness of her little dog by the Townsend girls, Sara was unable to keep her gaze from drifting back to Lord Bridgeton. He really was quite handsome.

"My sisters are visiting London for a few days and I thought they would enjoy some new books," he explained.

"Well, you have definitely brought your sisters to the proper place to remedy that," Sara said brightly. She then turned her attention to the girls. Something about them made her feel a little protective of them. "Lady Evelyn and Lady Gwyneth, it's so wonderful to meet you both. I'm sure we can find books to suit you with no trouble at all."

"Thank you. You're very kind, Miss Fleming. This bookshop is so lovely," Lady Evelyn murmured softly.

"I'd be happy to show you around," Mara offered, taking the lead in the situation. She had spent more time in the bookshop than Sara ever had and therefore was more familiar with where everything was. "Do you mind if I take your sisters with me, Lord Bridgeton?" she asked.

"They'd be delighted to go with you, Lady Mara," he responded, with a nod of approval to his sisters.

Mara guided the two girls to the fiction area, leaving Sara alone with Christopher Townsend near the staircase.

"Well, this is a most pleasant surprise," Lord Bridgeton said. "I wasn't expecting to see you here this afternoon, Miss Fleming."

"Well, I wasn't expecting you either, Lord Bridgeton," Sara added.

"You look much happier today," he observed with a wink of his eye.

"As do you, Lord Bridgeton," she replied, flashing a smile.

"Is it because you've gained a new friend?" he asked. Lord Bridgeton eyed Boots with amusement as the puppy recovered from the excitement of being fawned over by the girls and lay contentedly in Sara's arms.

"It is very likely that this little fellow has raised my spirits, but it also has to do with a new outlook on things. How about you?" she asked. "Are you faring better?"

He slowly nodded his head, but he did not reply.

She looked at him with skepticism. "That doesn't seem very convincing."

"Doesn't it?" he replied, attempting to sound innocent.

"Not in the least, Lord Bridgeton. Have you tried looking at your situation, whatever it may be, with a new perspective?" she suggested. Her talk with Uncle Jeffrey yesterday had considerably brightened her mood. "I've discovered that doing so helps tremendously."

"Not yet, but under your recommendation, I shall try."

"It will help. Trust me," she assured him with a smile. "Your sisters seem lovely," Sara added, her eyes drifting to where they followed Mara.

She wanted to ask what saddened the girls, for clearly

something did, and wondered if it had to do with the same issue that troubled Lord Bridgeton. Was the entire family feeling the weight of some terrible burden?

His eyes darkened somewhat and it seemed as if a shadow passed over his face. "They are lovely girls. But they've been very sheltered at Bridgeton Hall and haven't been to London since they were little girls. I thought it would be nice to show them a bit of the city. They both enjoy reading quite a lot, so when I saw the bookshop, I recalled that Phillip and Simon had mentioned to me that their mother owned this store, and I decided to stop by."

"Well, they shall certainly find plenty to read in here. My cousin will take good care of them." Sara paused and glanced up at him, holding his gaze. "You're rather a wonderful brother to take such an interest in your younger sisters. I always wished I had a brother or a sister."

"Yes, a brother would have been nice to have as well," he quipped.

"I think that's why I adore my cousins so much. They're the closest I've got to having siblings of my own." Sara slowly rocked the puppy in her arms as if she held a sleeping baby.

"From what I've seen you all have a remarkably close relationship."

"We do. I admit that I still feel a bit of the outsider, since I'm the American and I don't see the others as often. But I do love them and they all make me feel included when I'm here. It's also nice that they make a fuss over me when I arrive."

"You like the special attention?" He looked as if he were highly amused.

"I do. Quite a lot," she confessed.

"You see, that is where we differ, Miss Fleming. I don't usually like being made a fuss over."

Sara scoffed at him. "Oh, I doubt that very much, Lord Bridgeton. You're a member of the nobility. A handsome and eligible earl. You wouldn't know what to do with yourself if a fuss *wasn't* made over you."

"Yes, I can see your point," he acknowledged. "But simply because others choose to pay attention to me because I'm an earl, it doesn't mean that I enjoy it."

She eyed him skeptically. "I'm not sure I believe that. After all, you're a man. All men love attention being paid to them."

He arched a brow. "So do women. And I find that to be true for them much more so than men."

Lord Bridgeton, she was beginning to discover, had a quick wit about him. She liked that in a man. "Perhaps . . . I suppose it depends on the kind of attention one gets. For instance, my cousin Mara detests being the center of attention."

"As do I," he admitted once more.

"I simply adore it!"

"So I've been told."

They both laughed that their conversation ended up where they began.

"You know, it's interesting to me that you and Lady Mara seem so close," he said. "From what I can see, you both have opposite personalities. She is quiet and reserved, and you are . . ."

"And I am . . . ?" Sara prompted him, curious to know what he thought of her.

"You are fishing for compliments."

Sara sighed in defeat. "I'm afraid you see me too clearly, Lord Bridgeton."

"I don't know if that's a good thing for me or not." His laughter was rich. "So tell me, Miss Fleming, will I be seeing you at the ball tomorrow evening?"

Sara nodded. "Yes, I believe that Phillip mentioned something about it this morning at breakfast. Lady Wickham's, was it? Apparently, Phillip is in charge of my social calendar now."

"Knowing Waverly, I'm sure he is." He paused before asking, "Perhaps you could save a dance for me?"

She gave him her most flirtatious smile. "I might be able to arrange something for you."

He looked at her very intently before saying, "Miss Fleming, I can only imagine there was a long line of men dying of love for you when you left New York."

Sara stared at him again, looking deep into those chocolate brown eyes of his. There was something about his eyes that drew her in. "Why would you say such a thing?"

"You know exactly why."

"On occasion I have been told that I'm an accomplished coquette," she flirted with him. "Is that what you mean?"

He laughed heartily at her outrageousness. "Yes, that's exactly what I mean."

Sara wondered how it seemed he knew her so well, but she didn't mind it.

Aunt Paulette came down the stairs from her office just then. "I was wondering where you two girls had gone off to, but now I see that you've caught the attention of a handsome gentleman . . ."—she startled—"and you have a puppy!"

Sara then introduced Mara's mother to Lord Bridgeton and to Boots.

"It's a wonderful bookshop you have here, Lady Cashelmore," Lord Bridgeton said.

"Why, thank you very much. I'm quite proud of it, but it was not my accomplishment alone. My sisters and I all worked together to make it what it is today. Even Juliette, Sara's mother, helped us in spite of being far away."

"My mother is the least bookish of all the Hamilton sisters," Sara explained.

"I can sympathize with her," Lord Bridgeton admitted a bit sheepishly. "I'm not very book-oriented myself."

Sara couldn't suppress a smile and shared a conspiratorial glance with him. "Neither am I. I take after my mother in that respect."

Aunt Paulette shook her head in disbelief at the pair of them. "I'll never understand that mindset of not loving books."

Lord Bridgeton added, "Regardless, I must say your store is impressive, Lady Cashelmore. I've never seen one to compare with it. And your daughter, Lady Mara, whom I also met the other evening, is quite lovely. She is busy helping my sisters choose some books at the moment."

"Thank you again, Lord Bridgeton," Aunt Paulette said. "I know Mara will take good care of them. She's practically grown up here and I've trained her well."

Aunt Colette and Simon Sinclair arrived at the shop just then.

"We've come to see how you're getting along," Aunt Colette announced.

"I notice Sara is hard at work, just as I suspected," Simon said, obviously ready to tease Sara about her learning the family business. He was a handsome young man, who favored his mother with his brown hair and blue eyes.

"Ha, ha," Sara retorted to her cousin. She and Simon were the same age, so they'd always had a bit of a rivalry between them. Then she confessed with unabashed glee, "I haven't even made it upstairs yet."

"I knew it!" Simon declared in triumph. "Didn't I tell you that Sara wouldn't get any work done today, Mother?"

Colette laughed in amusement. "You did and I did not disagree with you. Sara is exactly like her mother was!"

Mara returned with the Townsend girls, who excitedly shared the books they had chosen, and yet another round of introductions took place. To Sara the two sisters seemed a little lighter than when they had first entered the shop.

"Well, hasn't this turned into a festive gathering?" Simon remarked.

Aunt Colette said, "Lord Bridgeton, it's so lovely to finally meet your sisters. We must welcome them to London properly. Is your mother in town as well?"

He shook his head. "Lady Bridgeton was not feeling well enough to journey with us this time."

"Oh, that's a shame. Please give her my regards when you see her." Aunt Colette continued, "Won't you and your sisters please join us for dinner at Devon House later this evening? We're having all of the family over so it may be a little louder than you're accustomed to, but we would love to have you all there."

Sara watched Lord Bridgeton glance at his sisters first. They both seemed eager, if also slightly nervous, to accept the invitation. Then his gaze fell on her. For some reason he sought her assent. Sara looked into his brown eyes and smiled warmly. She liked him. It would be nice to have him and his sisters to dinner.

Lord Bridgeton turned to her aunt. "Yes, thank you, Lady Stancliff. That is very kind of you. We'd be honored to join your family for dinner."

"Oh, that's wonderful," Aunt Colette said. "I know Phillip will be happy to have you and your sisters there as well."

"Thank you again. We look forward to seeing you all this evening," he said. "But we should be getting along now."

After their farewells, Lord Bridgeton and his sisters made their purchases and left the store. Aunt Colette and Aunt Paulette looked at Sara intently.

"What is it?" Sara asked, a bit puzzled by their expressions. "Has my face gone green or something?"

"Nothing at all." Aunt Colette smiled mysteriously.

"Sara, why don't you let Simon take Boots home with him and Paulette and I will show you how to manage the bookshop? We'll never get any work done with this little dog here."

"Yes, that's a wonderful idea, Colette. Let's go, girls, upstairs," Aunt Paulette directed them. "You both promised to work with me today. Let's try and get something done, shall we?"

Giving up, Sara handed Boots to Simon with great reluctance. He looked none too thrilled to be left taking care of a dog.

"You owe me for this," Simon muttered under his breath with a good-natured smile.

"I know, I know," Sara said. "And thank you." She kissed the top of Boots's head and followed her aunts to the second floor.

As they walked up the stairs together, Mara whispered to Sara, "You and Lord Bridgeton seemed to talk for quite a long time together."

"He's easy to talk to," Sara said, realizing how true her words were.

"What were you talking about?"

"Oddly enough, nothing of importance. I can't even recall it now really." But she had flirted with him and it had been fun. Uncle Jeffrey was quite right. She may as well have a good time while she was in London.

"Will he be attending the Wickham ball tomorrow?" Mara asked, as she absently twirled her finger around the ribbon of her bonnet.

"Yes, and he asked me to save a dance for him." And to her surprise, she found herself looking forward to that dance with the handsome Lord Bridgeton, as well as seeing him at dinner later that evening.

* * *

Lady Evelyn Townsend watched her brother very closely as they rode in the carriage back to their town house after leaving Hamilton's Book Shoppe. There was something markedly different about him this afternoon. He'd spent a great deal of time speaking with that American girl. His face lit up when he was near her. She had never seen Christopher act that way.

He seemed more alive and happier than she'd ever known him to be before.

And now they were going to have dinner with the American girl's family. They'd only been in London a day and already they'd gotten an invitation to dine! Evie could hardly wait. But she was also nervous. Although Lady Stancliff and Lady Cashelmore seemed quite friendly, as did Lady Mara, who showed them around the beautiful bookshop, it was all a bit overwhelming. She and Gwyneth were not accustomed to socializing at all.

Evelyn had been a bit in awe of the fashionable and expensively attired Miss Fleming, with her cunning blue-and-white striped jacket with leg o'mutton sleeves and a fetching little bonnet. She seemed so carefree and happy and confident. Evelyn doubted that anything bad had ever happened to Sara Fleming in her entire life. Beautiful, sophisticated, and polished, she was the epitome of glamour and style and Evelyn felt like a little brown country mouse in comparison in her pale lilac dress with a dated pattern.

"They were all so kind to us," Gwyneth said, her voice quavering a little.

"Why shouldn't they be kind to us?" Christopher questioned his younger sister. "I've been friends with Phillip Sinclair and his brother, Simon, for years."

"I think what Gwyneth means is that she was touched by their kindness to us." Evelyn patted her little sister's hand in comfort. Gwyneth was quite sensitive and Evelyn was very protective of her. "It's been so long since we've done anything social or even had fun, Kit, and you know that."

It had been far too long. Evelyn could not recall the last time her parents had entertained at Bridgeton Hall or had accepted an invitation to a party or a ball or even received a visitor. They had lived as veritable recluses and that invariably left Evelyn and Gwyneth alone as well. Once in a while Father would leave on mysterious trips for weeks at a time, for which they were all grateful, but Mother never left the estate. In fact, Mother had become quite irate that she and Gwyneth were leaving with Christopher yesterday.

Mother was so upset at the very idea of them going to London, Evelyn almost wavered in her decision to go. But her brother was determined that she and Gwyneth join him.

In the end the chance to escape won out over Mother's overdramatic and ultimately powerless wrath. It was much easier to defy her with Father gone. Oh, how Evelyn longed to get away from home more than anything! Just being in London made her feel better, as if she could breathe freely. Yes, even in this smog-filled, dirty city she could breathe better than she could at her home in the country. She was almost giddy with freedom. Being amidst so many people with so much going on filled her with elation. Anything could happen here. She could disappear into a crowd and never return if she chose to. The sights and sounds were music to her ears after the suffocating silence of Bridgeton Hall.

"We shall have a good time at Devon House," Christopher explained, with a touch more sympathy in his tone. "I've known Phillip and Simon Sinclair since we were lads at school and their very large family is quite wonderful."

"It is not like ours then, is it?" Gwyneth murmured, her sweet face sad.

"Not like ours at all," Christopher added vehemently.

Again Evelyn watched her brother carefully, as the

carriage jounced over the bumpy road. "I think you're smitten with Miss Fleming."

He laughed, but it rang a little hollow. "Even if that statement were true, Evie, and I assure you that it is not, it would be a futile pursuit. She is in love with someone else and I must marry a girl with money, remember? It's the reason we are in London."

Evelyn grew silent. He was right on that score. Even though she wished it wasn't true. Their family financial situation was probably more perilous than Christopher wanted her to believe.

"I'm nervous," Gwyneth murmured again. "They're all so much grander than we are."

"Nonsense," Christopher said in a tone so firm that it surprised Evelyn. His brows furrowed and he frowned. "Gwyneth, you and Evelyn are both just as good as any of them. You are ladies and born to the nobility. You are the daughters of an earl, from a long and distinguished family. You are their equals. Don't let anyone make you feel inferior. Ever."

No, that had been their father's job and he had done it quite well at that. Evelyn had been made to feel inferior her entire life. She was never good enough, or pretty enough, or smart enough to please her father. Or her mother. And they punished her for it regularly.

When she was eight years old Father had taken it into his head that she was too plump. In his eyes, it was unseemly for a Townsend girl to be overweight. So he had ordered that her diet be restricted and no sweets were allowed to be consumed at all. Barely surviving on the tiny portions she was allotted each day, Evelyn was so hungry that she would often sneak into the kitchen at night to steal food, anything she could get her hands on. When she was caught, her father locked her in her room each night at bedtime and only let her out in the morning when he deemed fit. And as further punishment, during mealtimes in the nursery, she was forced to stand with her hands bound behind her back and watch while her brother and sister ate whatever they wanted. That routine continued for months, until Evelyn had lost enough weight to satisfy even her father.

There was the time Mother, in a fit of rage over something she and Gwyneth had done to displease her, such as accidentally waking her when she was trying to sleep in the middle of the afternoon, chopped off all of their hair. The two of them looked like sad little boys, which enraged Father, who was disgusted by the sight of them. Instead of being angry with his wife for butchering their hair, he whipped his two daughters soundly with a strap and ordered that they not be seen by him until their hair grew back. Which actually turned out to be a blessing in disguise.

For a few precious months, she and Gwyneth lived peacefully, not bothered by their father. There, in the relative safety of the nursery, they escaped by reading books. The worlds within the written pages were far more hospitable and enjoyable than the world they lived in.

But that was only a fraction of the abuses and indignities imposed upon Evelyn and her sister by James Townsend over the years. Evelyn shuddered at the horrific memories. Things were only a little better when Christopher would come home from school for he always tried his best to protect them.

She shook her head as she gazed out the small carriage window, watching the busy streets pass by, wondering at the lives of all the people. Wondering if they endured abuses as she had. It was a miracle that the three of them survived their childhood. But her brother was quite right. No one would ever make Evelyn Townsend feel inferior or worthless again. No matter what happened.

8

Low Tide

Alexander Drake crumpled the letter in his hand. He should have known. He should have guessed. He felt like the world's biggest fool.

They had taken her to London of all places!

He wouldn't have suspected they would have gone somewhere so ordinary. He imagined that her spiteful parents would have spirited her away to some far-flung place in the Pacific to keep her from him. Or left on another one of their around-the-world voyages, which was what he suspected from the start. Yet he should have known all along. London. Of course.

The mother had family in England. He'd completely forgotten about that.

The Flemings had outmaneuvered him. Most assuredly. They had delivered him a devastating blow. And a costly one at that. But they hadn't won yet. No. Not by a long shot. There was far too much money on the line to give up. Not now. Not when things had been falling perfectly into place.

He'd just about given up hope that he would hear from

her. He thought all was lost and everything he'd planned so carefully was for nothing. A few weeks ago he called for Sara at their grand house on Fifth Avenue, only to find it shuttered and dark. The snide butler looked down his nose at Alexander and refused to tell him where the Fleming family had gone. Even the young housemaid he paid weekly to give him information about Sara had no idea what had happened or why the family had left. It was as if they had vanished into thin air.

And just like that all his plans had been for naught.

But Alexander knew exactly why the Flemings had left and it infuriated him.

His entire life he'd had to scrape and claw to get anything he wanted. Nothing ever came easily for him. Growing up on a farm in New Jersey with his churchgoing parents and his seven brothers and sisters, was not the life for him. He wanted more out of life than growing corn and marrying the girls from the neighboring farms, like his brothers did. Luckily, Alexander was very smart and his parents had sold their finest horses to send him to Columbia College, believing he needed an education if he wanted to make a better life for himself. It was the only thing he and his parents ever agreed on.

Once he left, he never returned to the farm again. Never saw his parents or his siblings again. He was determined to do more with his life.

While at Columbia he became friends with a few of the wealthier students and was introduced to some of the finer things. It was where Alexander acquired his expensive tastes and experienced a little of the life he knew he was meant to live. It was at school where he also learned to deeply resent these young men, who had everything handed to them on a silver platter simply because their fathers had money. Oh, they were all nice enough to his face, but he knew they looked down on him because he was not one of *them*.

Alexander had come from nothing and had nothing, while these boys had everything he desired. Fine clothes, expensive champagne, racehorses, and grand mansions. With his charm and good looks, Alexander began to lie and put up a façade of gentility and money in order to get invitations to the best houses.

The first time he stole from them was while at the home of a school friend at his Fifth Avenue mansion. It had been ridiculously easy too. Alexander pocketed an emerald brooch, which paid for the rest of his law school tuition, a nicer apartment, and a fine new wardrobe. As far as he knew, the woman was never even aware the emerald brooch was gone. It became easier and easier each time he took something valuable, while it gave him a perverse sense of pleasure to steal from people who pretended to be his friends.

Why should some people have so much while he had to struggle for so little? It wasn't fair. To his way of thinking, he was simply making things more equitable between them and him.

When Alexander realized he would never get the kind of money he wanted on his own, he was despondent. It would take him years to become a successful lawyer and make the money necessary to have the things he wanted right now, and even that wasn't guaranteed. No. He needed to gain it another way. Quickly. He needed to marry into one of those families with money. But those wealthy families would never allow their precious daughters to marry the likes of him, no matter how charming and handsome and educated he was.

That was when he heard about Captain Harrison Fleming and his million-dollar shipping empire. And his lovely young daughter, who would inherit all of it. The captain wasn't blue-blooded himself either. He came from less than nothing and therefore couldn't possibly look down on Alexander.

Alexander had had a decent chance to win Sara Fleming. And he'd done it too! The girl had fallen head over heels in love with him.

He felt the crumpled letter from Sara in his hand and grinned thinking of her words.

Forgive me, please. I did not leave you. My parents took me to London against my will. Please, Alexander, please come rescue me as soon as you can. I still wish to be with you. I don't care what my parents want. I love you with all my heart.

Her written words echoed in his head. The silly girl continued to want him and so the game was still on. He could marry her yet and win it all.

"Well," a soft, lazy voice asked, "what does she say?"

Alexander looked over at the beautiful woman who lay naked in his bed, her long blond hair tousled and her eyes sleepy, and his heart thudded in his chest. Lucy Camden had only just awakened when the letter from Sara Fleming arrived, even though it was well past noon. Then again, he had kept her up rather late last night.

He flashed her a triumphant smile. "It seems we're going to London, darling."

Lucy perked up at that. In fact she squealed with delight, sitting up in bed, her golden hair falling over her bare shoulders, and clapped her hands together. "London! How wonderful! I've always dreamed of going there."

"Yes, the little chit wishes for me to come 'rescue' her." He frowned in thought. Perhaps he shouldn't bring Lucy to London with him. That might be a bit too bold. Yet he couldn't imagine being away from her for that long. He needed Lucy like he needed air to breathe.

Lucy Camden was the only good thing in his life that had ever come to him easily. An orphan and the distant relation of the wealthy Ellsworth family, Lucy had earned her keep by being the companion to Margaret Ellsworth, the old matriarch of the family. And Lucy bitterly resented every minute of it, feeling that she was belittled and taken advantage of. Alexander met Lucy at a garden party last summer in Newport. Immediately struck by her sultry blond beauty, he fell hopelessly in love with her when he noticed her pocketing a pearl necklace from one of the young ladies at the party.

They were kindred spirits, he and Lucy, because they wanted the same things out of life. They lived on the edge of respectability and did what they needed to do to get what they wanted and they didn't care who got in their way. He'd been with Lucy since last summer and hadn't tired of her yet, as he usually did with other women. Because Lucy Camden wasn't at all like other women.

In fact it was his brilliant little Lucy who told him about Sara Fleming in the first place, having seen her as a guest at the Ellsworths' grand house in Newport last summer. Lucy was the one who devised the scheme for Alexander to meet her.

It was a shame that Sara's parents had ruined everything when he had worked so hard and planned it all so thoroughly. He had toed the line and played each move perfectly in his seduction of her. Sara quickly fell head over heels in love with him and she believed he loved her. In all honesty, it was ridiculously easy to do.

Sara Fleming was a very attractive, if a little spoiled and vain, young woman, and so very ripe for the picking. After playing the romantic hero for her with a few stolen kisses and sweet words of eternal devotion, she was his. It certainly wasn't a hardship to be with her. Alexander had actually enjoyed some of the time he spent with her. Her parents had been cordial to him and seemed to approve of him, at least outwardly. Why, he thought he'd totally won over the captain with his talk of being a self-made man! Hard work. Grit. Schooling. Gumption. Determination to make a better life for himself. All that sort of nonsense.

Alexander had fooled them all into believing he was an upstanding man of character with a bright future in the law, which was only half true. He'd stolen a small fortune to put up that front, to wear the proper clothes and appear as an up-and-coming lawyer. Aware that he couldn't hope to enter Sara Fleming's social circle with the Vanderbilts and the Astors, he'd even arranged for their accidental meeting that October afternoon in Central Park. It had been Lucy's brilliant idea to startle the horse, causing Sara to fall and creating a seemingly unplanned moment. And Alexander was right there to rescue her. He'd charmed her easily and their courtship was a simple affair filled with pretty words and gentlemanly ways. He'd even stolen a diamond engagement ring, intending to propose to her before she disappeared with her parents. It was another little trinket he'd lifted from an unsuspecting society matron.

"I've been thinking, Drakey." Lucy interrupted his thoughts, a sly little smile on her full lips.

"Have you now?" He stood and tossed Sara's letter into the fireplace. He made his way back to the bed, his robe falling open.

"Yes, I have." She reached her arms up to him and greedily pulled him down on top of her.

Easing his weight over her lush little body, he kissed her pouty lips before asking, "What are you thinking in that pretty head of yours, sweet Lucy?"

"I think I shall pretend to be your sister during our trip to London," she explained with an amused smile. "No one there will know and I can be with you all the time."

Alexander rolled off her and settled back into the pillows,

placing his arms behind his head. He loved the way her mind worked. "My *sister*?"

"Yes," she continued with excitement. "We can say I came to New York to visit you, and you had no choice but to bring me to London with you. It will appear much more respectable if you have your sister with you. It's perfect. We even look a little alike with our blond hair and light eyes."

He nodded, stunned by the brilliant simplicity of her plan. "Yes . . . It could work. I think I even mentioned my seven siblings to her once. She'd probably be thrilled to meet you too!" Alexander laughed at the thought, then turned serious. "Except that means that we will have to pay for two ship passages and all the hotels, travel, and meals. New clothes for the both of us. Going to London to marry her will be a very expensive and risky undertaking, Lucy. Her parents are already suspicious and will try to stop us. I'm going to have to elope with her there. That will cost even more money."

Lucy placed a kiss on his cheek. "We can sell the engagement ring."

Yes, they would have to part with the diamond. Alexander wanted to travel to London with Lucy in grand style and that would cost a pretty penny. He wished he could cover Lucy's entire body with diamonds. One day he would do just that.

"We must look the part when we arrive in London or it won't work, Drakey. We shall book adjoining rooms on the next ship to London. We need the money to do that, so we'll sell the ring. It's nothing compared to the millions we'll get our hands on when you marry that Fleming girl." Lucy positioned her naked body over his, straddling him, her long legs pressing against his thighs. "You can make it up to me then."

"That will most definitely be arranged, my love," he answered. "You've been such a sweet, patient girl and you shall be richly rewarded."

The plan was, once he got his hands on the Fleming millions, he would set Lucy up in a grand house of her own, with servants, beautiful clothes, jewels, and anything else she desired. She would never have to feel subservient again. Lucy didn't care about marrying Alexander, or any man for that matter. Lucy simply wanted to be rich enough to have whatever she wanted, and he couldn't blame her for that. In fact, he admired her for it, because they shared the same dreams.

Again, Lucy smiled that slow, seductive smile of hers that weakened him to her power every single time. He could deny her nothing when she smiled at him like that. "The best part will be . . ." Lucy said with a triumphant gleam in her eye. "You can introduce me to everyone as Miss Lucille *Drake*."

"My innocent little sister," he laughed wickedly as she moved her hips over him.

9

Trade Winds

Christopher Townsend, the Earl of Bridgeton, glanced around the crowded ballroom, his eyes searching for one woman in particular. He knew she was here, for he saw her mother just a moment ago. He finally spied her dancing with a young man he recognized from his club. With his heart thudding in his chest and echoing in his head, he made his way over to her as the dance ended.

"Miss Beckwith," he called, eyeing her pleasant face and soft brown curls. She wore a gown of white silk with enormous puffed sleeves, which gave her the ungainly appearance of a snowball. He steeled his resolve, recalling that her father had endowed her with a massive dowry, which would solve all his financial problems and then some, for years to come. "Isn't this our dance?" he asked, mustering his most dashing smile.

"Why, Lord Bridgeton, I believe you are correct!" she gushed, waving her fan and glancing up at him.

Hating himself for what he was doing, he took Bonnie Beckwith in his arms as the orchestra played. She chattered amiably about he knew not what nor could he respond except with the merest of acknowledgments. While meaningless words came from her cupid bow mouth, his heart was sick with dread. He must convince this woman, this odd little stranger with the wide eyes and the snowball dress, to marry him when he had no desire to marry her at all. In fact, he didn't even wish to be dancing with her. But he must.

He had to save his family. He had to save the estate. As the Earl of Bridgeton, Christopher was now obligated to pay his father's outrageous debts and care for his mother and sisters. And to do that he needed to marry this peculiar personage who babbled incessantly as he waltzed her around the ballroom.

It felt as if ice water ran in his veins.

Earlier that day he met with his investment partner about their shipping venture. The outlook was still not good. They might not see a profit for another year at least, and even then the amount wouldn't be enough to keep him solvent yet. He had gone to the meeting with the expectation of some good news, a glimmer of hope for a financial return in the near future, which would see him through. But it wasn't to be.

So Christopher was left with the only option available to him. Marriage. He'd done his research thoroughly. There were only two feasible prospects with enough money to resolve his financial trouble.

First there was Bonnie Beckwith. She was the pampered daughter of an immensely wealthy textile merchant who wanted to marry his daughter to a title and didn't care what it cost, and Christopher's title was definitely for sale. She was pleasant enough, if a little odd. The thought of spending his life with this round chatterbox with the big eyes made him a little queasy. With the way she batted her eyelashes at him, he figured he could win her over easily enough. His youth, good looks, and his earldom made that possible, in spite of his disinterest.

As the seemingly eternal dance ended, he escorted Miss Beckwith back to her mother and thanked her politely, leaving the girl slightly breathless with one of his smiles. It occurred to him that he still had no idea what she had said to him while they danced. She could have told him she ran around the house naked for all he knew, or cared, for that matter.

He sighed heavily with relief. At least the first step was taken. He gazed around the room once more, looking for his second option, which was only slightly more palatable.

Lady Constance Fuller. She was a tall, lanky redhead, and a very wealthy widow. As the daughter of the Earl of Granville she had been an heiress in her own right even before her marriage to a wealthy copper and tin industrialist. Now a widow with two young daughters, she was still quite eligible and the word was, now that she was out of mourning, she was looking to remarry. Christopher would be acquiring a ready-made family with Constance, but she was more physically attractive to him than Miss Beckwith.

He took a deep breath and began to make his way through the crowd toward Lady Constance, where she stood drinking punch near the refreshment area.

"Well, good evening, Lord Bridgeton!"

The familiar American accent immediately caught his attention and it seemed his heart skipped a beat. He paused and slowly turned his head. There she was, a vision of loveliness in yet another pale blue gown, showing off the elegant curves of her body, her silky dark hair piled stylishly atop her head, which accentuated the graceful curve of her neck. That floral scent of hers surrounded him and he couldn't help but grin.

"Miss Fleming. You are a sight to behold, indeed."

"Why, thank you, kind sir. You shall turn my head with

your pretty compliments. But I must say that you are just the man I was looking for," she said, an impish grin on her exquisite face.

He knew her words were just that, words. She was merely flirting with him, which she was an expert at. *You are just the man I was looking for* . . . Yet the sound of those particular words, coming from those sweet lips, caused his breath to catch in his chest.

However, Christopher managed to mutter carelessly, "Am I now? Why would you be looking for me, Miss Fleming?"

She waved her tiny dance card, her blue eyes sparkling as she spoke. "Yes, well, you see, I was supposed to dance this next set with a Lord Robinson, but apparently he left rather suddenly, and here I am without a partner. And then I recalled that yesterday you asked me to save you a dance and I thought to myself, I wish I knew where Lord Bridgeton was, and then you appeared! Isn't that remarkable? Just as I was thinking about you, here you are!"

What was truly remarkable was how much it thrilled him to imagine that she was thinking of him in any way. How he wanted to dance with her! For the briefest moment he glanced toward Lady Constance Fuller. She was being led to the dance floor by an older, gray-haired gentleman. Well, he'd apparently missed his opportunity to speak with her just now anyway.

He looked down at Sara Fleming, marveling at how petite she was. He wanted nothing more than to scoop her up into his arms and carry her out of there.

"Here I am, just when you were thinking of me." He held out his arm to her. "Shall we dance then?"

A bright smile lit her face and she took hold of him with the lightest of touches. He guided her to the dance floor as the orchestra began a waltz.

"Do you recognize this waltz, Lord Bridgeton?" she asked, her eyes dancing with merriment.

"Should I?" he replied, looking at her blankly.

"It's 'Tout à vous.' It's the one we danced to the first time we danced together! Isn't that funny? Now we've waltzed to it twice."

"Ah, yes. I recall you telling me about it now," he said, smiling at her. "Truly yours?"

"Yes, that's right." She gazed up at him. "I shall have to think of it as our special tune from this point on." She paused for a moment, listening to the music and humming a little. "It was wonderful having you and your sisters at Devon House last night."

"Yes, it was, wasn't it? Thank you again for having us. Your family is most welcoming and very special."

In all honesty he was fascinated by her family. There was so much connecting everyone. Admittedly, he had known Phillip and Simon Sinclair for years, and had dined with their parents, Lord and Lady Stancliff, a number of times, but he had never been with the entire family before. Sara's family.

Observing Sara with her parents had been quite interesting. There was definitely a little tension between them. However, there was also genuine love and warmth between the parents and their daughter, something he had never witnessed or experienced in his own family. Captain Fleming was a good man, and had amazing stories to tell about his travels, and Mrs. Fleming was quite a character herself. Sara had an unconventional upbringing and had visited places he had never even heard of.

Then there were all the aunts and uncles and other cousins. He'd had a devil of a time keeping everyone straight. Quinton and Lisette Roxbury and their three children. Lord and Lady Cashelmore and their two children, one of whom was Lady Mara. The Duke and Duchess of Rathmore and their three little daughters.

Aside from the sheer number of people, what struck Christopher most was the laughter and joking between them all. The good humor and camaraderie was astonishing. These people loved and cared for one another, respected one another and were happy to be in one another's company. He couldn't even articulate why it touched him so deeply. He only knew that everything his own family, his own child-hood, was lacking, was right there in the Hamilton family.

Something inside of him longed to be a part of it.

His own sisters couldn't stop talking about the evening either. It was as if a dark veil had been pulled off their eyes and they could finally see the world and what they had been missing out on all their lives. Yes, his sisters had read about loving families in books, but they had never witnessed one firsthand.

"I agree. My family is very special, but at times they can all be a bit too much. I'm always happy to see them, but I'm always happy to go home too. There's just so many of us!" Sara laughed lightly.

"I can understand that," he replied, seeing her point. He'd felt overwhelmed a few times last night with all of them there.

"You are a very understanding man, Lord Bridgeton."

"Is that a fault in your eyes?"

"No, not at all. I was merely stating a fact. But since you're the one fishing for compliments this time, I shall tell you that I find your sympathetic nature quite attractive."

"I am delighted to hear that." God, but she felt good in his arms. She was so pretty he could hardly take his eyes off her. He had a wild desire to lift her in his arms, carry her to a dark corner, and kiss her passionately for hours. It was a shame really, that he couldn't even consider marrying Sara. He'd heard that her father recently lost all his money and they were here in London living with the Sinclairs at Devon

House until they recovered and to hopefully see their daughter successfully wed.

When he'd discovered that he wondered if her story about her parents separating her from the man she loved was really to spare her the knowledge that her family was now bankrupt. Why, she was in the same position that he was, only she wasn't aware of it and didn't have to shoulder the burden of providing for the rest of the family, as he did.

"It was interesting to learn more about your exotic childhood at dinner the other night," he said. "You've been all over the world, Miss Fleming."

"Yes, there are some benefits to being a captain's daughter. I've seen some beautiful places. Have you done much traveling, Lord Bridgeton?"

"I can't say that I have, unfortunately. I had a very brief trip to France two years ago, before my father died. But that's the extent of my travels."

"Well, perhaps sometime in the future you shall get to travel."

"Perhaps," he said, shrugging. "I doubt very much that I can catch up with a captain's daughter!"

She grinned mischievously. "You are more than likely right."

As their waltz came to an end, which seemed far too brief to suit him, Christopher looked around for Constance Fuller. He had no choice. He had to get on with it. And the sooner the better. He had pressing business to attend to, however much he enjoyed the distraction of dancing with Sara Fleming.

"Lord Bridgeton?"

"Yes?" He stared into her blue eyes, surprised to discover that he had missed something she said.

"You seemed to have drifted away from me for a moment." She seemed almost bemused by that fact.

"I apologize. I have other things on my mind this evening."

"Yes, I can see that." A look of concern crossed her features. "Is there anything I can do to help?"

Touched by her offer, he only wished that she could. "Thank you, but I'm afraid not, Miss Fleming."

She favored him with an inviting smile. "Well, I was asking if you were free for a moment or two? Would you mind escorting me to the drawing room? I promised my aunt Yvette and uncle Jeffrey I would join them there after this dance and I'm not quite sure where it is."

"Nothing would give me greater pleasure."

With Sara Fleming on his arm, Christopher made his way through the crowded ballroom. There was such a crush of people it took all of his effort to protect her from being jostled about. He then recalled that there was an outside entrance to the grand Wickham drawing room. He'd spent many a night playing cards here with his friend Edward Wickham and Phillip Sinclair. It would be quicker and safer to walk Sara out through the patio and around to the drawing room, than fighting their way through the crowded ballroom and interior hallways and rooms.

"Come this way," he directed her, altering their course. She followed him willingly, her small hand tucked safely into the crook of his arm. When they finally escaped through the French doors to the outside patio, they both took a moment and breathed a sigh of relief.

"I've never seen this place so crowded," he said.

"Thank you," she murmured. "I couldn't even see where we were going. But I don't believe this is the drawing room, Lord Bridgeton," she added with a humorous grin, looking around at the marble terrace.

"I know a shortcut," he explained.

She acted a bit disappointed. "Oh, and here I thought you

were leading me to a shadow-filled corner down one of the garden paths."

Christopher had to shake himself from the illicit images her words invoked in his mind, for he would like nothing better than to whisk little Miss Captain's Daughter down one of those shadowy garden paths and kiss her luscious mouth slowly and seductively for hours.

"I hate to disappoint you, but no," he managed to say.

She arched a brow and giggled. "Well, we should continue on then, should we not?"

Once again he offered his arm to her and she accepted. Then he guided her down the steps and along the stone pathway that led toward the drawing room. The Wickhams had installed gaslights in their garden and the golden illumination lit their way. It was a short walk before they found themselves at the French doors to the drawing room, which stood wide open. They could hear the murmur of voices inside and the rise and fall of conversation punctuated with laughter.

"Here we are," he said, rather disappointed that their little journey was over already. But he did need to return to the ballroom and his pursuit of Lady Constance Fuller.

"That was indeed a shortcut, Lord Bridgeton. Thank you."

Christopher looked down and felt himself drown a little in her eyes. She was so utterly lovely. Her hand still rested on his arm and it took all his willpower to resist the urge to pull her to him. Instead he stood perfectly still, just looking at her.

She said not a word either, but gazed up at him, with an expression of wonderment on her face.

"Are you still in love with him?" The words escaped his mouth before he could consider what he was asking.

"Yes." She held his gaze and did not turn away. "I am."

"Is he coming for you?"

"I certainly hope so."

"So you have not heard from him yet?"

It was then she seemed to awaken from her little reverie. She glanced away. "Not yet, no. But I am sure I will hear something from him soon enough."

"I hope he is worthy of you."

She looked at him intently. "Why would you say something like that?"

Surprised by the sharpness of her tone, he responded, "Because you deserve to be with a man who realizes what a treasure you are."

"Oh, Lord Bridgeton, that was very sweet of you."

He suddenly felt the fool. "Yes, well then. I believe it's time you went inside, Miss Fleming."

She nodded and thanked him while he guided her up the steps to the entrance of the drawing room. He could see her aunt and uncle inside, the ones he met last night. Lord Sinclair and Lady Mara were with them as well and they were all talking and laughing.

He turned to go, a heavy feeling in his chest, and made his way back to the crowded ballroom. There was definitely something about that girl that drew him in and it took everything he had to fight it. He could never have her, so there was no point in dwelling on it. He had to look toward securing his future and saving his home and family. He walked over to the tall, pretty redhead who grinned invitingly at his approach.

"Good evening, Lady Constance," he said, forcing himself to smile.

10

Any Port in a Storm

Curled up on the cushioned window seat in the Devon House library with Boots snuggled in her lap, Sara watched the rain pouring down, splashing against the windowpane. The dark clouds and stormy weather matched her gloomy mood. It had been so long and she was tired of waiting. Surely she should have received a letter from Alexander Drake by now!

She glanced over at the small writing table where she had begun yet another letter to him. It lay there, unfinished, with cross-outs and scribbles. Admittedly, she wasn't the best of writers, but Sara had no idea if Alexander had even received her first letter, let alone the four that followed. And still there was no response.

Heartsick, she continued to stare at the rain, listening to the sound of it pelting the glass.

Am I wrong about Alexander? Are my parents right about him after all?

Perhaps it was too much of a bother for Alexander to

come to London. Maybe he really didn't love her enough to come get her.

A flash of lightning, followed by a rumble of thunder that shook the glass, caused her to jump and startle the sleeping puppy. She soothed him and sighed with despair, leaning her forehead against the cool window pane.

The glorious October day she met Alexander Drake seemed so far away now.

She had been riding in Central Park, admiring the golden leaves, bright blue sky, and the crisp autumn air. The brand-new riding habit that she'd worn for the first time that day fit her perfectly and showed off her figure. The smart black velvet jacket was her favorite, thinking it gave her a sophisticated air. She and her groom had just left the meadow and were circling back along the path, when Sara's horse suddenly startled. She never did discover what made him rear up, catching her by surprise and tossing her to the ground, but in the next moment she was lying in the tall grass, and staring up at the most handsome face she'd ever seen.

"Miss, are you all right?" he had asked with concern in his voice, his blond hair glinting in the afternoon sunlight.

Whether she was mesmerized by his startling green eyes or struck dumb from her fall, she wasn't sure which, but she was unable to speak. She could barely catch her breath. Her head swam dizzily and she could only smile at him.

"My name is Alexander Drake. Please allow me to assist you."

With the help of her groom, Alexander carefully carried her to his carriage and took her home. It turned out Sara had sprained her ankle and gotten a nasty bump on her head, but her parents had been so grateful for his help and care of their daughter that they welcomed him in immediately. And she had been utterly smitten with him from the start.

While she recovered from her fall, she had fallen in love, for Alexander Drake came to call on her each day. He brought her pretty bouquets of flowers, delicious little treats, and books of poetry to cheer her up. And suddenly he was a part of her life. She couldn't eat or sleep for thinking of him. Once she got well, they began to go riding together.

In spite of all the young men who vied for her attention in New York, Alexander Drake had been the only one that she wanted because he was somehow different from the other men she knew. With his golden looks, he was charming and funny and impossibly handsome. He made her feel as if she were the only girl in the world. When he smiled at her, she simply melted. And he was the most romantic man too! He treated her like a princess, wrote her adoring poetry, and whispered the most beautiful things to her. He was the perfect man, her dream come true as if from a fairy tale.

As their tender courtship progressed through the winter, Sara began to notice her parents' quiet disapproval of Alexander, but she simply attributed it to their being overprotective of her. Her mother began to softly suggest that she receive other gentleman callers. "Don't you think you are limiting yourself, dear? There are lots of other eligible men out there." Her father would make remarks, such as, "Is that Drake coming by *again* this evening?" Sara smiled and airily dismissed their comments, not paying them any mind.

She was too in love with Alexander by then to care what they said.

But by early spring, Alexander declared his love for her one night in the front living room of her house and she almost died from the sweetness of it. It was a chilly evening and they were seated near the fire. She had been wearing her prettiest rose-colored watered-silk gown with the most gorgeous red cashmere scarf. Her father was not home that night and her mother had left the room for a moment to check on something. That was when it happened.

Sara could hardly breathe as Alexander whispered the

words in her ear she had longed to hear from the moment they met.

"My dearest Sara, I fear I have fallen in love with you." He took her hand in his and looked deep into her eyes. "Please tell me I have your heart. Might I dare to hope that you could love me as well?"

"Excuse me, Miss Sara?"

Startled by the voice that pulled her from her reverie, Sara turned from the rain-drenched window and looked toward the Devon House butler, who stood at the doorway of the library, waiting patiently.

"Yes, Parkins?" she asked.

"Forgive me for interrupting, but Lord Bridgeton just arrived, looking for Lord Waverly. I'm not quite sure what to do with him," he explained. "He's quite soaked from the storm. Shall I show him in the drawing room to wait there? Or I should perhaps bring him in here? I can serve a light supper in here now for both of you, or in the dining room if you prefer."

"Why yes, of course, Parkins, you can show Lord Bridgeton in here. I'll speak with him. And it would probably be best to bring supper in here too, as you and I had planned. That would be thoughtful and most appreciated," Sara said. "And can you please send Thomas in to stoke the fire and bring some towels for Lord Bridgeton?"

"Of course, miss, right away," Parkins said before he left the library.

"Well, Boots," she whispered to the sleeping puppy in her arms, "we have company." Sara gently rose from the window seat and placed Boots on a cozy chair with a warm blanket for him to snuggle with. Deep in the throes of his nap, he barely moved. Then she scurried to put away the letter she had attempted to write to Alexander Drake, stuffing the papers back into her elegant rosewood writing box that Aunt Lisette had given her as a birthday gift one year.

Wishing she was wearing something prettier than the rather plain pink day dress she had thrown on earlier, she just managed to take a peek at herself in the looking glass on the wall and straighten her hair, when the library door opened and Lord Bridgeton entered.

"Forgive me for intruding, Miss Fleming," he said, looking a bit sheepish. His hair was indeed wet, and he had run his fingers through the thick black tresses, slicking it back from his handsome face. Drops of rain dripped down his cheeks. And once again she was struck by his height. He was quite an imposing figure.

"Oh, you're not intruding at all." Even though he really was, she found that she didn't mind at all. She was oddly grateful for the distraction from her forlorn thoughts of Alexander Drake.

The footman entered and handed Lord Bridgeton a towel and then began to stoke the fire to warm the library. He also lit the lamps and a few candles since the heavy rain clouds darkened the room much earlier than usual.

"Thank you, Thomas," Sara said before the footman left the library.

She watched Lord Bridgeton dry his face and hair as best he could while he moved to stand near the fire to allow his drenched trousers to dry.

"I was supposed to meet Waverly here an hour ago, but I got caught in the storm, as you can see," he explained, as he continued to remedy his rain-soaked attire. "But Parkins has informed me that Waverly isn't here yet. So I imagine he's stranded by the storm as I was. Hopefully somewhere dry." He laughed and turned to face her. "Thank you for allowing me to take shelter here. It's quite a deluge outside and I'm afraid I didn't take my carriage today, a decision I now regret. The streets are flooded and the wind has knocked down so many things, even the carriages are not getting through. I also did not have the foresight to bring an umbrella with me."

"Oh, but Phillip isn't in town today!" Sara told him. "He left early this morning with his father, my father, and Simon to look over their estate. They won't be back until tomorrow or the day after. Perhaps you had the date mixed up?"

Lord Bridgeton looked thoroughly puzzled. "That's odd. I was positive I was supposed to meet him this afternoon."

"Knowing my cousin Phillip, I'm sure the fault lies with him," she said. "But I'm afraid I'm the only one at home at the moment to entertain you. My mother and Aunt Colette are visiting with my aunt Lisette. So it's just me."

The smile Lord Bridgeton bestowed upon her actually gave her a little thrill. "I don't object to that at all," he said with an amused glance.

Parkins entered the library with a tray of piping hot tea and warm bread, assorted cheeses and fruits, cold chicken, and some teacakes with icing. He placed the tray on the table in front of the sofa. "Will there be anything else, miss?"

"No, thank you, Parkins, this is wonderful," Sara said, dismissing him. She had planned on a light supper anyway since she was the only one at home. Now she at least had some company besides Boots. And very handsome company at that!

The butler left the two of them alone in the library.

"How do you take your tea?" she asked Lord Bridgeton, as she arranged the china cups and saucers.

"Just a little sugar, please." He remained in front of the fire, warming himself by rubbing his hands together.

As she fixed Lord Bridgeton a plate of food and a cup of tea, she felt the domestic intimacy of the situation and found it oddly comforting on this late stormy afternoon. She looked back up to offer the tea to him and froze. The teacup rattled on the saucer and the tea spilled over the edge of the cup.

Transfixed, she stared as he stood before the fire, removing his fitted jacket and placing it over the back of a nearby

chair to dry. He slowly untied his cravat and laid it on the
end table, then loosened the opening of his white linen shirt
and rolled up his sleeves. Through the thin, slightly damp
fabric she could see the outline of his broad chest and the
bulging muscles on his arms and was completely stunned.

He was a beautiful example of the male form: tall, clas-
sically handsome, muscular, and exuding a quiet strength.
Involuntarily her pulse quickened at the sight. He was so
utterly male and she was all alone with him in this room.

"Your tea . . ." she managed to squeak when she was able
to find her voice.

"Oh, thank you!" he exclaimed, walking toward her.
Carefully he took the cup from her hands. "This isn't exactly what I had in mind, but it will do in a pinch."

Sara gave him a knowing look. "You'd prefer something
stronger, Lord Bridgeton? Whiskey, perhaps?"

"Have you any?" he asked in grateful disbelief. "It's been
a hell of a day." He immediately apologized. "Please forgive
my language, Miss Fleming."

She placed both hands on her hips. "Have you forgotten
I'm a sea captain's daughter, Lord Bridgeton? I've spent a
good deal of my life aboard ship surrounded by dozens of
sailors who did not always watch their language when I was
around, no matter how hard they tried to behave. Believe
me, I've heard much worse language than that."

"I do recall you telling tales of your seafaring childhood,
but I don't remember hearing anything about swear words."
He grinned mischievously at her.

Sara walked over to a large, well-stocked liquor cabinet
and rummaged through Uncle Lucien's elegant bottles. She
knew her liquors too. Spending her life on a ship dominated
by men had taught her a variety of useful things, including
how to serve drinks. She held up two crystal decanters.
"Would you prefer brandy?" she asked. "Or whiskey?"

He arched a challenging brow in her direction. "Whichever one you'll drink with me, Miss Captain's Daughter."

"Brandy it is then," she answered evenly.

Sara had never had a drop of either liquor in her life but for some reason she leaned toward the brandy. She wasn't about to back down from a dare, and Lord Bridgeton had definitely just laid down a challenge. Surprised by his wicked sense of fun, she gamely joined in. Deftly she poured two glasses full of the golden brown liquid. It smelled dreadfully, but she was determined not to show fear, having only had tastes of wine and champagne before. She walked toward him, holding out the crystal glass.

Smiling, he slowly set down the teacup and accepted the brandy, his fingers brushing hers. He held up the glass. "Cheers. To the storm."

"To the storm," she whispered back. She lifted the glass to her lips.

A bright flash of lightning lit the room, followed immediately by a tremendous crashing of thunder. Boots yipped and Sara jumped, spilling some of the brandy. They both laughed and watched as Boots hid behind his blanket. Again they raised their glasses to each other. The first sip burned her throat and she couldn't suppress a little cough. She noticed he was watching her carefully, so she gave him a smile.

"I am impressed, Miss Fleming," he said, clearly amused, yet with a gleam of admiration in his eyes. "I didn't think you'd go through with it."

"I told you, I'm a captain's daughter." The liquid seemed to warm her body wonderfully from the inside out. No wonder he wanted to drink it after being caught in the storm.

"Well, sip it very slowly. And please have a seat and keep me company," he suggested, indicating the dark green velvet sofa facing the fireplace, where the food was laid out on the low table in front.

Carefully carrying her glass of brandy, Sara made her

way to the sofa, and he followed, sitting beside her. His body took up a good deal of the sofa and she found she was sitting closer to him than she realized.

It was quite an unusual situation, being alone in the library with Lord Bridgeton on this cold and rainy spring evening. She didn't know why she felt so happy being with him, even knowing the risks she took if her mother or father or anyone else were to find her this way. But she didn't care. This wasn't an illicit affair she had planned. She was simply having a little fun. Uncle Jeffrey had even told her to try to enjoy herself while she was in London. And this was the most fun she'd had since she left New York.

Besides, she liked Lord Bridgeton very much. He was now a dear family friend. Not some stranger. She could certainly sit in the library with a friend who needed shelter from the storm. Surely there was nothing wrong with that? Lord Bridgeton didn't seem to think so.

"Just how many salty words do you know, Miss Captain's Daughter?" he asked, before taking a bite of some bread and cheese.

"Four." She stared at him. "No, seven."

"*Seven?*" He looked astonished, his voice incredulous.

"Shall I tell them to you?"

He suddenly laughed. "No, I don't think so, but I believe you. Some other time perhaps."

"Maybe I can teach you a few," Sara offered with a saucy smile. She liked surprising him.

"Oh, I've no doubt of that."

"My offer stands anytime you feel the need to swear."

Again his laughter echoed in the library. "This is not how I expected this day to turn out."

"Neither did I."

Sara eyed him carefully, while taking another tiny sip of brandy. The flickering firelight accentuated the classic angles of his face, the strong line of his jaw, and the noble bridge of his nose, making him seem even more handsome. In his loose white shirt, sitting casually on the sofa with a drink in his hand, he seemed the epitome of masculinity. The thick lashes that fringed his eyes closed briefly.

Then he turned and looked directly at her. "I don't know what we're thinking doing this."

"I like it," she whispered, settling back against the sofa.

"You like it," he said, echoing her words. He shook his head in disbelief before taking a sip of the brandy.

"Yes, I like it." Sara continued in a pragmatic tone, "No one is here. No one will know. If the storm is as bad as you say, I'm sure my mother and Aunt Colette will stay the night at their sister's house instead of trying to get back home. We're not really doing anything wrong. It's all completely innocent."

"I've never met anyone quite like you, Miss Fleming."

"I think you should call me Sara now."

"If you call me Christopher."

"Agreed," she said, smiling at him, and taking another sip of the brandy. It made her feel wonderfully warm. "So tell me then, why did you have 'a hell of a day'?"

He sighed heavily. "It's a long and involved story that I'm sure you'd have no interest in. Suffice it to say that it's all due to family problems."

"Ah, now that I do understand." She nodded her head toward him.

He chuckled ruefully. "You have no idea about family problems. You, my darling Sara, have the most wonderful family."

Why did the sound of him saying her name delight her so much, especially with the words "my darling" in front of it?

"You make it sound as if your family is dreadful. Have

you forgotten that I've met your sisters, *Christopher,* and they are as nice as can be," she pointed out, while emphasizing her use of his given name, which she liked using. Christopher was a good name. Not as good as Alexander, but good just the same.

"Yes, my sisters are nice"—he took a swig of brandy— "but you have never met my parents."

"How bad can they be?" she questioned. "They raised *you*, and you are perfectly nice. And so are Evelyn and Gwyneth."

He scoffed. "We turned out well in spite of their best efforts to do otherwise. And the girls, well . . . The girls bear a lot of ugly scars that you can't see."

Suddenly Sara felt as if she were about to learn something dreadful, something perhaps she didn't wish to know. But the utter look of sadness on his face pulled at her heart. She had no choice but to let him continue. Slowly she drew her legs up beneath her. "And you have these scars too?" she asked on a whisper.

He nodded and drank more of his brandy. "I didn't come here to discuss my childhood with you."

"But it's on your mind right now . . ."

With a quick movement of his wrist, he downed the last of his brandy. "You're the one on my mind."

Her heart thudded wildly in her chest. Had she misunderstood what he just said? "Christopher?"

He rose from the sofa without a word, strode across the room, and poured more brandy from the decanter. She watched him carefully as he returned to sit beside her.

He sighed so deeply she could feel his breath. "My childhood was not like yours, Sara. Not everyone is as lucky as you are, or is as lucky as your entire family is. I didn't have parents who loved and cared for me, who wanted me to do well and encouraged me. My father—" He broke off, as if he were quite angry.

Sara said not a word. She barely breathed, sensing he needed to share what he was about to say to her. The fire crackled on the hearth, the golden glow of flames flickering around them. She waited patiently.

Christopher began again. "My father was a vicious and cruel man who brutalized my sisters and me, while my mother did nothing to stop him. In fact, she often joined in. Our home was a house of horrors filled with humiliation and pain."

Silence enveloped them, broken only by the rolling rumble of thunder and the torrential rain outside. Sara was speechless. Not knowing the words to comfort him, she continued to remain quiet. Slowly she sipped from her glass of brandy, only this time it didn't warm her.

Lightning flashed across the room.

"My father's idea of fun was to torment his children, whether it was slowly starving one of us for months at a time, or beating us for the slightest infraction of his ridiculous expectations or irrational rules. He was worse to the girls. Much worse." He paused, and there was a hitch in his voice when he spoke again. "And I couldn't stop him. I could never stop what he did to the girls."

"Oh, Christopher." Her voice was so soft she wondered if he even heard her. Yet the pain of which he spoke was quite palpable.

"To the outside world, I suppose we appeared to be a normal family, but the Townsends were far from normal. Very far. Growing up, I always felt as if it were my fault somehow. That I did something wrong to make my father hate me so much, but I could never figure out what it was. So I just tried my best and worked my hardest to be the best son and brother I could be. But I was the lucky one, because I got sent away to boarding school. Evie and Gwyneth had to stay there with our mother and father, at their mercy. That killed me. Every time I had to leave them, I hated myself for going."

Barely able to imagine such a life, Sara remained silent. It was unthinkable, what he was saying to her. Picturing Christopher as a young boy, trying to protect his little sisters, she was overcome by emotions she couldn't even name. His words touched her deeply. She reached over and gently squeezed his hand.

"I hated myself because I was glad to leave. Yet I felt guilty for leaving Evie and Gwyneth alone, especially when they had no escape or refuge. My sisters were trapped in that house with them and I could do nothing to help them."

"I'm sure you did all you could and they know that," Sara said.

Christopher took a deep breath. "I tried. I always wished there was more for them. A safe place I could send them. But at least my father is dead now. He died a year ago and we are finally free from his cruelty. My sisters are only just learning to live their own lives."

"And what about your mother?" she asked in a hesitant whisper.

"Oh, she's still a miserable, vindictive woman, but she lost most of her power over us when my father died. She screams and rants and raves, but she's basically a recluse and won't leave Bridgeton Hall. As the head of the family, I'm the one in control now."

"I'm so very sorry." Sara would never complain about her parents again. Never had her mother or father raised their hand to her. Not once had she been treated cruelly or humiliated or harmed in any way. Throughout her entire childhood, she had only been loved and adored, and admittedly quite spoiled. Which made it impossible for her to comprehend the horrors that he and his sisters endured. She had a newfound respect for Christopher Townsend. For in spite of all the darkness in his life, one would never guess all that he had been through.

"There's nothing you need to be sorry for, Sara. It is what it is. And it's finally over. Or the worst part of it is anyway. The oddest thing is, I have never spoken of this to anyone before. Ever. Even my sisters and I avoid discussing our childhood at all costs. It's just something that's understood between us." He shook his head in disbelief. "I don't even know why I'm telling you any of this now."

Sara was more than a little overwhelmed by his confession and yet profoundly moved that he had chosen her as the one to whom he would reveal his darkest secrets. She'd never known anyone like him, anyone who had experienced what he had, and she wished there was something she could do to help ease his pain. "You told me because you know I care about you."

"Do you care about me?" he asked intently, his brown eyes questioning her.

"Of course I do!" she insisted. "I care about you very much, and in such a short amount of time, no less."

"But you're still in love with him?"

She knew he referred to Alexander Drake. Their conversation had suddenly taken an odd turn. A bit confused, she said, "One has nothing to do with the other, but yes. Yes, I'm still very much in love with him."

Once again his eyes fixated on her. "Why do you love this man? Whatever his name is."

Now Sara took a big sip from her glass of brandy. "I love Alexander because he's handsome and romantic and charming. And he loves me."

"Alexander." Christopher muttered the name dismissively and Sara was about to protest when he suddenly asked, "So what happened?"

"You mean why am I here in London and he's still in New York?" She sighed heavily. "I'm sure you can guess."

"Your parents don't approve of him. I've gathered that much. But why?"

A silence grew around them as Sara paused. She drank more of the brandy. "There is definitely something about him that they won't share with me yet, but basically it boils down to the fact that they believe he is not good enough for their precious little girl."

"So what happens now?"

"I wait for him to come to me. Or for my parents to bring me back to New York, I suppose. But I'm sure he will come here."

"With the intention of marrying you when he gets here?" he asked. His voice sounded rather husky.

"Yes. At least I hope he still plans to marry me. I haven't received a letter from him yet." It was so odd to be discussing her feelings for Alexander with another man.

"Of course he still wants to marry you. Who wouldn't want to marry a girl like you?" he muttered very low. "Do you still wish to marry him?"

Sara nodded her head slowly.

The rain pelted the windows and the fire crackled. For a moment neither of them said a word.

"So tell me, Miss Captain's Daughter, has this *Alexander* kissed you?"

Before she had time to consider what she was saying, she answered his impertinent question. "Of course he has."

Alexander had first kissed her in the living room of her parents' New York brownstone. She had been thrilled by the feel of his soft lips on hers, and he had been sweet and gentle with her, as a gentleman should always be with the lady he loved. There had been a few more stolen kisses when they were able to sneak away from the watchful eyes of her parents.

Christopher took another swig of brandy. And Sara did too, the warmth of the liquid finally flooding her body once more. It felt good again now. She relished the taste of it on her tongue and felt invigorated by it.

"So this man has kissed you."

"Yes, I believe I just said so." Sara jutted out her chin in defense, refusing to feel ashamed for kissing the man she loved and intended to marry. "I'm sure you've kissed your share of women."

He smiled roguishly. "Yes, I suppose I have done more than my fair share of kissing at that."

"Then why are you angry with me?" she demanded heatedly.

"Why am I angry with *you*?" he said with a rueful tone. "I'm not angry with you, my beautiful Sara. I'm angry with *him* for kissing you."

The brandy was making her a little light-headed, but she drank more anyway. She needed to make sense of what Christopher was saying. He just called her beautiful. *His* beautiful Sara, and again, it gave her the oddest sense of exhilaration. What was happening here? She stared at him, noting the light growth of stubble that covered his usually clean-shaven jaw. Fighting the impulse to reach out her hand and rub her fingers slowly across his cheek, she questioned, "You don't even know him. Why are you angry with him for kissing me?"

His words were sharp. "Because *I* want to be the one to kiss you."

"You?" Sara unexpectedly found it difficult to catch her breath. "You want to kiss me?"

"Yes." His eyes flickered across her face. "I want to kiss you."

"So kiss me then." Goodness gracious! Had she really said that aloud to him?

"Is that what you want?" he asked, his voice low and husky, his eyes focused on her. "For me to kiss you?"

Her heart was beating so loudly in her chest Sara was

positive he could hear it. Breathing became an agonizing chore. She didn't know if it was the warmth of the brandy, or his heartbreaking confessions about his childhood, or the raging storm outside, or the sight of his muscled arms in his loose white shirt, or the firelight playing across his handsome face, but she suddenly and desperately wanted Christopher Townsend, the Earl of Bridgeton, to kiss her more than anything in the world.

Carefully, she set her empty brandy glass on the table and turned to face him. "Yes. I want you to kiss me," she confessed softly. "I think I shall die if you don't."

For a moment, time stood still.

She waited with bated breath as he set his glass down. Again, he looked into her eyes, their gazes locked, as he reached for her with a throaty growl. Pulling her into his strong arms, he whispered her name as he brought his lips down over hers.

His embrace was warm and he tasted of brandy and his breath was hot. As his mouth covered hers, Sara was lost in the deep sensuality of being kissed by him. His soft lips pressed firmly against hers, tasting her, wanting her. Roughly positioning her across his lap, he held her in his arms as he continued to kiss her. It was amazing that a kiss could last so long. This was certainly nothing like any of the hasty and brief kisses she'd had with Alexander and the intensity of this kiss rushed through her veins, saturating every nerve in her body with a languid, molten heat.

Then he gently parted her lips with his tongue and she reeled from the sensation.

Her whole being spun with the beauty of it. As his tongue swirled with hers, the taste of brandy shared between them, Sara melted deeper and deeper into his embrace, his arms holding her to him. Slowly her arms found their way around his neck, pulling him even closer to her.

Just when she thought she might faint from the pleasure

of it, he gently drew away from her. He cradled her face in his hands, staring at her.

"Did he kiss you like that?"

For a second Sara couldn't remember who "he" was. Her brain felt a little foggy and it took a moment for her to recall Alexander's name. With slow deliberation she shook her head, whispering, "No. No, he never kissed me like that. I didn't know such kisses even existed."

"Good," he muttered before bringing his mouth down over hers again.

This time she was eager for him, opening her mouth, inviting him in. He groaned and held her tighter. That same molten heat and wickedly new sensations of desire raced through her entire body, leaving her breathless, incapable of doing anything but kissing him back. It felt as if she were drowning in him, becoming part of him. Yet it wasn't enough. She craved more and more of him as the kiss deepened. The faint, spicy scent of him enveloped her and her fingers curled through his thick, damp hair. The light stubble that covered his cheeks grazed her skin and she didn't care.

His hands were in her hair, loosening the pins, allowing the dark tresses to spill around them. His mouth hot on hers, his wonderful hands continued to move over her, caressing her back, the arch of her neck. The kiss seemed to go on and on, forever. They could have been kissing for hours or days for all she knew. Or cared.

She was lost in this magnificent kiss of his. Nothing else mattered, but this endless bliss, this cascade of feelings connecting her to this man in this moment. The feel of his lips, his tongue, his breath, his hands, his arms . . . she was surrounded by him, and yet she craved more from him. She pressed her own body against his, craving a closeness with him, a wild yearning to become a part of him.

With an agonized groan he drew back from her and she almost sobbed with the loss.

Panting heavily, he held her close to his chest as she rested her head on his shoulder. Her entire body trembled with a desire she didn't know she possessed and her head was spinning, whether from the brandy or from his kiss, she knew not which.

Gently he stroked her hair, soothing her. It felt wonderfully delicious to be held by him. So warm. So snug. So intimate. The room was quiet except for the steady rain that continued outside and the sound of his breathing. It was so warm. So utterly peaceful.

She could stay like this forever, she thought, as she slowly closed her eyes.

"Sara?" he whispered softly. "Sara?"

"Yes?"

"You fell asleep."

"No, I didn't," she murmured. "Not really." Had she fallen asleep? She couldn't have! For how long? Perhaps she dozed for just a moment. But only because it was so very warm and comforting in his arms. Christopher had the most wonderful arms. And he smelled so nice.

"Are you okay?" he asked.

She sat up then, and looked at him, blinking. Goodness, but he was handsome. "Yes, I'm fine." She placed a kiss on the tip of his nose. "Quite fine."

He looked a little surprised. "I feel I should apologize to you for this, but I don't want to."

"Why would you apologize to me? That kiss was simply magnificent. Didn't you think so?"

Very carefully, he lifted her from his lap and set her back down on her end of the sofa, softly kissing the top of her head. "As a matter of fact, I thought it was wonderful too. In all honesty, it was the best kiss of my life. But I have a feeling in your case, it's the brandy talking."

"The brandy talking . . ." Sara started to giggle then. She couldn't help herself. It was so terribly and ridiculously funny. "Christopher, brandy can't talk!" She dissolved in a fit of laughter, finally resting her head on the velvet cushions. Her head felt so very heavy.

Christopher smiled at her. He had such a nice smile. Then it seemed like he went away for a long time, because she couldn't see him, but he came back with a china teacup.

"Here. You should drink this, beautiful girl."

"I don't want any more tea." She motioned for him to go away. She was just too tired.

"It's not tea. It's brandy," he cajoled.

Oh, well, that was different. Sara sat up on the sofa, which was not the easiest move she ever made. "Thank you." Glad that she remembered her manners, she reached for the cup and took a sip. It wasn't brandy after all but cool tea and it was soothing and rather wonderful. She was suddenly very thirsty and found that she drank the whole cup.

"Would you like some more?"

Sara nodded and handed the empty cup to him. "You are quite nice, Christopher. Truly. You are the nicest and handsomest man I've ever known. Or ever kissed." Then she put her head back down on the green velvet pillow. She'd never felt so sleepy in her life.

She simply had to close her eyes for just a minute.

11

Lost at Sea

Christopher Townsend stared at Sara as she slept peacefully on the sofa, her beautiful face illuminated by the flickering firelight. With a gentle motion he covered her with a warm blanket that had been hanging over the back of a nearby chair. Then he crouched down on the floor beside the sofa.

Well, this was just awful.

He had gotten Sara Fleming drunk and taken advantage of her. What was wrong with him? What had he done? What if her parents or one of her many relatives suddenly walked in? What could he possibly say to them?

This was entirely his fault.

Yet she looked so serene, lying there, her dark hair loose, her sweet face at rest, wearing a simple pink dress and covered by a warm blanket. He reached out a hand and brushed a few stray, silky curls from her cheek. The pretty little captain's daughter. With her four—no, seven—swear words and her unconventional upbringing. Who would drink brandy just to show she could. Who would listen to him and sympathize with him about his god-awful childhood and not pity him. Who would kiss him seductively. Even eagerly.

She was quite astonishing.

The afternoon had taken such an unexpected turn. From getting caught in the storm, to being alone with Sara, to challenging her to drink with him, to confessing his childhood horrors to her, to kissing her passionately.

And it had been passionate. The most erotic and passionate kiss he'd ever had, and that was something in and of itself. She had been so willing and open. Sara *wanted* to kiss him. Wanted *him* to kiss her. Nor did she pretend as if she didn't want to, like some girls did. Hell, she had said she would die if he didn't kiss her. He'd never expected that.

Never even saw it coming.

Even if it was just the brandy talking, he would cherish that kiss with Sara Fleming for as long as he lived.

And what had prompted him to divulge to her the sordid stories of his childhood? He'd never spoken of that part of his life to anyone before. Not even to Phillip Sinclair, his closest friend. It was something he kept well-hidden. Secret. Separate from the façade he presented to the world. Yet the pity, the shame, and the recriminations he'd always feared did not materialize when he told her. She simply listened and seemed to care about him even more. He felt comfortable talking to her, which was surprising to him. Why should he confide in Sara Fleming? Of all people? A slip of a girl from America?

A sea captain's daughter.

She was different, this girl. Perhaps it was the very unusualness of her that drew him in. Her honesty. Her openness. Her fearlessness. Her lack of pretense. She was unlike any woman he'd ever met. That she was beyond beautiful didn't hurt either.

God, but she was lovely. He longed to kiss her again. To hold her in his arms.

Except now what?

He certainly couldn't marry her, even if she would have him.

Reluctantly he stood, stretched, and walked toward the window. The rain was still pouring down, but the sun had long since set. It was very dark out. The clock above the mantel struck eight thirty. He hadn't realized it was so late.

Earlier that day he'd called on Bonnie Beckwith and brought her a bouquet of flowers. She'd worn some bright yellow concoction of a dress that made her look like a giant lemon meringue. He'd suffered through twenty minutes of her babbling about he knew not what. Something about a musicale, maybe? Soprano? Pianoforte? She liked to sing basically. That was the gist of it. It was really quite astounding. He'd never before met anyone who could speak nonstop, yet say absolutely nothing of importance or relevance.

Christopher didn't know if he could do it. Shackling himself to that girl would be like living in his own personal hell for the rest of his life.

However, her parents seemed quite pleased with his visit though, and Bonnie herself was over the moon. She had batted her eyelashes over her wide eyes so many times it made him dizzy.

Christopher sighed heavily. Well, the wheels were set in motion now. He'd let his interest in Miss Bonnie Beckwith be known to her and her parents. But he knew without a doubt that he would never feel a fraction for her of what he felt for Sara Fleming.

A sickening knot formed in the pit of his stomach.

What about Lady Constance Fuller? Perhaps he should call on her once, before he completely ruled her out. Ever since she brazenly propositioned him during their dance at the Wickham Ball, he'd backed off. He suspected Lady Constance was a bit indiscriminate in her love affairs and wasn't sure that was a good attribute for his future wife to have. He doubted Lady Constance would be the type to retire quietly to the country. But perhaps that might be preferable after all? If he was going to enter into a loveless marriage, wouldn't it be better to marry a sophisticated widow who didn't have idealistic expectations about love and wouldn't mind leading separate lives?

Hell, he didn't want to marry either woman. Running his fingers through his hair, he gave a heavy sigh. He didn't know what was right anymore.

Certainly what happened between him and Sara Fleming just now wasn't right. He should be ashamed of himself for allowing her to drink brandy and kissing her that way. But good Lord, when she whispered that she would die if he didn't kiss her . . . How was a man supposed to resist such a temptation? If someone offered him a million pounds *not* to kiss her just then, he would not have seen a penny of the money.

Pressing his fingers against his temples, he sighed again. Christopher moved to the side table and poured more brandy into his glass, and took a long swig, letting the burn slide down his throat. He walked back toward the velvet sofa.

Sara still slept soundly there, blissfully unaware of his internal turmoil.

Maybe he should wake her and send her up to her room before either of her parents returned. He hoped her head wouldn't hurt terribly when she awoke. Staring down at her, he desired nothing more than to carry her to his own bed and hold her in his arms all night long.

If he admitted the truth to himself, this beautiful American girl, this little captain's daughter, was the one he wanted to marry. The one he wouldn't mind spending the rest of his life with. Life certainly wouldn't be dull being married to Sara Fleming.

Yet Christopher could never have her. She was already in love with and planning to marry another man and he needed to wed someone very wealthy. It was that simple and that complicated. And definitely not meant to be.

Just then the library door swung open and Phillip Sinclair burst in, dripping wet and making a lot of noise. Awakened by the sudden intrusion, Boots yipped in annoyance, then snuggled back into his blanket. Sara did not move an inch.

"It's a devil of a night out there! Sorry to keep you waiting, Bridgeton. Parkins told me you were here. Took me hours to get home. The streets are completely flooded, carriages are blocking the roads, and I just walked all the way from—"

Phillip suddenly stopped talking and stared, taking in the situation. The dimly lit room. The intimate setting. The remains of dinner on the table. Empty brandy glasses. Sara out cold on the sofa. Christopher knew it looked bad.

"What the hell is going on in here, Bridgeton?"

Christopher raised his glass of brandy. "Waiting for you, Waverly."

"Well, I can see that," Phillip said slowly, rain trickling down his face. He gestured his head toward the sofa. "What happened to her?"

"She had a little too much brandy."

"Blazes!" Phillip looked stunned. "Did you get my cousin foxed?"

"Guilty," Christopher confessed. "Now, before you deck me, will you please help me get her upstairs before someone sees her like this?"

"You're damn right I'm going to flatten you," he growled in outrage. "That's my cousin!"

"I am well aware of that fact."

Phillip paused, his hair still dripping. "But I'd like some of that brandy first."

Christopher tossed him the towel that he'd left on the chair and went to pour his friend a glass of brandy. "When

I arrived, your cousin told me you went with your father and brother out to the estate and wouldn't be back until tomorrow."

"No, no." Phillip shook his head while toweling his damp hair. "I was never going with my father today. Simon and my uncle went with him. Sara must have gotten it all muddled. I was at the club this afternoon."

Christopher handed him the glass. "Well, I got caught in the storm as well and arrived here about an hour later than we agreed on, as drenched as you are now. Your lovely American cousin"—he gestured to Sara—"was kind enough to keep me company."

Phillip stared at his cousin in utter disbelief. "Why the hell did you let her drink, Bridgeton?"

"Have you ever tried to stop her from doing something she wanted to do?"

With a chuckle, Phillip nodded his head. "I see your dilemma."

"She only had the one glass, but I think she drank it too quickly. For a captain's daughter, I thought she'd be a little hardier."

"Me too. I'm rather surprised actually." Phillip seemed puzzled. "But I supposed we'd better wake her and get her upstairs before Aunt Juliette sees her like this. And you're a damned sight lucky that her father isn't here tonight." He took a swig of brandy and then set his glass down. He walked over to the sleeping form of his cousin and tapped her on the shoulder.

"Sara," Phillip called. "Sara. You must get up now."

She mumbled something incoherent into the pillow, but did not awaken.

Looking completely flummoxed, Phillip announced in defeat, "She won't wake up."

"Let me try." Christopher set down his own drink and Phillip moved aside.

Kneeling next to the sofa, Christopher stroked her arm. Then using both hands, he gently lifted Sara to a sitting position, calling her name again.

Sara opened her sleepy eyes, stared at him, and suddenly started laughing. "Brandy can't talk, Christopher."

"Yes, yes, I know." Amused, he managed to hold her shoulders securely to keep her from flopping back down on the sofa. "It's time to go to bed now."

"Is it really?" she questioned, in utter disbelief. "What time is it? It feels like it must be midnight." Then she noticed her cousin. "Oh, hello, Phillip! It's so nice to see you! Where's Boots? Oh, there he is!"

Phillip traded concerned glances with Christopher. "She's still soused. This is going to be tough."

"I am not soused either," Sara said, somewhat offended. She brushed away Christopher's hands and attempted to stand up, but the blanket that had covered her had slipped to the floor and tangled around her feet, causing her to stumble back down onto the sofa. "Well. I suppose I am at that."

He and Phillip couldn't help but laugh. "Bring some of that tea over here," Christopher directed. "She needs a little more time."

He remained kneeling before the sofa and held Sara, propping her up, while Phillip went to get the tea.

"I'm fine really. Just very, very sleepy," she protested. Her tousled hair cascaded over her shoulders and the sultry little half smile she gave him made his heartbeat skitter. She looked more beautiful undone than she ever had with her stylish clothes and her perfectly arranged hair. She looked more natural and unguarded.

"I know you're fine," Christopher said in a soothing tone. He wished he could just enfold her in his arms and hold her until she felt better. "You simply need to drink a little more tea and rest here for a bit."

"All right," she said agreeably, staring at him, her blue eyes intent. Then she reached out a hand and gently caressed his cheek. "You're really quite a handsome man, you know."

His heart skipped a beat at her touch. He grinned roguishly for a moment, and said, "So I've been told." Reluctantly, he released his hold on her and stood, stepping aside for her cousin.

Sara giggled a little more as Phillip returned with a cupful of lukewarm tea and some bread. He handed the cup to Sara and instructed her to drink it all. Like an obedient child, she drank all the tea and dutifully ate the bread while Christopher and Phillip watched her closely.

"You mustn't stare at me," she said to them, becoming cross. "I'm not an infant, you know."

"We just want to make sure you're well," Phillip said, going to fetch more tea for her.

"You can stop fussing over me." Her eyes lingered on Christopher and her tone softened. "I'm quite all right."

"I can see that," he said to her. He could stare at her and fuss over her all day and not mind in the least. What was it about Sara Fleming that made him want to be near her? Want to care for her? Protect her? Want to kiss her? God, how he wanted to kiss her again!

Phillip handed her another cup of tea. "Drink it all," he commanded. "And perhaps I won't mention this little incident to your parents," he added quite firmly.

"Oh, Phillip, you wouldn't!" Sara cried, a slight note of panic in her voice, before she gulped down the tea.

He folded his arms across his chest. "Maybe I will. Maybe I won't. It depends."

Sara gaped at him. "On what?"

Phillip looked pointedly back and forth between Sara and Christopher. "It depends on a number of things. The

first of which begins with the two of you telling me just
exactly what happened here this evening."

"Nothing," Christopher and Sara said in unison. Surprised
at their coordinated answer, they both stared at each other
in amazement.

Phillip glanced at them skeptically. "Look at you . . . I
come home to find my sweet little cousin intoxicated.
Asleep on the library sofa. With her hair loosened. And all
alone with my best friend. You tell me what happened, or I
will jump to the only obvious conclusion."

Christopher spoke up. "Listen, Waverly, nothing untoward
happened here tonight, except Miss Fleming shouldn't have
had that glass of brandy. I came here this evening to meet
you, remember? I was drenched from the storm and Parkins
brought me to the library. Your cousin was kind enough to
keep me company while I dried off and waited for you
to arrive. She and I merely talked for a while and shared a
bite to eat and something to drink. For that I apologize. I
should have not encouraged her to have the brandy." He
looked directly at Sara, and with a veiled reference to
the scorching and passionate kiss they shared, said, "It's the
only thing that I feel deserves an apology from either of us."

Christopher certainly would not reveal to Phillip that he'd
kissed his cousin. That was between Sara and him. He definitely didn't regret it and he hoped that she didn't either.
Hell, he would treasure that moment between them for the
rest of his life.

Then Sara added, "Lord Bridgeton is correct. There's
nothing to concern yourself over, Phillip. I regret having
had the brandy and I promise I shall never do so again. Trust
me." She slowly pressed her fingers to her temple. "Other
than that, we just spent the time talking."

Phillip remained suspect. "I want to believe you both, but
something tells me otherwise."

"Well, you're wrong," Christopher said. "I assure you that nothing improper happened between us."

Sara suddenly seemed to regain her composure. "Honestly, Phillip, you're making quite a fuss over nothing." She stood up straight, carrying herself almost regally. "Now I am going to retire for the evening and take my leave of you two gentlemen. Please don't get into fisticuffs on my account." She stared into Christopher's eyes. "Thank you for a lovely, if unusual, evening, Lord Bridgeton. It was most . . ." She paused and he could swear she winked at him. "It was most . . . enlightening."

With that, Sara scooped Boots into her arms and calmly strode from the library.

Phillip turned to look at him, his face incredulous. "We definitely need a drink now."

Sighing heavily, Christopher said, "I couldn't agree with you more."

12

Mal de Mer

Feeling a little under the weather, Sara awoke much later than usual the next day. The storm from the previous evening had cleared, leaving the sky a crystal-clear blue, but Sara kept the blinds drawn, in no mood for the bright sunshine. She remained in bed, with Boots cuddled next to her, unwilling to face her parents, or her cousin Phillip or any other members of her family in light of what had happened with Lord Bridgeton the night before. She didn't believe they were aware of what had transpired in the library, but still . . .

Christopher.

Good heavens! Not only had she drunk a glass of brandy, she had kissed Christopher Townsend. Quite passionately. For a good length of time too. And enjoyed it immensely.

Touching her fingers to her lips now, they felt almost bruised, as if she could still sense his lips pressing against hers, the coarseness of the stubble on his face. She could still taste the delicious heat of his tongue in her mouth, could still smell the intoxicating male scent of his body pressed close to hers, could still feel the secure warmth of his muscled arms wrapped around her, could still hear the rapid pounding of his heart, could still see the ardent gleam in his brown eyes.

Being with him had been an all-consuming, unique experience and it amazed her how easily it happened. If she were completely honest with herself, she had to admit that she wanted it to last longer than it had. She had most definitely wanted more . . .

Feeling her cheeks burn scarlet, she wondered how she could ever face him again. She had acted like a reckless wanton. What on earth had she been thinking to kiss him like that? That was just it! She hadn't been thinking at all.

But it had all been very exciting. Probably one of the most exciting evenings she had ever spent with anyone, including Alexander Drake. The kiss she shared with Christopher had been unlike anything she ever shared with Alexander. Alexander had kissed her softly, quickly, chastely. It had been thrilling, of course, but nothing like that tumultuous, all-encompassing, mind-melting, knee-shaking kiss with Christopher. It was quite perplexing that she should so enjoy a kiss with a man she did not love.

A knock on her door interrupted her illicit thoughts of Christopher Townsend. Her mother entered. With a look of concern on her face, Juliette Hamilton Fleming came to stand beside the bed.

"Leighton just told me you weren't feeling well. Aunt Colette was expecting you at the bookshop today." Juliette placed a gentle hand on Sara's forehead. "You feel a little warm and your cheeks are flushed. Perhaps you should remain in bed."

"I'm fine, Mother." Embarrassment caused her cheeks to redden even more. "I just have a headache."

"Are you certain?" Juliette hovered over her, biting her lip.

"Yes. I already told you I'm fine." Sara didn't mean to

sound harsh, but it came out that way. After what Christopher had told her about his family, she felt terribly guilty for the way she had treated her parents lately. She had barely been civil to them since they arrived in London, and she'd been especially cold to her mother.

Having Christopher Townsend confide in her in such a manner touched something within her heart. No one had ever entrusted her with such deep, dark secrets before. These were real, honest-to-goodness soul-baring revelations. And Christopher had chosen to share them with her, of all people.

Christopher had been right about something else. Sara's own childhood had been quite idyllic in comparison to his, or most anybody's. His pointed remark made her feel spoiled and petty for being so angry with her mother and father for simply trying to protect her from Alexander Drake, however wrong they might be.

Her parents had only the best intentions for her, which could not be said for Christopher's parents. The whole evening had been an eye-opening experience. About life. About her own life. About how privileged and fortunate she was to possess a wonderful and caring family who loved her.

She now felt like an ungrateful little brat.

"I'm sorry, Mother," Sara apologized, reaching out to grab her mother's hand. "I didn't mean to snap at you. I'm simply grumpy because I didn't sleep very well. Thank you for checking on me."

Juliette seemed flustered by her apology but pleased too. She squeezed Sara's hand tightly. "Oh, you're welcome. I didn't mean to disturb you. I'll let you rest now. Come down when you are ready, but I'll make sure a tray is sent up to you in the meantime. Please eat a little something at least. It will help you feel better."

"Thank you again," Sara said, nodding and attempting a

smile. "I will. Can you please let Aunt Colette know that I will be over to the shop just as soon as I can?"

"Of course." Her mother placed a kiss on her forehead, gave her a little smile, and exited the bedroom.

Sara sighed heavily. She and her mother had always been close, but now things were decidedly awkward between them. Sara was still very angry with her mother and her father for what they had done, but knowing they had done it out of love for her made it harder to remain upset with them. It was all so confusing.

Last evening also left her bewildered regarding her feelings for Christopher Townsend after their torrid kiss. What did he think of her? Had he romantic feelings for her? When he said that he was angry that Alexander had kissed her . . . What did that mean? He acted as if he were jealous.

But that simply couldn't be! Christopher couldn't love her. She dismissed the possibility as ridiculous. And even if he did love her, it didn't matter. Not when she loved Alexander.

Suddenly she cringed.

Alexander would be devastated if he discovered that she had been kissing another man! Just as she would be completely heartbroken to discover if he had kissed another woman. Well, she simply had to ensure that Alexander never found out about Christopher Townsend. That was all. Determined that she would not think of Lord Bridgeton or allow him to kiss her anymore, she vowed silently to herself to never be untrue to Alexander again.

Glancing at the little ormolu clock on the mantel, she saw that it was well past noon. She'd hidden in her room long enough. Reluctantly, Sara rose from the blue toile–covered four-poster bed and rang for Leighton, her lady's maid. After a warm bath and dressing in a simple gown of pale yellow lawn, she made an effort to eat from the tray of food that had been sent to her room.

"Well, Boots," she whispered to the sweet little puppy who stared at her so adoringly with soulful brown eyes, "I suppose we should just get it over with and go downstairs."

He seemed to agree with her, so she kissed the top of his head, and headed for the door with Boots in her arms.

To her surprise, her cousin was standing outside her bedroom door, about to knock, when she opened it. Her heart sank to her toes. His tall body and purposeful demeanor blocked her way. There was no hope. She had to face him, the only other witness to her scandalous behavior from the night before.

"Phillip."

"Good afternoon, Cousin Sara," he said cheerfully, a slight gleam in his green eyes. "I was beginning to worry about you, but I'm happy to see you up and feeling well."

"Thank you. I overslept and I just . . ." her voice trailed off. She wasn't fooling him.

"Have a headache?" he asked, seemingly amused by the thought.

"A little one," she admitted, feeling guilty. She squared her shoulders. "But I'm on my way downstairs just now, so if you'll please excuse me . . ."

"Oh, but I have something that might just make you feel better." The smug look on his handsome face irritated her. "But if you'd rather not have it, by all means go right ahead . . ." Phillip made a gallant gesture of letting her pass by, his arm outstretched.

It was then that Sara saw something in his hand. A letter.

Her heart skipped a beat. It could just mean one thing. She had not received one single letter since she had arrived in London. This one could only be from Alexander Drake in response to hers. None of her New York friends even knew she was in England for she hadn't written to any of them. Her mouth went dry and she could barely breathe in anticipation.

"Is that a letter for me?" she asked, trying to sound nonchalant.

"It might be." He grinned devilishly. "I just happened to be at the door when the post arrived today. And lo and behold, if there wasn't a letter addressed to my sweet little cousin, who wasn't to be seen at breakfast this morning. Who, I heard, was not feeling well. That very same cousin who was drinking brandy alone in the library last night with—"

"Phillip! Shush!" Glancing down the hallway, she hoped her voice did not sound as desperate as she felt and she prayed that no one had overheard the words of her roguish cousin who seemed bent on tormenting her this afternoon.

He paused. "I might be inclined to give it to you in exchange for some information."

"Phillip," she managed to utter once more. "What is it you want?"

He stalked toward her, forcing her to walk backward into her bedroom. He stepped inside and shut the door behind him.

"Have a seat, my dear cousin," he instructed with a note of glee in his voice.

Sara suddenly regained her spirit and set Boots on the floor. "Phillip, I don't have time for your silly games. Please give me my letter and allow me to go about my day." She made a grab for the letter but he moved his hand behind his back too quickly for her to get it.

"Not so fast there!" He laughed at her feeble attempt to retrieve the letter.

Growing impatient and annoyed with him, she snapped, "What in heaven's name do you want, Phillip?"

"I told you. Just a little information," he said, feigning sweetness. "Have a seat, Sara."

She wanted that letter with every fiber of her being. "Fine." She sat upon the divan near the window and crossed her arms in silent protest. "Now what is it you wish to know?"

"Well," he said with irritating slowness, obviously enjoying her discomfiture. "There are a couple of things I'd like cleared up before I give you this letter, which you seem to want most desperately."

"And they would happen to be what?"

Phillip gazed at her intently. "Well, for starters, I'd like to hear your version of what happened last night with Lord Bridgeton, now that you are sober. I want to see if it matches up with what he told me happened between you."

"I'm sure it does, since we were both there. And I believe we went over all this last night in the library," Sara retorted, unable to hide a distinct note of condescension. Well, she certainly hoped their stories matched. Christopher wouldn't have told Phillip that they had kissed, would he? "However, I don't care for your tone, Phillip."

"Do you want this letter? It's all the way from New York too." His expression was quite self-satisfied. "Perhaps I should just give it to your mother. She would—"

"Oh, Phillip, don't!" Sara pleaded. If her mother got her hands on that letter before she did, Sara would never get to read it. "Please."

"Ah, now I see, you're being a little more cooperative. Will you tell me what happened?"

"Yes," she said with great reluctance. Boots yipped loudly, after dropping one of her old gloves at her feet, which was his invitation to play. She picked up the glove and tossed it across the room and the puppy scampered after it.

"What more do you want to know?" she began. "Everything happened just as we told you. Lord Bridgeton came here to meet with you. He was soaked from the rain and Parkins brought us some supper in the library where I was reading and planned on eating by myself anyway. As Lord

Bridgeton was drying off, he made a joke about needing a stronger drink than tea, which I completely understood. I offered him some brandy and for some reason I decided I'd join him in a glass. And yes"—Sara put up her hand to prevent her cousin from speaking—"before you interrupt, I know that was foolish of me. What's done is done. Lord Bridgeton and I chatted while he ate and I suppose the effects of the brandy caught me unaware and I fell asleep on the sofa. Then you came home. The end."

Phillip eyed her suspiciously. "Why don't I believe that?"

"I honestly have no idea. But that is exactly what happened."

It was mostly true anyway. She only left out the specifics of exactly what they discussed and the fact that they had kissed each other. Quite passionately. His mouth hot on hers. His hands caressing her face, her body. Sara's cheeks grew warm again at the memory.

He looked a bit crestfallen at the simplicity of her tale. "That's just what Bridgeton said."

"Because that is all that happened. Now can I please have my letter?"

"What did you two talk about all night?" he asked, eyeing her carefully.

Sara let out a frustrated sigh, before taking the glove Boots had retrieved and tossing it across the room for him to chase once more. "If you must know, he confided in me some things about his rather unhappy childhood, which I promised not to share with anyone else. So I shan't tell you more than that."

"He did?" Phillip was incredulous. "Why would Bridgeton discuss his childhood with you of all people? Why, he barely knows you!"

"I've no idea. You'll have to ask him that." Sara really didn't know why Christopher told her those things about his family. And although he hadn't actually asked her *not* to tell anyone what he'd revealed, she just innately sensed those were things not shared with others. He trusted her. Besides, they were not her secrets to tell. She rose from the divan and held out her hand. "May I have my letter now?"

"Did he kiss you?"

"Of course not!" she protested heatedly. Good heavens! She had practically begged the man to kiss her! *I think I shall die if you don't.* But Phillip did not need to know that. It was mortifying enough that she'd spoken those words aloud to Christopher. Maybe it was due to the brandy that she'd acted so wantonly? Yes, that was it. She'd blame it on the brandy.

"Then why was your hair undone?" Phillip questioned.

"Because it's more comfortable to lay your head on a pillow without pins in your hair, believe it or not." Growing more annoyed by the minute, she continued, "Now you're just being ridiculous, Phillip, and looking for trouble where there is none. Aside from my having one glass of brandy, which I promise you I now regret, nothing illicit happened between Lord Bridgeton and me last night. I'm sorry if the truth disappoints you."

He looked somewhat hurt. "I'm actually just trying to protect you."

"I understand and I do appreciate that sentiment. Truly I do. But there's nothing to protect me from. Christopher was a perfect gentleman." Who called her "his beautiful Sara" and kissed her and caused her blood to race in her veins and made her want to kiss him all night long. But no, nothing happened.

Phillip arched an inquisitive brow. "So it's *Christopher* now, is it?"

"Well, yes," Sara reasoned, and spoke as if explaining it all to a small child. "He confided in me and we are friends now. I gave him leave to call me Sara. It is what happens between two friendly adults. None of that is a crime."

"I suppose . . ." he muttered, still not totally convinced.

"Are we finished now?" she asked, growing quite impatient with him. "My letter?"

"You're awfully anxious to have this letter from New York . . ." he said, examining the envelope closely. "I wonder who it's from? It must be someone you don't wish your mother to know about . . ."

Oh, how she wanted to strangle her cousin! Not even when they were children had he annoyed her more. "Phillip, please."

"Tell me who it's from or I will tell your mother and father about last night in the library and hand over this letter to them."

"You wouldn't!" she gasped, as panic began to overtake her. She would die if she didn't have that letter. If either of her parents got their hands on that letter she would never know what Alexander had written to her. "You wouldn't be so cruel to me!"

He held the letter above her head, out of reach. "Try me."

"You're being positively evil today, Phillip."

"If I were being truly evil I would have read the letter first myself, then given it to your mother already." His earlier teasing tone vanished and his dark green eyes were steady on her. "So I consider myself to be acting quite reasonably, given the circumstances of my innocent cousin being whisked away from an unscrupulous suitor by her parents to the safety of my home. After what I witnessed last night, and then discovering this letter today, I'm simply trying to do what's best for you."

"Am I a simpleton or something?" Sara cried, torn between bursting into tears and screaming in fury. "Why does everyone think they know what's better for me than I do?"

Ignoring her, he demanded, "Who is the letter from, Sara? It's from him, isn't it? The one your parents took you away from?"

"I assume so yes," she admitted angrily, through clenched teeth. "But I won't know until you give it to me and let me read it!"

"I've known you your whole life, Sara Juliette Fleming, and if you believe I'm doing any of this to be mean to you, or to hurt you, then you don't know me at all," he said very quietly before he handed her the letter.

Slowly she reached for it. "Thank you."

Phillip merely stood there, staring at her. "Tell me."

Taking the letter in her hand, she immediately recognized Alexander's handwriting and her heart quickened at the sight. He'd written to her! Finally! She glanced back up at her cousin. "Yes, it's from him. Are you going to tell my mother?"

He shook his head. "Don't do anything foolish, Sara. I'll be watching you, not just because it's my duty as your older male cousin, but because I love and care about you."

With that Phillip turned and left her room, closing the door behind him.

Sara stood motionless for a moment, barely breathing. She slowly sank back on to the divan, with Boots at her feet happily chewing on her glove. With a trembling hand, Sara broke the seal on the envelope and began to read the long-awaited letter from Alexander Drake.

My Dearest Sara,

It is with the greatest joy in my heart that I received your sweet letter from London. I have been distraught with worry over your whereabouts and inconsolable with grief at not being able to locate you. The fear that I had lost you forever and the despair of believing you no longer loved me placed my poor heart in a constant state of agony each day and night we have been apart. I am most relieved to discover that you are quite well and that I remain locked in your heart and affections.

However, it saddens me deeply to learn that your parents do not approve of me nor wish for us to marry, for I do not believe I ever gave them cause to deserve such censure. My love for you is pure, steadfast, and true, and my intentions are most honorable. If they disapprove of my humble circumstances, there is naught I can do to change that. I am frankly stunned that your father's dislike of my person is so great he felt it warranted such drastic measures to keep us apart. And you must believe that I would love you if you hadn't a penny to your beautiful name.

Yet as it is still your fondest wish, and mine as well, I shall sail on the next ship for England to be with you, my dearest girl. We shall have to remain careful, and indeed, I hope this letter finds its way to your dear hands and is seen by your beautiful blue eyes only. I am coming for you, my sweet, and we shall be together when I do. Whether you have received this letter or not, I shall find my way to you and rest assured, we shall be married. I vow this to you. You have my undying love and devotion always.

Ever Yours,
Alexander

Sara continued to stare at the page until the letters blurred together, making them illegible. She reread the letter a second and third time. Then she pressed the letter to her heart.

He was coming for her.

Alexander was coming to marry her! He still loved her and wanted to marry her! She smiled with joy at the letter in her hands, filled with relief that he had finally written to her and could be halfway across the ocean by now. He could arrive in London in a matter of days!

Oh, how wrong her parents were! Alexander just proved it. *And you must believe that I would love you if you hadn't a penny to your beautiful name.* She knew he didn't love her for her fortune. He even said so! She knew he loved her for herself only.

Or did she? Perhaps he hadn't yet received her second letter. The one in which she'd written that her parents would disinherit her if they married, just as Uncle Jeffrey suggested she do. Alexander didn't mention loving her even if she was disinherited and wanting to marry her anyway. There was a difference.

Boots hopped up beside her, climbing into her lap and sniffing quizzically at the letter in her hand.

More than a bit confused, Sara didn't know what to do next.

13

Ebb Tide

Lady Mara Reeves stared at the two of them, her eyes following the dancing figures around the ballroom. They seemed quite out of place together, rather an odd pair. For some reason, they didn't look right to her but she couldn't pinpoint just what it was exactly. The gentleman was very handsome and quite striking in his manner and the woman seemed to pale in comparison to him. Her eyes lost track of them for a moment as other dancers moved in front. The dance floor was filled with dozens of couples swirling in time to the orchestra's music.

She could see Sara dancing with a nice-looking young man who seemed to be trying to grow a set of whiskers. There was her cousin Simon with a lovely little brunette as his partner. Mara's parents were at the other end of the room in conversation with another couple she was not familiar with. Yes, Lord and Lady Cabot's ball was in full swing.

But there was something about that man that riveted her attention. Had she met him before? She didn't think so, but he seemed vaguely familiar. Something about him intrigued her.

"Why aren't you dancing, Mara?"

Startled from her thoughts, she turned to her cousin Phillip Sinclair. He stood beside her with a questioning expression on his handsome face. Phillip had been like an older brother to her for as long as she could remember, alternately protective and playful, and Mara loved him dearly.

Giving him an arch look, she said, "I could ask the same of you."

"Touché," he admitted, handing her a glass. "But I'll have you know, I was dancing earlier, but I'm taking a bit of a break now. Here. Have some punch. It's quite good."

"Thank you." Keeping her eyes on the dancing couple, she took the glass from him. "And I'll have you know, I'm taking a little rest as well." She smiled at him before taking a sip of the fruity punch.

Mara wasn't overly fond of dancing and had deliberately left her dance card unfilled. She'd only attended the Cabots' ball because of two reasons: One, she promised Sara she would spend the Season attending parties with her, and two, her parents were here this evening as well and so she arrived with them. Essentially, there was no avoiding this night out. Consequently, she'd spent most of the evening wandering around and people watching. She found it fascinating and it was one of her favorite things to do. Ever since she was a little girl, Mara preferred remaining quiet and observing what was going on around her.

"Phillip, who is that tall red-haired lady dancing with Lord Bridgeton just now?" Mara asked.

"I believe that's Lady Constance Fuller. Why do you ask?"

"I'm curious, I suppose. I've not met her before," Mara noted. Lady Constance Fuller had a certain manner about her. She was very interested in Lord Bridgeton; that was quite obvious. She leaned in far too close and seemed to cling to him like a vine. While Lord Bridgeton, on the other hand, was clearly disinterested; his back was stiff and his smile did not meet his eyes.

"Mara . . . May I ask you something?"

Surprised by Phillip's serious tone, she turned to stare at him. "Of course."

"Has Sara talked to you about her gentleman in New York?"

Mara paused, unsure how to respond. She had promised Sara her utmost discretion in regard to her forbidden romance, as Mara had taken to calling it. Yesterday afternoon Sara had rushed over to her house with the letter she'd just received from Alexander Drake. First they'd celebrated that he was finally coming for her, and then the two of them had pored over every word he'd written, in an attempt to discern any possible meaning. Did he know about the disinheritance or not? They'd never drawn a definitive conclusion.

Mara gazed at Phillip now. Genuine concern was reflected in his eyes. "Yes, of course, she's told me about him," she said. "And about how you tormented her with the letter yesterday."

"I almost didn't give it to her. I've had nothing but second thoughts since I did. Perhaps I should have let Aunt Juliette know about the letter after all. I just worry about her, Mara."

"There's no need to worry."

"No?" Apprehension was etched in his face.

Mara wrestled with her conscience for a moment. Sara's fate was on the line. Sara, whom she loved with all her heart. And Phillip, who loved Sara too. They all wanted the best for her, including Sara's parents. She believed that Sara did truly love her American and that he loved her. It was all terribly romantic.

"No. There's nothing to worry about, Phillip. Everything is fine."

Phillip sighed, his brows relaxing somewhat. "I am aware that she tells you everything and I also know that you care about what happens to her. Will you please let me know if you think something is going to happen? Will you do that for me? If you have the slightest feeling that something is not right?"

"Do you mean if she decides to run off with him or something to that effect?"

He gave her a brief nod.

"I promise that I shall let you know if I learn of anything that would put Sara in danger," Mara said. And she meant it.

Phillip paused for a moment. "Did she mention anything to you about what happened with Lord Bridgeton?"

"Lord Bridgeton?" Mara was confused. "Why should Sara mention him?"

"I'm not sure exactly," Phillip said. "They were both alone in the library together the other evening during the storm and it felt like I had walked in during a private moment. I had the feeling that something . . . romantic happened between them, but I suppose I was wrong. I asked both of them and they denied that anything went on there. If anything like that had happened, Sara surely would have told you."

Astounded, Mara stared at Phillip. This was a surprise. "Something romantic? Between Sara and Lord Bridgeton?"

This thought hadn't occurred to her before, but then Mara recalled the two of them talking at great length in the bookshop that afternoon. Now that she considered it a little more, they had seemed to hover near each other quite a bit the night Lord Bridgeton and his sisters joined them for supper at Devon House. This was a thought-provoking new development. Sara and the handsome and eligible Lord Bridgeton?

Mara suddenly grew dizzy.

It was happening again.

She was having one of her premonitions. She hadn't had one in quite a while. Since she was a very young girl, she would get a peculiar feeling that foretold her something about the future. Some called it intuition or signs or instinct.

Whatever it was called, Mara sensed it right now. The dizziness and the strange tingling sensations that were the precursors to the misty images she would see in her mind had begun and there was nothing she could do to stop it. Her heart raced and her jaw clenched. Every nerve in her body lit up. Pressing her fingers to her temple, Mara closed her eyes and held her breath. Images began to form in her mind.

Her family. Lots of people in a cathedral. Sara wearing a wedding gown. Flowers and her little cousins with garlands in their blond hair. Lord Bridgeton smiling with happiness. Feelings of joy and love. A celebration.

At least this was a happy presentiment and not a sad one. She liked thinking of Sara and Lord Bridgeton together. They suited each other.

"Mara, are you feeling all right?" Phillip asked, placing his hand on her arm and looking at her with alarm.

"Yes, I'm just fine," she murmured, her eyes fluttering open. Taking a deep breath to calm herself, she attempted a smile. Her premonitions were never wrong, even if at times they were hazy. But Mara rarely shared her premonitions with anyone. She feared everyone would think she was a more than a little daft.

"You didn't look fine to me," Phillip said, holding on to her and observing her carefully. "Your face had the oddest expression just then. I thought you were going to faint."

Mara took a sip of her punch before saying, "It was just a little dizzy spell. I get them from time to time. Nothing to worry about."

The dance ended and couples began milling about the ballroom, changing partners and readying for the next set. The couple she had been surreptitiously watching earlier disappeared into the crowd and a sense of disappointment crept over her. That handsome gentleman was gone.

"Who are you looking for?" Phillip asked, still looking at her curiously.

"No one." Embarrassed, she didn't wish to tell her cousin about the handsome man who caught her eye. Mara didn't even know his name! But she'd spied him earlier and for some reason couldn't keep her eyes off him. She was also too shy to ask anyone about him, especially Phillip. If he teased her about it, even in his affectionate way, she would die of mortification. No. She'd just keep this to herself. "Weren't you dancing with Elizabeth Cabot earlier?"

"Why, yes, I was." Phillip gave her a roguish grin. "Poor girl. She's quite smitten with me. But then again, all the ladies are."

Mara sighed and shook her head, grinning. Phillip was amusing, even if he was a bit full of himself at times.

Just then Lord Bridgeton joined them. "Good evening, Lady Mara. Waverly."

"Good evening, Lord Bridgeton." Mara glanced up at him. He really was quite a handsome man. Tall, masculine, and commanding.

Lord Bridgeton laughed at Phillip. "Hiding, are you?"

"Just taking a break," Phillip retorted. "It's only considerate to give the pretty ladies a rest once in a while, Bridgeton."

After smiling at his little joke, Lord Bridgeton turned his attention to her. "The next set is about to begin. Would you care to dance with me, Lady Mara?"

Surprised by his offer, Mara accepted even though she was not inclined to dance. Across the room she saw Sara on the arm of yet another young gentleman. Her cousin certainly was enjoying herself this evening. Mara nodded and handed her cup of punch to Phillip before taking Lord Bridgeton's arm. He guided her to the dance floor just as the music began. They began to waltz in time to the music. For such a tall man, he was surprisingly light on his feet.

"Thank you for dancing with me, Lady Mara," he said, his warm brown eyes searching hers. "I was hoping to have a private word with you this evening."

"With me?" Mara asked, taken off guard. Before she could think about what she was saying, she blurted out, "I would assume you would rather speak with my cousin Sara."

He looked amused. "That is precisely who I wished to discuss with you, Lady Mara."

"You wish to discuss Sara?" Now Mara was quite intrigued, especially in light of the little premonition she had and what Phillip had just told her. *Had* something romantic happened between the two them after all? And what on earth could Lord Bridgeton want to speak to her about?

"Yes, in confidence, if you don't mind," he said.

"Yes, of course," she said, as the dance continued.

"I understand that the two of you are close and that she confides in you," he began, "and I am aware that she has an interest in a certain gentleman from New York."

Shocked, Mara's mouth fell open for a moment. "Sara told you about him?"

"Yes, she did."

This development really confounded her. Why on earth would Sara discuss Alexander Drake with Lord Bridgeton? The pair were closer than she realized! "I'm rather astonished that my cousin told you about him."

"He *is* the reason her parents brought her to London, isn't he? They wanted her away from him?"

"Yes," Mara admitted reluctantly. If Sara was telling Lord Bridgeton such details . . . Well then, this was definitely the beginning of something between the two of them. "But what has any of this to do with you?"

"Nothing really." Lord Bridgeton gave her a beguiling smile. He was a very charming man. "But I have grown fond of Miss Fleming and I just wondered what you know about this man . . . And is he good enough for her?"

Mara looked at him closely. He really did care for Sara. "I don't know for certain, Lord Bridgeton, but it's fairly obvious that her parents don't think he is."

"Yes, of course. But I am more interested in what your opinion of him is."

"Judging from his letter, I'd say he seems utterly devoted to her."

"She received a letter from him?" he asked. The note of panic in his voice touched Mara's heart.

"Lord Bridgeton, have you feelings for my cousin?" she couldn't help but inquire, even though she already knew the answer. She had seen it.

He laughed, but it sounded a bit hollow to her ears. "Of course I care about her, as I care about your entire family, who has been inordinately kind to me and my sisters. But if you are asking if I have any romantic intentions toward Miss Fleming, you would be mistaken, Lady Mara. I simply wish to rest in the assurance that she is being looked after properly and is not in a position to make any dangerous decisions regarding this gentleman."

Mara smiled at him. He was quite jealous of Alexander Drake and she felt a bit of sympathy for him. "I promise you, Lord Bridgeton, that Sara is in no danger."

As the dance came to an end, he guided her back to the alcove where she had been standing with Phillip earlier.

"Thank you, Lady Mara. For this lovely dance and for your discretion in the matter we discussed."

Mara gazed up at him, intrigued by his interest in Sara. Her intuition told her that Christopher Townsend, the Earl of Bridgeton, was a genuinely good man who cared deeply about her cousin. "Your secret is safe with me."

"I don't have a secret," he said, looking slightly uncomfortable.

"Don't you, though?"

"Lady Mara, I am merely concerned for your cousin's welfare. That is all."

"Of course you are." Mara gave him a knowing look. "Thank you for the dance. I quite enjoyed it, something I don't usually do. May I ask a favor of you before you go?"

"Anything," he replied. "I am in your debt."

Mara gestured casually to the very handsome man standing near the entryway. The one she had been watching earlier. "Do you happen to know the name of that gentleman over there?"

A wry grin lit Lord Bridgeton's face. "Why, Lady Mara . . ." His eyes followed to where she pointed. "I'm presuming you don't mean the balding gentleman, but the tall one with the full head of hair?"

Mara couldn't help but blush. She nodded.

"I believe that's Foster Sheridan, the Earl of Sterling. I'm afraid I don't know much more about him than that." He smiled warmly.

"Thank you, Lord Bridgeton. Very much." She whispered the name to herself, storing it away for later. *Foster Sheridan, the Earl of Sterling.* Mara liked the sound of it.

"Would you like me to find out about him for you?"

"What?" Startled, she glanced back at Lord Bridgeton. "Oh, no, thank you. That's not necessary."

"If you change your mind, just let me know." He gave her

a wink. "Again, Lady Mara, I thank you and wish you a good evening."

"Good evening," she murmured.

Mara watched him go, thinking what a wonderful gentleman he was. She truly liked him. It was a shame that Sara was still preoccupied with her American. But she believed wholeheartedly that Christopher Townsend had deep feelings for Sara, even if he didn't quite realize it, and that Sara felt the same.

"Were you just dancing with Lord Bridgeton?"

Mara turned at the sound of Sara's voice. Her cousin had walked up behind her, looking stunning in a gown of royal blue silk, with long white gloves, and an ostrich feather in her hair.

"Sara, you startled me!"

"Forgive me. I didn't intend to." She patted Mara's arm in apology. "I thought I just saw Lord Bridgeton walking away from you."

Mara nodded. "Yes, I just danced with him."

"You danced with him?" she asked in surprise. "He hasn't asked me to dance."

They both watched as the tall figure of Lord Bridgeton moved across the ballroom and asked a rather short, brown-haired girl with wide eyes to dance.

"Do you know who she is?" Sara questioned. "The girl in the ridiculous bright green dress?"

Mara was not familiar with a great many people, but this girl she recognized immediately. It was difficult to forget someone who dressed the way she did. "I believe that her name is Bonnie Beckwith. I met her last year at a dreadfully dull musicale. She sang that night. And not very well, as I recall."

"Why on earth would Lord Bridgeton be interested in someone like her?" Sara murmured more to herself than to Mara.

Mara watched her cousin closely now. Here was Sara Fleming, beautiful, fashionable, and sought-after and supposedly in love with her handsome American, yet looking rather put out that Christopher Townsend, the Earl of Bridgeton, had not asked her to dance.

"Maybe he's just being polite," Mara conjectured.

"Most likely," Sara agreed, seemingly satisfied with that answer, waving her fan in a careless manner.

"Have you spoken with Lord Bridgeton yet this evening?"

"No." A puzzled smile crossed Sara's face. "It's odd. I haven't spoken to him at all tonight. He seems quite preoccupied with dancing with everyone else though. Mara, I have the distinct impression that I am being ignored this evening."

"Why on earth would he ignore you?" Mara asked.

"I'm not sure," Sara answered. "But my dance card is quite full." With a flounce of her skirts, Sara moved toward a young man who came to claim his dance with her.

Amused, Mara smiled. There was definitely a bit of jealousy there. Both Sara and Lord Bridgeton were not yet aware of their feelings for each other.

14

Dead Ahead

"Lord Bridgeton? Did you hear me? I was asking you a question. Yoo-hoo! Lord Bridgeton?"

At the sound of his name, Christopher stared blankly at the lady across from him. "Forgive me, Miss Beckwith. I was distracted by the horses." He honestly had not a clue what she'd been saying. It had been a dismal outing and he had simply ceased listening to her.

"I asked if we would be out here much longer, Lord Bridgeton. Something in the air is making me sneeze. I detest sneezing. Don't you?" Bonnie Beckwith scrunched up her little nose in distaste. "Are we heading back home yet? It's dreadfully hot out this afternoon. I'm simply parched and would love something to drink. I believe it is time to return home now, don't you?" She sneezed three times.

They had been riding through Hyde Park in his barouche. The sun was warm and the early June skies were surprisingly clear. There definitely was a hint of summer in the air. The path was busy as many people were out enjoying the fine weather. In a concerted effort to court her, Christopher had invited Bonnie Beckwith to go riding with him and his sisters. He sorely regretted his decision not two minutes into the ride.

Miss Beckwith and his sister Evie did not get along right from the start, as they bickered over where to sit, and Miss Beckwith had done nothing but complain the entire time. The sun was in her eyes. She was too warm. A bumblebee buzzed near her face. She was afraid of bees. The barouche was uncomfortable. They were traveling too fast. The path was too bumpy.

"Is it not yet time to return, Christopher?" Evie asked, and he knew by the tone of her voice she wished the ride to end as much as he did.

"I believe so, ladies," he agreed. Then he gave instructions to the driver to return to the Beckwiths' town house.

Christopher turned back to face Miss Bonnie Beckwith, who sat across from him beside Gwyneth. Poor Gwyneth had not opened her mouth to say two words, not that she could get a word in edgewise with Bonnie jabbering on and on. His sweet little sister in her plain, pale blue bonnet looked like a little wren compared to Bonnie, in a riot of bright pink and lemon organza with enough feathers on her hat to stuff a pillow, looking like a demented parrot. The garish colors somehow seemed even worse next to the sedate hues on his sisters.

He had now paid two calls on Miss Beckwith, sent her a small bouquet of flowers, and danced with her at the Cabots' ball. By inviting her to ride in Hyde Park with him today, he was taking another step closer to asking for her hand. Her parents were bursting with pride when he'd called for her this afternoon. They could smell marriage in the air and for the time being it seemed that Christopher was in the lead. He knew of two other gentlemen who were courting her, but their ranks weren't as high as his. Christopher had an earldom to offer, and Mrs. Beckwith seemed quite keen on her daughter becoming a countess, as did Mr. Beckwith.

He had yet to divulge to them that his coffers were empty. Somehow he did not think they would mind, eager as they were to marry off their only daughter. And to Christopher's way of thinking, they were going to have to hand over a great deal of money to any man to take Bonnie off their hands. So they might as well give it to him.

As the barouche made its way out of the park, Christopher sighed in relief that the painful outing was drawing to a close. It might be best if he simply spoke to her father right away and made an offer for Bonnie's hand. He had to get it over with. Once they were married, he could set her up in a separate residence and not have to see her too often. The thought of actually sharing a bed with this whining, feathered chatterbox was too much for him to bear at the moment.

"This road is so terribly bumpy," Bonnie grumbled, her face pinched in a frown. "Why did we go this way? I suppose it is faster, but good heavens, I am being jounced and jostled to bits!"

No one answered her, for she did quite well answering her own questions. Catching Gwyneth roll her eyes at Bonnie's most recent complaints, Christopher smiled to himself. His little sister hadn't lost all her spirit.

He'd allowed Evelyn and Gwyneth to stay in London with him longer than he'd first anticipated. The girls seemed so happy to be away from Bridgeton Hall that he did not have the heart to send them back to their mother. His sisters deserved to live life and spread their wings a little. It was the least he could do for them for right now. Once he had money again, he could give them anything they wanted. He intended to spoil them rotten.

When the barouche stopped in front of the Beckwith town house in Mayfair, Christopher stepped out to help

Bonnie down and escort her inside. Her mother hovered eagerly around them. She had a similar look as her daughter, minus the garish clothing.

Bonnie gazed up at him with wide, blinking eyes, the pink feathers in her bonnet bobbing as she spoke. "Thank you for a lovely afternoon, Lord Bridgeton. I can't recall when I've had such a nice time."

Stunned that she would describe their ride as lovely when she was completely miserable the entire time, Christopher could only agree with her. "It was my pleasure," he lied.

"Oh, Lord Bridgeton," Mrs. Beckwith began, preening a bit. "My husband, Alfred, and I would like to invite you to dine with us next week and I know it would please Bonnie greatly to have you here. Would you be able to join us for supper on Tuesday evening, by any chance?"

So they were forcing his hand then. Speeding things up. This dinner was obviously meant to have Christopher meet with Alfred Beckwith and discuss a dowry. A very, very large one, that was for certain.

"I would be honored to join you, Mrs. Beckwith," he replied evenly, afraid to even think about it. There would be no going back after this. "Thank you very much."

Bonnie batted her eyelashes at him. "Oh, Lord Bridgeton, we're so pleased you will be able to join us!"

With that, he bid the Beckwith women good-bye.

Climbing back into the carriage, Christopher gave the driver special instructions instead of going directly home. Settling into the seat, flooded with relief now that Bonnie Beckwith was no longer in his presence, he grinned broadly at his sisters, ignoring the knot forming in his stomach.

"Who wants some ice cream?" he asked, hoping to liven them up. They all deserved a little reward for suffering through the last hour. "I know a wonderful place nearby that makes the most delicious chocolate ice cream."

Gwyneth clapped her hands in delight and squealed, "Oh, Kit, yes, please!"

"That does sound divine." Evelyn finally lost her frown.

"Well, we're on our way," he said, as the barouche lurched forward.

"You can't do this, Kit."

Christopher stared at Evelyn, who had moved across to sit beside Gwyneth, and now they both faced forward in the carriage. They stared at him determinedly.

"Not her," Gwyneth added with a shake of her head.

He sighed. As if he had any other option but to marry Bonnie Beckwith! "There's not much hope for it, girls."

"But she's dreadful, Kit. You simply can't marry her!" Evie cried. "I won't let you be shackled to the likes of that babbling idiot for the rest of your life. You deserve better than that."

"Well, I doubt you'd like my only other option any better. Bonnie is actually the wiser choice," he explained, hoping he sounded positive.

"Surely there's another way, Kit?" Gwyneth asked, the sadness in her voice making him uncomfortable.

"Well, if either of you wish to find a man rich enough to marry and willing to save the rest of us within the next few months, please go right ahead. Be my guest, because it's certainly not my wish to wed someone like Bonnie Beckwith, but this is what needs to be done to protect our family and our home."

Christopher's words came out much harsher than he intended and he knew immediately from the look of their faces that he'd hurt them. He would no sooner sell his sisters in marriage than he would cut off his own arm.

Women in general had been given a tough enough lot in life. After all his two sisters had been through, he couldn't fathom trapping either of them into loveless marriages. It appalled him how few options his sisters had other than to marry or to remain living at home. He wished he could do more for Evelyn and Gwyneth. Someday he would, when he had the means. He just wasn't sure what, aside from giving them as much freedom as he could.

"I'm sorry for what I just said," he muttered low.

"No, we're the ones who are sorry," Evie began, looking contrite. "We should be making this situation easier for you, not more difficult than it already is."

Gwyneth added in her sweet way, "It's because we know you don't even like her, Kit. It's not fair that you should have to marry someone like that."

"Life is not fair." Then he added, "We know that already, don't we? There are worse things in life than marrying little Bonnie Beckwith. Like not having a place to live or food to eat. Marriages like this happen all the time. Bonnie is not so bad, actually. I think she's rather harmless." Christopher didn't know whom he was trying to convince more, his sisters or himself.

They grew quiet for a moment as his words sunk in.

"There's really no chance for you and Miss Fleming?" Evie questioned him with a note of hope in her voice. "You seemed to truly like her . . ."

Oh, yes. But he more than liked Miss Fleming. In fact Christopher was beginning to think himself half in love with her. Since the night of the storm he'd thought of nothing else but her. Her beautiful face. Her quick wit and self-confidence. Her sense of humor. The way she kissed. The way she made him feel when he was with her.

If only he could marry her.

Yes, marrying Sara Fleming would be his first choice. A life with her would be almost perfect. Having her at his side as his wife and in his bed . . . He simply couldn't let himself think about it. It was too painful to contemplate, because a future with her was not meant to be.

His conversation with Lady Mara Reeves at the Cabots'

ball the other evening confirmed that. Sara had received a letter from her American and he was more than likely coming for her. Christopher wondered what would happen when the man arrived and if her parents would be able to stop her.

He hadn't spoken to her since the stormy night they kissed in the library. Of course, he'd seen her at the Cabots' ball, but he'd done his best to stay away from her. She'd looked exceedingly tempting in her royal blue gown that clung to her curves and displayed her delectable figure all too well. He had deliberately avoided her and felt terrible about it.

"I have explained to you that Miss Fleming is almost certainly going to marry the man she is in love with. Who is not me," he said bluntly, making sure they understood. "Besides, she does not have the money we need to save us. While Miss Beckwith, as chatty and colorful as she is, has more than enough money to suit our needs. The choice is clear, isn't it, girls?"

Both of his sisters remained completely silent, and Christopher couldn't deny the heavy weight that settled over him.

15

Close Quarters

He was finally here.

Alexander Drake was in London!

Sara stared in disbelief at the note that was passed to her while she was helping out at the Hamilton Sisters' Book Shoppe the next afternoon. A pretty blond woman, an American judging from her familiar New York accent, walked up to her where she was working near the back of the store and quietly asked if she was Sara Fleming. Intrigued, Sara said yes.

With a furtive glance around, the woman whispered, "I'm Alexander's sister. Lucille Drake. He asked me to give you this." With a benevolent smile, she passed a folded note to Sara. "He is so looking forward to seeing you."

Sara was unable to utter a word in response.

"I'll come by the shop again this time tomorrow afternoon if you'd like to give him a return message, which I can only imagine that you do." The woman, who seemed quite sympathetic to their plight, patted Sara gently on the arm, reassuring her. "I'm afraid I must go now. But I hope to see more of you."

Struggling to recall if Alexander had ever told her that he had a sister, Sara murmured a befuddled, "Thank you."

And just as suddenly as she appeared, the woman walked calmly out of the shop.

With a trembling hand, Sara looked at the folded note. Her name, clearly written in Alexander's penmanship, was all that was on it. Her heart raced. He was here! He had come for her!

"Who was that?"

Hastily shoving the note into the pocket of the dark green apron she wore, Sara looked up at Aunt Colette. "Just a woman. She said she had forgotten the title of the book she was supposed to get for her husband and would return tomorrow."

"Well, when you've finished putting those books on the shelf, how would you like to help me arrange the new front window display? I've an idea for giving the window a summery theme, with some floral prints, parasols, and ribbons." On her arm Aunt Colette held a basket full of materials and she seemed very excited to have Sara assist her. She added brightly, "It will be fun."

"Yes, of course." Sara smiled at her aunt, trying to appear calm. She felt terrible about lying to Aunt Colette about the woman who gave her the note and surprised herself how quickly the lie sprang from her lips. Normally, she would be happy to help and decorating was something she enjoyed. But right now she would have agreed to jump in a vat of hot oil, if it meant she could have a private moment to read Alexander's note first.

"Yes, of course. I'd love to! I'll join you just as soon as

I finish with these. It shouldn't take me long at all." Sara placed her hand on the stack of brand-new books on the table beside her that she was supposed to place on the shelves.

Assisting at the bookshop with her aunts a few afternoons a week was something she had grown to enjoy. Although she wouldn't say she loved working in the bookshop, Sara had discovered an appreciation for what her aunts had accomplished and admired them all the more for the impressive business they had grown. Besides, she liked organizing the books and found she was rather good at it. She also enjoyed the leathery smell of the place and the ringing of the bells over the door when a costumer entered.

Sara relished the sense of purpose at having a place to go each day where she was expected to contribute and be a part of something outside of herself. It reminded Sara of how she had always loved helping sail her father's ship when they were traveling the world. She had been a part of the crew then.

The last few years in New York she'd done nothing truly productive with her time. Instead she'd been overly preoccupied with pursuing her social activities, acquiring a fashionable wardrobe, and focusing on her romantic dreams to the exclusion of all else. As much as Sara was loath to admit it, her mother's suggestion that she work in the bookshop had been a good idea. However, at that moment all she wanted to do was get out of the shop as quickly as possible.

"Well, come join me up front when you can." Aunt Colette walked away, toward the front of the store, with her basket of decorations in her arms.

Sara let out a shaky breath. Glancing around to ensure that no one was watching her, she removed the note from her pocket and unfolded it, her heart in her mouth, as she read Alexander's words.

My Dearest Sara,

As I'm sure you are aware by now, I am finally in London and you have met my lovely sister, Lucille, who has agreed to help us. I arrived a week ago and determined that the safest way to contact you was through the bookshop. I don't know if you ever received the first letter I sent to your aunt's house and I did not wish to risk your parents intercepting yet another missive from me, so I sent Lucille as emissary for us.

I long to see you, my darling, and have thought of nothing but you during these endless weeks apart. I hope this remains true for you as well. Have I still your heart? If so, let us make plans to be away from your parents and wed as soon as we can. That is the only way we can be together, for you are my love, my life. Once you are my wife, then all our dreams will come true. Please send word through my sister when I can see you.

> *Your soon to be husband,*
> *Alexander*

With her heart pounding, Sara read the note a second time. And then a third before carefully placing it back into the pocket of her apron.

Alexander had come for her, just as she had known he would! He still loved her and wished to marry her. And he was here, somewhere in London, waiting for her. Filled with happiness, she glanced up and gazed out the wide shop windows. The streets were bustling with dozens of ordinary people, going about their daily business. Alexander Drake, the love of her life, was out there in this city. He had crossed the Atlantic Ocean to be with her. He had thought about her and figured out where she would be and found her at the bookshop!

He was here! He was here! He was finally here!

The words echoed over and over in her head as she hastily put the books away on the shelves, not paying attention to whether they were in the right place or not. She desperately wished Mara was working at the shop with her today, for she would love to show her the note and share the good news. But Mara and Aunt Paulette had gone to the other Hamilton bookshop in Mayfair this afternoon.

Sara hurried to join Aunt Colette at the front window. So filled with nervous excitement and thoughts of her immediate future, she was unable to concentrate on what she was doing. After Sara accidentally knocked over the display table, not once, but twice, sending Colette's artful arrangement of books spilling to the floor, she gave up.

"Honestly, you're like the bull in the china shop this afternoon, Sara! Whatever is the matter with you?" Aunt Colette asked, growing a bit impatient.

Wringing her hands together, Sara apologized. "Forgive me, Aunt Colette. I don't know what's wrong with me today. I'm afraid I didn't sleep well last night and I'm simply overtired."

With a little shrug and a half-hearted grin, Aunt Colette threw her hands up in the air. "Would you prefer to go home for the day, Sara? Maybe a nap would help? However I think you've done all you can to help at the shop today."

"Yes, perhaps that would be best. Thank you." Relieved to be sent home, Sara hugged her aunt. "I promise I'll be better rested next time."

"It's quite all right, Sara. Please don't concern yourself with it. I hope you feel better," Colette suggested, before her attention was refocused on repairing the damage to her pretty window display.

Hurriedly running upstairs, Sara took off her apron, remembering first to remove Alexander's note and place it safely in her reticule. As she gathered her things and put on her bonnet and gloves, she hoped the walk back to Devon House would be just what she needed to clear her head and calm her jumpy nerves. With her head literally spinning with thoughts of Alexander Drake, she felt she couldn't breathe.

He was here! He was here!

She could possibly be married to him by the end of the week.

That thought caused her heart to skip a beat.

She needed to get outside and breathe. She needed to move.

Flying back down the staircase, she called good-bye to her aunt and to the girls who worked in the shop. Just as she was exiting the bookshop, she stopped short. Lord Bridgeton stood on the sidewalk, looking as if he were about to enter the shop. Her heart dropped to her feet.

She was not in the mood to see Christopher Townsend just now. He'd been rather cool to her at Lady Cabot's ball last week, which left her feeling oddly disappointed. For the first time since she'd met him, there was an awkward uncomfortableness between them. They had not spoken to each other since their kiss in the Devon House library, which was fine with her, since she'd rather forget it ever happened.

Especially with Alexander Drake in town.

"Good afternoon, Miss Fleming," Christopher said, sounding rather chipper. "You are just the person I wanted to see."

"Oh, hello, Lord Bridgeton. I'm terribly sorry," she said hastily, anxious to be on her way. "I'm actually headed home, but I'm sure my aunt or one of the other girls inside could help you with whatever you're looking for."

His brown eyes searched hers intently. "I didn't come to the shop to buy a book, Sara."

"Oh." Feeling a bit annoyed, she glanced over at the window area where Aunt Colette was working. Still quite intent on the display, she didn't notice Sara standing there with Lord Bridgeton. "You came here specifically to see me then?"

"Yes." He offered her a charming smile. "I saw Waverly earlier and he mentioned you were at the shop with his mother this afternoon. I would like to speak to you for a moment or two, if I may."

"I'm in rather a hurry," she said, avoiding his eyes. He was the last person she wanted to spend time with right now.

"Then please allow me to give you a ride home in my carriage? It's right here." He gestured to the large black carriage hitched to two fine matching horses waiting on the cobblestoned street. "I promise not to delay you."

Giving in, she sighed in exasperation. "Fine."

Christopher flashed her a triumphant look. He certainly wasn't being cold or distant toward her today, she observed wryly. As he helped her into the carriage, Sara glanced back and saw Aunt Colette in the shop window, watching them. She gave them both a little wave and a nod of approval. Sara waved back. After instructing the driver, Christopher climbed into the enclosed carriage after her and shut the door.

As the carriage rocked into motion, she settled back on the cushioned leather seat and nervously smoothed her peach-colored day gown edged with white lace and adjusted her pretty matching bonnet. Christopher sat opposite her, his muscular presence almost overpowering the small space inside the elegant carriage. Glancing surreptitiously at him, she was reminded again how devilishly handsome the man was.

He'd taken off his tall black hat so she could see his dark hair was slicked back. He looked quite nice in his tan coat and high-collared white shirt, black trousers, and boots. She admired the look of his clean-shaven face, for it accentuated the classic line of his cheeks and jaw. Slowly he removed his gloves, laying them on the seat beside his hat.

"Well?" she asked, growing impatient with him. "What is so important you were required to whisk me away like this?"

He paused a moment and then just said it. "I felt I needed to apologize to you."

"Apologize?" Frowning in confusion, she asked, "Whatever on earth for?"

"For quite a few things, as a matter of fact." He gazed at her openly, his expression earnest and a bit contrite. "I've behaved rather badly toward you and I've felt terrible about it."

She shook her head. "If you're referring to the night in the library, I—"

"That's a large piece of it," Christopher interrupted her, seemingly intent on saying what he needed to say. "But there's more to it than that."

Sara remained quiet, twisting her hands in her lap. It suddenly grew unbearably warm inside the carriage. She took off her gloves as well and shoved them in her reticule. Glancing up, she saw that he was waiting patiently for her attention.

"Excuse me," she murmured.

"We haven't had a private moment together since the evening of the storm, and given the unusual circumstances, with the brandy and all, I admit I took advantage of you and the situation. For that I am deeply sorry. I don't know how to explain away what happened between us, Sara, and quite frankly, I can't. But I'd very much like you to know that I care about you and would never intentionally do anything to hurt you."

She was touched by his admission, and a riot of emotions flooded her already overwhelmed consciousness. He had blamed himself for what had happened between them and was acting as if he had committed some sort of crime against her. Which he most certainly had not.

"Christopher," she began, "I don't think that—"

"Also," he interrupted her once more. His brown eyes were locked on hers. "My caddish behavior continued when I ignored you the night of Lady Cabot's ball, because I was too ashamed to face you. I apologize for my behavior that night also. That was not well done of me and you deserved better than that. Much better. I fear I've not been very fair to you, Sara."

"Christopher, I—"

"In the short amount of time that I've known you, I've grown to value your friendship and I hate myself for how I treated you that night in the library. And ignoring you afterward at the ball only made everything worse. The more I thought about it, the more I realized I had to apologize to you and clear the air between us." He finally paused.

"May I speak now?" she asked.

"Yes." He flashed a smile. "I'm sorry for interrupting you." He sat back against the seat, a little more relaxed after baring his soul to her.

"First of all," Sara said, searching for where to begin, "I accept your apology for snubbing me at Lady Cabot's ball. I was quite bewildered by that, if you must know. I feared I had done something to offend you. Secondly, I—"

"I knew that I'd hurt you that night and I've felt terrible about it ever since."

"Christopher Townsend, if you interrupt me one more time, I shall scream!"

He laughed aloud, and the sound made her smile. He put

his hand over his mouth in an exaggerated show of silence. The absurdity of his pose almost caused her to laugh too.

Instead Sara shook her head, feeling a bit self-conscious now that he was quiet and staring at her expectantly, looking ridiculously handsome as he did so. "As for the night in the library, I take full responsibility for my own actions. I'm a grown woman of twenty, almost twenty-one, years. I, myself, made the decision to drink the brandy with you. You certainly didn't force me, Christopher. Please don't feel badly about that. As for our kiss . . ."

He remained absolutely quiet, with his hand still covering his mouth.

"As for the kiss . . ." Her voice faded away once more, as she was overcome with a nameless emotion. She had tried to forget that that kiss occurred. Had wanted to pretend that it never happened for it only complicated the already quite complex matters in her life. But she'd been unable to erase it from her memory. It haunted her. That heavenly kiss had been unforgettable and she didn't want it to be. She didn't want entanglements with Christopher Townsend.

Yet her breath still caught when she thought about it and her whole body warmed at the memory. That he would make apologies for kissing her, left her feeling decidedly wretched. There was a lump in her throat too. "That kiss was the most . . . It was . . . I don't have the words to describe that kiss, but I am quite positive that *I* shamelessly asked *you* . . . to kiss me, Christopher . . . and I . . . I—"

Between her shattered nerves over the news of Alexander Drake's arrival in London and being alone with Christopher Townsend again, discussing the intimate kiss they shared, wild emotions washed over her, making her feel strangely lost. Amidst a sudden rush of inexplicable sadness, an unexpected sob escaped her and Sara began to cry. Hot tears sprang unbidden, spilling down her cheeks.

Before she knew what happened, Christopher was seated beside her and pulling her into his strong arms. He wrapped her in his warm embrace and at once she felt calmer, as if she could breathe again. He smelled good, familiar to her now, and she inhaled deeply, and it was heavenly to be held by him.

"Sara, Sara, my beautiful Sara," he murmured softly. "Please, don't cry. I didn't intend to make you cry."

For some reason, his sweet words made her cry harder.

"What is it?" he whispered. "Why the tears?" He cupped her face in the palms of his hands, forcing her to look at him.

"I don't know," she said with a forlorn sob.

He handed his handkerchief to her and she began to dry her eyes.

"Was it something I said?" he asked softly. "Something I did?"

Gazing at him, she saw something in his expression she'd never seen before and it took her breath away. With a shaky sigh, she repeated, "I don't know, Christopher . . . I just . . . I feel so . . ."

His mouth was on hers before she could finish speaking. He was kissing her and she didn't care. She was glad of it. Glad that she didn't have to ask him to kiss her this time. Thrilled by it. Had been secretly waiting for this to happen again. He kissed her gently, with utter tenderness, his lips warm and soft, as if comforting her still. Her tears forgotten, Sara melted against his body, leaning into the kiss.

It was then that he began to kiss her with more intensity, demanding more from her, which she willingly gave. Opening her mouth for him, he slipped his tongue inside and a delicious wave of heat washed over her at the intimacy of it. This kiss was different from their first one because now, oh now, she knew what to do!

This time she met his tongue with hers, twirling around

each other, delighting in the taste of him in her mouth. Their breath intermingled and she sighed with deep pleasure. Slowly his hands left her face and slid around her shoulders, pulling her closer against his chest. Their kiss deepened. In his arms, with his kiss, she forgot everything else except the exquisite feel of him surrounding her.

As he held her tightly against him, a heavy heat grew between them. Her hands circled around his broad chest and reached along the back of his neck. Her fingers gently splayed into his thick black hair. Meanwhile, he had managed to remove her hatpins and her dainty peach bonnet, tossing the hat with one hand to the other seat, all while still kissing her.

It was too wonderful. It was too perfect. This wickedly delicious sensuousness that enwrapped her in swirling sensations she never knew existed before him. She only knew now that she couldn't get enough of him. Needed more of him. Of this. Their mouths. Their hands. Touching. Breathing. She was drowning in him and didn't care.

"Sara," he murmured her name into her hair as he pulled her so she was seated across his lap. "My beautiful Sara," he said once more before covering her mouth with his and the intimate dance began again.

It was wrong that it delighted her so to be called his. She was not his. But for now, just for now, it didn't matter. Now she *was* his, and only his. He was her whole world at that moment. The rapid pounding of his heartbeat echoed her own, as they kissed and kissed and kissed. He held tight, one arm holding her securely while his other hand caressed her cheek. That very same hand languidly moved down across her neck, above the swell of her chest.

She held her breath for a moment, waiting in anticipation, every nerve in her body taut with suspense and longing. With deliberate slowness, his hand glided over the front of her peach gown, and firmly cupped one breast. She sighed into his mouth and he groaned back, squeezing her a little harder. His warm fingers found their way over the lacy edge of her gown, reached between her corset and sought out her naked breast.

She gasped his name from the sheer pleasure of his touch, instinctively arching her body toward him. He kissed her harder.

The caress of his bare fingers on her naked flesh was the most wanton and wonderfully erotic sensation. If she could remove all her clothes right then and there she would. Every article of clothing she wore screamed, begged, and ached to be taken off by him. The weight of her gown alone was crushing and confining, suffocating. She longed to feel his naked body next to hers.

His mouth still hot on hers, her hands made their way around to the front of his jacket and her fingers began to undo his tie, loosening his collar. Eager to feel the naked-ness of his chest, she opened his shirt, her fingers splaying through the hair on his chest. As she marveled at the warmth and strength that emanated from his muscled body, her hands fluttered over the broad expanse of him.

So lost in her own decadent exploration of him, she barely noticed his hand moving up her stocking-clad leg, underneath her gown, gently caressing her. By the time she was aware of it, his fingers were circling the thin strap of the garter on the top of her bare thigh. Sara could hardly catch her breath. He stopped kissing her, and stared at her, his face impossibly close to hers, his breathing heavy. He searched her eyes, seeking an answer to an unasked ques-tion. For the briefest instant she considered telling him to stop, but the thought merely evaporated into thin air before she could grasp a proper hold of it. Softly she kissed his cheek, moving her lips across his smoothly shaven jaw, and down his neck until she pressed a kiss to his bare chest.

"Sara." Her name was a plea for she knew not what, but in that moment she wished only to give him everything he desired.

And it was desire, white hot and rampant, that raced through her entire body when he ravaged her mouth with a kiss so fervent she felt it all the way down to the tips of her toes. Every fiber of her being was on fire for him. She ached for him to touch her, and she longed to touch him. And then his hand began to move beneath her gown, his fingers caressing her, stroking her most intimately and she almost cried out at the intense pleasure of his touch. As she lay across his lap, an insistent throbbing heat grew within her and demanded all her attention.

She clutched the front of his jacket, holding on for support as her body weakened. Her eyelids drifted closed and she laid her head against his chest. Breathy gasps escaped her mouth, almost in sobs, as his fingers worked their rhythmical magic on her, weaving a spell of pleasure so exquisite she feared she would die. Feeling as taut as the string of a bow, she moved her hips against his hand, the motion building to a peak that almost shattered her with its bliss when it finally arrived.

When she could breathe normally again, she slowly opened her eyes to find Christopher staring at her, an unreadable expression on his face.

"You are the most beautiful woman I have ever known." His voice was low and hoarse.

"Again . . . I don't have the words to describe how you just made me feel. And I don't even wish to know *how* you knew what to do to make me feel that way."

She leaned up and kissed him. He wrapped his arms around her once more and held her for some minutes. It could have been an eternity for all she knew, for time had ceased to exist once she got in his carriage. His fingers stroked her hair, which had come loose or he had loosened it, she didn't know. The feel of his hands touching her still delighted her. She could stay in his embrace, with her head on his strong shoulder like this, forever and not mind at all.

Good God in heaven! What had they just done? What had happened? She didn't wish to contemplate what it might mean. Or the right and wrong of it. For now, she simply wanted to remain safe in his arms, awash with this peacefully languid feeling.

"Sara?" he whispered at last.

"Hmm?"

"You fell asleep."

"No, I didn't."

He chuckled. "Open your eyes."

"Don't," she pleaded softly. "Not yet." She simply couldn't move, even though she knew he was right.

He kissed her cheek. "We can't stay in this carriage forever."

"Can't we though?"

"I'm afraid not." He shifted and gently lifted her off his lap, positioning her on the seat beside him.

As the carriage rocked along, they both began adjusting their clothes in silence. It was going to take some work to get her hair back in order, but she hadn't the energy for it just now. Christopher reached for her hand, his fingers intertwining with hers. Bringing it to his mouth, he placed a soft kiss on her palm, then he held her hand to his heart. The sweetness of the gesture touched her deeply.

"It seems I owe you yet another apology," he said slowly.

"Please don't or I shall cry again." She couldn't bear for him to feel sorry for what they had just done.

"Well, it needs to be said. I don't know what happens

when I'm around you, Sara. I lose all sense of decency." He gave her a rueful smile and kissed her hand once more before bringing it back to his chest. "I ought to marry you after what we just did."

The lump returned to her throat and Sara felt as if she were suffocating. "I can't marry you, Christopher."

"I am aware of your position," he said, his voice edgy. "I can't marry you either, but it doesn't mean that I don't know that this situation warrants a proposal. You're a lady. A woman I care for deeply and hold in high regard, as well as being the cousin of my oldest friend. I am supposedly a gentleman." He scoffed at himself. "But I haven't treated you as a lady at all. I've done things only a husband should do with you, Sara."

All she heard him say was, *I can't marry you either.* An irrational flash of jealousy stabbed her in the chest. It was ridiculous. She was going to marry Alexander Drake in a matter of days. Why should she care that Christopher said he couldn't marry her?

Yet she did.

But why though? Why would he say that he *couldn't* marry her? That's what had her wondering. Was he in love with someone else too?

The very idea shocked her to her core. She'd never considered what his feelings were before and for that she felt like a fool, as well as for feeling jealous.

"It's fine, truly. I'm fine. Please don't worry. I wanted this just as much as you. There's no need for you to propose to me, either, although you are sweet to think you should. I'm not completely naïve. I know there's more to it than that and that I'm still chaste enough."

She made a vague gesture with her other hand to indicate the rest, for she was not strong enough to say the actual words aloud. Of course, she knew what sex was and that she had not technically crossed that line over to the primrose path. "And please don't tell me that you're sorry. It cheapens what we did." She gazed into his warm brown eyes. "It was much too special to be sorry about, Christopher."

"In spite of your sweet words, this was wrong, Sara." He leaned over and kissed her with great tenderness. "For all that, I agree with you."

He still held her hand in his. She did not wish to let go either. They rode in silence for a few moments.

A thought suddenly occurred to her. Puzzled, she asked, "Shouldn't we have reached Devon House by now?"

"About that . . ." He looked a bit sheepish. "Well, the thing is I wanted to give you my apologies uninterrupted, so I told my coachman to drive around until I gave him word to head to Devon House."

"Do you mean we've just been riding to nowhere in particular all this time?" Sara couldn't help but laugh. "Where are we?"

"I've no idea," Christopher said, shrugging carelessly. "The park, perhaps? Shall I tell him to drive toward Devon House now?"

Sara squeezed his hand. "Not just yet."

He squeezed her hand back. "I thought you were in a hurry to get home?"

It was funny. She had been quite anxious to get home and write to Alexander. Now that all seemed so far away and not quite real. Nothing in her life seemed as real as what just happened between her and Christopher Townsend.

Slowly she shook her head. "Not so much anymore."

This unexpected encounter with Christopher had turned her day upside down. Her thoughts had been of Alexander Drake all afternoon, until she was alone with Christopher in this carriage. She had the oddest desire to just ride away with him. Again, the thought entered her head. *I can't marry*

you either. Why couldn't he marry her? Irritated by the fact
that it bothered her so much that he couldn't marry her, she
was about to question him.

"So you've heard from him then?"

Christopher's voice pulled her from her thoughts.

She nodded. "Yes." Was it her imagination or did his whole
body tense up?

"Is he here in London?" he asked.

"He will be soon." Sara wasn't sure why she evaded his
question. She simply didn't want him, or anyone else for
that matter, to know that Alexander Drake had arrived just
yet. Since she had no idea what their plans were together
she thought it best to involve as few people as possible.

"And you'll marry him when he gets here, won't you?"

She nodded, unable to utter the words. He knew this already. Why must he ask her about marrying another man at
this moment? After what they had just done together?

He grew quiet. As did she.

Letting go of her hand, he reached across and slid open
the panel and spoke to the coachman. Slowly Sara brought
her hand to her cheek. It was still warm from where he
held her.

After speaking with the driver, he turned back to her with
a helpless shrug. "Apparently, we've traveled to the other side
of town, but we'll head toward Mayfair now."

Time to go home. Their magical little interlude was
coming to an end.

Reluctantly, Sara began to repair the damage to her hair.
Wishing she had a looking glass with her, she managed to
scoop up as much of her hair atop her head as she could.
Christopher handed her a few hairpins that were on the floor
of the carriage, and rather deftly helped her arrange her hair
with an ease that astounded her. Placing her peach bonnet
atop her head for her, he flashed her an enigmatic smile and

winked. Again, she didn't wish to know just how he gained such knowledge. The very thought of him with another woman put a funny little knot in her stomach. Yet the idea of her being jealous was quite preposterous, for she was madly in love with Alexander.

"Do I look respectable enough now?" she questioned, posing a bit, smoothing her dress.

He captured her chin with his hand, and held her face for a moment, his brown-eyed gaze suddenly quite serious. "You, my beautiful Sara, have touched my heart in ways you cannot imagine."

Finding it difficult to breathe, she again fought an un-bearable sadness and felt that she might cry. "I don't know what to say, Christopher."

"There's nothing to say. I did not intend for this to happen today, any more than I did the night of the storm. Any more than you did. I can't explain it, for I've never felt this way before. This was something special between you and me alone. Something beautiful, as you described it. No one else need ever know about it but us." Placing a kiss on her cheek, he released his hand from her chin and sat back on the seat beside her with a heavy sigh.

It made no sense. What was happening made no sense. The sad feelings welling inside of her made no sense. She straightened her shoulders and took a deep breath. It was time to go home and put this behind her. Like he said, no one would ever know about it but the two of them. And without a doubt she knew she would cherish this time with him for the rest of her life.

It occurred to her then that once she married Alexander Drake and sailed back to New York, which was just a matter of days now, she would most likely never see Christopher Townsend again.

Sara reached for his hand, clasping her fingers with his.

Again he brought their hands to his lips and kissed her palm. All the way back to Devon House, he held her hand next to his heart and uttered not a word until the carriage stopped.

He lifted her easily down from the carriage in one graceful motion. They stood there briefly for a moment, before he whispered close to her ear, "Good-bye, my beautiful Sara."

Afraid to look back at him, Sara hurried up the steps to Devon House with tears welling in her eyes once more.

16

Below Deck

"**W**ell, I gave it to her," she announced.

"You've been gone long enough," Alexander Drake uttered, rising from where he'd been reclining on the large bed when Lucy Camden entered their room at the elegant Savoy Hotel. "It's been hours. I was beginning to worry about you."

Lucy gave him a superior smile and a little wink. "I can take care of myself, Drakey. You know that."

"I do know that. But what did she say?" Alexander asked, his eyes watching her every movement, appreciating her curvy figure and graceful gestures. "Do you think she'll still go through with it?"

"I didn't stay around long enough to ask her. Remember? That was the plan. Not to cause suspicion. I just gave her the note and left the bookshop as quickly as I could," Lucy explained, sounding a bit peevish.

She stood in front of the large gilt-framed mirror in their hotel room, preening and posing, admiring herself in the smart violet gown she bought before leaving New York. She played with a feathered hat, tilting her head to one side, then the other, while adjusting the long veil that adorned it. Removing the hatpins, she carefully placed the dainty black and white silk concoction on the table. Then she began smoothing her artfully arranged blond curls. Her every motion seemed provocative and erotic somehow, and Alexander was hopelessly captivated by her.

"She's much prettier than I remember her being." Lucy turned and faced him with an accusatory glance.

Alexander never said that Sara Fleming wasn't beautiful. No one could deny that. "What she looks like is irrelevant, my love. We'd be here even if she weighed a ton and had a face like a shovel, and you know it. All that matters are the millions of dollars in her bank account. What's important now is how did she seem? Do you think she'll be there tomorrow with a note for me?"

Lucy thought for a moment, biting her lower lip, which she knew drove him mad. "She seemed more surprised than anything to see me. Almost as if she didn't believe that I was your sister. Maybe she even recognized me." She smiled ruefully. "I guess she's a little smarter than we thought, isn't she?"

With languid movements Lucy moved to the bar area and poured herself a glass of champagne from the open bottle that lay in a bucket filled with melted ice on the table near the window. They had celebrated a little prematurely this afternoon before she left to deliver the note to Sara. Rising from the bed, Alexander joined her there. They sat across from each other at the elegant table. She poured him a glass of champagne as well.

When they'd first arrived in London, he'd been hesitant to contact Sara at her aunt and uncle's rather large mansion in Mayfair. Afraid to risk her parents learning of his presence and once again spiriting their daughter away, he'd spent the better part of a week carefully watching the house and the comings and goings of Sara Fleming. When he discovered that Juliette Fleming's family owned two Hamilton bookshops in town, it had taken some doing on his part to figure out that the pampered and spoiled Sara Fleming was actually working in one of the stores. That was when he knew the bookshop was the perfect venue through which to contact her.

The champagne was a little warm and flat now, but they drank it anyway.

"I saw her get in a carriage with a man." Lucy paused with a knowing expression. "A very tall, handsome man."

Alexander raised an eyebrow. "Well, it's probably nothing. It could have been one of her cousins or an uncle. There are scores of them."

Shrugging a delicate shoulder, she said, "I just thought you should know." Then she sighed. "I would have followed that carriage if I could have, because it was right after I gave her your note. I wanted to know where she was going. I watched the shop for a while, wondering if she would come back. Nothing happened. So I wandered around Mayfair for a bit. I bought myself that little hat over there." Smiling brightly, she asked, "Do you like it?"

"Everything looks beautiful on you," he replied.

Alexander tried not to be annoyed, but it seemed as if they were going through their money far too quickly since they arrived in London. They'd each had to steal from the other guests in the hotel to pay for their stay and Lucy certainly didn't need another expensive hat, and he was positive it was expensive, not after the wardrobe she acquired before leaving New York. However, once he had his hands on Sara Fleming's millions, Lucy could have as many pretty little hats as she wanted.

But he had to marry the chit first.

All he wanted to know now was what Lucy thought Sara

would do. How did she seem? Was she still willing to marry him? Lucy, however, seemed intent on telling the story in her own time, almost taunting him with it.

"So then I got to thinking . . ." Lucy sipped her warm champagne and then ran her pink tongue along the rim of the glass. "What would I do if I were her and just received a note from you, my true love? I'd want to go home and write you back immediately, of course. So I wandered over to that big white house where her family lives and I watched for a while." She paused dramatically in the breathless way that Lucy had. "And what do you think I saw?"

Alexander sighed, but was beginning to feel a bit uneasy. "What did you see?"

"I saw our little Miss Fleming come home in that same carriage, with that very same tall, handsome gentleman."

"So? What's wrong with that?"

"Well, Drakey, you know me. I can tell things about people. I have an eye for noticing things. Even the smallest, seemingly insignificant, details."

Alexander couldn't help but smile. He knew that Lucy was exceptionally good with her observations of people. It was what made her such a cunning little thief. And part of why he loved her so much. "What did you see?"

"First off, I noticed that the handsome gentleman certainly didn't act like a cousin or an uncle and he didn't live in that house, because he rode away after Sara got out."

"So?"

"So, it was *how* they were with each other. I had my suspicions when I saw the two of them in front of the bookshop. Just a feeling. It was the way he looked at her, how he moved with her. They didn't see me through the window of a shop across the way, watching them. But when I saw Sara Fleming get out of that carriage when she returned to the big white house, I just knew." She paused expectantly, waiting for him to react.

"Knew what, Lucy?"

She beamed at him in triumph. "Her hair was completely different."

Not having a clue what she meant, he was beginning to lose patience with her. "Lucy . . ."

"You men can be such dunces." She smiled at him wickedly as she slowly shook her head. "Drakey, what happens to my hair when you kiss me? When you really kiss me? In bed? Does it stay all neatly arranged? No. It comes down, because men like a lady's hair to be down. They like to run their fingers through it and feel it in their hands while they kiss us. But afterward, we ladies have to put our hair back up in a hurry, don't we? Especially if we don't want anyone to know that we were being kissed."

"What are you saying?" Feeling a bit horrified, Alexander didn't want to believe what Lucy was insinuating.

Sara Fleming was a sweet, innocent, virtuous girl. And she was madly in love with *him*. She was ready to defy her parents to be with him. He'd taken great care to treat her with the utmost respect, giving her nothing but a few chaste kisses to lure her into believing that he was a proper gentleman who idolized her. He couldn't even imagine her with some other man. Acting like a loose woman. Not his Sara. No. It was not possible. He didn't believe it.

Lucy drained her glass of champagne and licked her pouty lips slowly. "I'm saying that Sara Fleming's hair came down sometime this afternoon while she was with that tall, handsome man, and she had to put it back up in a rush. And if I'm not mistaken, I think he whispered in her ear, too. Before she went into the house."

Alexander let out a very long sigh. "What do you think it means?"

She gave him a very frank look. "I think it means she may have found someone new. And you should have listened to me, lured her into bed, and gotten her pregnant first. Then her parents would have *had* to let you marry her."

He'd tried to do things the right way. He'd played by the rules with Sara Fleming and had treated her like a lady for six months, and he refused to be cheated out of marrying her by some other man! He had worked too hard at this to lose her and her millions now.

By God, he wouldn't stand for it!

"You have to go back there and talk to her, and make her believe that I love her. You and I have too much at stake, have spent too much money, and have come too far to lose her at this point. It's not fair. I won't have it!" Alexander shouted, and flung his glass against the wall. The crystal shattered in a magnificent crash, spraying the rose-covered wallpaper with the remains of his champagne.

Lucy didn't flinch. With a steady gaze, she offered him her champagne flute. Overcome with fury, he threw that against the wall with a splintering crack. Then, with a wicked smile, she gave him the empty champagne bottle. The re-sounding clatter it made when it smashed against the wall satisfied them both.

Slowly, one by one, Lucy began to remove the pins from her hair, until the thick blond tresses fell in luscious waves around her shoulders. Alexander watched in fascination, his sudden anger turning to lust.

"Oh, I am going back to that bookshop tomorrow, make no mistake about that," Lucy uttered in the breathy voice that drove him wild. She began unfastening the buttons at the front of her high-necked gown, her blue eyes fixed on him. "And she'll be there, waiting. I know she will. Because she loves you. And she'll have a note for me that says she wants to see you right away."

Lucy could do that to him. She had that power. She could drive him to despair in one minute and then make him believe anything was possible in the next breath. She could seduce him and make him forget everything, everything but her, just as she was doing now. Alexander hated her for it and loved her for it. His mouth grew dry as he watched her elegant fingers opening the front of her gown until he could see the swelling curves of her ample breasts spilling over the top of the black corset she wore underneath.

"How can you be so sure she'll be there?" Alexander demanded of her. "And still want to see me? Let alone go through with an elopement?" He wasn't even sure anymore, but he needed that reassurance from Lucy.

She raised the ruffled skirt of her violet gown and placed her shapely leg on the table. Running her hands up and down the length of her long leg, she unfastened the garter that held her stocking. In a languorous motion, she began to roll down the black silk stocking as she spoke, revealing her pale, creamy skin. He longed to run his tongue over it. With a graceful swing of her legs, she placed her other leg on the table and begin to remove that stocking as she spoke.

"Oh, I can be sure. I'm a woman, if you haven't noticed, Drakey. I know how women think. And our little heiress is a good girl. She's promised to love you, so she'll be there. Even if she may be torn between you both. And when you marry her, you had better get her with child as soon as possible. Then the parents can't get rid of you. And when you do, you'll think of me the whole time, won't you?"

He nodded wordlessly. He would do whatever Lucy wanted him to do.

After a pause, she instructed him with a wicked gleam in her eyes. "Now, remove those trousers and come and kiss me."

Lucy had made an interesting point, but Alexander had

no time to entertain it. For she was about to make him forget everything but her. Which was just how she liked it. After undoing the front of his pants, he lifted her onto the table rather roughly. He brought his mouth down on hers, grabbing a fistful of her thick blond hair. She squealed in delight and wrapped her long legs around his waist.

"Tell me you want me," she commanded, her voice husky with desire.

"I want you," he said between gritted teeth. God, how he wanted her. She was all he wanted.

"Tell me *how much* you want me, Drakey."

"More than anyone. More than all the money in the world." His breathing was coming in short gasps as he thrust into her as hard as he could. She moaned and the sound made him dizzy with wanting her.

"And you love me better than Sara Fleming?"

"Yes," he ground out. "You know I love you. You're the only one I love. The only one I ever will love or want."

"And you'd do *anything* for me?" she breathed close to his ear, sending shivers down his spine. The small, elegant table groaned under the weight of the two of them.

"Anything you want me to do, Lucy." He thrust harder as she moved her hips to meet him. "Anything, anything for you." The crazy thing was, he meant it. He truly did. He would do anything for her.

"Promise me?" she whispered.

He lost himself in her, thrusting in and out. She was everything to him. "I promise. I swear I would do anything for you. Anything you want."

"I want to make Sara Fleming suffer. I hate her and I have hated her from the moment I met her. And we are going to torment her and make her life miserable when she's your wife? Aren't we?" she said, digging her sharp little fingernails into his back.

"I'll do whatever you want," he panted through clenched teeth.

"Wouldn't it be convenient then, Drakey, if Sara Fleming were to meet with a terrible accident after you were married? Perhaps as soon as she has your child?"

He closed his eyes in bliss. He could have all the Flemings' millions and keep Lucy, maybe even convince her to marry him. And that spoiled captain's daughter would get just what she deserved for cheating on him. It was the best he could imagine. He groaned as pleasure washed over him in a heated rush. "Yes, oh God, yes!"

Lucy screamed his name, which brought him more pleasure than anything.

17

Cast Off

"I was going to suggest a hand of cards, but you seem miserable this evening, my friend," said Phillip Sinclair, the Earl of Waverly, a bit of concern in his voice.

Christopher Townsend answered with a weary sigh, "Because I am."

He'd done it. He'd actually done it.

Earlier this evening he had offered for Bonnie Beckwith's hand in marriage, and her father had rewarded him most generously for doing so. They'd agreed to dowry terms and, surprisingly, Alfred Beckwith hadn't balked when Christopher revealed that his earldom was in dire financial straits. The man seemed to take it in stride. It was merely the price he had to pay to make his daughter a countess. Contracts were being drawn up tomorrow.

Now Christopher would be able to pay off his father's debts, set Bridgeton Hall on the road to solvency, make the necessary repairs, and care for his sisters. It was what any responsible man in his position would do. It was the most rational, most reasonable, most financially sound course of action. Marriage was solely a business transaction, as Mr. Beckwith pointed out, rather surprisingly given the fact that it was his daughter who was being traded. It was a transfer of assets and an investment in the future. Everyone would get what they wanted. Bonnie would get her title. The Beckwiths would get their daughter successfully married and secure an entrée into more exclusive social circles. And Christopher would get the money to save his estate and support his family. It suited all their needs quite perfectly.

Christopher should feel elated.

Yet, here he was depressed beyond belief, drinking whiskey with his oldest friend. After an uncomfortable supper with the Beckwith family earlier, he had gone to his gentleman's club, desperately needing a strong drink and not to be alone with his thoughts.

Phillip raised a brow. "What's wrong?"

Christopher could not even begin to explain that he'd basically just gotten engaged to a woman he couldn't bear being in the same room with. Because then he would be required to explain *why* he had to do this and he still was not able to admit his financial problems. The shame was far too great. Too humiliating.

Then there was what happened with Sara Fleming that very afternoon.

The day had been a disaster from the very start.

His intention in going to the bookshop to see Sara had been just as he had explained to her. Knowing that he was offering for Bonnie Beckwith this evening, he had wanted to clear the air between Sara and him. He also felt the need to apologize for taking advantage of her in the library and his callous behavior toward her at the Cabots' ball. Sara was entitled to that much from him. He also thought Sara deserved to know he was about to become engaged as well. He would make amends and then he would put what happened with her behind him and focus on his upcoming marriage with a clear conscience.

Yes, that had been the plan. Simple. Straightforward.

He certainly hadn't planned on seducing her in his carriage. And he couldn't even blame the brandy this time. For either of their behavior. It was entirely his fault. What had come over him?

It was her tears that set him off. He couldn't bear the sight of her crying and the instinct to comfort her overwhelmed him. And then once he had her in his arms, well then . . .

He didn't know what the hell happened when they were alone together. It was as if all reason and propriety ceased to exist. All that mattered was the two of them.

Being with Sara that afternoon in the carriage had been the most erotic and sensual encounter he'd ever experienced. And that was saying something. She'd been so beautiful and sweet and willing. She did something to him. Made him feel things. Made him wish he could have her as his. Made him long for a life with her. Which was just torturous because it could never happen.

He needed to marry money. She was determined to marry her American gentleman.

And yet she was all Christopher thought about.

Despite how wrong what happened between them today was, it had felt so perfectly natural to be with Sara. It was as if they could read each other's thoughts, anticipate each other's desires. They understood each other. Liked being together. He'd been with other women before in his life. But not like that. Nothing like what he felt with Sara Fleming. Not even close.

Still, he shouldn't have done that to her. He hadn't even been able to tell her about his upcoming engagement because he simply could not utter the words, for they had lodged in his throat. He'd said absolutely nothing. It was so wrong. Everything was wrong. Which brought him back to his friend's question of concern. *What's wrong?*

Christopher let out a heavy sigh. Everyone was going to find out soon enough anyway. The Beckwiths were wasting no time and making an engagement announcement on Saturday. This would be a short engagement. He would likely be a married man by the end of August.

He might as well get it over with.

He said to Phillip in a quiet voice, "I got engaged today." The words sounded as horrible aloud as they had felt within.

"If you say so!" Phillip guffawed carelessly with a wide grin and a dismissive wave of his hand. "You had me believing you there for a second."

"No. I really did get engaged this evening. It'll be announced Saturday."

Christopher watched the expression on Phillip's face turn from amusement to confusion. Then complete disbelief. "You're joking, Bridgeton, aren't you?"

"I'm afraid not." He drank the whiskey, needing the fortification. "I'm quite serious actually."

"I don't understand . . . You got engaged today?" Phillip was baffled. "But why? And more importantly, to whom?"

"It's a rather long story. And my future bride is . . ." Christopher paused, hardly able to bring himself to say her name aloud. ". . . Miss Bonnie Beckwith."

Letting loose a relieved smile, Phillip howled loudly. "Well, now I definitely know you're jesting!"

Christopher remained quiet. Unsmiling. Letting the news sink in. If only it were all a big joke. Unfortunately, the joke was on him.

Slowly the laughter stopped and the smile left Phillip's face. He stared at Christopher, eyes wide. "Wait. You *are* serious, aren't you?"

"Yes." With a quick nod, he confirmed Phillip's worst suspicions. "Care to congratulate me?"

"Hell, Bridgeton, what'd you go and do something like that for?" Phillip's incredulous expression was tinged with something akin to horror. "Surely you're not in love with a chit like that?"

"God no. Of course not." Christopher shook his head. "But she's a nice girl, from a respectable family. We suit each other well enough, I guess. Most marriages start off this way. It will be fine." At least that was what he hoped. Yet when he looked at the long span of years ahead of him, with this particular woman tied to his side, a sickening dread crept over him.

"Well, hell . . ." Phillip was utterly dumbfounded. "I just had no idea you were in the market for a wife just now."

"It has to be done eventually. You know how it is. We have to marry, carry on the line, and all that." Christopher downed the remainder of his drink.

"I know, but still . . ." Phillip protested with a shake of his head. "I know her father's got buckets of money, but she's not worth it. What's the big rush? We're young yet. You have plenty of time to find a bride you love . . . or even like a little . . ."

"It has to do with family reasons."

"You've never mentioned that before." Phillip's brows drew together in confusion. "Was this something your father arranged before he died?"

If his father hadn't left a mountain of debt and mortgaged the estate to the brink of bankruptcy, then Christopher could have had his choice of bride. So in a sense, yes, his father had arranged this. "You could say that."

"Oh. I see." Yet clearly Phillip was still just as befuddled as before. "Well, I understand now why you're miserable." He called for a refill of their glasses from one of the servants.

"We're definitely drinking more tonight, Bridgeton. Whether we're celebrating or commiserating your engagement."

The two were quiet while their drinks were brought to them.

Christopher rubbed his hand on the back of his neck, hoping to ease the tension. It had been quite a day, going from heaven with Sara Fleming to hell with Bonnie Beckwith in a span of a few hours. Yet he couldn't wish away or regret what had happened with Sara, in spite of knowing that it never should have occurred in the first place. He'd enjoyed it too much and he knew she had too.

Phillip finally spoke a bit hesitantly. "Bridgeton, maybe I'm out of line with this, but I can't help thinking there was something between you and my cousin."

Christopher remained silent.

"Wasn't there?" Phillip prodded. "You both denied that anything happened that night of the storm, but I had a sense there was something between the two of you in the library. You and Sara seemed to . . . really like each other. There was an air of intimacy or something about you both that night. I know I sound like an idiot, but I was rather happy to see it."

And then, Christopher just said it out loud for the first time. "I might as well confess that I'm in love with her."

Phillip whistled low. "That makes your engagement news even more awful."

Christopher grimaced. "There's no hope for it. Sara is determined to marry her man from America."

Phillip sighed. "Yes, I am aware of that, but he's not here and you are. My aunt and uncle don't approve of him and took measures to prevent it, as I'm sure you've surmised. But I don't think coming to London has deterred Sara in the least." He paused and raised an eyebrow. "I was hoping perhaps you'd have helped her change her mind on that score."

"What is it her parents find so disreputable about him?"

Phillip shrugged. "They haven't said anything to me about him, but I know they've been having him investigated. My mother said something about getting proof to show to Sara, whatever that means. So I've been staying out of the whole affair, to be honest. The important thing to me is that I love my cousin and want only what will make her happy. Whether it's the chap from New York. Or you." He gave him a pointed look. "Because I noticed something between the two of you and thought that'd be nice. You and my cousin together."

Yes. That would be nice. Being married to Sara. Being a part of this wonderfully large and loving family. Having Sara by his side every day. Having her in his bed every night. Raising a family of their own together. He could picture it all with a clarity that surprised him. And it made him infinitely sad to know it would never come to pass.

Phillip let loose a prolonged sigh. "There must be something we can do about this. Break off the engagement to Beckwith. Don't do this to yourself, Bridgeton."

Christopher said nothing. What could he say? He had no choice except to marry Bonnie Beckwith. "Sara's hopelessly caught up with the American."

Phillip added, "Yes, I noticed that as well. She got a letter from him a few days ago and seemed quite happy about it."

"Yes, I am aware," Christopher said with a grimace.

"What has she told you about him?"

"She hasn't said much. Just that she's in love with him and wants to marry him. Apparently, he is coming for her."

Phillip shook his head. "Well, this should be interesting. I don't see Uncle Harrison taking too kindly to that."

"I just want her to be safe," Christopher said, and he meant it. "I hope this man is worthy of a woman like your cousin. She's quite special."

"She is at that," Phillip agreed. "Even when she was a

little girl. She always managed to be the life of the party and was always able to get her own way."

Christopher tried to imagine Sara as a pretty child, with her soft, dark curls, flashing blue eyes, and laughing smile. He'd bet she was quite a handful.

"Good evening, boys. Up to no good, are you?"

Startled, Christopher looked up as three older gentlemen joined them. It was just what he needed to top off his day. Sara's father, Captain Harrison Fleming, took a seat in one of the brown leather armchairs while her two uncles, the Marquis of Stancliff and the Duke of Rathmore, took seats at the table.

"Father!" Phillip said with a welcoming grin. "I didn't know you and Uncle Harrison and Uncle Jeffrey were going to be here this evening. I thought it was past bedtime for the likes of old men like you."

"We're not as old as you think," Lucien Sinclair, the Marquis of Stancliff, said to his son with a mischievous grin.

Christopher knew that Phillip's father was married to Colette, the eldest of the five Hamilton sisters, and Sara's father was married to the second oldest sister. And Jeffrey Eddington, the Duke of Rathmore, was married to Yvette, the youngest. The two other uncles, Quinton Roxbury and Declan Reeves, married to the third and fourth Hamilton sisters respectively, were not there this evening.

Keeping track of Sara's family tree took some doing. But since he'd met each of them that night at Devon House, he thought he had it all figured out. He'd gathered that the three men had been friends since back in their bachelor days and he found it rather amusing that they'd all married one of the Hamilton sisters.

Christopher shook hands with them, feeling more than a little guilty when Captain Fleming clapped him on the shoulder good-naturedly. If the captain had any idea what

Christopher had done with his daughter just hours ago, he'd call him out right there. And Christopher knew he deserved it.

The three men ordered drinks and began ribbing one another about events from their past, jokes that were lost on Christopher and Phillip, but they definitely got the gist of them.

"Let's play some cards," Phillip suggested, reaching for the deck in the center of the table. "Uncle Jeffrey, I think you owe me some money from the last time I beat you."

Captain Fleming shook his head. "You all can play. But my reason for coming here this evening just arrived. I have a meeting with someone. I'll see you gentlemen in a little while. If you'll excuse me." With that he stood, drink in hand, and walked over to a table on the other side of the room.

A lanky, balding man with his hat in one hand and a leather case in the other hand was waiting for him. The two sat down at the table nearby and began a lengthy conversation.

"Whom is Uncle Harrison meeting with?" Phillip asked, eyeing them with curiosity, as he shuffled the deck of cards.

His father answered, "An investigator from New York. The one who's been looking into the affairs of the man that Sara wants to marry."

Christopher's heart quickened at those words. The other three men continued to talk to one another, have drinks, and start a card game, while they were discussing something about the masked ball tomorrow evening at the Duke and Duchess of Rathmore's. But Christopher's attention was riveted on Sara's father and the man with whom he was meeting.

They appeared very intense and there was much discussion. Opening the large leather case he'd brought with him, the lanky man pulled out some papers and showed them to Captain Fleming.

As Christopher gathered up the cards that had been dealt to him, he would have given every cent he had to know what was in those papers, but judging from the grim look on Captain Fleming's face, things did not bode well for Sara's American gentleman.

18

Steady as She Goes

"Have you seen her yet?" Mara whispered for what seemed like the hundredth time, while she glanced furtively around the Hamilton Sisters' Book Shoppe the next day.

Sara shook her head, so nervous she could barely speak. The note she had written to Alexander Drake felt as if it were burning a hole in the pocket of the green apron she wore over her dress.

Last night she had shown Mara the note she'd received from Alexander Drake yesterday. Together the two of them devised what they believed to be a good plan and penned a response. She had written that she wanted to see him as soon as they could arrange it, offering to meet him anywhere he wanted.

Now, with her heart racing in her chest, Sara waited in the bookshop for Alexander's sister to appear. The store was quiet that afternoon, with not many customers. She hoped Lucille Drake would hurry up and arrive already. The suspense was unbearable.

Grateful for Mara's presence, she gave her cousin's arm a squeeze. Mara smiled nervously and moved to one of the shelves to arrange the books, while Sara pretended to restock the stationary display.

Although she confided in her cousin about the note from Alexander, Sara did not tell Mara about what happened with Lord Bridgeton in his carriage yesterday. She simply could not bring herself to say the words out loud. For there was no way to describe how it happened or how magical she had felt with him. Oh, but it had been wonderful! Not knowing what came over her yesterday, she cringed slightly at her shameful, completely wanton, behavior. Yet at the time it did not seem shameful at all to be with him in such an intimate manner. In fact, it seemed like the most natural thing to be with Christopher, and she had no idea why it should be like that with him, of all people.

Why should she feel this way about a man she wasn't in love with or even planning to marry? Especially when she had the man she *did* love ready and willing to marry her? A man who loved her so much, he crossed the ocean to be with her. Alexander Drake was here and still wanted her. And she wanted to be with him. She had from the moment she met him.

Sleep was elusive for her last night. She lay in bed tossing and turning, thinking about Christopher Townsend and Alexander Drake. Why had she kissed Christopher like that? What possessed her to allow him to take such liberties with her when she'd never allowed Alexander to kiss her that way?

She'd pondered that question all night long and came to no definitive answer.

Yesterday, such a great feeling of sadness at never seeing Christopher again had taken over her and she had felt powerless to stop herself when offered the chance to be with him. As soon as Christopher took her in his arms, she melted and any pretense of asking him to stop simply evaporated into thin air. Once his warm lips touched hers, the word "no" was nowhere to be found. She had wanted, needed, everything he offered her yesterday. He'd been quite passionate, desiring her as much as she desired him, while also acting remarkably sweet and tender toward her afterward. She'd been lost in the all-consuming sensations of the experience while her desire for him overwhelmed all else. And it had been exquisite.

But as Christopher had said to her, this was something she need never tell anyone about. Not Mara. Not even Alexander. *Especially* not Alexander. She could never confess to him what she had done with another man.

But all of that was behind her now.

Christopher Townsend, the Earl of Bridgeton, was completely behind her now. She needed to forget him. Forget all about him. He, and his seductive kisses, belonged in her past.

Her future belonged only to Alexander Drake.

She rearranged the same stack of notecards for the hundredth time, her nerves as jittery as the sails in a windstorm. She wondered where Alexander was and when she would get to see him.

And suddenly there she was. Lucille Drake. Alexander's sister.

Sara froze in place, simply staring at her.

Lucille meandered casually through the store, perusing the book displays, and acting as if she were a regular customer. She was smartly attired in a day gown of black and white stripes, with huge puffed sleeves and a matching black-and-white-feathered bonnet, with a pretty veil. Alexander's sister was quite beautiful. They both had the same coloring, blond hair and fair skin, but her lips were full, almost pouty. There was a raw earthiness about her, in spite of her fashionable attire. And there was something else . . .

There was something vaguely familiar about her and Sara found it difficult to pinpoint what it was.

With slow deliberation, the woman made her way toward her.

Her heart thudding against her chest, Sara placed her hand in her pocket, her fingers brushing the thick writing paper she had carefully folded for him to read. Oh, she had so many questions! Where was Alexander? Was he somewhere nearby? When could she see him? How had he found out about the bookshop and known she would be there? When could they get married?

"Good afternoon, Miss Drake," Sara murmured.

"It's so nice to see you again, Miss Fleming." Her grin was almost blinding. "I was a bit worried I wouldn't find you here today."

Again Sara glanced around the shop in nervousness, thankful that Aunt Colette was at home today and Aunt Paulette was upstairs in her office, busy with accounting the inventory. Only Mara was watching them with great curiosity, while she pretended to organize a bookshelf. The other women who worked in the shop were going about their own business, taking no notice of the exchange between Sara and the other American woman.

"Is Alexander nearby?" Sara couldn't help but ask, hoping that he was. How she longed to see him again!

Lucille Drake shook her blond head, looking at her intently. "No. My brother and I thought it would be too risky, should he be recognized if your parents happened to be here. They aren't, are they?"

"No, they're not here." Sara stared at her, a bit fascinated by this woman she'd never really known about before. Excited to finally meet a member of Alexander's family, she'd realized that he had never talked about them in detail, just made a vague reference to a large family on a farm in New Jersey. It was only now that it seemed odd that

Alexander had a sister, close enough to him that she'd want to assist in his romantic life and sail to London with him, yet he never once mentioned her by name to Sara.

Yet, she'd already met both of Christopher Townsend's sisters, Evelyn and Gwyneth.

Lucille Drake did not seem like a woman who grew up on a farm. Then again, neither did Alexander. Sara needed the answers to so many questions! Why had she never thought to ask them before?

"Well, that is a good thing that your parents are not here. We thought it best that we keep our little meeting secret." Again, that blinding smile. Lucille Drake was startlingly pretty. A bubbly laugh escaped her full lips. "Unless, of course, your parents have suddenly had a change of heart about you and my brother marrying."

"No, unfortunately, they have not." Sara had been careful not to even mention Alexander's name to her parents since they arrived in London.

"I thought not." Lucille gave her a sympathetic glance. "So, Miss Fleming, have you a message for my brother?"

"Yes, I do." With a trembling hand, Sara reached into the pocket of her green work apron and retrieved the letter. Handing it over to her, she asked, "Why did Alexander never tell me about you, Miss Drake?"

"Please, call me Lucy. We're about to become sisters soon, aren't we? There's no need to stand on ceremony, since we'll be spending so much time together after you're married. And since Alexander loves you, I know I will too. He and I are *very* close."

"Then why is it that he's never mentioned you to me, if you're so close?" Sara couldn't help but ask.

"Men. Who knows what goes on in their little heads?" Lucy shrugged daintily and gave her a knowing smile. "But I suppose since I'd been away, visiting our cousins in Virginia the entire time he was courting you, he didn't think to mention me. I suppose he only had eyes for you, since you're quite the beauty. He must have forgotten all about his little sister. But when I returned to New York last month, I found him despondent over losing you. You were all he talked about. How bright, and charming and beautiful you were! I happened to be with him the day he received your letter. He begged me right then and there to come to London with him. How could I refuse any man in such a heart-broken condition, let alone my own dear brother? I had to come with him! Besides, I was dying to meet the woman who'd captured my brother's heart. And now not only am I so glad that I agreed to come to retrieve you, but now I know exactly why he fell in love with you."

"You're kind to say so, Lucy." It delighted Sara to think of Alexander heartbroken and despondent over losing her. "Thank you so much for all your help."

Lucy tucked Sara's note into her reticule. "Thank you for making my brother so happy. I've never seen him like this. He's quite devoted to you."

"I'm equally devoted to him." Sara's heart swelled with longing. "Where is he?"

"We're staying at the Savoy Hotel."

"When did you arrive in London?" Sara was bursting with questions.

"About a week ago. Alexander was very careful not to be seen, but he watched you and figured out that this shop was the safest way to contact you."

A little shiver went through Sara at the thought of Alexander watching her without her knowing. But she understood why. If her parents believed him to be in London, she would be on her father's ship before she knew it, sailing for God knew where.

"He was smart to consider that." She wondered why she hadn't thought of it herself.

"My brother is very, very smart." Lucy stared at her with

an odd look on her face. "So, can I expect him to receive good news when he reads your note?"

"Yes, of course." Sara nodded.

"That's wonderful! He will be so happy to have this. I cannot wait to give it to him." Lucy leaned in closer to Sara, whispering in a conspiratorial tone, "Yours is the most romantic love story I've ever known about. I'm so excited to be able to assist you and my brother in getting married!"

"Thank you for all your help." Sara paused. "Lucy, are you quite sure we've never met before? There is something so familiar about you."

"I imagine I seem familiar to you because I remind you of Alexander. But I don't think we've ever met before. I would definitely remember meeting someone as lovely and stylish as you, Sara," Lucy said, her eyes glittering with envy.

"Thank you," Sara murmured. "I suppose you do simply remind me of Alexander." Yet Sara couldn't shake the feeling she had met this woman before.

Lucy paused for a moment, then suddenly said, "Sara, I just had the most wonderful idea. Why don't you come with me right now?"

"What do you mean?"

Her smile sparkled and her blue eyes danced with the excitement of her proposal. "Why not just come with me back to the hotel, right now? This very minute. We could surprise Alexander! Then we can be on our way and you and Alexander could be married as early as tomorrow!"

Sara's heart skipped a beat at the possibility. She wanted nothing more than to fling off the green Hamilton's apron and follow Miss Lucille Drake to the Savoy Hotel and right into Alexander's waiting arms. It could be so easy. So simple. After weeks of longing for him, missing the sound of his voice, the light of his smile, and yearning to be his wife, it could all be hers in a matter of minutes. She only had to walk out of the bookshop with his sister. No one knew. No one would stop her.

Yet suddenly faced with the immediate possibility of leaving her parents, her family, everyone she loved, with no clear idea of when she would see them again, or how they would receive her after her marriage, she hesitated. And Boots! She couldn't leave without Boots. No, now was not the time. It was too sudden.

She wasn't ready just yet.

"I'm not sure, Lucy . . ." There was something about Alexander's sister that gave her an uneasy feeling as well. What was it about her exactly that caused her to feel that way? Sara couldn't say.

"Why not?" Lucy's voice held a note of pleading entice-ment. "Your parents aren't here to keep you apart. Alex-ander is waiting for you. You both wish to wed and there's nothing now to prevent you from doing so. Come with me, Sara . . ."

An unexpected, cold rush of fear washed through Sara. Her words came out rather quickly. "No . . . I don't think so. I'm not quite ready. I'd planned for the day after tomorrow, as I told him in my letter. There are things I wish to bring with me and I need to pack some clothes. I need to say good-bye to my parents, without their knowing I'm saying good-bye, of course. No, Lucy," Sara said, with a firm shake of her head. "I can't come with you just yet."

"Don't you wish to see my brother?" she questioned, a delicately arched eyebrow raised.

"Oh, of course I do!" Sara protested. "I've thought of nothing but him since I left New York. As a matter of fact I want—" Sara suddenly had an idea of her own. "Lucy, my aunt and uncle are hosting a masked ball this evening. Hundreds of people will be attending. Why don't you and Alexander attend? Only my parents would recognize Alex-ander, but not if he were wearing a mask! There wouldn't be any reason for them to suspect that Alexander was there. With so many guests there, you would blend in easily. Then he and I would have a chance to see each other before I leave with him the day after tomorrow, as we planned."

"A masked ball . . . That could be perfect. And rather amusing too." Lucy gave her an admiring look. "You are a clever girl, aren't you?"

"Do you think Alexander would agree?"

Lucy grinned. "I know how to ask him in such a way that he can't refuse me."

Quickly Sara took a sheet of paper from the display case and with a fountain pen began to write the address of Uncle Jeffrey's home and instructions on how to gain entrance and where and when to meet her in the house. Her hand trembled so much she hoped they could read her writing. She suddenly needed to see Alexander first, see his face and hear his voice, before she ran off with him to get married. It'd been far too long since they had seen each other.

Lucy took the sheet of paper, waving it to let it dry, before she placed it securely in her reticule. "This is so exciting. And fun. I've never been to a masked ball!" She patted Sara's hand, whispering, "We shall see you tonight!"

With that, Lucy Drake exited the bookshop.

Sara released a shaky sigh. This was it. This was the beginning of her new life. Everything was about to change.

Immediately, Mara was by her side, her green eyes wide with curiosity. "Well, what happened? You spoke for quite a long time."

"They're coming to the masked ball tonight."

"What?" Her mouth hung open in surprise.

Sara stared at her cousin. "I need to see him again, Mara. I need to see Alexander first before I can leave with him. So I invited them to Aunt Yvette and Uncle Jeffrey's masked ball tonight."

Mara gasped in astonishment. "Sara, have you gone completely insane?"

Sara gave a little laugh, which may have bordered on hysterical. "Perhaps I have. But I need to see him first, Mara. And I'm going to need your help in making sure no one finds out about this."

Her cousin hesitated, her gray-green eyes filled with worry. "Oh, this could be too risky. Your parents are sure to find out."

"Well, it's too late now. I've already asked him to come." Sara shrugged. "In any case, we should both hurry home. We have to get ready for the ball." Knowing she had the most gorgeous emerald gown to wear, with a cunning little crystal studded mask, Sara grinned with excitement at the prospect of finally seeing Alexander again.

19

Batten Down the Hatches

"When do you want to tell her?" Captain Harrison Fleming asked his wife that same afternoon. He gestured to the sheaf of papers he had laid out on the desk in front of her in their suite of rooms they shared at Devon House. After meeting with his New York investigator last night, Harrison shared the evidence with his wife.

Juliette Fleming stared in dismay at the carefully prepared pages, which documented in great detail the sordid past of Alexander Drake and his companion. "I was hoping we were wrong, you know."

"I was too. Honestly. Which is exactly why we didn't say anything to her," he said. "But now Sara has to know the truth."

"Every page I read, it just gets worse and worse. He's a despicable character, and we let him in our home, and let him court our daughter. It makes me sick to think of it." Juliette sighed and closed her eyes, rubbing her fingers on her temples. She opened them again, her blue eyes looking toward her husband. "And we're positive that he's here? In

London? She must have written to him, but I never expected him to follow her. I thought he'd just lose interest."

Harrison began to pace back and forth, his feet moving over the thick ivy-patterned carpet. "I didn't think he would come after her either, even if he'd found out where we'd taken her. But we underestimated him. He's definitely at the Savoy Hotel, with the woman. McCafferty, the investigator, sailed on the *Campania* to follow Drake. He's a very thorough investigator and the reason I hired him."

Lines of worry drawn on her face, Juliette asked, "Yet we don't know if he has contacted Sara since he has been here?"

"That he did not know for certain." He looked at her knowingly. "But let's assume that he already has. Have you noticed a change in her?"

Juliette shook her head. "It's difficult to say. Aside from being cold to me, she's been behaving quite normally. She even seems happy enough, socializing with Phillip, Simon, and Mara, and with Phillip's friends. Why, she's even taken a liking to assisting at the bookshop."

Harrison repeated, "The bookshop."

Juliette's eyes widened. "Oh, dear God. He could have been into the shop any day this week and seen her. She's there right now with Mara and Paulette."

"Paulette won't let any harm come to her." Harrison placed a comforting hand on her shoulder. "And McCafferty would have mentioned if he'd seen Drake visit the bookshop. At least I hope so. In any case, we need to have a talk with her before Drake does make it to the shop." He gestured to the papers littering the desk, and the one photograph that could not be ignored. "I think seeing all this will prove to her that we were justified in our concern."

Juliette picked up the grainy black-and-white photograph of the handsome Alexander Drake, with his arm around a beautiful blond woman aboard the steamship *Campania*.

The camera caught them both smiling, while the wind seemed to blow her skirt as they stood beside the railing on the deck of the ship. It looked as if they were about to kiss each other. "How did Mr. McCafferty manage to photograph them?"

"Apparently, he carries one of those new cameras with him. He said he made it appear that he was photographing the horizon and not them, so as not to arouse suspicion. I have to admit, it's a very effective tool in his line of business. It'll be hard for Sara to refute the findings when faced with photographic evidence."

Juliette cringed in distaste. "It's so very crude. We're going to show her all of it?"

"Absolutely. It's what we've been waiting for. Proof in black and white. It's not just hearsay or our suspicions any longer, Juliette. Even Drake couldn't explain his way out of this. Sara cannot read all of this and not see him for the man he truly is. It's not just that we know he was after her money. Any man would be tempted by that. It's his character, or lack of, that I take offense to. He is a thief. A swindler. A liar. The list goes on and on. He is devoid of any kind of moral compass and I refuse to have my daughter wed to this good-for-nothing reprobate."

"Oh, Harrison," Juliette sighed in weariness. "I hate to do this to her."

"We didn't do this to her. Drake did." His voice was firm. "And we're saving her from him. We're doing the right thing."

"Of course we are, and I realize that. I do. I suppose I was just hoping that she would forget about him while we were here, perhaps fall in love with someone else, so she wouldn't care so much when we told her. I hate to see her hurt."

Harrison kissed his wife's cheek. "I think you under-estimate our girl. She's a lot more like you than you realize, my sweet Juliette. I believe Sara's going to be more angry than hurt by him when she learns the truth. She'll be so furious at being duped and taken in by his charming façade that she will want nothing to do with him. And knowing my girl, she'll probably take a swing at him."

"I hope you're right." But Juliette did not sound hopeful.

"Let's go talk to her now." He began gathering the papers from the desk.

Juliette insisted, "Oh, let's not tell her now, please, Harrison. Not with Yvette and Jeffrey's ball tonight. The whole family's been looking forward to it and I don't want to spoil anyone's evening. We'll be there with her and so will everyone else, so I don't want her to be sad or so upset she refuses to go. Let's allow her to have fun tonight. It can wait one more day. We will talk to her about it in the morning."

Unable to deny his wife anything she wanted, Captain Harrison Fleming agreed. "If you insist, my love." He kissed her again. "We'll tell her tomorrow."

Lady Mara Reeves bit her lip in worry, as she stood at the entrance of the Duke of Rathmore's ballroom that evening. Wearing a dark pink mask dotted with crystals that matched her rose silk gown, Mara had arrived at the ball with her parents, but all she could think about was Sara. She scanned the sea of colorful, glittering, bejeweled, and feathered masks covering the faces of the five hundred guests, looking for her cousin. It was more than a little difficult to discern who was who.

Earlier that day, Sara had been so elated that she'd arranged to meet Alexander and Lucille Drake this evening, that Mara was swept along in her high spirits and agreed to help Sara if she could. But now, Mara was beginning to have a bad feeling about the entire evening.

Unable to spot Sara in the crowd, Mara groaned with

frustration. This was not one of her premonitions. This was common sense and Mara felt that whatever Sara was planning with Alexander Drake was going to end badly. For everyone concerned. Inviting him to the ball was a terrible idea.

She needed to find Sara before it was too late and let her know that meeting Alexander Drake tonight was a dreadful mistake. Perhaps she ought to tell someone that Drake was arriving? Heavens, he could be there already! Mara took the few steps down into the main ballroom and began to wander through the gathering crowd, as more and more guests arrived. Becoming lost in the swell, she changed her mind and headed out of the ballroom. Exiting through the side door, she moved into a less crowded salon.

"Lady Mara, is that you?" a voice asked.

She turned toward the voice. "Lord Bridgeton?" she asked, squinting through her own mask at the tall, imposing figure of Christopher Townsend. Dressed in elegant black eveningwear, he wore a simple black mask covering his eyes that seemed to accentuate the classic lines of his face. She sighed with relief. She had been hoping to find Phillip, but she knew Lord Bridgeton would help her. She gave him a grateful smile.

"I thought it was you," he said jovially. "But it's difficult to know who anyone is this evening. You look quite lovely, by the way. The color pink suits you."

"Thank you." She paused, wondering the best way to say it.

"Have you seen any of your cousins?" he asked. "I arrived a quarter of an hour ago and I've yet to see Waverly or Sinclair . . ."

Mara instinctively knew that he was really looking for Sara. "I need your help, Lord Bridgeton."

His expression grew serious. "Yes, of course. I will help you in any way I can, Lady Mara."

"It's to do with Sara."

"I see." He escorted her to a more secluded area, near some large potted plants, clearly eager to lend his assistance. "What do you need me to do?"

Hesitant to reveal her cousin's plan, Mara bit her lip again. It was now or never. "Lord Bridgeton," she began. "I feel I can trust you."

"Please . . . Call me Christopher."

Mara nodded. "May I count on your utmost discretion in this matter?"

"That goes without saying," he agreed readily. "You have my word."

Satisfied, she began to explain. "Do you recall our little discussion at the Cabots' ball, about Sara's gentleman from New York? Alexander Drake?" She paused, waiting for the nod of affirmation from him. "Well, he's here."

Even through his mask, his expression was incredulous. "He's here at the ball? At this moment?"

Mara grimaced. "Yes."

His dark brows drew together in concern. "Does Sara know about this?"

"She's the one who invited him."

"What was she thinking? Her father will surely call the man out if he sees him. Is the plan for the two of them to leave tonight?"

She shook her head. "No. She wants to see him first. But I have a terrible feeling about it all. I didn't know whom else to turn to, although I've really no idea what you can actually do to help me. Or her. I simply need some advice."

Lord Bridgeton asked, "And no one else is aware of this?"

"No one. Just me. It only came about this afternoon, when his sister visited the bookshop. For a moment I thought Sara was going to leave with her then and there. Instead she asked them both to come to the ball tonight.

I've no idea if they've arrived, or even if they will, and I have no way to recognize them if they did. But I feel I must tell someone, even though Sara swore me to secrecy. Suddenly I'm very worried." Mara's words had come out in a mad rush. She could hardly stop them.

Lord Bridgeton placed his hands gently on her shoulders, calming her. "It'll be fine, Mara. You are right to tell me. Someone besides you needs to know what is going on, just to have another person to protect Sara."

Reassured by his commanding presence, she took a deep breath. "Perhaps I should find Aunt Juliette and tell her what I know, although Sara may never forgive me for doing so."

"Listen to me, Mara. I was with Sara's father last night at our club and I saw him meeting with the man whom he'd hired to investigate Drake in New York," he explained in a low voice. "Although I was not privy to the details of this meeting, Captain Fleming was clearly not happy with the outcome. From what I gather, this Drake is not a reputable character."

Mara's heart pounded and wild thoughts rushed through her head, increasing her dread of something terrible happening. "Do you think she's in danger?"

"I can't say for sure, but I agree with you. I'm worried about her too. He may not wish her bodily harm, but I wouldn't want to see our Sara married to a man with such a base nature."

When Lord Bridgeton said, "our Sara," Mara's heart skipped a little beat. "You do care for her," she whispered. She'd been right about him all along.

"I do." He nodded. "A great deal."

She stared at him. What a wonderful man he was! It was a shame that Sara was so besotted with her American that she couldn't see what was right in front of her eyes. Mara's intuition told her that Lord Bridgeton wished Sara could see it too.

"But enough about that," he said, dismissing the moment of sentiment. "Where is Sara now? Where can I find her?"

"I'm not sure. I haven't seen her yet tonight. But I know she's wearing an emerald gown, and a half mask just like mine, only in green. We had them made together," she explained.

A rueful smile played across his face, knowing as well as she did that finding anyone in this disguised crowd would be a challenge. "Well, that helps narrow it down a little."

Mara shrugged helplessly. "It's all I know."

"Do you know if they had a designated meeting area?"

"If they do, she didn't tell me where."

"Then I'll just have to keep looking until I find her. Hopefully before Drake does. In the meantime, you can look for Waverly and tell him what's happening. And if you feel you should, let Sara's parents know."

Mara felt better already knowing that they had a plan. If Sara was angry with her for breaking her promise and divulging her secret, then so be it. Her cousin's welfare was more important. Mara would never forgive herself if something happened to Sara and she hadn't done anything to protect her. Because the sensation that something dreadful was going to happen this evening still gnawed at her.

"Yes, I'll do that."

"Do you have any idea what this Drake fellow looks like?"

"Oh, yes! Sara told me that he's tall with fair hair and blue eyes, and he'll be with his sister, who is also blond and very pretty."

"That doesn't help much, but at least it's something. Thank you for telling me about this, Mara." He suddenly leaned down and quickly kissed her on the cheek. "Now let's go. And good luck!"

* * *

Jeffrey Eddington, the Duke of Rathmore, pulled his niece aside. "You're looking lovely this evening, Sara."

She smiled at him. "Thank you, Uncle Jeffrey. You're looking rather debonair yourself, in your black mask. It suits you."

"I am debonair, aren't I?" He grinned broadly, enjoying the attention, as he always did. "How are things going?"

"Just fine," she said a little too brightly. But things were not fine in the least.

She'd been on pins and needles all evening, constantly on the lookout for Alexander Drake. She'd instructed him to meet her near the bottom of the main staircase, but it seemed her aunt Yvette and uncle Jeffrey had taken up residence there, greeting guests as they entered the ballroom. Now she had to hope that Alexander would see her and somehow wait to approach her when it was safe. She also had to hope her parents didn't see him first. Luckily for her, the masks made doing so unlikely.

"You've been enjoying yourself then?"

"Of course, Uncle Jeffrey." Was she mad to have suggested that Alexander meet her here? What had possessed her to make such an outlandish suggestion?

Jeffrey lowered his voice and leaned in. "Have you heard from your young man? Did you tell him about being disinherited if you married him?"

"No." Sara shook her head and murmured, "I haven't heard from him."

There was no possible way she could explain to her uncle that not only had she heard from Alexander Drake, but that he was more than likely somewhere in the ballroom that very moment, waiting to speak with her.

"I'm sorry, my dear," he said kindly. He looked genuinely

hurt for her. "Then it's probably for the best that you see him for what he truly is. Not worthy of a beautiful girl like you."

Unable to reply, she merely nodded. She fumed in silence. Uncle Jeffrey didn't know Alexander. Had never even met him. How could her uncle possibly know what was in Alexander's heart? Or how much he loved and adored her? There was no way Uncle Jeffrey could know if Alexander loved her only for the money.

"And how has it been for you without the burden of being an heiress? I've quietly made it known that your father lost all his money through many foolish investments, which I must say has brought me great fun. I've been needling your father about his 'financial losses.' Have you enjoyed playing at being penniless?"

"I suppose," she said noncommittally. To be honest, Sara had quite forgotten about the little ruse they'd come up with the day Uncle Jeffrey had gifted her with Boots. Nor had it been important for her to have perpetuated that story, at least from her point of view. Her father's money hadn't come up in any situation.

Mainly because the topic of marriage had not been broached to her. She supposed all the gentlemen she'd been introduced to while in London were aware of her newfound financial status, but she'd never gotten close to or interested enough in any of them to make such a discussion necessary. Her mind had been consumed with other thoughts. Thoughts of Alexander Drake. And Christopher Townsend, whom she had to admit, surprised her. She'd found herself thinking of him more often than not.

Especially after the carriage ride yesterday. There was something about the way he held her that made her feel . . . cherished. If that made any sense. Yes. He made her feel special. And yet here she was, waiting breathlessly for Alexander Drake to arrive.

"Jeffrey! There you are!" Yvette Eddington, the Duchess of Rathmore, walked toward them, wearing a stunning pearl-studded mask that matched her elegant black-and-white gown. "Oh, Sara." She gave her a kiss on the cheek. "You look so lovely. Your parents were just asking me if I'd seen you. They're in the card room now, I believe."

"Thank you, Aunt Yvette. I'll go to them right away."

"Enjoy your evening, Sara," Yvette said before she took her husband's arm and pulled him toward her. "Come with me, darling. I must introduce you to someone!"

Uncle Jeffrey gave Sara a wink through his mask and grinned.

As her aunt and uncle disappeared into the crowd, Sara made her way to a little alcove by the steps to the ballroom, to watch and wait for Alexander Drake.

She wondered what Uncle Jeffrey would say when he found out that she'd eloped with a fortune hunter. Would he be hurt or disappointed in her? She knew her parents would be both of those things. But she would prove them wrong.

Sara would prove everyone wrong when she was happily married to Alexander. She knew he loved her for herself. He was everything she'd ever dreamed of in a man. She loved him. And he'd come for her. He had proven his love. She didn't believe he was only after her for her money. In all honesty, Sara didn't care about the money and Alexander didn't either. Not once while they had been together had the subject of her money ever come up.

No, she knew without a doubt that he loved her. Now she simply needed to see him again, to hear his voice, to calm the doubts she had about running away with him. She wished they didn't have to run away, but her parents had given her no choice. Would she rather have a grand wedding with her family and friends around her to celebrate? Instead of skulking off and getting married in some unfamiliar little place? Of course she would! But if that's what it took to marry the man she loved, then that's exactly what she would do!

Sara had taken a great risk in inviting Alexander here tonight, but then he had taken a greater risk in coming to London. It demonstrated just how much they loved and trusted each other.

At that moment Aunt Lisette and Uncle Quinton walked by her. Sara felt as if she were running a gauntlet with her mother's family this evening, but she greeted them warmly.

"Why aren't you dancing, Sara?" Aunt Lisette questioned. With her auburn hair arranged elegantly and her mauve mask, it could have easily been her mother standing there with her. All the Hamilton sisters looked remarkably alike.

"Oh, I was dancing earlier," Sara said breezily, smiling. "I'm just taking a little rest."

"Will you save a dance for your old uncle Quinton?" he asked with a little wink.

"Of course I will. I shall join you both in the ballroom shortly."

With butterflies in her stomach, Sara watched nervously as her aunt and uncle walked into the ballroom without her. Now it was after nine-thirty. Having instructed him to arrive at nine, she worried if Alexander was going to show up after all. Perhaps something happened to delay his arrival? A carriage accident?

"Sara?"

A voice so familiar she wanted to cry with joy at the sound of it whispered beside her. She turned toward it, recognizing him instantly. And there he was, in all his golden splendor. Alexander Drake. The love of her life. Wearing black evening clothes with a gold embroidered vest and an elaborate golden mask, he stood tall and dashing. His deep blue eyes danced with happiness behind the gilded mask, which accentuated his light blond locks that were slicked back from his face. His incredibly handsome face. Even hidden by the gold mask, she longed to touch it.

"Alexander," she said softly, although she really wanted to scream his name aloud. "I can't believe it's really you. That you're really here."

He smiled at her with his perfectly straight teeth. "I am finally here, my darling, for you and you alone."

20

Gangway

Christopher searched the crowd with mounting panic, not even entirely sure why he was so worried. Sara was more than likely perfectly fine. Yet still, the idea of her with that American man caused his blood to boil. If anything happened to her tonight, he would never forgive himself.

He'd come to the ball tonight to have a last night of freedom unencumbered by escorting a fiancée around before his engagement was announced Saturday. To add to his good mood, Miss Bonnie Beckwith and her family were not invited to this particular soirée. The Duke of Rathmore's guest list was varied to be sure, but discerning at best. And of course, a marriage to Lord Bridgeton would allow Bonnie and her parents entrée to exclusive and sought-after events like this masked ball.

Masks! Christopher groaned inwardly. What a night for everyone's faces to be obscured. Searching for the beautiful face of the woman he loved would be difficult when it seemed as if every other woman at the ball was wearing some shade of green.

Frustrated, he continued his way through the crowd for some time, eyeing every green dress carefully.

It was then he saw her. He knew by the way she moved, the graceful sway of her hips, the delicate curve of her neck. Sara was walking away from the ballroom, her emerald gown trailing elegantly behind her. Had she been speaking with the blond couple who were now walking in the opposite direction? Was that tall gentleman in the golden mask the American and the woman with him his sister? His first thought was to go after him, confront him. Toss him out, if need be.

Instead, moving on pure instinct, he followed Sara. He had to know she was safe and that she wasn't planning on leaving the house to meet up with the American somewhere. Not sure what she was up to, he watched her exit through a small doorway off the main hall, closing it behind her. He trailed after her. When he was on the other side of the door, he found himself in another hallway with a number of closed doors in front of him. Quietly he began to open each door, one by one, searching for her. With a resigned sigh, Christopher looked into a storage closet, a stairway to the servants' quarters, and a powder room, before he finally found her alone, gazing out the front window of a small drawing room lit by a single gas lamp.

At the sound of the door opening, Sara spun around, startled. She'd removed her mask, the green silk ribbons still clutched in her hands. Clearly unnerved by the intrusion, she asked, "Who is it?"

It was then he realized he still had his mask on. "Don't worry. It's just me." With a smile, he reached up and untied the black ribbons holding his mask in place. He tossed it on a nearby table.

She visibly relaxed, placing her hand over her heart. "Goodness, Christopher, you gave me a fright."

"I apologize." He stepped toward her. "It was not my

intent to frighten you." She looked so beautiful he could hardly breathe at the sight of her. The green dress fit her perfectly, accentuating her lush curves, and the low décolletage revealed the tempting swell of her breasts. Her soft cheeks were faintly flushed, her lips slightly parted. Was it only yesterday that he'd held her in his arms and kissed her in his carriage? It seemed like a million years ago.

"But what are you doing in here?" she asked, confused by his presence. "Did you follow me?"

"I did."

Her blue eyes widened. "Why?"

"I wanted to make sure you were safe."

She laughed a little. "What makes you think I'm in any danger?"

He moved closer to her. Now the familiar floral scent she wore wafted over him, evoking memories of her sitting on his lap, willing and eager. "You were just speaking with him, weren't you? Your American. I know he's here."

She gasped, her expression shocked, and took a step backward. "How did you know that?"

"I saw you talking to him just a few moments ago. What did he say? Are you planning to meet him later?"

"Christopher, how did you know that?" she cried. "How could you possibly know I was talking to Alexander of all people? I could have been speaking to anyone!" Her voice was a bit panicked and he knew she wondered if anyone else saw her with him.

He took another step toward her. "Is he coming back for you? Tell me you didn't make plans with him, Sara."

She gave him a defiant look. "Who are you to demand such things? I don't have to tell you anything at all."

"Don't be foolish."

"What does it matter to you what I do?" she flung at him.

"I care what happens to you, but you're too stubborn to realize it."

"Well, I think you were spying on me, and I don't care for that in the least!" She squared her small shoulders and jutted out her dainty chin.

"What if I was? Is it wrong that I was trying to protect you?"

"Yes." She raised her voice. "Because I don't need any protection, let alone yours!"

"Someone needs to protect you from yourself," he said, annoyed at her casual dismissal of him. "He's not who you think he is."

"You don't know anything about him." She took another step backward.

He moved forward, the desire to kiss her as he did yesterday grew minute by minute. "I know more than you think I do."

"You have no idea. You know nothing about him or what we mean to each other."

He glared at her. "Why are you in this room? Is he meeting you in here?"

"What?" She looked baffled. "No."

"Then you've just made plans to go away with him?"

"That"—she took a defiant stance and placed her hands on her hips—"is absolutely none of your business!"

He took a deep breath, his anger and frustration mounting, and he fought the overwhelming urge to take her into his arms and kiss some sense into her. "I care what happens to you, Sara. So, yes, it is my business." He was so close to her now.

Her eyes blazed and she spoke vehemently, pointing her finger in his direction. "No. It's really not your business. Whatever plans I have or have not made with Alexander Drake has nothing at all to do with you. You have no say over anything in my life, Christopher Townsend. You have no claims on me. I have enough people trying to control me and telling me what to do. I. Do. Not. Need. You."

That was it. Her words set him off and he reached for her, pulling her roughly into his arms. "Don't you need me, though?"

She shook her head at him. "No, I don't need you," she protested, but her eyes were locked with his.

"Yes, you do." He held her tightly, bringing his face closer to hers. "You need me and you want me just as much as I need and want you. Say it. Say you want me, Sara."

For a moment, time hung suspended between them, lost in the silence of the room.

"I want you," she murmured breathlessly, as she dropped her mask to the floor and tilted her face toward his.

He brought his mouth down on hers and he was lost. It was as if they both had been waiting for this moment. He knew it was wrong, he knew he shouldn't kiss her again, shouldn't hold her like this, but he was powerless to stop it. He couldn't have pulled away if he was offered all the gold in the treasury.

And she melted into him, her body warm and pliant the instant he touched her, which of course, made any thought of letting go vanish into thin air. No, she couldn't deny it either. She wanted him to kiss her just as much as he wanted to kiss her.

By God, he loved kissing her. Her lips were soft and full, her mouth warm and inviting. Never had a woman made him feel this way. A complex mixture of powerless and powerful, of need and desire, of possession and possessed. He wanted her. It was as simple as that.

And as complicated.

He wanted Sara Fleming more than he'd ever wanted anything in his whole life. And God help him, if he was going to spend the rest of his life shackled to a chatting parrot of a woman in order to save his family and his estate, and if Sara was going to disappear from his life with her American scoundrel, then he was going to take this moment to himself. This one moment with her. He would at least have this.

He didn't deserve more than that.

If she allowed it . . .

And then, she reached up and her arms circled his neck. Her mouth opened and her sweet tongue entered his mouth. Her fingers ran lightly along the back of his neck and then splayed into his hair, caressing him.

His heart almost burst at the tenderness of her eager touch. Again, it was her very willingness, her desire for *him*, that was his undoing. He couldn't resist such temptation. He simply could not. He wanted her too much.

Surrounded by the sweetness of her breath and the now familiar perfume of flowers that she wore, he kissed her with more intensity, and she pressed her body against his. His hands roamed over her, down her back, along her arms, which clung to him. He carefully pulled the pins from her hair, letting the dark tresses fall loose around her delicate shoulders.

He found his own fingers slowly undoing the fastenings at the back of her gown. One by one, he unhooked each clasp that held her silky green gown in place, until it slowly opened and the material fell in a pool at her feet.

A slight moan escaped her into his open mouth. He lifted her off the floor slightly, moving her away from the swell of material that was her dress.

For a moment, they broke away from their kiss. She gazed up at him with heavy-lidded eyes, her breathing thick with desire for him. He cupped her face in his hands, her achingly beautiful face. Her lips were full from kissing him and her soft cheeks were flushed pink. Unable to speak, Christopher stared into her blue eyes, seeking her consent.

He would die if she said no.

Without words and now clad only in her corset and silk stockings, she leaned up on her tiptoes and kissed him on the mouth. Her answer was clear and all he needed. He swept her up in his arms and carried her to the large velvet sofa in the room. She was as light as a feather, such a tiny thing. He laid her down and managed to remove his own clothes in record time.

He lay down beside her, wrapping her in his arms, his mouth covering hers once again. She responded with complete abandon, with almost a reckless, crazed passion that made him want her even more. The sight of her scantily clad body next to him, the feel of her silky skin pressed against his, the sound of his name whispered on her lips, her breath hot, the touch of her soft hands clinging to him, drove him over the edge of reason.

He didn't care that they were in a little drawing room at her uncle's house in the middle of the grandest ball of the Season, surrounded by hundreds of people. He didn't care that the man she really loved was out there somewhere, waiting for her. All that mattered was that she was here with him now. For now, right now, Sara Fleming was his. She belonged only to him. They belonged only to each other. It was just the two of them, alone in a dimly lit room, the rest of the world forgotten.

What mattered now was caressing her, his fingers slowly undoing the front clasps of her corset, the straps of her garters, freeing her from all the constraints that kept her from being completely his. The sight of her naked body, her long legs, her pale skin, the gentle curve of her hips, the swell of her breasts . . . she was stunning. Truly the most beautiful woman he had ever seen. He covered her with kisses, her breath coming in gasps, as she murmured his name over and over.

As he moved over her, she moved beneath him, her hips pressing close against him.

Sara opened her eyes and stared at him, his muscular body positioned over hers. There was no going back now even if she wanted to. And she didn't. And she knew without a doubt in her heart, that if she asked him to stop, he would. But she didn't want him to stop. She wanted this. As crazy as it seemed, as reckless as it was, she wanted to be with Christopher Townsend more than she ever wanted anything before in her life.

It made no sense that she'd just allowed this man, this naked man, to undress her and carry her to the sofa. It made no sense that she wanted Christopher to have her after she'd already promised herself to another.

She'd just spoken to Alexander Drake and a flood of conflicted feelings surfaced, leaving her off kilter. Their reunion hadn't been quite like she'd envisioned. Perhaps it was the awkwardness of the masks or because his sister had been there too, so he couldn't say the things she'd needed to hear from him after all this time apart. Although she'd agreed to meet him at his hotel tomorrow afternoon, she had to admit she had more than a few misgivings about the whole elopement.

After seeing him and his sister, Sara escaped from the noise of the ballroom to this little drawing room to have a moment to collect herself. She hadn't been in there more than a minute or two when Christopher suddenly appeared. It surprised her how glad she was to see him, even though he had annoyed her by telling her what she should do, along with everyone else in her family, thinking he knew what was better for her than she did.

The next thing she knew, he was kissing her, his mouth hot and demanding on hers, making her forget she was annoyed by him. Making her forget about Alexander Drake. She wanted to forget everything in that kiss with him. Far, far away in the back of her mind a tiny alarm bell was ringing, but she forgot that as well during this crazy night.

Nothing made any sense to her anymore and at that moment she did not care. *Good sense be damned!* She was powerless to stop the feelings that flooded her entire body. The heady desire that carried her to this decadent place.

All that mattered now was the two of them, together.

She arched her back and leaned into him, gripping his muscled arms as he entered her. She held her breath, unable to move or think as he gently pushed his way inside of her. With a gasp, she trembled from the feel of him, blinking back tears. This was not how she felt when he touched her in the carriage. Not at all. This was entirely different. Not knowing what to do next, for a split second she panicked, wondering if she'd made a terrible mistake.

His lips brushed her cheek and he whispered her name with utter tenderness. Slowly, gently at first, he began to move inside of her. Growing accustomed to the new sensations that inundated her, she began to relax. Her arms hugging him to her, he murmured words in her ear. Sweet, tender, comforting words that soothed her, aroused her.

Sara had never known anything could feel this all-encompassing. That someone could possess her so completely, so intimately, so thoroughly. That she could be so close to another human being. That he was a part of her. It was a revelation. A completely glorious revelation.

She began to move with him, matching his thrusts with her own, as a newfound desire began to build within her again. She wanted him. Reveled in the feel of his skin, now slick with sweat, pressed close to her. She was surrounded by him. He was all she saw, his body covering hers. He was all she felt, as he thrust in and out of her, his strong arms securely on either side of her. He was all she could taste as his kisses rained down on her. He was all she could smell, as the scent of him filled her. He was all she could hear, the sound of his breathing, his heart pounding, the soft words he whispered in her ears.

She was completely enveloped by Christopher Townsend. And loved every second of it. Couldn't get enough of him. Wanted even more from him. The intimacy of it touched her in a way she never imagined.

And then the pleasure began.

As he began to move within her with more urgency, she felt the sensations that overtook her in the carriage yesterday. She ached to have more, moving her hips against him, which caused him to thrust even harder. Heavenly sensations built within her, pushing her further and further along, closer and closer to that elusive explosion of pleasure that had overwhelmed her when he caressed her yesterday.

Together they moved in rhythm, meeting each other with their desire, seeking, wanting, giving, taking. More. And more. Sara thought she would die of the sheer wanting of him. Wanting him closer and harder and tighter and faster. It was so primal. So carnal. And torrid. And beautiful. And not like anything she had ever been told about sex, however fleetingly, or how it would be among the hushed whispers and speculations of her close friends.

Words could never describe this.

Suddenly wave after bliss-filled wave of pleasure cascaded over her, radiating from her core and flooding through her entire body from her head to her toes and ending in an explosion of ecstasy. Unable to catch her breath or center her thoughts, she simply floated back to earth, as he continued to thrust within her. He called her name as the same ecstatic sensations gripped him. That she could bring him as much pleasure as he gave to her was a thrilling new sensation.

Then they both lay still, unmoving, breathing heavily, arms and legs intertwined, her hair tangled around them. Sara couldn't have moved even if the room were suddenly engulfed in flames.

He finally kissed her face and gently lifted himself off her. He wrapped her in his arms as if he would never let her go. She clung to him, suddenly afraid to face what came next. Satisfied to just stay there, safe and secure in his strong arms, and not think of later or tomorrow, she burrowed into him. He stroked her hair, languished kisses on her head, her cheek, her hair. Filled with lethargy and a newfound peace, she slowly closed her eyes.

"Sara."

She snuggled closer to him, wishing she had a blanket.

"Sara," he whispered, placing little kisses along her cheek.

Her eyes fluttered open. "What?"

"We have to get up and get dressed now."

"Not yet," she objected, closing her eyes again. It was so nice. Lying here like this with him. She didn't want to move.

"So it wasn't the brandy at all," he laughed. "This is just you."

"What do you mean?"

"You're very difficult to move, once you get comfortable. Did you know that? Are you like this first thing in the morning too? Hard to wake up? I bet you are." His soft laughter made her smile.

Eyes still closed, she shrugged her shoulders helplessly. "Maybe I am."

"Come, my beautiful Sara. We must get up and get dressed."

She murmured, "Why?"

"As much as I would love to spend the rest of the night here with you in my arms like this," he whispered in her ear, sending thrilling little shivers down her spine, "it's not a very good idea. There's a rather large party going on out there, if you haven't forgotten, and your family may be looking for you, and we're in a slightly compromising position if someone should walk in."

"Fine," she grumbled unrepentantly. "I suppose you're right." She finally opened her eyes. Christopher was staring down at her, his brown eyes tender.

"You are so beautiful, Sara. I can't stop looking at you."

Feeling inexplicably shy, she looked away. Where were her clothes and how could she reach them? Oh God, how would she get out of this room?

"Are you sorry?" His voice was low.

Still looking away, she said, "No. Are you?"

"Not in a million years would I regret this night with you."

Again a little thrill raced through her at his words. It made no sense. The whole night made no sense. But he was right. They should get dressed and get out of there and back to the ball as soon as they could. She was sure to have been missed by now.

"I don't regret it either," she managed to say without looking at him. And oddly enough, she didn't. She had wanted this. Had wanted him. Had wanted that to happen.

Slowly she met his gaze.

He leaned down and kissed her mouth. He caressed her cheek. She longed for . . . something . . . she didn't know what. Again that overwhelming sadness that had possessed her yesterday in his carriage came over her again. All during their lovemaking there had been no need for words, no reason to speak. They both knew what the other was thinking. It had been all feeling and sensation and instinct. But now, now words needed to be said. Inexplicably, she could not speak. Too many words were lodged in her throat.

Blinking back tears she began to sit up. She refused to cry again. He sat up too.

Rising from the sofa, he began to collect his clothes. Watching with wide eyes, she was quite appreciative of his male form as he pulled his trousers on. He really was an extremely good-looking man, even in the dimly lit room. Tall. Muscular. Incredibly masculine, from the curve of his calves to the muscles of his arms and broad shoulders. She could watch him all evening and not grow tired of the sight.

Wordlessly, he handed her the pale pink chemise and corset, which had been tossed carelessly on the embroidered rug during the heat of passion. Feeling shy and awkward, she stood and began to put them on. Her elegant emerald gown still lay on the floor near the window. Shirtless, he had only his pants on as he moved toward her. Wearing just her corset, she looked up at him.

"Sara, I know—" he began to say, before she stopped him.

"Don't," she interrupted him with a hitch in her voice, holding up her hand, feeling the sting of tears once more.

Confused by the roiling emotions inside of her, she feared what he would say. And really, what could he say? That this should never have even happened? She knew that as well as he did. Was he going to apologize for taking her virginity? No. She didn't want to hear that from him. No recriminations. No regrets. No apologies. She changed her mind. If words weren't necessary before, then they weren't necessary now. "Don't say anything, please, Christopher. I simply can't bear it."

With a silent nod, he pulled her back into his arms. He kissed the top of her head and she reached around and held him tight. This was crazy. Utterly, utterly crazy. But for one last moment, she rested her head on his broad chest, breathing in the warm scent of him, listening to the beat of his heart, taking comfort in being with him.

Suddenly the door to the drawing room opened.

And there stood both of Sara's parents.

Appalled at the sight before them, Harrison and Juliette Fleming were speechless. Her mother actually shrieked and then covered her face with her hands.

Before she could stop them, all seven of the swear words that Sara knew came flying right out of her mouth.

21

Toeing the Line

Horrified, Christopher instinctively stood in front of Sara, trying to shield her half-naked body from her parents, not that they couldn't clearly see what had been going on between them. The evidence was plain. He and Sara were both in a state of undress, with their arms around each other, and the rest of their clothes strewn around the room. There was only one conclusion they could draw and he was quite certain they had drawn it.

This was not good.

He wasn't sure what had shocked him more at the time, the sudden appearance of Sara's parents or the vile string of curse words that came out of her pretty little mouth.

Captain Fleming, his face thunderous, said in a tense, imperious voice that left no doubt that the man could command a ship full of sailors, "I'm going to close this door. When I open it again, I want to see you both properly dressed and ready to explain yourselves. If you can. Hopefully, I'll be calm enough to talk by then without killing you for touching my daughter, Bridgeton." With that proviso, he and his stunned wife stepped back into the corridor, closing the door forcefully behind them.

Christopher turned his attention to Sara, whose face had gone from the rosy glow of kissing him to completely ashen. He placed his hands on her shoulders. With her blue eyes wide, she stared up at him in mutual horror.

"Oh my God," she whispered in desperation.

"I'm so sorry," he said. They were both in serious trouble and there was no denying it.

Panicked now, she broke away from him and began to hastily pull her clothes on. Her hands trembled as she struggled to roll up her stockings. "I've never seen my father so angry with me."

He began to dress as well, hurriedly shrugging into his white dress shirt. He certainly didn't intend for Sara's mother and father to see him half-naked again. "I've never heard such language from a lady in my life, Sara," he pointed out. "You weren't kidding me when you said you knew swear words. You swore like a sailor."

Sara didn't answer him. All her attention was focused on getting dressed as quickly as she could. He fastened the back of her ball gown and then he helped her put her long hair back up in a somewhat respectable fashion.

Again the door swung open and her parents walked in, their expressions understandably grim.

Christopher slowly lowered his hands away from Sara's hair. It probably wasn't a good idea to be touching the captain's daughter right in from of him. Sara gave him a nervous glance, and he motioned for her to sit on the sofa. Mrs. Fleming sat upon the chair across from them. Christopher joined Sara on the sofa. Captain Fleming remained standing near his wife's chair.

The room grew tensely quiet.

Deciding it was up to him to take responsibility,

Christopher spoke first. "Mrs. Fleming, Captain Fleming, there is no excuse for this. I can't apologize enough for—"

"You're damn right you can't! I should wring your neck right here and now," Captain Fleming threatened angrily.

"Father!" Sara cried out in alarm.

"Really, Harrison, is that kind of talk necessary?" Juliette Fleming murmured, placing a calming hand on her husband's arm. "Now let's sit and discuss this rationally, shall we?"

Captain Fleming was seething. "How can I be rational about this man who was seducing my daughter right in front of me?"

"Harrison. Sit. Down," Juliette commanded in a steely tone that brooked no argument. Her blue eyes, so like her daughter's, sparked with anger and determination.

With great reluctance, the tall captain yanked a chair over next to his wife's and sat down. His expression was thunderous and he fumed silently as he crossed his arms over his chest.

A little taken aback that Captain Fleming had capitulated so quickly, Christopher was impressed with Mrs. Fleming's technique. He imagined that Juliette Hamilton must have led her husband on a merry chase when they were younger. She was quite beautiful and it was clear from whom Sara inherited her looks. And temperament.

Juliette Fleming then turned her gaze on Christopher and it felt that she could see right through him. "You were saying, Lord Bridgeton . . . ?"

"I would just like to apologize first," Christopher began. "Although I know that it doesn't change or make up for what happened here, I am very sorry. It was never my intention to harm Sara in any way. I accept all the blame. This is entirely my fault, not hers. I should never have taken advantage of her in such—"

"Don't say that!" Sara protested, raising her voice. "It

was not *all* your fault! What happened is just as much my fault as it is yours! I'm so tired of everyone thinking I can't think or act for myself!"

Christopher wasn't going to be able to say a word in this discussion with the way the Flemings interrupted him. But when he looked at Sara, she was visibly upset. He couldn't blame her. The evening had become a nightmare. He gently put a hand on her arm to comfort her.

"Get your hand off my daughter."

"Harrison," Mrs. Fleming warned her husband. Then she sighed in weariness and turned her attention back toward them. "Sara, when you start comporting yourself like a dignified adult, we shall treat you like one. Now, Lord Bridgeton, although my husband and I appreciate your apology—"

Captain Fleming coughed loudly as a way of scorning him.

Juliette gave him a scathing look. She began again. "Although my husband and I appreciate your apology and the sentiment behind it, there isn't much else to say. It's quite clear what happened between the two of you in this room tonight. You have compromised our daughter. So there is only one thing to be done." She paused for a moment, gazing at him expectantly.

Christopher couldn't breathe.

He knew exactly what Juliette Fleming was suggesting. Hell, he even agreed with her. He'd just taken their daughter's virginity on a drawing room sofa. What the devil had he been thinking? He should ask for Sara's hand in marriage. It was the only decent, gentlemanly thing to do. He had to marry her. Nothing would make him happier, but, oh God, what a mess he was in now! Forfeiting the Beckwith fortune would cause him to lose Bridgeton Hall, his home in London, everything.

Everything was ruined. *He* was ruined. He'd been an

idiot and only had himself to blame. His reckless behavior tonight just cost him everything. How would he support a wife, let alone his sisters and his mother? His stomach roiled with anger. Anger at himself.

He'd have to somehow explain to Mr. Beckwith that he'd changed his mind and couldn't marry his daughter after all. This was just disastrous.

The tension in the room was palpable. Again he glanced at Sara, seated beside him. She was so lovely, her dark hair softly coming loose from the hastily applied pins, her elegant hands folded in her lap. With her head facing down, she would not look at him. He knew she was thinking of Drake and it made him irrationally angry.

Christopher faced Sara's parents. He had no choice. Clearing his throat, he began, "I would like to ask for your daughter's hand in marriage."

"I accept your offer. We'll plan the wedding for this Saturday." Captain Fleming spoke so calmly and rationally that Christopher was confused by the sudden turnaround in his mood. Was there the faintest hint of a smile on his face when he spoke?

Captain Fleming rose from his chair, his hand outstretched to seal the deal. Christopher stood to meet him. Mrs. Fleming stood as well, a grin on her face. Christopher felt as if he had missed something.

"Does anyone even care what I think about any of this?" Sara exclaimed, clearly agitated. "Does it matter to anyone in this room that perhaps I have plans of my own?"

"No, it doesn't," her father said, dismissing her while shaking Christopher's hand.

"Father," she implored. "Please, listen to me. This is not what I had—"

"No, Sara. It's done," Captain Fleming said to his daughter, ignoring her protests. "You've compromised yourself.

There's no help for it. You'll marry Lord Bridgeton on Saturday."

"Captain Fleming, I must tell you that—" Christopher began to explain his predicament.

"Father, please! Just listen to me for a moment," Sara begged, rising from the sofa to better plead her case. "Mother, you must understand my point of view."

"Sara, that's enough," her mother intoned. "It's all settled. Lord Bridgeton has done the only honorable thing a gentleman in a situation like this can do and has asked to marry you. And that is exactly what will happen. I know you both must care for each other in order for this to have happened here this evening." She raised her hand yet again to prevent Sara from speaking, giving her daughter a pointed look. "Have you considered the possibility of a child, Sara?"

After a short gasp, Sara grew quiet, her cheeks turning scarlet. Clearly, she had not thought about that fact.

For a moment Christopher's heart almost stopped completely. He hadn't had time to consider that possibility yet either, but he certainly should have. He knew better than that and had always taken precautions in the past, but everything had happened too quickly between them this evening. To say the very least, he had not been thinking clearly at all. However, her mother was right. Marrying Sara was the only choice now.

Nothing this night had turned out the way he expected.

And now he suddenly found himself engaged to two women at the same time.

"I have no objection to marrying Sara," Christopher said, finally breaking the awkward silence. "It's the right thing to do and I care for her, and with the possibility of a child, of course, there's nothing else for us to do but marry. However, there is something else I must take care of first before I can marry her. I am already . . ." His voice trailing off, he felt like a fool.

The three of them looked at him curiously.

Christopher just had to get it over with. "I'm afraid I'm engaged to someone else already. Our engagement is going to be announced on Saturday."

Another curse word slipped from Sara's mouth. Her parents were watching them both very carefully.

"You're engaged to be married?" Sara cried in utter disbelief, finally looking him in the eye. "Since when?"

"Since last night," he said. There was no denying that Sara was angry with him.

"What?" The look of astonishment on her face only grew. "Whom on earth are you engaged to?"

He hesitated. "Bonnie Beckwith."

Her mouth agape, Sara stared at him in confusion. Then she actually laughed. "You must be jesting!"

"No. I am not."

"When were you going to tell me about this?" she demanded, her hands on her hips, anger replacing her brief amusement.

He countered with, "When were you going to tell me about Drake?"

Having no answer, Sara pursed her lips together.

Christopher turned back to her parents, who both had something akin to amusement on their faces. "So you see, I need a little time to take care of this other matter before I can marry your daughter."

Mrs. Fleming murmured rather sympathetically, "Yes, that is understandable, Lord Bridgeton."

"It seems to me that if you were engaged to another woman, you certainly shouldn't have been dallying with my daughter this evening." Captain Fleming eyed him with clear disapproval. "Just when will you be attending to this 'other matter'?"

"First thing in the morning I will speak to her father and withdraw my offer," Christopher said, squaring his shoulders.

"Then I shall secure a special license and get things in order. The wedding will take place Saturday at Devon House." Captain Fleming actually smiled at him.

Christopher looked toward Sara. She was not smiling at all. In fact, by the set of her jaw, she looked positively furious.

22

Abandon Ship

Juliette Fleming lay in her husband's arms in their bedroom later that night, still reeling from what had happened at the masked ball. They'd managed to get Sara home before anyone there had been aware of what happened. Harrison had then ordered Sara to her room for the night, with instructions that they would finish their discussion with her in the morning.

"Boy, oh boy, is she your daughter." Harrison chuckled, kissing her cheek.

"That's not funny, Harrison," Juliette scolded good-naturedly. "And you completely overreacted, by the way!"

"I wasn't completely overreacting," he said softly. "I really was furious with that boy!"

"I know and I don't blame you. But I was worried when Mara told us that Drake was at the ball. And I was so terrified that we'd find Sara with him that it was such a relief to discover her with Lord Bridgeton that I almost laughed!"

"It still wasn't a laughing matter no matter how you look at it," Harrison concluded, his brows drawn together.

"I know, I know. But it was better than finding her with Drake! Don't you agree? I like Lord Bridgeton, and I'm rather pleased that they'll marry. In spite of the rather shocking circumstances we found them in tonight, I believe Sara's actually in love with him, but she's just too stubborn to realize or admit it. Did you notice how angry she got when she discovered he was engaged? She was jealous!"

"Well, Bridgeton is clearly besotted with her."

"He is, isn't he?" Juliette smiled in satisfaction. "I was hoping something like this would happen. Oh, not the discovering them half-naked like that, no!" she quickly amended. "I certainly could have done without seeing *that*."

"Honestly, I don't know what was worse, the expression of horror on your face or theirs!"

"It was quite a shock, I'll tell you," Juliette said. "I was just mortified for her, that's all. For both of them, actually. But I liked how protective he was of Sara."

"I'd have liked it a lot better if Bridgeton had been more protective of my daughter's virtue in the first place and not seduced her at my sister-in-law's party," Harrison grumbled.

Juliette nudged him with her elbow. "Harrison . . . have you forgotten how it was with us? On your ship? We were just like them, only we were lucky. We never got caught by anyone."

"Sara is just like you, Juliette, you forward little hussy. Headstrong and stubborn and wants her own way. She probably took advantage of him," he teased.

"Harrison!" Juliette laughed. "You always say that I seduced you, but you know it was mutual!"

"It was at that." He placed a loving kiss on her cheek.

"They're both young and so in love with each other they can't even see it." Juliette softly sighed. "It's fortunate that we caught them together, or Christopher Townsend may have ended up marrying that other girl and not Sara."

"I wouldn't have thought of it that way, but you may be

right," Harrison admitted. "Bridgeton is a good man and I've nothing against him, except for this evening. I actually played some cards with him at the club last night. I like him a lot. I believe he'll be good for her."

"Yes, she'll be safe married to Lord Bridgeton rather than that awful Drake. And I think she'll be very happy too, if she'll allow herself to be. I had hoped all along that she'd meet someone she loves better than that awful Drake character."

"I just think she'll take the news about Drake better, now that she has Bridgeton," Harrison added.

"I don't see how Drake can possibly even be an issue anymore, Harrison. If Mara said that Drake was at the ball, then why on earth was Sara with Lord Bridgeton and not him?" she asked.

"I've no idea. I'm just as confused by her behavior tonight as you are." He shrugged. "I can't even pretend to understand you women."

Juliette elbowed her husband again, and he pretended it hurt, while chuckling. "Well, we'll talk to her tomorrow," he said. "And I'll have to try not to seem too happy about her having to marry Lord Bridgeton."

Very early the next morning, Sara held Boots in her arms as she stared out the window of her bedroom, watching a misty fog roll across the street below. She'd need to leave soon, before anyone woke up and tried to stop her. Due to the late hour they returned home last night, she'd told Leighton, her lady's maid, that she needed to sleep and instructed her not to wake her until noon. No one would expect to see her before then. Everyone would be sleeping late as well. Thinking she could send for the rest of her things later, she'd packed only a small valise. It was all she could carry, especially if she had Boots with her. She certainly couldn't leave him behind.

Kissing the top of his little head, she rocked the tiny Yorkie in her arms.

Her parents had planned to talk to her this afternoon about all that had happened and her impending marriage. Well, they would be in for another shock when they found her gone. Sara had had enough of them telling her whom she should and shouldn't marry. She was finished with anyone telling her what to do.

She was almost twenty-one years old. She was old enough to make her own decisions about her life. About what she wanted to do and who she wanted to marry, most certainly. She knew her own mind. The time for anyone, her mother, her father, Christopher, Phillip, Uncle Jeffrey, or any of them, telling her how to live her life was over.

Last night had been awful.

Well, most of it.

Having her parents discover her undressed in Christopher Townsend's arms was not the proudest moment of her life, that was for certain. That she had been utterly mortified was an understatement. Afterward, she and Christopher never even had a moment to talk and her parents hadn't given her a chance to say a word either. It was as if she wasn't there and her opinions didn't count. They'd ushered her out of Uncle Jeffrey's house, telling her aunts and uncles that Sara wasn't feeling well, and whisked her home. Grateful for the fact that at least her whole family didn't know of her shameful behavior, she had remained quiet the entire ride home. As did her parents. Luckily, they spared her the lecture on her shocking conduct when they got back to Devon House, promising her instead a good long talk the next day about the disgraced state of affairs in which she now found herself.

Humiliated, Sara couldn't even look her father in the eye.

She had to admit that her parents' knowing about her involvement with Christopher Townsend weakened her case for marrying Alexander Drake. How they seemed to know that Alexander was at the ball was still a bit of a mystery to her. Had her parents recognized him somehow? Had they run into one another? Or was it Mara? She was the only one who could have told them. Would Mara have betrayed her? She hated to contemplate that. But she hadn't even seen Mara all evening! Where had Mara been? Or perhaps Phillip had gotten it out of Mara and *he* was the one who told her parents?

In either case, she wasn't waiting around to find out the answer. Not today anyway.

As for why she had done what she'd done with Christopher, that remained the greatest mystery of them all. She had no earthly justification or rationale to explain what had happened with him in that drawing room last night. One minute the two of them were talking, the next they were arguing. Which they'd never done before. Before she knew it, she was in his arms and they were kissing. And she simply could not stop. Nor did she want to. For some reason, her brain ceased to function properly when Christopher kissed her.

But it didn't mean that she wanted to marry him either. Especially not when her parents were now telling her that she *had* to marry him. Besides, *he* was already engaged! To that ridiculous little Beckwith girl, of all people! At least now Sara understood why the other day in the carriage Christopher said he *couldn't* marry her. Well, fine. Bonnie Beckwith could have him. She didn't need or want Lord Bridgeton!

It was Alexander Drake she really loved and wanted to marry. He was the one she dreamed of and longed to be with. Yet no one believed her. Marrying him was what she had wanted all along. And that was exactly what she intended to do.

With her little tapestry valise in one hand and Boots in the other, she left her room and tiptoed down the hall. Taking the servants' staircase, she silently left Devon House in the misty dawn and walked determinedly down the street, headed for the Savoy Hotel, where she had promised to meet her future husband.

Later that same foggy morning, the Earl of Bridgeton paced impatiently in the overdecorated and gaudy drawing room of the Beckwiths' grand London town house. Every feature in the place fairly screamed money, as was Mrs. Beckwith's intention. While his footsteps covered the expensive Persian rug, Christopher glanced at the ornate gilt clock on the marble mantel. He knew it was ridiculously early to be paying a call, but he had no choice. Anxious to get on with it, he wished Mr. Beckwith would hurry and make an appearance.

He had to end this engagement with Bonnie Beckwith as soon as possible.

Her father was not going to be pleased at all. Luckily for Christopher, they'd only been engaged one day. It was doubtful that any of the paperwork was completed and since the engagement hadn't been announced yet, it should be easy enough to withdraw.

As soon as this was done he had to meet with Captain Fleming. There was no getting around it. Although he'd agreed to marry Sara, he had to disclose his dire financial situation to her father. Perhaps the captain would rather have his daughter wed to a man with better prospects than his. Sara was a girl used to having nice things, and even given their family's reduced circumstances, being his wife was not going to elevate her monetary position at all.

He'd also made the decision to sell Bridgeton Hall last night, as he lay sleepless in bed reliving the humiliating scene in the drawing room and taking stock of his unbelievable situation. There was nothing else to be done for it. After hundreds of years, Bridgeton Hall would not belong to a Townsend. He'd already written a letter to his solicitor this morning, asking him to begin proceedings to sell the estate.

As much as it pained him to do so, there was also a sense of freedom with the letting go of it. Just as his sister Evie had suggested, maybe it would be better to be free of the burdens of the manor house that had held mostly nightmares for them and start over somewhere new. With what little money was left, he'd find a nice place for his family to live. Then he would get a position somewhere. This morning, since he hadn't slept all night, he'd managed to write a series of letters to various friends, seeking employment. Although raised to be a gentleman of the nobility, there was no reason at all why he shouldn't work to earn money to support his family. His two sisters would understand and be ecstatic to learn that he wasn't marrying Bonnie Beckwith after all. He actually couldn't wait to tell them the news this evening.

The brightest spot in all of it was Sara.

He would be marrying Sara Fleming.

It still stunned him to think of it. A burgeoning sense of hope and happiness filled him, in spite of losing the estate and the Beckwiths' money. Even without a cent to his name, he would rather marry Sara than have all the money in the world with Bonnie Beckwith.

"Well, well, my lord . . . What is it that's so important that I needed to be called from my breakfast?" Alfred Beckwith said as he blustered into the drawing room.

Christopher faced him. "Good morning, sir. I'm afraid I've had a change of circumstances regarding our arrangement."

Beckwith waved his hand carelessly. "Oh, if you need

more money, that's not a problem at all. We can manage to work something out, my boy."

"No, Mr. Beckwith, I'm afraid that's not the case. Not this time." He paused. "Unfortunately, I must withdraw my offer of marriage to your daughter."

"Are you serious?" he asked, completely baffled by the news.

"Yes, I am," Christopher said briskly. "We've not signed any papers as of yet, so it should be a fairly painless diverging of ways. I thank you for everything and wish you and your daughter only the best in the future. I'm sure she will find someone who will make her happier than I ever could."

A piercing shriek issued from the doorway. Startled, both men turned to see Bonnie, still in her nightclothes, standing there. She'd clearly overheard their conversation. "No, Lord Bridgeton, no! You cannot do that!"

"Bonnie! Get back to your room this instant, young lady!" Alfred Beckwith commanded, horrified by her presence. "You're not even dressed!"

Ignoring her father completely, she glared at Christopher with angry brown eyes. "You said you would marry me! You said it!" Furious, she stamped her pink-slippered foot. "You can't unsay it. You promised to marry me. You *have* to marry me now!"

Christopher stared at this little woman whom he *had* agreed to marry just days ago. With a ruffled, high-necked pink robe wrapped around her and her long brown hair falling about her shoulders, she looked like a child. A very spoiled little child having a tantrum.

"I apologize, Miss Beckwith, for any hurt feelings my change of heart has caused you," he said soberly. "But following much consideration, I don't believe that we would be well suited after all." What had he been thinking to contemplate shackling himself to this mini-tyrant for the rest of his life? Money made people do desperate things.

Bonnie began to cry then. Not delicate ladylike tears or a gentle sob, but a full-on wail of grief and frustration and utter confusion as to why she was not getting her way.

Her father went to her, and while patting her shoulder, said soothingly, "Oh, don't cry. There, there, my sweet darling. You mustn't cry. We can find someone better for you, I promise."

"Nooooo, Papa! I waaaaant to marry him! I wanted to be a cooountesssss!" she cried with a great gulping sob, fat tears streaming down her reddened face.

Alfred Beckwith turned back to Christopher with imploring eyes. "Really, Lord Bridgeton, can you not see what you are doing to my daughter? Look at her! She is completely and utterly devastated. Bonnie had her heart set on you! And now you are breaking it. I beg you to reconsider what you are doing here."

Bonnie paused from her histrionics long enough to stare up at him, to see what impact her father's words had on him. She cried again, "Lord Bridgeton, you said you would marry me . . . You said you would!"

Christopher had no doubt that Mr. Beckwith would buy his overindulged daughter another man with a title with which to console her. The Earl of Bridgeton was no longer for sale.

He squared his shoulders. "Once again, I apologize to you both for wasting your time and causing you any unnecessary disappointment. Mr. Beckwith, I've no patience for scenes like this, so as you can see, I'd not be the kind of husband your daughter would require after all. When all is said and done, she will be much happier without me. Miss Beckwith, I wish you only the best in any future marriage. Good day to you both."

Tipping his hat to a speechless Mrs. Beckwith on his way

out of the drawing room, Christopher left the house as quickly as he could.

He'd never felt more relieved in his life.

That same morning Lady Mara Reeves rushed over to Devon House just as soon as she could. She had to find out what had happened to Sara last night. Aunt Juliette and Uncle Harrison had whisked her home before Mara had had a chance to talk to her. When she'd seen Lord Bridgeton, he remained tight-lipped as well and left immediately after the Flemings did, leaving Mara to speculate on what had happened. She had just known something terrible was going to happen that night and she had a feeling it had come to pass.

Mara also sensed by now that Sara was angry with her for telling her parents that Alexander Drake was at the ball. Not only did Mara need to find out what happened to her cousin last night, she needed to apologize to her.

The Devon House butler opened the door and let Mara in. "Good morning, Lady Mara," he greeted her with his usual solemn voice.

"Good morning, Parkins," she said rather hurriedly. "I've come to see Miss Sara."

"I don't believe she's come down yet, my lady," he explained. "Lord and Lady Stancliff and Captain and Mrs. Fleming are breakfasting in the dining room already, if you care to join them."

"Thank you. But I think I shall just go directly up to Sara's room first." This was perfect. Mara could speak to Sara privately this way. She fairly flew up the wide staircase and down the hall to Sara's room.

Knocking softly upon the door, Mara heard only silence from the other side. How could Sara still be sleeping? Filled with impatience, Mara turned the knob and entered the room. Sara wasn't in there and it looked as if the large four-poster bed hadn't been slept in. A dreadful feeling began to overtake Mara.

She reached for the long, tasseled bell cord, ringing for Sara's lady's maid. While waiting for her to arrive, she looked carefully around the room. Boots was gone, but most of Sara's things were just where she would have left them.

Leighton, a sweet blond girl with kind eyes, arrived, looking confused at seeing Mara but not Sara. "Excuse me, my lady, but where is Miss Sara?"

"That's just what I was going to ask you, Leighton," Mara said, knowing instinctively that Sara had gone to Alexander Drake. "When was the last time you saw her?"

"Why, last night before she went to bed, of course," the girl said in a worried tone. "She instructed me not to wake her before noon. It's only just eleven now, your ladyship."

"She didn't say anything to you about going anywhere?"

"Not a word."

"Can you tell me if any of her things are gone?"

The girl looked hurriedly through the wardrobe. "A small valise is missing and some of her personal items."

"Thank you, Leighton. Please don't worry. I think I know where she is." Mara comforted the stricken maid. Then she turned to head downstairs. She had to tell Aunt Juliette and Uncle Harrison that Sara had left.

Just as Mara reached the bottom of the main staircase, Parkins was opening the front door to admit Lord Bridgeton. He looked as if he hadn't slept all night.

"Why, Lord Bridgeton! What on earth are you doing here?" she asked. It was rather early for paying calls. Yet from his manner, she knew a friendly visit was not on his agenda.

"Good morning, Lady Mara," he said quietly. "I've come to discuss something with Captain Fleming."

"Do you have any idea what happened last night?" She rushed over to him, wringing her hands together. "Oh, and I have the most terrible suspicion that Sara ran off with Alexander Drake."

"What?" he said, clearly alarmed, a shocked expression on his face. "You mean to tell me that Sara is not here?"

She shook her head. "No. I just arrived myself, but she's not here. I was just up in her room. Everyone thinks she's still sleeping, but from the looks of things, she hasn't been in her bed all night."

Frowning, he asked, "Where are her parents?"

"Parkins told me everyone is in the dining room having breakfast. Come with me." She grabbed his arm and guided him toward the Devon House dining room. Her heart racing, Mara hoped against hope that Sara hadn't already married Alexander Drake.

Her two aunts and two uncles were having a leisurely breakfast when they interrupted.

"Mara? Lord Bridgeton?" Colette Sinclair looked up from the table as they entered, quite surprised to see them both. She smiled at first, then she saw their faces. "What's wrong?"

"Excuse us for intruding, Auntie, but . . ." Mara took a deep breath. "Aunt Juliette, Uncle Harrison, have you seen Sara yet this morning?"

Harrison Fleming stood up so quickly his chair fell backward, causing both Juliette and Colette to gasp in surprise. "Where is she?"

"That's just it, Uncle Harrison. I don't know," Mara began to explain. "I only arrived a few moments ago to see her. Her room is empty and her bed hasn't been slept in. Leighton said she hasn't seen her since last night. I have a feeling she may have . . ." It was too awful to say the words aloud.

Captain Fleming looked toward Lord Bridgeton. "What do you know of this, Bridgeton?"

Christopher shook his head. "I just arrived myself as I have something very important that I need to discuss with you before Saturday, Captain Fleming. But I'm just as shocked as you are to find Sara gone."

Confused by Lord Bridgeton's statement, Mara looked between him and her uncle. What had happened last night? And what had Saturday to do with anything?

Juliette stood, her face pale. "She's gone to him, hasn't she? She's run off with that awful Alexander Drake."

The room grew quiet as tension mounted and they all feared the worst.

"Let's go get her," Lord Bridgeton declared, his face full of determination. "Let's go after her. Maybe it's not too late to stop them."

"He's right," Lucien Sinclair said, also rising from his seat. "We can try."

Everyone looked at Mara. Juliette asked, "Mara, do you have any idea what their plans were?"

Mara shook her head.

"The investigator told me Drake was staying at the Savoy Hotel," Harrison said in a voice tinged with edginess. "But I doubt they'd still be there at this point. I don't see Drake wasting time. Where were they planning to get married? And where were they going afterward? Do you know, Mara?"

"I'm sorry, Uncle Harrison . . . Sara only talked of them marrying, but she never told me anything specific. Just that Alexander Drake wanted to marry her as quickly as possible."

Harrison scoffed, "Of course he wanted to marry her in a hurry."

Colette offered anxiously, "Well, if they were planning to marry as soon as possible, chances are they've probably left for Gretna Green by now."

"Oh, Harrison, we must stop them!" Juliette cried, looking toward her husband with worried eyes.

"Well, they're two Americans unfamiliar to how things work in England. I don't know if Drake could have gotten a special license while he was here," Harrison said, walking to his wife to comfort her. "They could be marrying anywhere. They're both of age."

Lord Bridgeton, sounding impatient, said, "Let's split up and search the churches in London first." Mara thought he looked quite panicked.

Lucien spoke up. "That's exactly what we shall do. In the meantime, I can also inquire with the archbishop to see if a special license has been issued to Drake. If that's not the case, then we'll head to Gretna Green."

Harrison began to make plans. "Mara, let's send for your father to help us. And we'll get Roxbury and Eddington as well. We should hurry for we've no time to lose."

Phillip and Simon sauntered into the dining room just then, hungry for breakfast. "Good morning, all!" Phillip greeted them with a chipper voice and a smile. Then he stopped short, upon seeing Mara and Lord Bridgeton and everyone's grim faces.

Simon asked with a frown, "What's going on here?"

Captain Fleming spoke up. "Well, boys, it seems that Sara has run off to marry the man from America we were trying to keep her from and we need to go find her, hopefully before it's too late. From what I learned from the investigator I hired, not only is Alexander Drake a heartless fortune hunter, but he is also a common criminal. A jewel thief and a swindler, who has had more than one arrest with the New York and New Jersey police. He may even be violent. And the woman with him is *not* his sister, as they are claiming she is. Her name is Lucy Camden and they are more than . . . merely good friends."

Mara gasped in surprise. "Oh, Uncle Harrison, I saw that

woman! She was in the bookshop yesterday talking with Sara! She told Sara that she was Drake's sister and naturally Sara believed her."

Crestfallen, Juliette placed her hand over her heart. "This is all my fault. Now I wish we had told Sara all of this last night, instead of waiting until today. Now it may be too late."

"It may not be," Lord Bridgeton said. "We have to search for her. Come with me, Waverly."

Mara, appealing to Lord Bridgeton and her cousin, said, "I want to come with you. I can be of help too."

Phillip and Lord Bridgeton exchanged glances with his father.

Lucien looked back at her and said, "All right. Mara, you can go along with Phillip and Lord Bridgeton. But be careful! Simon, you'll be faster at getting the word to Jeffrey, Declan, and Quinton. Let's get going, everyone, we've got a lot of ground to cover."

Mara hurried out of the house, joining her cousin and Lord Bridgeton in his carriage to search for Sara and Alexander Drake before it was too late.

23

All Hands on Deck

"They could be anywhere. This is hopeless," Phillip Sinclair grumbled as the three of them made their way down a busy street after searching a handful of London churches with no luck.

Christopher had been thinking the same thought, but there was something inside of him that would not let him give up. He had to find Sara. He had to. He loved her. She was his now. He'd just given up everything and changed his life for her. She was his. Or at least she would be his on Saturday after he married her. And he'd be damned if he'd allow this lowly American thief to take what belonged to him.

From the moment Christopher had heard the news that Sara had left, he'd been panicked.

Why had Sara run off? Christopher hadn't dared to hope that she was in love with him, but he would have at least hoped she didn't find marriage with him so unappealing that she risked losing her family for this other man. Especially after what they'd done last night and knowing there was a possibility that she was carrying his child. *What was she thinking?* In any case, Christopher was the one who was going to marry her. Not this Drake fellow.

When they reached his carriage, he assisted Lady Mara back inside and he and Phillip climbed in after her.

"Where to now?" Phillip asked, gazing intently out the small window, watching the people on the street, hoping to catch a sight of Sara among them.

The entire Hamilton family had paired off and headed out to search London for her. In fact, Mara's parents, Lord and Lady Cashelmore, had already left for Gretna Green, in case Drake had taken her there. Captain Fleming and Mrs. Fleming had gone straight to the docks to see if perhaps Drake had decided to sail back to New York with her. Lisette and Quinton Roxbury and the Duke and Duchess of Rathmore were searching churches, just as they were, while Lord and Lady Stancliff were checking with the archbishop to see if a special license had been issued. Simon Sinclair was acting as messenger, relaying messages between all of them. It amazed Christopher how strong the familial bond was between them. Not one of them questioned what needed to be done to rescue Sara, they simply did it, because they loved her and she was part of their family.

It stunned him to think that this would become *his* family too when he married Sara. If they found her in time, that was. Yet he couldn't think about that.

"I think there's a little church down this street here," Phillip suggested, his eyes on the buildings ahead. "Do you see that spire? We should look there."

Lady Mara folded her arms in frustration. With her lilting Irish accent she said, "I don't know why we just don't check the Savoy Hotel first. Maybe Uncle Harrison is wrong and they haven't left yet after all. Or maybe the clerk or someone there might have seen or heard where they were going. It certainly couldn't hurt to ask. We may end up with more information than we have right now."

Both Christopher and Phillip stared at her in stunned amazement. Mara was right. Why didn't any of them think to check the hotel first, instead of running around searching churches?

"Lady Mara, you're brilliant. That's exactly what we're going to do," Christopher said. Then he gave directions to the coachman to take them to the Savoy Hotel.

Mara gave them both a disdainful glance. "I said those exact words when we first left Devon House and the two of you ignored me."

Shrugging sheepishly, Phillip apologized. "We men are dolts sometimes, Mara. You know that. We're just too worried about Sara to think straight. We're sorry for not listening to you earlier."

Smiling in satisfaction, Mara said, "I forgive you."

As the carriage headed toward the Savoy, an unsettling thought that had been nagging him since they left Devon House floated to the surface. Christopher questioned the two of them. "May I ask why a fortune hunter would be wanting to marry Sara? It doesn't make sense, if her father no longer has a fortune."

Phillip Sinclair looked at him as if he had two heads. "What the devil are you talking about, Bridgeton?"

"Well, I'd heard that Captain Fleming recently lost all the money he had. That's why they're staying with your family at Devon House," Christopher said. "So if Sara has no fortune to inherit, then why is a fortune hunter so keen to marry her?"

Clearly shocked, Lady Mara's mouth fell open. "Oh, Lord Bridgeton, the Flemings are worth millions and millions of dollars! Sara is an heiress who will inherit all of it. It's the main reason her parents separated her from Alexander Drake. But once they were in London, Uncle Jeffrey thought it would be safer if everyone believed Sara to be penniless, so he started the rumor that Uncle Harrison lost all his money."

Christopher couldn't breathe. It was unbelievable. "You mean Sara *is* an heiress?"

"Yes." Phillip chuckled in amusement. "I thought you knew."

"I'm marrying her on Saturday and I had no idea. Not a clue."

Christopher was stunned by the news. After all that, after everything, Sara was worth millions. After believing he couldn't afford to marry her even though he loved her, after putting himself through the agony of proposing to the likes of Bonnie Beckwith, he could have pursued Sara Fleming all along.

"What did you say, Lord Bridgeton?" Lady Mara cried, her gray-green eyes wide.

"What do you mean you're marrying Sara on Saturday?" Phillip demanded, his expression one of disbelief. "You told me you were engaged to Bonnie Beckwith!"

"You're engaged to Bonnie Beckwith?" Lady Mara stared at him in utter astonishment.

The muddled conversation would have made Christopher laugh if it weren't all so serious, and if he weren't on the verge of losing Sara Fleming forever. He looked at Sara's two cousins staring at him in confusion.

"Well, at the ball last night . . ." Christopher began to explain to them what happened the night before as delicately as he could. "Sara and I were alone in one of the empty rooms, and unfortunately, her parents walked in and caught the two of us . . . in a rather . . . compromising position, shall we say? So as an honorable gentleman I offered for her. Her parents agreed and we planned for the wedding to take place on Saturday. I broke off my engagement to Miss Beckwith first thing this morning. And here we are. I believe you know the rest."

Utterly speechless, Lady Mara covered her mouth with her gloved hand and continued to stare at him, while Phillip broke into a wide grin.

"Well, that is simply fantastic!" he exclaimed happily. "Why didn't you say something to me last night? You and Sara! I knew it! I told you that just the other evening that I wished you would marry my cousin. I'm so relieved you're not marrying that Beckwith chit. You'd have been miserable with her."

"Oh, I'm aware." Christopher shuddered at the idea of Bonnie Beckwith as his bride. Instead, he'd be able to have the life he'd wanted all along. A life with Sara Fleming as his wife. But first he needed to find her. "Lady Mara, are you well?"

Her complexion had gained a little color at his news. But she slowly lowered her hand from her mouth, and smiled shyly at him. "Oh, I'm happy for you, Lord Bridgeton, but it's just that . . ." She broke off, looking a little embarrassed.

"What is it?" he asked.

"Well, it's just that if Sara knew she was going to marry you on Saturday, but she still ran off to be with Drake, I don't believe that that speaks well for your future together, even if we do find her in time," she said with a touch of hesitation.

It was that very thought that he didn't wish to entertain and had ignored all morning. Sara was still in love with Alexander Drake. Even though she kissed Christopher willingly, passionately, and allowed him to make love to her, Sara would still rather marry the American. In spite of knowing that her parents disapproved of the man. That really stung.

Sara Fleming did not love him.

Meanwhile, he was completely and thoroughly head over heels in love with her. And he had fallen in love with Sara Fleming the moment he met her. It just took him a little while to fully realize it.

Christopher looked directly at Mara. "I love Sara, which

is much more than we can say for Drake. I'll take better care of her in that regard." Recalling how Sara melted in his arms and sought his kisses last night, he added, "And I think she cares for me more than she realizes. When we find her, which I have no doubt that we shall, I will marry her. In the end I think we'll be quite happy together."

At least he hoped so.

When the carriage arrived at the grand Savoy Hotel, the three of them hurried through the elegant lobby to the front desk. To their great surprise, it turned out that Mr. Alexander Drake had not yet checked out of the hotel and was still in his room.

"I told you so," Lady Mara could not resist saying to them with great satisfaction.

As they took the electric lift to the fourth floor, Christopher wondered why Drake hadn't fled with Sara in tow. Then an awful thought occurred to him. If Sara had left Devon House early this morning, perhaps they were already married? When they knocked upon the hotel room door, Christopher could discover that Sara was Mrs. Alexander Drake when it opened. His heart sank. But if they hadn't already wed this morning, then what had they been doing at the hotel all day? It was close to two o'clock in the afternoon now.

With his clenched fist, Christopher pounded loudly on the door. Holding his breath, he waited, impatient and angry.

Finally the door opened just a crack. A blond woman peeked out. "Who's there?" she asked suspiciously.

Wasting no time, Christopher shoved the door wide open, sending the woman stumbling backward in surprise with a startled little shriek. Mara gasped in alarm. He continued to push his way into the room, striding forward with Phillip close behind him. Sara's little dog, Boots, yipped vociferously at the intrusion, running around the room, wild with excitement.

Then Christopher saw her.

Sara was seated at a table with who could only be Alexander Drake across from her. They held each other's hands and looked as if they had been deep in conversation, but both looked up in surprise at the sudden and explosive intrusion. Christopher stopped short at the sight.

"What the hell is going on here?" Drake yelled angrily, rising to his feet.

Ignoring him, Christopher only had eyes for Sara. "Did you marry him?"

"What are you doing here?" she cried, shocked by the sight of him and her cousins. And she seemed none too pleased to see the three of them. Boots continued his little barks, scurrying from person to person, excited by the sudden commotion.

The blond woman, who had picked herself up from the floor, glared at Christopher with a disapproving scowl. "This is the man I told you about, Drakey."

Frowning, Alexander Drake ordered, "I don't know who you are or why you're here, but this is my room and I'm ordering all of you to get out! Now!"

Christopher stared at Sara, demanding to know the answer to his question. "Tell me it's not too late, Sara. Are you already married to this man?"

Drake moved toward him, his stance menacing, and pointed at the still open door. "That's none of your business. Now get the hell out of here!"

"We're not going anywhere unless Sara comes with us!" Phillip declared.

Sara rose to her feet, her expression a mixture of worry and annoyance. "Alexander, it's quite all right. Let me handle this, please. These are my cousins, Lady Mara Reeves and Lord Waverly. And that is Lord Bridgeton."

Her words had no effect on the man. Drake stood as if poised for battle, his chest puffed out. So this was the infamous gentleman from New York, the man Sara was madly and foolishly in love with. He didn't seem like all that much. Christopher had to admit the man was good-looking if one liked those golden-haired, boyish types. Although Drake was tall, he was no match for Christopher. There was not a doubt in his mind that he could take Drake if it came to blows. He almost wished it would. A part of him felt ready to smash the fellow's pompous face in and relish doing so.

"What are you doing here?" Sara confronted the three of them, her tone exasperated. To keep Boots from barking she scooped the puppy into her arms, attempting to soothe and quiet him. "There was no need for you to come bursting in like that. As you can see, I'm fine. There's no cause for worry, you know. I can take care of myself."

"Oh, Sara, you mustn't marry him!" Lady Mara blurted out.

Sara's face grew angry. "I can marry whomever I choose." Boots squirmed so much in her arms that she set him down again.

"You're marrying me on Saturday." Christopher's implication was unmistakable, his eyes locked with hers. There was no way she was not marrying him. "Or have you forgotten that little detail, Miss Fleming?"

"I haven't forgotten, *Lord Bridgeton*," she said in a brittle voice and he noted her use of his formal title with a tinge of bitterness. "But *I* never agreed to marry you. My parents made that arrangement *with you*. I was never asked or consulted. I merely was told I had to marry you." She squared her delicate shoulders and took a deep breath. "I'm sorry if you were misled into believing there was to be a wedding

Saturday, Lord Bridgeton, but I'm marrying Alexander tomorrow."

In spite of feeling relief at discovering that she hadn't yet married Drake, something inside of Christopher snapped and anger flooded through him. How dared she spurn him like this? How could she still wish to wed this thief from New York who was only after her for her money? After what happened between the two of them last night in the drawing room? He'd made love to her just a few hours ago, for crying out loud! "You'd marry this man knowing that you may already be carrying my child?"

The room grew suddenly quiet, as the meaning of Christopher's words sank in. Sara stood motionless, her cheeks slowly turning scarlet, as she glared at him. He knew he shouldn't have embarrassed her this way, but he couldn't let her marry Drake. He loved Sara Fleming with all his heart and if there was the slightest chance she was carrying his child there was no way on earth he was going to allow her to marry another man.

Finally breaking the tense silence, the blond woman let out a long, low whistle, as she sauntered over and stood beside Drake. Christopher realized this must be Lucy Camden, the woman posing as Alexander Drake's sister. She was quite attractive in a somewhat coarse way.

Lucy turned to confront them, an amused expression on her face. "Well, well, well. We seem to have a bit of a problem here, don't we? It appears little Miss Fleming isn't so perfect after all . . ."

24

Run Aground

Sara was mortified. Absolutely mortified.

She could barely look at Mara and Phillip, let alone
Alexander. Oh, what Alexander must think of her! Would
he even want to marry her now, suspecting that she was
carrying Lord Bridgeton's child? How dared Christopher
mention what happened between them! Last night wasn't
anyone's business but theirs. And to throw it in her face like
that! As if it didn't mean anything. Stung by his cruel cal-
lousness, Sara blinked back tears, replacing them with
outrage. She would not cry . . .

What was Christopher thinking anyway? Coming here
and bursting in on her this way! Who did he think he was?
Why, she'd only just arrived at the hotel herself not a half
hour ago. She and Alexander were just getting reac-
quainted and making plans to travel to Gretna Green first
thing tomorrow.

As soon as she'd snuck out of Devon House that morning,

she'd realized that it was far too early to show up at Drake's hotel. At the ball last night, Alexander had told her to come to the hotel this afternoon and she agreed. As much as she longed to be with him, a lady could not just arrive at a hotel at the break of dawn and ask for a gentleman's room! Sara had her standards, in spite of everything. After walking aimlessly for a few blocks and not knowing where else to go, she suddenly recalled that she had a key to the Hamilton Sisters' Book Shoppe in her reticule.

With great pride Aunt Colette had presented the key to her just last week, as a gift, welcoming Sara into the family business. So this morning Sara had unlocked the door and let herself into the empty shop, since it was far too early to be open. Sara crept upstairs to Aunt Paulette's private office, which had a wonderfully soft sofa. Exhausted from the events of the masked ball and not having slept all night, she lay down among the velvety cushions with a blanket and little Boots snuggled beside her, and quickly fell into a deep and dreamless sleep.

Sara awoke a little after noon, feeling, if not better for having slept for almost six hours, then definitely more awake. Everything that had happened last night with Christopher now seemed like a faraway dream. Could she simply brush it away like the wispy clouds of a reverie? Could she just erase it from her memory and pretend it never happened? Well, she would have to do so to marry Alexander.

Sara fed Boots some small scraps of chicken she'd packed in her bag for him, but she didn't eat anything herself. She was far too nervous, wondering if her family had discovered she was gone yet and imagining how it would feel when she saw Alexander Drake again. Using the small stove and kettle in the office, she made herself some tea and hoped it would calm her somewhat. After freshening herself up, she quietly let herself out of the store, ignoring the raised eyebrows of the shop assistants who were now busy running the bookshop.

When she arrived at the Savoy Hotel, she bore the disapproving scowl of the hotel manager, who pursed his lips in distaste, but told her Alexander's room number even though he clearly didn't believe he should tell her. Her stomach fluttered during her ride in the electric lift knowing her life together with Alexander Drake would begin in a matter of moments.

He and his sister Lucy were warm and welcoming to her. Alexander had placed a sweet kiss on her cheek and took her hand, telling her he'd never been so happy to see anyone in his life. While Lucille played with Boots, Sara and Alexander had sat down together to talk. He'd been sweet and romantic to her, saying everything she needed to hear.

"I've dreamed of this moment, my dearest Sara, when you would be with me again." His blue eyes sparkled and he looked at her longingly. "I won't rest easily until we're safely married, then no one can ever take you from me again."

"Oh, I've missed you so, Alexander," she murmured, suddenly feeling shy and awkward with him.

"And I've missed you, my darling. Seeing you at the ball last night was like seeing a vision. I'd almost forgotten how beautiful you are," he whispered low.

She squeezed his hands. "Oh, Alexander."

"Does anyone know where you are?" he asked.

She shook her head. She had been very careful about that. "No. I didn't tell anyone where you were staying and no one saw me leave the house."

He seemed to visibly relax at that bit of news. "Then we shall hire a carriage and leave for Gretna Green first thing in the morning. I'll feel safer once we're legally wed. Then no one can ever take you away from me, my lovely. Once we're married, we'll confront your parents and it will be too late for them to do anything about it." Alexander smiled slowly. "You can stay here with me tonight."

Well, she really didn't have much of a choice now, did she? Sara had left the security of her home and family and hadn't thought further ahead than that. Her eyes drifted to the large four-poster bed draped with velvet curtains. Feeling slightly embarrassed at the thought of spending the night here with Alexander, she suggested, "Perhaps it might be best if I stay with your sister in her room? Until we're married . . ."

"Forgive me for being impatient, my love. I didn't mean to suggest that . . . But then we can discuss it later." He eyed her carefully, but smiled.

"If Sara likes, she can stay in my room and I can stay in here with you, Alexander," Lucy called.

Unaware that his sister had been listening to their conversation, Sara glanced over to see Lucy seated on the floor, playing tug of war with Boots. There was something about the woman that left Sara feeling uneasy. For all of Lucy's show of friendly helpfulness and sisterly support of their situation, there was an air of disdain about her, or a sense of superiority, as if she knew something that Sara didn't. The uneasiness just increased after her remark about sharing a room with her brother. Sara also could not shake the feeling that she had met the woman before, but where and when she could not recall.

"We'll discuss the sleeping arrangements later, Lucy dear," Alexander said with a bit of an edge to his voice. He took Sara's hand in his, and brought it to his lips, pressing a kiss to her fingers. "Now, Sara darling, I need to ask you something rather unpleasant. Have you any money with you?"

"Money?" she asked, stunned by the sudden change of

topic, and a slight shiver ran down her spine. Was this what her parents predicted? Her heart dropped to her toes.

"Money. Such a distasteful subject, isn't it?" He flashed her his most winning smile. "I'm sorry to bring it up, you see, but this hotel is very expensive and I can't draw on my funds in New York until next week. But never you mind. Don't worry your pretty little head about anything as sordid as money, my darling. As your husband, I will see that you are always well taken care of."

A very small alarm bell began to ring in the back of Sara's mind and she recalled her conversation with Uncle Jeffrey. "Alexander," she began slowly. He still held her hands. "We've never discussed my money before . . ."

"Yes, of course I realize that. But certainly you must be aware that I don't possess nearly the amount of money that your family does. No one does! But none of that matters in the least to me, darling. You know I would love you just the same if you hadn't a penny to your name." He gave her hands a little squeeze.

"And I would love you the same if you hadn't any money," she said. Now was the time to say it. She paused, feeling a little nervous. "But I should let you know that my parents are still quite against our marrying each other. They made it very clear that they would disinherit me if we wed, leaving me without a cent to my name."

"Your parents can't do that!" Lucy cried in outrage.

Sara gave the girl a pointed look, wishing her to stay out of her conversation with Alexander. This had nothing to do with Lucy.

"Surely they are just threatening you, Sara. They love you too much to do something so dreadful to you," he said, a slight hint of worry in his eyes.

"They are not just threatening me. My father means it. I won't get a cent. But that's all right with you, isn't it, Alexander?" she questioned him, hoping against hope that he really meant that he would love her even if she hadn't a fortune. "You make more than enough to support us, don't you?"

Her words were just registering on his face when there was a loud banging on the hotel room door. Lucy hurried to answer it, and that's when Lord Bridgeton burst into the room with Phillip and Mara. Just as Sara was about to learn what Alexander was going to say about her inheritance, their moment was ruined!

Ruined by Christopher Townsend and his imperious demands that she marry him and shaming her in front of everyone. Lucy's snide comments about her innocence added insult to injury. Now they all stood in the hotel room in complete silence, the implications of Christopher's words quite clear.

Finally Alexander questioned her in an icy voice, "Sara, is what this man says about you true?"

With great reluctance, Sara nodded, meeting Alexander's gaze with unflinching honesty.

A confused expression on his face, Alexander murmured, "In spite of your inconstant behavior, I shall forgive you, Sara. I still want to marry you more than anything in the world."

Sara stared at him. Alexander still wanted her to be his wife even though she had been unfaithful to him, and he believed that her parents would disinherit her.

"Of course he still wants to marry you, Sara. He's a lowly thief and a fortune hunter and you're the greatest prize he could ever hope to steal," Christopher declared.

Instinctively Sara defended her future husband. "He is *not* a fortune hunter!" Still, something about the entire situation was not quite right. She couldn't pinpoint what it was. Just a feeling that something was wrong.

"How dare you say such things about my brother!" Lucy exclaimed heatedly.

"And this woman is most definitely *not* his sister," Christopher stated emphatically. "Are you, *Miss Camden*?"

Sara's heart skipped a beat and she whipped around to stare at Lucy. *Lucy Camden*. There was something about that name . . . *Miss Camden*. Somewhere in the back of her mind a memory was awakening. Where had she heard it before? If she was not Alexander's sister, then who was this very beautiful woman? What was she to Alexander and why was she here in London with him? A sick feeling of dread as thick as syrup seeped through her veins as unthinkable and indecent images found their way into her mind.

Lucy placed her hands on her hips in righteous indignation, her pretty face full of scorn. "I am Lucille Drake, Alexander's sister!"

Mara, who had been standing there quietly holding Boots in her arms, finally spoke up. In her soft Irish accent she said, "This woman is definitely not his sister, Sara. Your father hired an investigator to look into his background and he followed them here to London. I know you don't wish to hear this, but it's the truth. The man is a thief and he *is* only after your fortune." Mara gestured toward Alexander. "Why don't we have Mr. Drake explain who this woman is to him?"

"It's not true!" The desperate words rushed from Sara's lips, even though the inevitability of their truth belied their meaning. This had all turned into a terrible, terrible nightmare.

Alexander and Lucy remained silent, as if assessing the situation.

"It is true, Sara," Phillip said, not unkindly and looking at her most earnestly. "If it weren't true, I would wish you well in marrying this man, if it was what you wanted. I only want you to be happy. But my sweet American little cousin, Drake is lying to you."

If what her cousins were telling her were true, the money was one thing. Sara could almost accept that. It *was* a lot of money. She wasn't naïve enough to expect a man to not want that much money. But this other woman . . . that was something else entirely. If Alexander came to London to marry her, with this Lucy Camden or Lucille Drake or whoever she was, pretending to be his sister but in reality she was actually his . . . his mistress! Well, *that* was more than Sara could bear.

That meant that Alexander Drake really did not love her after all.

There were definitely lies involved. And Sara had no choice but to believe Alexander was the one lying. Her parents would never make this up. Phillip and Mara wouldn't lie to her about something like this. Christopher wouldn't either.

Trembling, Sara turned again to look at Alexander's face. The boyish, handsome face she had loved for so many months. "Who is she?" she whispered, barely able to breathe.

"It's not what you think, Sara," Alexander began with another of his charming smiles. "Please let me explain to you, my darling. Everything has been exaggerated and blown out of proportion. I'm not a thief! The very idea is ridiculous! I never took anyone's jewels. It was all an innocent misunderstanding. I'm a lawyer, Sara! You know that. Your parents know that. I couldn't do anything against the law! And admittedly, no, Lucy is not my sister. Not really. But our families were very close growing up and she has been *like* a sister to me. She only wants my happiness, our happiness, and she agreed to come to London with me, because she understands just how much I want to marry you. That's all." He paused, letting his words sink in.

Then Alexander continued smoothly. "As for the fortune hunter business, I've already told you that I grew up poor, on a farm in New Jersey. Unlike you, I didn't come from money. But just like your own father, I've worked very hard to get where I am, Sara. I put myself through college and obtained my law degree. Someday I plan to earn a lot of money to support you, but at the moment, I don't have much. Is that a crime? No. Should I have brought that fact to your attention sooner? Yes, but your parents whisked you away before I could properly state my case. Was I embarrassed by my financial situation compared to yours? Absolutely. It's not an easy thing for a man to admit. Will your money, your millions, be much appreciated and put to good use until I can support us in style? Yes, of course. If that makes me a fortune hunter, then so be it."

Again Alexander smiled at her, that familiar golden smile that made her heart melt the day she had fallen in love with him that very first afternoon in Central Park. He'd gallantly rescued her and made her heart sing. Oh, how she longed to believe him! His words seemed to make sense. Almost rang true. She could quite easily slip under his spell again . . . and believe that everyone else was wrong about him. Her parents. The investigator. Her cousins. Christopher.

But she suddenly saw Lucy's smug expression, and recalled her odd comment about sharing the room with Alexander tonight. She eyed the woman again. Carefully.

Lucy stood there with that scornful, slightly mocking look, almost as if she were daring Sara to believe that she was Alexander's sister. Nothing about her conveyed the air of a supporting and loving sister. No, there was a mixture of possessiveness and jealousy in those brittle blue eyes. A woman's instinct, an intuition, a deep knowing told her that Lucy Camden was, indeed, Alexander's mistress and had been all along.

Alexander had lied to her. About everything.

It was suddenly crystal clear.

As cold realization dawned, her blood ran hot with anger. Sara had been made a fool of by the man she had loved with all her heart, the man she wanted to spend the rest of her life with. The man she was defying her parents to be with.

He never really loved her.

If he really loved her he would have been hurt, jealous, and angry with her to discover that she had been unfaithful to him with Lord Bridgeton. Instead, he acted quite calm. As if it didn't matter that she could be carrying another man's child. His love for her was all an act to convince her to marry him. A ploy to seduce her for her great fortune.

A ghastly thought occurred to her then. What would have happened after tomorrow? After she married him? He was still going to keep Lucy with them, to flaunt her right under Sara's nose, allowing her to continue to believe that Lucy was his sister, wasn't he?

It was that moment when she stepped toward Alexander Drake and struck him across the face with all the force she could muster. Her hand made a satisfying smack against the smooth flesh of his cheek. She saw the shock register in his eyes, which immediately flashed with wild rage. Just as she withdrew her hand, he grabbed her by the wrist, holding her in a viselike grip to prevent her from attacking again. Alexander began to twist her arm behind her back.

Before Sara knew what was happening, she sensed the commanding presence of Christopher Townsend behind her. With a yelp, Alexander released her hand just as Christopher punched Alexander squarely in the face. The sickening crunch of bone reverberated around her as she turned in time to see Alexander fall backward and land on the floor with a heavy thud, his face covered with blood.

Lucy screeched in horror and dropped to his side, calling, "Drakey!"

"If you ever put your hands on her again, I will do more than break your nose. I'll kill you," Christopher threatened in an icy voice, acting every inch the Earl of Bridgeton. He pulled Sara into his arms, holding her tenderly. "Did he hurt you?"

Stunned and still angry, she shook her head. The warmth

and security of Christopher's strong arms around her almost made her cry.

"Oh, Christopher," she murmured, resting her head against his broad chest. "Let's get out of here."

"I hate you, Sara Fleming!" Lucy suddenly screamed, rising to her feet. "From the moment I met you last summer, I've hated you!"

Turning her head, Sara stared at Lucy, as a foggy image began to form. "Last summer?"

"You have had everything handed to you on a silver platter and it's not fair. You're spoiled and self-centered and you always get everything you want!" Lucy cried. "You couldn't even remain faithful to Alexander, could you? You're so selfish and stuck up, you don't even remember meeting me in Newport, do you?"

It was then a dim memory arose within her. Sara had spent last summer in Newport with her friend Amanda Ellsworth. Lucy had been a servant at the house. That was it! That was where Sara had seen her before! Lucy was the companion of Amanda's grandmother, Margaret Ellsworth, who had been ill and confined to a wheelchair. Searching her memories, she could recall seeing Lucy sitting with the elderly woman on the terrace once, and thinking to herself that the young woman looked quite unhappy. They must have been introduced to each other at one point, but Sara couldn't recall the exact moment. She had spent most of her time in Newport preoccupied with a devastated Amanda, who was recovering from being jilted by her fiancé.

But there had been some incident while she was at the house in Newport. What was it? Again Sara reached into her memories from almost a year ago. There had been a lovely garden party one afternoon with hundreds of guests and Amanda's pearl necklace had been stolen.

Sara narrowed her eyes at Lucy. "Oh, I remember you now, Miss Camden."

"It's not fair that you rich girls get everything and other girls get nothing!" Lucy's voice was full of bitterness and venom. "Other girls have to work their whole lives, for miserable old crones, for a pittance. While you get pretty new gowns and expensive jewels and are waited on hand and foot and get to go to fancy parties. It's just not fair!"

Slowly Sara said, "You hate me for that, but you don't even know me."

"Of course I hate you!" Lucy spat out.

"Lucy, stop," Alexander mumbled, with his hand covering his blood-streaked face.

Trying to comprehend what was happening, Sara asked them, "So you and Alexander came up with this plan to fool me into marrying him?"

"And you fell for it, you vain little twit!" Lucy grinned wickedly. "You think you're so smart. So high and mighty! We had you convinced that Alexander loved you, when it's me he really loves! Yes, I'm the one he loves. And when you married him, we were still going to be together. He was going to set me up in a fine house and buy me everything I wanted and all the time I'd know that I'd be hurting you and making your life miserable."

The vitriol with which Lucy's words were spoken unsettled Sara. Someone she barely knew hated her and wanted to deliberately hurt her because of what she had. "You want the things I have? Is that why you steal jewelry? Like a pearl necklace?"

"I don't steal," Lucy hissed, her face a mask of bitter resentment. "I take what I *deserve* to have."

"Well then," Sara said, gesturing to Alexander with disgust. "You can take *him*. He's all yours. I don't want him anymore. You are absolutely right, Lucy. You deserve him. You both deserve each other."

"I hate you!" Lucy cried, dropping back down to sit beside Alexander.

"Let's go home, Sara," Christopher said, gently guiding her toward the door. "We'll alert the authorities that two American thieves are in this room when we get downstairs."

They left Alexander Drake lying on the expensively carpeted hotel room floor with blood streaming from his nose, and a despondent Lucy Camden seated beside him.

25

Safe Harbor

Back at Devon House again, Sara spent the rest of the night explaining to her parents the events of the last hours with Alexander Drake. And apologizing. She apologized to her parents for the way she had acted. She apologized to her aunts and uncles for causing them so much worry and trouble. And she apologized to her cousins. Embarrassed and rather humiliated, Sara felt like a great fool. Although her parents were more than relieved to have their daughter safely home again, there was no doubt that Sara was still in disgrace over her recent behavior.

During the carriage ride home with Phillip, Mara, and Christopher after leaving the Savoy Hotel, Sara had remained silent, unable to discuss anything with her cousins or Lord Bridgeton. She simply had too many tumultuous thoughts racing through her mind to speak, as she tried to come to grips with the fact that her courtship with Alexander Drake had all been a ruse for him and Lucy Camden to get their hands on her fortune. Not only had Alexander not loved her, he had deliberately plotted and schemed with another woman to dupe her into marrying him.

Deeply hurt and undeniably angry, it was almost too much to bear.

Six months ago, Sara had innocently fallen in love with a dashing and handsome stranger who gallantly came to her assistance one fall afternoon, not having a clue that the whole thing was prearranged and orchestrated to take advantage of her. She had given Alexander her heart and he had manipulated her.

Heartsick and furious at having been so misled by Alexander Drake, Sara retired to her room and spent the night crying in bed. She didn't cry so much for losing Alexander, but for being so easily tricked by him and Lucy. The spiteful words Lucy had flung at Sara had stung as well, because they bore a mark of truth.

Was Sara so vain and foolish, so self-centered and used to getting her own way, that she had been so gullible and smoothly taken in by Alexander's captivating and charming ways? It certainly seemed that way. Perhaps that awful Lucy Camden was right after all. Sara had had everything she wanted handed to her quite easily all her life, and the first time that she didn't was when her parents whisked her away from Alexander. And her parents had been right, while Sara had acted like a spoiled child, pouting and angry because she wasn't getting her way.

It wasn't her fault that her father made millions of dollars, but looking back over her life, perhaps she *had* spent more than a lot of her time and money on frivolous pursuits like acquiring expensive and fashionable clothing and attending social events in New York. She thought only of herself. It was only when they'd arrived in London that Sara had worked in the bookshop. And she had simply done it for fun. As a lark. Not taking into consideration that so many of the women who worked at their jobs had no choice but to work to earn their money to survive.

Sara was very lucky, indeed. And she had not been very grateful for all that she had. Instead she complained about being an heiress.

More than feeling like a fool, she felt truly ashamed of her behavior. From the way she treated her parents to how she ran away and caused her entire family to worry about her, to how she had behaved with Lord Bridgeton the night before.

Christopher Townsend.

She had behaved dreadfully with him and treated him terribly as well.

She hadn't seen Christopher since he'd brought her home from the hotel, but according to her parents their wedding was still set for Saturday. The day after tomorrow she would become Lady Bridgeton. The thought sobered her, for she could not imagine what her life would be like now that she would remain in England. Mixed feelings for him and their impending marriage were just as confusing.

After a fitful sleep and a long night of tossing and turning, Sara arose early the next morning. She dressed in a soft pink gown with her hair simply arranged and headed downstairs to breakfast, leaving Boots with Leighton. To her surprise, Parkins told her that Lord Bridgeton had just arrived and was in the library with her parents. What was Christopher doing here so early? Why had she not been called to join them? Sara hurried down the hallway and flung open the library door.

"Sara!" her mother called in surprise, looking up from where she sat on the sofa. Her father and Lord Bridgeton stood before the mantel. "We thought you were still asleep."

Sara stared at her parents and Lord Bridgeton, curious as to why he was here and why she was not being included in this little gathering which she was certain had some bearing on her future.

Her father said, "Sara, could you please excuse us? Lord Bridgeton has something he wishes to discuss with your mother and me."

"I'd prefer to stay, if you don't mind," she said softly.

"Actually, Captain Fleming, it might be best for Sara to hear what I have to say to you," Christopher said, his expression grim. "This affects her as well."

Although his tone was rather somber and she worried what he might be sharing with them, Sara was pleased that he wanted to include her. She gave him a hesitant smile, which he did not return. Christopher looked as handsome as ever though, tall and commanding. He'd been quite forceful with her yesterday at the Savoy Hotel and had surprised her by trouncing Alexander so soundly while protecting her.

Her father agreed. "Very well. Please join us, Sara."

She moved quickly to the sofa to sit beside her mother.

Christopher nodded to her. "I was just about to tell your parents the reason why I asked them to meet with me." He looked to Sara's father. "I had wanted to say this to you yesterday and it was why I was at Devon House when we discovered that Sara had left. But with the events that followed, we never had time to talk. So here I am."

Sara and her parents looked at him expectantly. She couldn't imagine what all this was about. And to think she would have missed it, if she had stayed in bed! What on earth did Christopher have to say? Was he going to announce that he didn't wish to marry her after all? Was that it? Her heart skittered in her chest.

Christopher cleared his throat. "Captain Fleming, the other evening when you discovered your daughter with me, I told you I was already engaged. Which I was. To Miss Bonnie Beckwith." Briefly his eyes flashed to Sara. "I told you I would break off my engagement with her first thing the following morning. Which I did. I am now free to marry your daughter as we arranged. However, I must tell you why I was engaged to Miss Beckwith in the first place."

Her mother laughed lightly and waved her hand. "Really, Lord Bridgeton, that is not necessary for you to share with us."

"I'm afraid it is most necessary," he said, looking solemn.

Sara was on pins and needles. Since the other night she had wondered why on earth Christopher had been engaged to the likes of Bonnie Beckwith and wondered why he had kept it a secret from her. She couldn't imagine that he loved the girl.

Christopher looked directly at Sara with his chocolate brown eyes. "You see, Miss Beckwith is an heiress."

Sara sucked in her breath at his words and it felt as if both her parents did too. She had not been at all aware that Bonnie Beckwith was an heiress.

"I was not in love with her, nor did I even like her, to be brutally honest," Christopher said, looking humble. "I was simply marrying her for her money."

"I see," her father said with a frown.

Confused by what he was saying, Sara stared at him, still wondering why.

Somberly, Christopher continued to explain. "My father died over a year ago and when he died, I inherited his earldom, his title, and the family estate. I also inherited a mountain of my father's debts, a grand but crumbling manor house in dire need of extensive repairs, and two younger sisters and my mother to look after and care for." He turned toward her mother. "In England, as you know, Mrs. Fleming, a gentleman such as myself, an earl, is not expected to work for a living nor are we trained to do anything but manage our own estate, provided the money is there to do so. Consequently, the only options available to me were to sell my birthright or acquire a wealthy wife. Bonnie Beckwith solved this problem for me and her parents were thrilled to have their daughter marry a penniless earl in exchange for her becoming a countess. In the meantime, I met and fell in love with your lovely daughter."

Christopher paused, gazing briefly at her, and Sara's heart skipped a beat. He was in love with her?

"Yes," Christopher admitted, "I think I fell in love with Sara that first day she arrived in London and I met her here in this house. I was completely unaware that she was an heiress. As a matter of fact, I was told that you had lost all your money, Captain Fleming, and were in rather dire straits." He looked to her father.

Harrison said with a regretful grin, "Yes, that was my brother-in-law's idea to protect Sara while she was in England."

"So you can see why I believed that I could never marry her, even though I wanted to, because I had a duty to save my family first. Information that I did not share with Sara," Christopher said. "However, Sara and I managed to find ourselves growing closer, and then, the night before last, you happened upon us."

Heat flooded Sara's cheeks at the memory of the night in the drawing room and she avoided looking at her parents.

"Naturally, I asked for Sara's hand, not only because it was the honorable thing to do, but because I love her," Christopher continued. "Yet I was in a quandary because, not aware that Sara was an heiress, I realized by ending my engagement with Bonnie Beckwith, I would be forfeiting my last chance to save my home and my family."

"Oh, Christopher," she whispered, her eyes searching his face.

Once again, Sara felt like a selfish little fool. How on earth had she not known this? How had she not known that Christopher was in such an awful position? The night of the masked ball all she had thought about was herself and how *she* was humiliated and not being given a say in her own life. Not once had she given any consideration to what Christopher had been feeling. She had been just as culpable as he was the night he took her innocence. Yet while Sara had been furious at being obligated to marry him, when she really wanted to be with Alexander, she never once stopped to think about what their sudden and forced marriage was doing to Christopher.

Sara stared at him, riveted.

"Yesterday morning, as I promised, I ended my engagement with Bonnie Beckwith. I also put Bridgeton Hall up for sale and inquired into a few positions with a banker whom I know and a few other friends, hoping to find gainful employment to support my mother, my sisters . . . and my new wife. Then I came straight over here, to speak to you about this, Captain Fleming. I thought you needed to know that although you believed your daughter was to be wed to a wealthy British earl, I am, in fact, quite broke." Christopher paused, his eyes finally meeting hers. "As much as I love Sara and truly wish for her to be my wife, I couldn't foresee her living the simple life I could provide for her. In spite of what happened between us the other night, I wanted to give Sara the option to decline my offer of marriage."

They all remained silent.

Sara could barely breathe. Christopher had given up everything to marry her. Everything. He'd lost his ancestral home and had given up securing a fortune, believing Sara had nothing, and still he was willing to wed her without the slightest protest. He was prepared to work to support her. Touched beyond measure at his incredible sacrifice, she didn't know what to say. She suddenly thought of Evelyn and Gwyneth Townsend and how lucky they were to have a brother who cared for them so much.

Christopher continued, "But when I arrived at Devon House yesterday morning to tell you all of this, Captain Fleming, it was to discover that Sara had fled. My only thought after that was to help find her and to make sure she was safe and unharmed. During our search, Lady Mara told me that Sara was a wealthy heiress. Imagine my surprise." Christopher shook his head in disbelief. "So, I'm here today to explain all of this to you. And I still would like to give Sara the opportunity to decline my offer. I know that she loves another man, in spite of what happened between us. I don't wish for her to marry me if that is not what she wants."

Her parents were silent. Sara could not breathe or speak. Her heart was too full. For an entire minute, no one uttered a single word.

Finally Captain Fleming cleared his throat. "Well, Lord Bridgeton, I don't know what to say."

"Thank you for sharing all of that with us," Juliette said softly, her expression full of sympathy. "It can't have been easy. But it helps clear up some questions I had about the two of you as well." She looked toward Sara.

Sara stared at her hands in her lap, her fingers clenched tightly together, tension running through her entire body. She could not even look at him. She didn't know what to do or say. She felt like screaming. Or crying. She willed the tears not to come but they stung her eyes. When was he planning to explain this to her? He had come here to tell her parents and Sara just happened to stumble into the library. What if she hadn't come downstairs this morning? When was Christopher going to talk to her about any of this?

"I'm willing to do whatever Sara wishes," he stated calmly.

"Lord Bridgeton, perhaps you could give Sara, and give us, a little time to discuss this privately first?" Juliette asked.

"Yes, of course," Christopher said with a nod. "I shall take my leave of you now and return tomorrow, if that suits you?"

"Yes, that will be fine. Thank you," Juliette said, looking curiously between him and Sara.

He thanked them and exited the library.

Meanwhile, Sara had avoided his eyes and could not watch him leave.

26

Coming Around

"You mean we are really selling Bridgeton Hall, Kit?" Evelyn asked, her brown eyes wide with astonishment.

"Yes," Christopher explained to his sisters at the Townsend town house later that night. "It's the best solution. We'll have some money to live on from the sale of the estate, and once I am gainfully employed I can support us."

"I'm just so relieved that you're not marrying that horrid Bonnie Beckwith, that I don't care what happens to us," Gwyneth added, a smile on her sweet face.

The three Townsend siblings sat in the main drawing room before the fire later that evening after he'd spoken with the Flemings. A heavy rain was coming down outside and Christopher had just explained his recent plans to his sisters. He had specifically omitted his engagement to Sara, since he was not certain what their state of affairs was after he left Devon House. Would there still be a marriage between Sara and him after all? In the meantime, his sisters had been relieved that he'd ended things with Bonnie Beckwith, as he knew they would be.

Even though he had originally intended for them to stay in London only for a few days, a month had now passed. Evelyn and Gwyneth were enjoying life in the city more than he had expected, and he couldn't bear to send them back to their mother at Bridgeton Hall.

"If things go well with the sale of the estate, maybe we could simply lease a little town house like this in London," he suggested to them.

"I would love to live in London!" Evie cried with glee. "Perhaps we can even have Mother go live with her older sister in Scotland. How wonderful that would be!" She waved the letter they had just received from their mother, demanding that the girls return to Bridgeton Hall immediately.

"It's certainly a possibility, for Mother can't very well stay at Bridgeton Hall when it's sold." Christopher smiled, caught up in his sister's enthusiasm. A new sense of freedom had taken over him since he made the decision to end the engagement with Bonnie Beckwith and sell the estate. Once his father's debts had been cleared, he wouldn't be beholden to anyone anymore. He would be a free man. It was quite a novel feeling. The fact that his sisters were supportive of his decision made him feel even better.

"Excuse me, my lord," said the butler, entering the drawing room. "There is a Miss Fleming here to see you."

Christopher stood up in surprise. Sara was here? At this late hour? Glancing at the clock, he saw that it was well past nine. After he left Devon House early that morning, he didn't think he'd hear from the Flemings again today. What was Sara thinking coming here at this time of night? Did her parents know she was at his house? Somehow he doubted it.

"Miss Fleming is here?" Evie asked, her eyes dancing,

obviously thrilled by this development. "Please, by all means, show the lady in, Jensen."

The young man paused. "Shall I serve tea, my lady?"

"No, I don't think that shall be necessary," Christopher said, recovering from his surprise. Sara was here. At his house.

Gwyneth smiled in satisfaction. "What is Miss Fleming coming to see you about, Christopher?"

"I'm not quite sure, but I would ask you both to give us some privacy, would you?" he asked his sisters.

Evelyn and Gwyneth exchanged amused glances. "Perhaps," Evie said with a mischievous smile.

"Now, listen you two, Miss Fleming may need to discuss some things of a personal nature with me, so I'd like—"

"Good evening. I apologize for the late hour."

Sara Fleming stood in the doorway of the drawing room. Wearing the same simple pink gown she had on earlier this morning, she had a thick shawl wrapped around her shoulders to protect her from the rain. Her hair was loose and damp and not covered by a bonnet. She looked as if she had just run right out of the house. Her blue eyes bright, she appeared more naturally beautiful and alluring in her simplicity than she had in her most stylish and elegant gown. His heart pounding, Christopher couldn't look away from her.

"Miss Fleming!" Both Evie and Gwyneth exclaimed in delight.

"It's so wonderful to see you," Evelyn said, welcoming her in. "Won't you please come and join us? Have a seat over here by me."

"Thank you." Sara seemed hesitant, but made her way over to the sofa where Evelyn was seated. With a brief glance at him she said, "I bet you're all wondering what I'm doing here so late."

"The thought has crossed my mind," Christopher quipped, still standing near the fireplace.

"It is a rather rainy night to be out . . ." Gwyneth said.

Sara turned to his sisters with a warm smile and a bit of a conspiratorial look. "Lady Evelyn and Lady Gwyneth, would you mind giving your brother and me a moment alone together? I have something private that I must discuss with him."

"Why, of course!" Evie exclaimed. "Come, Gwyneth. We were just saying how tired we were and that it was past time for bed. Won't you please excuse us, Miss Fleming?"

The drawing room grew silent after his two sisters left.

Christopher stared at Sara with an expectant look. "So exactly what are you doing here, at this hour, on a night like this?"

She gazed up at him from her seat on the sofa, her blue eyes warm and appealing. "I had to see you."

"And it couldn't wait for a more civilized hour?"

She shook her head, her dark wavy tresses spilling over her shoulders. "I needed to see you right now."

He looked at her with a bit of worry. "Do your parents know that you are here?"

"No." Sara shook her head again. "They think I'm asleep in my room."

Christopher ran his hand over his face. "It's a wonder they don't keep you under lock and key."

Sara smiled at him with a wicked gleam in her eyes. "But they don't."

"Well, they should. How did you even get here? It's pouring out!"

"Phillip took me in the carriage."

"Waverly. Of course." None of this made any sense. "Where is the esteemed Phillip Sinclair, Earl of Waverly, right now?"

Sara shrugged, the shawl falling from her shoulders. "On his way to his club, I would assume."

"Your cousin just left you here?" he asked in disbelief.

What on earth was Waverly thinking? Or Sara, for that matter? Coming here like this?

"Yes, he did. I asked him to."

Her matter-of-fact answer unnerved him. "Remind me to have a little chat with Waverly the next time I see him. In the meantime I feel that I'm going to need a drink this evening." Christopher sighed heavily and strode to the liquor cabinet. Sara's showing up at his house could only spell trouble. With her he never knew how things would turn out. He poured two glasses of brandy from the decanter. He walked back to the sofa and handed one of the glasses to Sara. Hers had half the amount of brandy in it as his did. He quipped, "I also have a feeling you need this as much as I do, but I don't want you falling asleep on me either."

"Thank you." She took the glass from him while appearing slightly abashed at the mention of the last time they had brandy together.

He noticed that her hand trembled slightly as she reached for the brandy. So . . . his little Sara was nervous, was she? He sat down beside her on the sofa. "Well, Miss Captain's Daughter, what is so important that you snuck out of the house in the rain at this late hour to see me?" he asked.

She sipped her brandy first. "I needed to apologize to you."

"Oh?" This ought to be interesting.

"I want to apologize to you for so many things, I'm not sure where to start."

He drank some of his brandy. "Go ahead." This evening was eerily reminiscent of the night of the storm in the Devon House library. The rain. The brandy. The two of them alone, talking earnestly.

Sara paused, and looked toward him, her eyes tinged with regret. "Christopher, I am so very sorry for everything I've done wrong. I'm sorry for being a selfish brat and only thinking of myself. I'm sorry most of all for running off to marry Alexander after you asked to marry me. I'm sorry you gave up everything to marry me, although what you did touched my heart more than you can ever know. I'm very sorry I had no idea what a difficult financial position you were in and I'm sorry you felt you couldn't share that with me. I'm sorry for worrying you and making you run around town looking for me. And I am very sorry for not being able to say any of this to you when you were at Devon House this morning. But I'm also not sorry."

"Not sorry for what?" he asked, intrigued by her mood and moved by her sweet apologies.

"Well, I'm not sorry you found me at the hotel and kept me from marrying him. I'm not sorry that you stopped Alexander from hitting me. I'm not sorry that you hit him so hard that you broke his nose." Sara's voice caught a little and she took a breath. "I'm not sorry that we made love that night. I'm not sorry that you said you loved me. And I'm not sorry that you asked me to marry you."

Christopher reached out and brushed away a stray tendril of hair from her cheek. "You're not?"

She shook her head before taking a sip of the brandy. "No. I'm not sorry for any of those things."

He asked the question that had haunted him since he had known her. "And so do you still love Alexander?"

"No." Her eyes met his. "All this time I think I was only infatuated with him and the idea of him. But no, I don't love him. I thought I did, but I was mistaken."

"And seeing him yesterday?" Christopher couldn't forget the worry in his heart yesterday as they searched for her. The fear that Sara had married Drake had been quite real.

"Seeing him again was what made me realize that I didn't really love him at all. He didn't love me either, that was quite obvious. But now that I understand what love is and what real love feels like, I know I never felt that way about him."

"So, what is it you want, Sara?" He wanted to hear her say the words to him.

"I want . . ." She faltered for a second. "I want you to know that I love you. And I think I've loved you for a while now, but I was too blinded by what I thought was love for Alexander to realize it."

His heart turned over in his chest. Sara Fleming loved him. It was too good to be true. Wanting nothing more than to kiss her, he leaned in, reaching for her.

Placing her small hand upon his arm, Sara stopped him. "Please. Let me explain."

"Very well," Christopher murmured, sitting back against the sofa. "I'm listening."

She took a deep breath. "I've come to realize that what I felt for Alexander, what I thought was love, wasn't really love at all. He was merely a romantic ideal that I had already built up in my imagination. A knight in shining armor. I knew nothing about Alexander except that he was handsome and charming and whispered pretty things to me. We never talked about anything of importance, or anything that mattered, or even of our future together. But because of you, I know now that wasn't really love I felt for him."

She paused and sipped her brandy. Then she settled her blue eyes back on him. "If I really loved Alexander, I couldn't have kissed you the way I did, If I truly loved him as I claimed that I did, I wouldn't have let us do the things we did together in the carriage that day or in the drawing room the other night. But I didn't, did I? Because deep down I guess I didn't truly want to be with Alexander. Because I have realized that you are the one I love."

"How do you know that?" he couldn't help but ask, his heart pounding at her words. "How do you know that I am the one you love and not him?"

"Because, Christopher, you are the one in my thoughts when I first wake up in the morning and before I go to sleep at night. You're the one I think about all day long. You're the one I care what happens to. You're the one who makes me feel things I have never felt before. I love your kindness and your honesty. I love how you care for your sisters and your family. I love that you are honorable. I love that I can talk to you about anything and that you make me laugh. I love that you want to care for me and want to protect me. I love that you gave up everything to be with me. I love that I feel at home in your arms. I love the sound of your voice, your handsome face, your perfect mouth, and your gorgeous brown eyes. I love how you kiss me. I love that you can make me forget everything except being with you. I love everything about you. I *love* you, Christopher Townsend."

He feared it was all some kind of fever dream. Was Sara Fleming really here, at his house, confessing her love for him? But as his eyes rested on her beautiful face, he knew it wasn't his imagination. She was truly there with him, saying these things to him.

"Sara," he whispered, filled with emotions he didn't know what to do with. "I've loved you from the moment I first saw you."

She placed her delicate hand on his cheek, caressing him lightly. "Please tell me that you forgive me for being a complete idiot?"

"I forgive you," he said. "And I'm sorry too."

"Whatever for?" she asked, a note of surprise in her voice.

"I'm sorry for embarrassing you yesterday at the hotel. When I said you might be carrying my child in front of everyone. I regretted it the moment the words were out of my mouth," he explained. He'd just been so desperate to stop her from marrying that man, he probably would have said anything at the time.

"No," she responded. "You were right to say it. It was nothing but the truth. I don't know what I was thinking in running to Alexander after what happened between us. It was not well done of me. I was being willful because I didn't like my parents telling me what I should do. In the end I honestly don't think I could have gone through with marrying Alexander, even if I hadn't discovered the truth about him and that awful Lucy Camden. I was having doubts even before I arrived at the Savoy Hotel. When you walked in that room, Christopher, in my heart I think I knew I loved you then. I acted angrily, but I was really quite happy that you had showed up."

"I would have turned London upside down to find you."

Her expression full of wonder, she asked, "You would?"

"Without question. Anything to stop you from marrying Drake."

"They arrested him, you know. And Lucy," Sara said. "My father and Uncle Lucien spoke with the authorities this afternoon. It turns out they were both stealing from other guests in the hotel. They even found some of the missing jewelry amongst their belongings."

"Well, that is good news. They were despicable characters. I hate to think what would have happened to you if you married him." Christopher didn't know what he would have done if they hadn't found her in time.

"I'm happy that they were caught too and I'm even happier that all of this is over. But I'm happiest of all that you cared enough to come to find me."

"That is because I love you more than I can say." Christopher spoke in a low voice. "And I want you to be my wife, Sara. Do you still wish to marry me, knowing I have nothing to offer you?"

"Yes," she answered. "I want to marry you. And *you*, Christopher Townsend, have more to offer me than money. And honestly, I don't care about the money. I never have. It was always my parents who worried about it. And it seems that they love you too and wish for the two of us to marry. They've already secured the license and everything is arranged for Saturday morning. That is, if you'll still have me?"

"Will I still have you?" He shook his head in disbelief, then turned to look in her eyes. "Of course I will still have you, my beautiful Sara. You're all I have ever wanted. With or without your money."

"But we will have my money," she said with a very serious expression on her face. "My parents said so. There's nothing to worry about. We've already discussed it after you left this morning. They're going to give us five million dollars as a wedding gift."

"I can't take that money," he blurted out, before choking a little on his brandy. It was a reflexive reaction and the words flew from his mouth before he could even think of what he was saying. The staggering sum of money was more than he could have imagined. His head spun. Five million dollars!

"Why not?" she asked rather breezily. "I'm sure it's more than the Beckwiths were going to settle on Bonnie."

"It is." Christopher could barely speak. "Quite a bit more." Five million dollars was a bloody fortune.

"You don't have to sell your family home now," Sara said softly. "You can take care of your sisters and your mother. You can repair the house. You can do whatever you like."

Yes, he would be able to do all that, and much more, with five million dollars. Good Lord, what *couldn't* he do with that much money? The money didn't seem to matter to him when he was marrying Bonnie Beckwith. Because he didn't love her, the money was compensation for marrying her. It truly was a simple business transaction: their money for his title.

But with Sara . . . That was quite a different affair. He loved her. He couldn't take money for marrying the woman he loved. It just didn't seem right.

"Christopher," she whispered his name. "The money doesn't matter."

"Says someone who has never had to worry about money in her life."

"Are you jesting?" she asked, a bit incredulous. "For as long as I can remember, I was told I had to be careful of fortune hunters and swindlers and people who would use me for my money. I've always been worried about money. Just in a different way than you think."

He paused and placed his brandy glass on the end table. Perhaps Sara had a point. He'd never thought about it that way before.

"So when I tell you that my parents' giving us five million dollars doesn't matter," she said pointedly with a little shrug, "it doesn't matter. Not to me. *Not* marrying me for my money is just as ridiculous as marrying me *for* my money. And you may as well know now, Lord Bridgeton, that I shall inherit a great deal more than that amount of money when they die."

Christopher hadn't even considered that fact. Good Lord, just how much money did Harrison Fleming have anyway, if five million dollars was just a fraction of his fortune? For a sea captain, he seemed to have acquired an awful lot of wealth.

"But I've been thinking about the money, Christopher," Sara continued in a pensive tone. She placed her unfinished glass of brandy on the table next to his. "I've always looked at my fortune as a burden and a nuisance. Like a weight around my neck, never knowing if people liked me for myself or because I had money. And I've been quite spoiled. Yes, I freely admit that. I spent without a thought of the cost. And it made me quite happy to tell you the truth. But now . . . I'd like to do something good with the money." She paused for a moment, a bit nervous. "And I would like you to help me."

"What do you mean?" he questioned, preparing himself

for whatever she might suggest. This evening had taken quite a turn and anything seemed possible at this point.

"When you told me about your family, and how your father abused your sisters . . . I haven't been able to get it out of my head. In a way, it's haunted me."

"I'm sorry," he said. "I should not have told you any of that." He still didn't understand why he revealed his family secrets to her, except that he felt a connection with Sara he'd never felt with anyone before in his life.

"No, Christopher," she protested gently. "I'm glad that you shared with me about what happened to you and your sisters. Especially about your sisters. My whole life I've been blessed with parents who adored me and I couldn't ever imagine being locked in a situation like that. But I keep thinking that there are many more girls who are not as lucky as I am. Girls who are imprisoned in their own homes with nowhere else to go. I was wondering if there wasn't a way we could help those other families. Other girls like your sisters. Could we help them escape their homes and live somewhere safe? Could we create a peaceful place for them to go? A place where they could learn to live their own lives?" she asked, her voice soft.

A lump formed in Christopher's throat at Sara's words and the possibility of her idea. He wondered what it would have been like if his sisters had been able to escape from their father. How would their lives have turned out? Would they still have the scars? Would they be happier, less afraid? The thought of other young girls out there in the same situation moved him. Yes, he would move mountains to help them. There was no question.

"I didn't think it was possible to love you more than I already do, but you just made me love you infinitely more," he said, as he looked at this beautiful American girl who had turned his world upside down.

"So is that a yes?" she asked.

"It is a resounding yes, Sara, to everything. Yes, I love you. Yes, I want you to be my wife. Yes, together I want us to do something good with all that money. Yes, I think you are the most wonderful woman I have ever met."

"I love you."

Unable to hold back any longer, and giving in to the desire he'd been fighting since she arrived, Christopher leaned over to kiss her.

In an instant, his arms were around her and she moved effortlessly into his embrace. Their mouths met and she melted into him with a sweet sigh of satisfaction. Holding her was everything. Being with her this way, knowing that this lovely woman was his, and his alone, caused his heart to constrict. He loved her so.

He whispered her name, as his mouth covered hers again. She pressed herself against him, opening her mouth, inviting him in. Their tongues met and a slow heat blossomed between them. She was warm and sweet and so very eager for him. Her hands were in his hair, just as his own hands were moving all over her body. Oh, how he wanted her!

With a groan he broke away. "No," he murmured low.

"Yes, oh please," she begged, breathless from their kissing, clearly wanting more. The little minx.

"No, Sara, not like this. The next time I have you, you will be my wife and we won't have to be rushed and furtive on a sofa, worried that someone is going to walk in unexpectedly and discover us together. No. When we're married the day after tomorrow, my beautiful Sara, I'm going to make love to you in my bed all night long."

"Oh my!" She gasped in anticipation, then whispered, "That sounds perfectly heavenly."

"It will be, I promise you that. But for now, my love, we need to get you home. Before your father discovers that you are missing and calls me out. I think he might actually kill me if he finds us together again." He flashed her a wicked grin.

"He wouldn't dare," she said with a meaningful look. "He knows how much I love you."

"We can only hope that he does. Now let's go."

"But I don't want to leave you," she murmured in his ear.

"Well, after we are married, you won't ever have to leave me again." That idea made him very happy indeed.

"Oh, how I love that thought!"

"Me too." He placed a final kiss on her delectable mouth. He could kiss her for weeks on end and still want more. "But it's rather late and I've learned how impossible you are to move when you're sleepy. Now, get your things together, my little captain's daughter, and I'll have them bring my carriage around. Hopefully, you won't get discovered returning to the house."

"Oh, all right then," she grumbled, but smiled at him.

Reluctantly, they both rose from the sofa, and he took her hand in his.

27

Smooth Sailing

"I'm so happy that you've married my brother," Lady Gwyneth Townsend said, hugging her new sister-in-law, her sweet little face alight with happiness.

Sara smiled with unabashed joy, as she stood in an elegant white silk gown trimmed in Belgian lace, which she'd had made on a whim when she was still in New York. "Well, I'm so happy that in addition to my handsome husband, I now have two lovely sisters. I have always wanted to have sisters."

After the ceremony on Saturday, everyone had gathered at Devon House to celebrate Sara and Christopher's marriage with a wonderful wedding breakfast. The wedding itself had been quite special for all that it was last minute. Mara was her maid of honor, Christopher's two sisters had been her attendants, and her three little Eddington cousins, Victoria, Violet, and Vivienne, were the sweetest flower girls. It was a very intimate affair, just Sara's family and Christopher's sisters.

Sara was disappointed that Christopher's mother did not

attend their wedding. Lady Bridgeton had claimed that she was too ill to leave Bridgeton Hall, but extended an invitation to her and Christopher to visit as soon as possible. Sara was quite interested to meet the woman and looked forward to their trip to Bridgeton Hall. After that, New York!

"And you will both come to New York with us, won't you?" Sara asked eagerly.

"Oh, yes!" Evelyn fairly beamed with excitement. "We can't wait to go! We're so looking forward to it, Sara."

She and Christopher had decided to visit New York as a honeymoon trip, sailing together on the *Captain's Daughter* with her parents. Sara was anxious to show her new husband the city she called home, before they settled in England and she took up the role of the Countess of Bridgeton. She also wanted Evelyn and Gwyneth to come with them, thinking that a whole new wardrobe and a visit to New York would be a wonderful adventure for the two girls. And Christopher had agreed.

"You'll love it there. There are so many wonderful things I want to show you when we get to America." Sara hugged both of her new sisters-in-law.

"Cousin Sara! Cousin Sara, look!" Vivienne Eddington called, her voice filled with delight. "Look at Boots! Look what we did to him! He's a flower *dog*!"

Her three little cousins were dissolving in peals of childish laughter at the sight of Boots. Sara's adorable Yorkie puppy had a few of the orange blossoms from her bridal bouquet fastened into a pretty garland around his neck. She had no choice but to laugh at the comical figure, for Boots looked thoroughly put upon, and not a little embarrassed, at being at the mercy of the three blond flower girls. They had certainly made him a flower dog!

"Be gentle with him, girls," Sara said, still smiling.

"Oh, we promise!" Violet exclaimed. "We love Boots!"

Then Sara caught the eye of her husband across the room where he was talking with her father and her uncle Jeffrey. Christopher winked at her, and she could not help but smile at the man she loved with all her heart. And indeed, her heart was full. She had everyone she loved in one room, from her husband to her parents to her aunts, uncles, and all her Hamilton cousins.

The best part was that she was at peace with her parents again. The estranged feelings she had cultivated between them over Alexander Drake were no longer there. Sara had thanked them for all they had done for her and her mother and father were happy about her marriage to Christopher, making no secret of their fondness for him. All was well again in her world.

An amused voice said behind her, "May I congratulate the bride?"

She turned to see Phillip standing beside her with a glass of champagne in his hand. He gave her a wry look, acknowledging her wedded bliss. "Well, Sara, I don't know how you did it, but somehow you managed to get your own way once again, in spite of your efforts to do otherwise."

"It seems I did." Sara laughed with her cousin. "But I was very lucky this time."

"I'll say you were! If we hadn't rescued you in time, you might have married that bounder!"

She shuddered to think what would have happened if Christopher and her cousins had not arrived at the Savoy Hotel that afternoon. Being married to the likes of Alexander Drake was no longer a prospect that pleased her. And to think just a few short weeks ago while on her father's ship, Sara had contemplated jumping overboard and drowning herself in the ocean merely at the idea of being separated from him. Everything had changed so much, that it was almost hard to believe that she was the same person. Now she'd rather push Alexander overboard! Yet in all seriousness, she had come to realize how grateful she was to have parents and a family who cared about her so much.

"Thank you for that, Phillip," she said, her tone much more somber. "I'm a fortunate girl to have you as my cousin."

He kissed her cheek. "I'm happy everything worked out and now you've gone and married my best friend. It couldn't have turned out better if I planned it, *Lady Bridgeton*. But I like to think I had a bit of a hand in this romance. I *was* the one who introduced the two of you, if you recall . . ."

Sara could never forget the day she walked into the drawing room at Devon House and first saw Christopher Townsend. Even then she was struck by his good looks and had been intrigued by him, in spite of her blind infatuation with Alexander Drake. "Yes, I suppose I should thank you for that."

"Yes, you should!" Phillip laughed, then looked toward Mara, who had just joined them. "Now I have to see that this one gets safely married . . ."

"Oh, don't worry about me. I may not ever get married," Mara murmured softly, her cheeks turning a little red.

"You keep saying that, but oh, yes, you will, Mara," Phillip said quite unequivocally. "But you'll at least be considerate enough to not put all of us through the trouble that Sara did. At least I hope you will!"

Sara stuck her tongue out at Phillip. He would always tease her as an older brother and she loved him for it. "Well, we'll just see what happens when you finally get married, Phillip!"

Smiling, Mara said, "I'm so very happy for you and Lord Bridgeton, Sara. I always had a good feeling about the two of you."

"Well, I have a good feeling that things will turn out well for you too, Mara," Sara responded. "And don't think that I have forgotten that I'm on the lookout for a wonderful gentleman who is perfect for you!"

Sara had spent last night talking with her cousin Mara, discussing all that happened since the night of the masked ball. Mara felt terrible for betraying her by telling Sara's parents that Alexander Drake was at the ball. Normally, that would have upset Sara, but if Mara hadn't told her parents, then her mother and father wouldn't have come looking for her that night. If her parents hadn't caught her with Christopher in the drawing room, then she and Christopher might not have been forced to recognize and admit their feelings for each other. As Phillip said, it all worked out in the end.

Again, Sara had her family to thank for everything.

After all the trouble she'd put them through, her parents still loved and wanted the best for her.

Yes, Sara was a lucky girl, indeed.

She was even luckier now that she was married to Christopher Townsend, the Earl of Bridgeton.

Sara grinned as her husband came walking toward her. He looked strikingly handsome in his dark morning suit and a little thrill went through her at the thought that he belonged to her. He was her *husband*. Being his wife made her inordinately happy. When she thought about it, it was rather strange. She had been acquainted with Alexander Drake for over six months, but didn't truly know him at all. Yet in less than a month, she had fallen head over heels in love with Christopher Townsend and knew more about him than she would have thought possible.

"Good day, Lady Bridgeton." he said, his eyes alight with mischief. Then he leaned in close, whispering in her ear, "But it will be an even better night."

"Why, Lord Bridgeton!" She playfully swatted his arm, but she was thrilled by his words. She longed for tonight as much as he did, when they could finally be alone together all night long and she could sleep beside him with his strong arms around her.

"Are you happy, my beautiful bride?" he asked, embracing her and holding her close to him.

Breathing in the scent of him, Sara looked up into his brown eyes and her heart fluttered. She had her whole life ahead of her with this man at her side. "Happier than I ever imagined I could be, because I love you so much. You're the one who has made me so happy."

"That makes two of us." With a smile, Christopher kissed her sweetly. "Because I couldn't be any happier with my little captain's daughter."

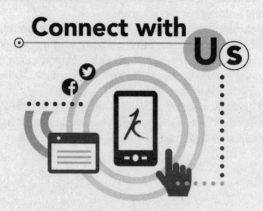